BOUND
WITH GOLD

*But gilded chains are no
substitute for love!*

Complete your collection with
all four books!

In February:
Blackmailed With Diamonds
In March:
Shackled With Rubies
In May:
Bought With Emeralds

Glamour, passion and jewels: what more can a woman ask for?

Four fabulous collections of stories from your favourite authors

February 2010: He can shower her with diamonds, but can he make her his bride?

Blackmailed With Diamonds

Lucy Gordon
Sarah Morgan
Robyn Donald

March 2010: He can bind her with rubies – but can he keep her for his own?

Shackled With Rubies

Lucy Monroe
Lee Wilkinson
Kate Walker

May 2010: He can adorn her with emeralds – but can he conquer her heart?

Bought With Emeralds

Sandra Marton
Katherine Garbera
Margaret Mayo

MISTRESSES
BOUND
WITH GOLD

SUSAN NAPIER
KATHRYN ROSS
KELLY HUNTER

All the characters in this book have no existence outside the imagination
of the author, and have no relation whatsoever to anyone bearing the
same name or names. They are not even distantly inspired by any
individual known or unknown to the author, and all the incidents are
pure invention.

BOUND WITH GOLD © by Harlequin Books SA 2010

The Revenge Affair © Susan Napier 1999
The Frenchman's Mistress © Kathryn Ross 2004
Priceless © Kelly Hunter 2006

ISBN: 978 0 263 87725 0

24-0410

Harlequin Mills & Boon policy is to use papers that are
natural, renewable and recyclable products and made from
wood grown in sustainable forests. The logging and
manufacturing processes conform to the legal environmental
regulations of the country of origin.

Printed and bound in Spain
by Litografia Rosés S.A., Barcelona

THE REVENGE
AFFAIR

SUSAN NAPIER

Susan Napier is a former journalist and script-writer who turned to writing romantic fiction after her two sons were born. She lives in Auckland, New Zealand with her journalist husband, who generously provides the on-going inspiration for her fictional heroes, and two temperamental cats whose curious paws contribute the occasional typographical error when they join her at the keyboard. Born on St Valentine's Day, Susan feels that it was her destiny to write romances and, having written over thirty books for Mills & Boon, still loves the challenges of working within the genre. She likes writing traditional tales with a twist and believes that to keep romance alive you have to keep the faith – to believe in love. Not just in the romantic kind of love that pervades her books, but in the everyday, caring-and-sharing kind of love that builds enduring relationships. Susan's extended family is scattered over the globe, which is fortunate as she enjoys travelling and seeking out new experiences to fuel her flights of imagination.

Susan loves to hear from readers and can be contacted at PO Box 18-240, Glen Innes, Auckland 1130, New Zealand.

CHAPTER ONE

AS THE lift doors opened Regan smoothed her sweaty palms down the side-seams of her classic black sheath and took a deep breath, beating back the niggle of doubt which had invaded her rebellious confidence during the swooping upward journey.

She had come this far—she couldn't chicken out now!

She stepped jerkily out of the padded lift into the stark luxury of a marble foyer, her slim body taut with tension. The rarefied air was unnaturally still and quiet, as if the ragged end of the evening rush-hour funnelling through Auckland's inner-city streets far below didn't exist.

Regan looked around, her straight black brows arching in faint disapproval. There was nothing warm or welcoming about the formal entranceway to the three apartments sharing the fourteenth floor. The lush tropical foliage growing out of huge glazed pots only partially offset the chilly atmosphere of intimidating elegance. The glossy, impervious surfaces and pale biscuit-coloured matt paint on the upper walls created a neutral environment which bordered on the boring. The only jarring note was the glaring red eye of a state-of-the-art security camera placed high up against the ceiling.

The lift doors hissed shut behind Regan's back with unexpected swiftness, the discreet thunk and faint whine of the descending mechanism making her nerves jump as she realised that she was temporarily cut off from her quickest avenue of escape.

It seemed somehow symbolic, as if Fate was making the choice for her—urging her to proceed with her audacious plans for the evening, chiding her for her cowardly hesitation.

Regan's fingers bunched into unconscious fists, her plum-dark nails digging into her clammy palms as she studied the gold numbering etched into the marble wall opposite the lift.

A discreet arrow directed her to the left, where a short corridor framed a dark wooden door recessed deep into the pale wall.

As she moved towards her destination she was uncomfortably aware of the video camera on the wall behind her. The notion that some faceless security man might be watching her even now, and speculating on the reasons for her visit, made her want to break into a guilty dash, but she forced herself to maintain a graceful stroll as she moved out of sight around the corner.

It had never occurred to her that her presence might be recorded on video. She had naively imagined that, for the protection of both sides in this arrangement, everything would remain conveniently off the record.

In the unnatural hush the delicate, gold-chased heels of her black evening sandals sounded out tiny exclamation marks against the veined marble floor, punctuating her nervous progress.

Just think of it as a date, Regan repeated to herself, trying to emulate the brash attitude displayed by her nineteen-year-old flatmate and her trendy clique of friends. Unfortunately the thought wasn't very liberating for a woman who hadn't had a casual date in over five years!

Oh, it was all very well for Lisa and her cynical cousin Cleo, whose modelling careers had taught them to regard males as interchangeable accessories, but such casual insouciance was alien to Regan's experience of men. In the five months since she had answered the ad to share a flat with the scatterbrained Lisa and cheerfully laid-back

Saleena she had come to realise how sheltered she had been in her previous existence. She had always naively believed that mutual respect and shared interests were the essence of any relationship between a man and a woman. Her strict upbringing had precluded the startling idea that one might choose a man purely according to one's mood, rather than because he appeared to be a sound, long-term emotional investment.

Tonight promised to be a revelation in more ways than one!

Regan moistened her dry lips. Oh, she had plenty of confidence in her social skills when it came to playing hostess, or circulating amongst groups of friends or business acquaintances, but she knew little of the modern protocols governing the intimate entertaining of a man one-on-one, so to speak.

One-on-one…

A shiver of delicious apprehension sizzled down her spine at the wanton image that sprang immediately to mind. Her pale skin warmed to a delicate blush as she pictured the searingly intimate circumstances in which this evening would probably end.

Of course, that was only if she *wanted* the evening to end that way, she reassured herself. It was purely ladies' choice—or so she had been told—but she wasn't so naive as to believe that the man she had come here to meet wouldn't have intimate expectations of his own.

Erotic expectations that *she* was supposed to fulfil to the max…

Regan's courage hit another serious speed wobble. Oh, God, she must have been mad to think that she could carry this off! She was an utter fraud. How did a woman who couldn't even inspire passion in the man she loved expect to be believable in the role of sexy, sultry playmate to a total stranger?

The moral teachings of a lifetime rose up to haunt her. This was the first step down the slippery slope to complete depravity. To what depths had she sunk to even consider such wickedness? Wasn't she disgusted with herself for betraying her cherished ideals?

No! A hot thrust of bitter remembrance stiffened her wavering resolve. She tossed her midnight-dark head in a gesture of angry defiance, fanning the blunt ends of her silky-straight bob across creamy shoulders laid bare by her sleeveless dress. Below the scooped neckline the snug black fabric tightened across her small breasts as she sucked in another steadying breath, struggling to control the acid rage which had been brewing and bubbling inside her for weeks, blistering her with shame, and self-contempt for her own weakness.

No! Regan's violet eyes glittered with repressed pain and fury. She had nothing to be ashamed of…she was betraying nothing that hadn't already been proved utterly unworthy of her faith.

She was no longer a pathetic, self-deluded, gullible fool, hiding her head in the sand to avoid having to confront the crude realities of life.

And the reality was that up until now it had been *Regan* who was morally out of step with the modern world.

Plenty of women her age—ordinary, *normal*, well-adjusted twenty-five-year-old women—wouldn't see anything wrong with what she was going to do. Regan was unattached, independent and answerable only to herself. No one was going to be hurt by her actions tonight. It was about time she adopted an outlook more in tune with the rest of her generation—more open-minded and willing to experiment with what life had to offer.

To catch up with the sexual revolution!

Tonight she was going to prove that Regan Frances was a sophisticated, passionate, desirable woman—a sexual being who could treat the giving and taking of pleasure with the same casualness that men seemed to enjoy. Then, and only then, would she feel truly liberated from the travesty of her marriage, and the crushing humiliations of the past few weeks.

She came to a halt before the deep-set door, breathlessly aware that the definitive moment had arrived.

Just treat it as a date.

Reaching out to press the doorbell, Regan was dismayed to see the fine tremor in her hand that twice made her finger miss its target. In the shiny brass surround she saw a distorted view of her own face, all mouth and eyes. She licked her dry lips, adding extra gloss to the dark plum colour which Lisa proclaimed was the ultimate in sultry glamour, and steeled herself to take another stab at the button.

As she did so the thin white strip on the ring-finger of her left hand mocked her timidity, and another hot jolt of temper kicked the normally tender bow of her mouth into a vengeful curve.

Wouldn't Michael be astonished to see his boring little sexless doormat of a wife *now*! she thought viciously, giving the silent bell a second defiant jab.

Except, of course, he couldn't—because to her certain knowledge Michael Frances wasn't gazing benevolently down from a blissful heaven of the soul; he was too busy burning in fiery hell!

On that deeply gratifying thought the door opened...and Regan's heart dropped like a stone into her sexy shoes.

CHAPTER TWO

INSTEAD of the virile, attractive, sexy sophisticate Regan had been praying for, a skinny, swarthy, wrinkled old man as bald as a billiard ball stood in the doorway.

Even though she was only five-foot-three, Regan towered over him in her slender heels, and not even his faultlessly cut black suit could disguise a shrunken frame and unmistakably bandy legs. As if to compensate for his shiny pate his salt-and-pepper eyebrows were luxuriantly bushy, springing upwards in fanning tufts which give him a permanently surprised expression.

He had to be sixty if he was a day!

Thunderstruck, Regan's first impulse was to bolt, but she mastered the knee-jerk impulse and swallowed hard as the wizened gnome dipped his head to one side.

'Bonsoir, mam'selle.'

A horrified giggle swelled in her throat. Was he really French, or did he think a suave foreign accent would make him more attractive to women?

Oh, God, it had never occurred to her that she might have to vamp a rich old fogey! On the contrary, Cleo had boasted that all the 'social liaisons' arranged by her ambitious ex-boyfriend were with perfectly agreeable single men who were simply too busy making gobs of money to sustain ongoing relationships with women. They preferred the no-maintenance alternative provided by Derek's informal network of 'friends'—attractive, sophisticated, obliging women, who could be relied upon to accept an invitation to a good night out without pouting about short notice and who cheerfully vanished when their attentions were no longer required to boost the male ego—or libido…

Knowing Cleo's elastic standards, Regan should have realised that her idea of 'perfectly agreeable' covered an awful lot of ground. 'Seriously rich' was probably her main criteria of judgement.

The old man was still patiently awaiting a response to his greeting, and the puzzled enquiry in the shrewd blue eyes caused a faint flicker of hope in her breast. But a quick sideways glance at the number by the bell told Regan that she hadn't made a mistake.

'Uh—good evening,' she ventured, pinning on a smile that quivered with effort around the edges as she realised that she didn't even know his *name*!

To give herself time to think she ducked her head to fumble in her beaded evening bag for the card which had been thrust into her hand a scant hour earlier.

'I know I'm a little late, but—uh—Derek sent me,' she blurted, holding out the business card with the apartment's address scribbled on the back.

A gnarled hand accepted the card, the startling eyebrows rumpling like woolly caterpillars as he frowningly studied it, then her.

'But you are not who is expected,' he said suspiciously, still standing squarely in the doorway, barring her entrance. His gaze roamed down over the shimmery black stockings encasing her slender calves, and back up to the hemline modestly skimming her knees and the regrettably slight cleavage exposed by the low-cut bodice. He shook his head, his thin lips pursed in what she instantly interpreted as disappointment. 'You are *not* Mam'selle Cleo…'

Perversely, Regan was outraged by his rejection. Instead of gratefully seizing on the excuse to withdraw with her dignity still intact, she lifted her chin, her small, triangular face paling with anger, her wide-set violet eyes darkening to the colour of fresh bruises as she prepared to do battle for her wounded pride.

Adrenaline pumped through her veins, fresh fuel to the smouldering anger inside her. How dared he dismiss her with such effortless ease?

This time she was not going to meekly bow to male judgement of her feminine worth. Since Michael had died she had learned that he had cheated her out of a lot more than just money. No man was going to get away with making her feel like a failure—not ever again!

It suddenly became vital that she wrap this contemptible little weasel around her little finger.

So she wasn't what he had expected—she wasn't a tall, willowy, full-breasted redhead, with emerald eyes and legs that went on for ever. That didn't mean she was any less of a woman!

'Cleo couldn't make it,' she told him coolly. 'She's indisposed.'

That was putting it delicately! Not half an hour ago Lisa's beauteous cousin had been sprawled on her hands and knees on a cold bathroom floor, her flawless complexion a putrid shade of green, her glamorous red hair dangling over the white china toilet bowl as she alternately retched and moaned, vile curses spewing from her pale lips as she vowed never to mix curry and cocktails again.

'And so…this means Monsieur Derek asks for you to come in her place?'

Regan sucked in her cheeks, trying for that haughty, bored model look that she had seen Lisa practising endlessly in the mirror.

'It was very much a last-minute kind of a thing—Cleo got sick and I was available,' she said, adroitly avoiding an outright lie.

She hoped that he wasn't going to suggest checking her story with Derek. But why should he bother? As Cleo had pointed out, there was nothing illegal involved, no need for fear on either side. Derek Clarke's discreet little sideline, designed to ingratiate himself with potentially useful colleagues and clients, was successful precisely because it was so casual.

'I see,' he said slowly, relaxing his stance. 'And you are…?'

'Ev—' She bit her lip. She had already decided that Regan was too distinctive a name, too easy to trace. She *had* intended to shelter behind her middle name, but now it occurred to her that Evangeline was just as singular as Regan. 'I— It's Eve,' she corrected hurriedly. 'My name is Eve.'

'Mam'selle…Eve.' His deliberate hesitation and wry intonation suggested he knew she was lying, and she flushed with guilt.

'I am Pierre.' He smiled suddenly—a splitting grin which rendered him uglier than ever. He turned sideways, inviting her inside with a broad, sweeping gesture of his arm.

'Unfortunately, Monsieur is running rather late this evening,' he said, his accent rolling off his tongue in an unmistakably genuine purr. 'He has rung to say that he is held up in a business meeting and asked me to deliver his apologies. He says that he will be home as soon as possible. Fortunately, he informs me, the dinner you are to attend does not begin until a fashionably late hour. In the meantime he suggests that you relax and enjoy a drink, and make free of the apartment while you are waiting. Monsieur has an excellent home entertainment centre…'

'Monsieur?' Regan repeated faintly, the blood pounding in her ears as she realised how close she had come to making a fresh idiot of herself.

The blind date that she had hijacked from Cleo wasn't with a wizened old gnome old enough to be her grandfather!

Pierre wasn't the man she was supposed to flirt with, flatter and seduce.

Regan's hopes soared as the evening ahead regained its tantalising promise...the wicked allure of pleasures previously denied her by her husband's secret indifference—the perfect revenge for years of his perfunctory lovemaking!

Her smile of euphoric relief was so dazzlingly different from the strained rictus that Regan had worn since the door opened that Pierre blinked.

'You're the *butler*,' she guessed happily as she floated past his bandy figure into the apartment, mentally scolding herself for jumping to hasty conclusions. If he couldn't even spare the time to pick up his own women, a wealthy workaholic businessman would scarcely be likely to be answering doors!

'I don't believe I have a title, as such,' said Pierre. 'I merely assist Monsieur with his domestic arrangements.'

The self-effacing comment was belied by the ring of pride in his voice as he preceded her down a short flight of stairs which wrapped around the curving wall of glass bricks screening the entranceway from the main body of the apartment.

'I bet you do the lion's share,' Regan murmured drily, her heels sinking into thick white carpet that she imagined would require meticulous care.

'*Mais, non.* Monsieur does not own such a pet,' Pierre said blandly. 'Except when the survival of the species is at stake, he does not approve of wild beasts being held in captivity...'

Regan swallowed a grin. 'Is that why he's not married?' she shot back, her flippancy cloaking her urgent need to assure herself that the little information she *did* have was at least correct on that one, all-important point.

Pierre's eyebrows twitched in acknowledgment of her riposte. 'Monsieur is the most intelligent and civilised of men,' he observed primly as he reached the bottom of the stairs and turned to watch her join him, 'although a certain degree of wildness is only to be expected of healthy males in their prime.' The fugitive gleam of mischief in the old eyes glowed even brighter. 'He certainly does not yet regard himself as being on the endangered species list...'

So... Unmarried. Healthy. Intelligent. Prime...with a dash of wildness thrown in for good measure. Regan lowered her lashes to hide her surge of terrified elation.

No wonder Cleo had been so furious about having to cry off!

She had come hammering on the door of the flat a scant hour earlier, stridently upset when she'd discovered that her cousin wasn't home and Regan had no idea of her whereabouts.

'There was a message on the answer-machine when I got back from work to say that she was going out to some party and wouldn't be here for dinner,' Regan had said, still annoyed that Lisa had conveniently forgotten that it was her turn to cook.

'But she can't be out! I was sure she'd be here—I need Lisa *now*!' Cleo wailed. 'It's a matter of life and death!' She barged inside with none of her usual grace. 'What about Saleena?' she demanded raggedly. 'Is *she* here?'

Regan fell back, shaking her head. 'Evening aerobics classes.' Saleena worked part-time at the local gym to supplement her student loan while she studied for a degree in Sport and Recreation. Like Lisa, she was extremely pretty and always game for a laugh, although—being two years older and a great deal more intelligent—her behaviour and attitudes were thankfully more mature.

Cleo screamed, a low, heart-felt shriek of frustration.

'Can I help?' Regan sighed, too accustomed to Cleo's histrionics to be truly concerned. Perhaps she had run out of nail polish for her synthetic talons. Dressed to the glittering hilt, and made up to model-girl perfection, she was obviously on her way somewhere trendy and expensive.

'*You!*' Cleo uttered an insulting laugh that ended in a muffled choke as her exquisite face turned suddenly from honey-gold tan to swamp-green and she dashed towards the bathroom, clutching her concave belly.

When she tottered out and collapsed on the couch in the lounge without bothering to artistically drape her limbs for the best visual effect, Regan knew that she was genuinely at the end of her tether.

It turned out that what Cleo had convinced herself was merely a lingering all-day hangover had developed into something debilitatingly nasty at both ends, and she was frantic to find a substitute for some hot date that an ex-boyfriend, Derek, had fixed her up with for that night.

'I've been trying to call Derek to tell him I didn't think I could make it, but he's not answering his stupid phone,' Cleo shrilled, 'and I haven't been able to find anyone to fill in for me, not this late on a Friday night…

'I thought I might manage it if I took a few pills, and they seemed to work for a while, but now I feel even worse,' Cleo groaned. 'In the taxi I thought I was going to throw up, so I told the driver to drop me off here—I knew Lisa would help…' She looked up at Regan through a tangle of red hair, her green eyes tearful with angry self-pity. 'I'm supposed to be there in half an hour and I *can't* simply not turn up, because I was supposed to escort this guy out to some fancy dinner— Oh, God!'

The mere suggestion of food prompted another mad scramble to reach the bathroom on time.

When she finally emerged on wobbly legs Regan offered to call a doctor, but Cleo was adamant that she didn't need one. 'I just want to lie down for a while,' she said shakily, homing in on Lisa's cluttered bedroom and crashing gratefully across the unmade bed. 'I have to warn Derek,' she moaned piteously. 'His phone number's on his card in my evening bag—I think I dropped it in the lounge—keep trying him for me, will you? And if you get through, tell him what's happened.'

'Why don't you just phone your date yourself and tell him you're ill?' Regan asked, unable to understand her obsession. What did one broken date matter to a woman who hardly ever went out with the same man twice?

'Because I don't have his phone number, that's why— only Derek's card, with the address I'm supposed to go written on the back and the time I'm supposed to be there!' Cleo croaked, rolling over onto her back. 'Hell, Derek'll *kill* me if I mess this one up for him—he said he could get some really good accounts from this guy.' Her former boyfriend was in advertising, and staying on friendly terms with him had landed Cleo several plum modelling assignments. 'But what in the hell am I supposed to do, for God's sake?' she said, panic turning to petulance. 'It's not my fault I got sick!'

She dragged her arm from across her bloodshot eyes and glared belligerently at Regan, who wisely held her tongue. In her opinion Cleo's hectic, party-loving lifestyle involved too much alcohol and too little food, and Lisa's puppyish admiration for her glamorous elder cousin was leading her down the same path.

Her silence appeared to mollify Cleo, who interpreted it as sympathetic agreement, and in between violent bouts with the re-emerging curry she allowed the rest of the story to emerge: how Derek regularly set up dates for Cleo and some of her girlfriends with wealthy single men, the kind of men who were happy to reward a pretty woman who escorted them around town with expensive trinkets if she was willing to round off the evening in bed.

'You mean Derek is a *pimp*!' Regan gasped, her eyes

rounding as Cleo's busy social life suddenly acquired a shocking new perspective.

'Of course he's not!' Cleo roused from her torpor to snap. 'He just does a few favours for people who might one day be in a position to do *him* a business favour in return, that's all. None of us makes any *money* out of it; it's not like it's a call-girl operation, for God's sake—so you can stop looking so bug-eyed with disapproval! It's just consenting adults being introduced to each together and...well, consenting!'

After her initial mental recoil Regan was filled with a morbid fascination. 'But...you said that the men rewarded you for sleeping with them...' she probed.

'Yes, but only with jewellery, not *money*,' Cleo tossed back scornfully, as if it made all the difference in the world. And perhaps it wasn't just semantics, thought Regan, her emotions churning in dark turmoil. At least both participants in the transaction knew the score, and there was no intention to deceive with any romantic pretence of love and caring.

What would it be like to make love with someone on a purely physical basis? she wondered with a shivery thrill. Without the pretences. With a stranger. Someone who had no preconceived notions about your desirability, or your ability to respond, who just wanted a lusty romp in the hay with no questions asked...

An idea, as bizarre and impractical as it was wicked and daring, slyly insinuated itself into her consciousness. After all that had happened was she going to continue to allow herself to be a victim, crippled by the lies with which Michael had ruthlessly manipulated their marriage, or was she prepared to reach out and grab at a chance to shatter his power over her for ever?

'A glamorous party, some recreational sex and a gold bracelet or a pair of diamond studs to wear home afterwards...what more could a girl ask of a date?' Cleo boasted feebly, waving a limp hand and drawing Regan's attention to the thick chased-gold bangle clasped around her bony wrist.

She stared at it as if hypnotised, goaded to ask, 'But how can you? I mean, what would happen if you found the man—you know...physically repulsive?'

'I don't *have* to have sex with them if I don't want to, it's not *compulsory*,' Cleo said through gritted teeth, distracted by another threatening liquid rumble in her belly. 'Derek never promises a guaranteed score—that would be tacky. Anyway, sometimes all *they* want is to show up somewhere with a flirtatious woman dangling off their arm. But most times it doesn't end up platonic, because I don't see anything wrong with sleeping with a guy you've just met if he turns you on, and since Derek only does favours for the movers and the shakers of this world...well, power's a great aphrodisiac in itself, isn't it?

'It so happens most of them are a hell of lot more virile and attractive than the average Joe Loser who tries to pick you up in a bar and thinks the price of a drink entitles him to a night in the sack! As if!'

Regan had been an earnest, nineteen-year-old virgin studying pre-law at university when she had first met Michael. She had never been picked up in a bar either before or since. She had never even wondered what it might be like.

Until now.

Now she was wondering about all sorts of things that she had never before considered.

'What's his name?' she ventured. 'The man you're supposed to meet tonight?'

'Oh, God, who *cares*?' Cleo groaned, rolling off the bed to hit the floor running. 'Look, just get hold of Derek and let him sort things out, OK? I don't give a stuff what happens—all I want is to be left alone to spew my guts out in peace!'

So Regan left her wallowing in her misery and went to rifle the contents of the sequinned purse she picked up from the floor of the lounge. From it she extracted Derek's business card, and, after a moment of shocked contemplation, one of the packets of condoms that Cleo obviously considered essential dating equipment. Surely she hadn't expected to use all four packets in *one night*!

Pushing that daunting thought aside, and acutely conscious of time ticking away, Regan hurried through her nervous preparations, hampered by her restricted access to the bathroom. Luckily she had washed her hair that morning before work, so a quick shower sufficed, and she borrowed some of Lisa's manufacturers' samples to experiment with a bolder style of make-up which made her violet eyes look provocatively large and heavy-lidded. Her hand shook as she carefully applied a thick coating of black mascara, her mother's oft-repeated catch-phrase ringing silently in her ears: *A painted woman is the devil's handmaiden.*

Fortunately for her nagging conscience, Saleena arrived home just as Regan was ready to leave, and she was able to gratefully hand over the responsibility for their miserable guest.

'I was going to study for next week's exam,' Saleena had protested mildly, her exotic brown eyes taking in Regan's uncharacteristic glamour. 'But I suppose I can keep an eye on Miss Chunderful while I'm at it, to make sure she doesn't drown in the toilet. Where're you off to?'

'I have a date,' Regan replied, fussing with her hair in the hall mirror so that she didn't have to look her flatmate in the face.

'No kidding? Cool!' Saleena approved the unprecedented event with her customary laid-back nonchalance. 'Who with?'

'Oh, no one you'd know,' said Regan vaguely, not about to confess that she didn't know either. For all her fun-loving personality, Saleena had a tendency to be a little over-protective where Regan was concerned, perceptive enough to realise what a culture shock it had been for her to move from a ritzy house in the suburbs to a cramped inner-city flat with two gregarious bachelorettes.

'OK. Have a good time.' No one could claim that Saleena Patel couldn't take a subtle hint to mind her own business. She flashed a cheerful smile. 'Did Lisa at least do the food shopping for tonight, do you know?'

'No, but after I listened to her message I went and got a few things down the road.' Regan was halfway out of the door before she recognised a serious flaw in her plan. She hurried back to find Saleena in the kitchen, unpacking the small plastic shopping bag that Regan had left on the bench-top.

'By the way, if Cleo asks, tell her not to worry—everything's sorted out as far as Derek's concerned and she can forget all about it, because the whole thing was apparently all off anyway…'

'What thing?' Saleena asked, opening a packet of dry pasta, and when Regan's face pinkened betrayingly she grinned and rolled her eyes. 'Oh, one of Derek's high-flying pals was supposed to be in town looking for some action, huh? No wonder Cleo's yowling so loud in there—she thinks she's missing out on her next jewellery fix!'

'You *know* about that?'

'Sure,' Saleena admitted casually, snacking on a brittle strand of spaghetti. 'She even tried to get me interested in joining Derek's swinging circle at one stage, but I told her I'd rather choose my own partners, thanks…'

Saleena was so blasé in her acceptance that Regan was once more made aware of her embarrassing naivety. What had been a shock to her was already common knowledge to her flatmates, and probably most of their friends. None of them was married, and all of them seemed to be sexually active, so doubtless they didn't see anything so shocking in Cleo's behaviour.

Regan contrived to act blasé now, as Pierre ushered her further into the huge, fan-shaped living space dominated by a wraparound view of the city skyline. Soft up-lights on the smooth walls and on slender free-standing lamp-bases revealed a room that was a symphony of delicate colour—subtle, warm hues blended and contrasted to present an impression of exquisite harmony. Outside the full-length windows, the wide, sweeping curve of a marble ledge echoed the various curves within—the round support pillars, the round marble coffee table centred between two long, half-round couches in blush-coloured leather and the semi-circular padded chairs dotted about the room, facing the fanned-out city. Away to one end, a few more steps led up to a raised dining area with a huge oval wooden table, and beyond that, presumably, to the kitchen. At the other end of the room was a curving corridor whose even subtler lighting suggested…the bedrooms?

Regan hastily turned her head, forcing herself to concentrate on the main room.

'It's beautiful!' she murmured, and then was annoyed with herself for sounding awed. A sophisticated woman of the world would take such beauty for granted. Knowing Cleo, the first thing she would have done was demand an ashtray! 'Monsieur has impeccable taste,' she added, with a suggestion of dry mockery.

'Merci.' Pierre shifted his bandy legs, clicking his polished black heels and inclining his head. 'This is a corporate apartment, used by many executives, so it must fulfil many functions. It was I who hired the interior designer and advised on and approved her designs, as well as supervising the physical decorating work.'

'You!' This time her jaw did drop at the idea of this ugly little man helping create such beauty.

'Appearances can be deceptive,' he replied modestly, un-offended.

Tell me about it! thought Regan evilly, her hand spasming on her purse as another spurt of anger shot through her veins. Michael had been blessed with sunny good looks—blond hair, boyish features, guileless blue eyes, and a white smile that predicated a charmingly frank and open manner.

Who would have believed that behind that golden façade had been a lying tongue and a cheating black heart—a man without honour? Not Regan. Right up to the night that Michael had wrapped his precious BMW status symbol around a tree she had believed that they had a secure and happy marriage, with only minor problems to cloud their shared contentment. She had admired her husband's dedication to work and respected his ambition to succeed. Only after he had died and the huge, unexpected bills had started to roll in had she begun to re-examine her former contentment, and come to realise that her willingness to overlook the flaws in their relationship had played right into Michael's cheating hands.

Over the following months, as the mess his lies had created had grown to staggering proportions, she had gradually been forced to the painful conclusion that, to all intents and purposes, she had been sleeping with a stranger for the four years of their marriage!

So what she was going to do tonight was not so very different after all, she thought bitterly, as she watched Pierre begin to put his personal orders into action.

He moved across to open the curved doors of a teak cabinet, revealing a wide-screen television and the most complex stereo system that Regan had ever seen. Concealed in a false support pillar next to the cabinet were racks of video tapes and CDs, arranged with alphabetical precision.

Pierre settled her on one of the demi-couches with the re-mote controls and furnished her with a vodka and tonic with a twist of lime in a chilled crystal glass, setting it down on a round side-table on top of a deftly folded cocktail napkin. He told her that the bathroom was down the curving corridor to her right and if she had a question, or required a refill for her drink, she could summon Pierre merely by pressing one of the hidden buttons strategically placed around the room, or she could help herself from the super-latively stocked bar which opened out from yet another mock-pillar.

Left alone, Regan drank her vodka quickly, in the hope that it might help her to relax. Except for warming the pit of her belly it didn't seem to have any appreciable effect, so she guiltily fixed herself another, embarrassed at the idea of summoning Pierre back so soon…he might think he had a rampant alcoholic on his hands!

Sipping more slowly, she ignored the television and chose a CD of smoky ballads from the wonderfully eclectic selection of music, and after a bit of clumsy experimenta-tion managed to get the remote control to set the volume and balance at the perfect level for her position in the room. As she lounged back on the feather-soft couch in her splen-did isolation she reflected that she could get used to being ultra-rich!

The most difficult part about flatting was the lack of pri-vacy. As an only child Regan had been closely monitored by her over-strict mother, but Michael had worked such long hours—or at least, he had *said* that he was working—that during her marriage she had got used to the quiet free-dom of having the whole house to herself for hours on end. In the flat there seemed to be a constant flow of visitors and phone calls and emotional upheavals, accompanied by the loud, head-banging music that Lisa adored.

However, all the activity *did* serve as a welcome distraction from her own weighty problems, Regan acknowledged. And although Lisa and Saleena outstripped her in street-smarts, Regan was the one they turned to when they wanted down-to-earth advice on practical matters—like how to get a pizza stain out of a silk camisole or how to fill in their tax returns. Because she had studied law, she was a valuable source of information for friends who had disputes with their landlords or whose sleazy boyfriends had stashed a joint in their handbags. It didn't matter to them that Regan had dropped out of her degree the previous semester, a year before she was due to graduate, it only mattered that her informed opinion was free. To Regan what mattered was that she felt *valued*, something that her shredded confidence had badly needed.

Pierre drifted back with more murmured apologies for the elusive Monsieur and offered her a small plate of delectable canapés and a glass of champagne. Thinking that it would be unwise to mix her drinks, Regan declined the latter and hungrily consumed the former.

Her stomach gurgled in gratitude. Lunch had been a hurried sandwich at her desk and breakfast had been a mere kick-start from a cup of espresso. In the last few weeks her normally healthy appetite had dwindled to almost nothing, but now she found herself suddenly utterly ravenous.

She pressed the button concealed under a side-table, and when Pierre appeared with startling speed and stealth she sheepishly asked if there were any more canapés.

'They really were delicious,' she added, to excuse her greed. 'You must have a splendid cook.'

'But that is me.' After a couple of vodkas, his ugliness of grin seemed actually endearing. 'I am, after all, a Frenchman, and we excel at such things. I am pleased that you enjoy them.'

The ballads drifted to an end, and Regan realised that she had been waiting in the apartment for over an hour.

Somehow, it hadn't seemed that long. She put on some moody jazz, and turned up the volume.

Placing her empty glass on the bar, she yielded to nervous curiosity and practical necessity and wandered down the hall to find the bathroom. It was as luxurious as the rest of the apartment, boasting a multi-head shower and an oval sunken bath almost twice the size of the entire bathroom back at the flat. Big, fluffy towels warmed on a heated towel-rail, and to Regan's amusement the toilet seat was also kept at a cosy temperature! Every conceivable toiletry a guest could require was thoughtfully provided, including—she discovered when she opened one of the drawers—a selection of various brands of tampons and condoms, nestled side by side in ironic juxtaposition.

She couldn't resist peeping into the half-open doors further down the hall to discover an office, two huge single bedrooms and, at the far end, an even bigger room with a sprawling king-sized bed which looked, to Regan's magnified awareness, as if it would sleep an army.

Most definitely the master bedroom, she decided, backing out…but not before she had noticed the black silk sheets, the tubular wooden slats on the teak bed-head and ends, unnervingly reminiscent of prison bars, and the vast mirror on the wall opposite the bed.

At least it wasn't fixed on the ceiling! she thought as she hurried back to the bar, wondering what she would do if 'Monsieur' turned out to be seriously kinky.

She diluted another icy vodka with a splash of tonic. She still wasn't entirely confident that she could handle a normal man's basic requirements, let alone satisfy one who demanded a performance artist in bed. But Pierre had said that the apartment was designed for use by a number of corporate executives, she reminded herself, in which case the master bedroom was generic, and not the personalised domain of the current occupant.

In fact, she thought, looking around the living area with a more critical gaze, there were no personal touches that she could see in the whole apartment. Like a plush hotel suite, or a photograph in an interior design magazine, it was sterile of private clutter. Unlike a permanent residence there were no books, photographs, knick-knacks or stray possessions to give any clue to the character of the present occupier.

When she tired of mooching around she absently kicked off her shoes and curled up on the wide, squashy cushions of the couch, sipping her drink, nibbling snacks and closing her eyes to soak up the music. She had almost dozed off when, coinciding with the end of the jazz disc, Regan heard the distinctive closing clunk of a heavy door and a rumbling exchange of masculine voices.

She leapt up from the couch, almost tripping over in her haste, smoothing down her dress and then her hair, unconsciously biting on her lower lip as she looked towards the entranceway. The voices faded briefly to a murmur and then became more distinct, Pierre's and one other...deeper and more staccato, edged with a weary impatience.

Suddenly Regan realised that she was curling her stockinged toes into the thick carpet, and she looked desperately around for her discarded high heels. She scooped them up and was hopping on one leg, still cramming the first shoe on her foot, when a living cliché came sauntering down the stairs.

He was tall, dark and handsome, wide-shouldered and lean-hipped, and he moved with the fluidity of an athlete.

Regan was stricken. She had gone from the ridiculous to the sublime in the space of a few hours!

This was going to turn out to be another nerve-shattering case of mistaken identity, she just *knew* it! Her whole mad plan had been doomed from the start.

He couldn't *possibly* be the man she had been waiting for; he was simply too unbelievably perfect!

CHAPTER THREE

'ALLOW me…'

Regan hadn't realised that she had dropped her other shoe until he stooped to pick it up.

'Uh, thank you…' she faltered, still balanced like a stork on her bare foot, stunned by the impact of his appearance.

Close up, the new arrival wasn't as classically handsome as he had first appeared. But he was certainly tall—over six feet—and his black suit and midnight-blue shirt and tie accentuated his dark colouring. His raven hair was thick and well-shaped, springing back from a slight widow's peak to brush his collar at the back. He was somewhere in his mid-thirties, she guessed, and already carrying a tiny trace of grey at his narrow temples.

There was intelligence in his gaze and cynicism in the hard cast of his features—a gambler's face, tense and watchful but betraying little of his own thoughts.

His eyes, which she had somehow expected to be also dark, were a light, penetrating steely-grey, slightly hooded under their heavy lids, and his stern Roman nose was framed by prominent cheekbones and a granite jaw. For such an athletic-looking man his skin was surprisingly pale and fine-grained, except on his lower cheeks and upper lip where it was roughened by a blue-black growth that was well beyond a five o'clock shadow.

Regan had to look a long, long way up at him, and as he inclined his head to meet her curious gaze she noticed the tracery of scars writhing up the left side of his lean throat and licking up under his jaw: the unmistakable scars

28

of an old burn. To leave such a permanent stamp the injury must have been serious, and agonisingly painful.

So...he was damaged too—only his scars were on the outside...

Regan's eyes flickered down to the flimsy black shoe cupped in his large hand as she fought to reject the dangerous rush of empathy. She saw that his hands, too, bore evidence of scarring, but it was absurd to think that a man like him would ever want, or need, her sympathy.

'I—I took them off,' she explained breathlessly, lowering her shod foot to the floor and transferring her weight to it, going on tiptoe with the other to maintain stability.

He smiled at her redundant comment, a slow curve of his well-defined mouth that made her wobble on her uneven perch.

'So I see,' he murmured on a light, teasing note that was totally at odds with his air of hard-bitten cynicism and the hooded wariness of his eyes.

His stroking thumb measured the length of the delicate spike heel in his hand. 'Were they hurting you?'

His voice was deep and rasping, the husky edge abrading her senses like velvet sandpaper.

'No—I—I was just lying down...'

He arched his graceful brows and she was aghast to feel herself blush as she was visited with a sudden mental image of herself languishing nude on black silk sheets, like a slave girl awaiting the arrival of her lord and master.

'On the *couch*,' she firmly emphasised, her mouth unknowingly prim.

'Of course,' he agreed, the quicksilver amusement in his penetrating eyes making her wonder whether he could read her skittish mind. She went hot all over. Naive she might be, but surely she wasn't *that* transparent?

She tossed her head, rejecting the appalling notion, and

adopted a pose of haughty confidence which came immediately under assault.

'May I?'

Without waiting for an answer he knelt on the white
carpet and encircled the ankle of her stockinged foot with
lean fingers, tugging lightly to lift it from the floor.

Regan squeaked as she teetered off balance on her spin-
dly heel, and grabbed at his shoulders to stay upright. Even
through the padding of expensive fabric she could feel the
shifting layers of solid muscle.

'What are you *doing*?' she gasped, wondering if he was
some kind of weird foot-fetishist. 'Oh…'

She watched him slide her shoe back onto her foot, wiggling it from side to side to ease the fit. 'Thank you…you
needn't have bothered,' she mumbled, embarrassed.

He tipped his head back, making no effort to rise. 'I
enjoyed it,' he said, meeting her wide-eyed gaze, his fingers
still lightly encircling her fine-boned ankle. 'You have very
pretty feet. And legs…' he added, brushing his fingers
gently up her calf to linger in the sensitive hollow at the
back of her knee.

Regan stiffened as a violent tingle shot from her toes to
her groin. Her heart beat furiously in her chest and her
breathing quickened. She was no longer in any doubt. This
was it. This was *him*. 'Thank you,' she said again, hoping
that she didn't look as flustered as she felt.

'I'm sorry you had such a long wait. I hope you weren't
too bored.' Having thoroughly disconcerted her with his
Prince Charming act, he rose slowly back to his full height.
Regan felt as if he was surveying every inch of her on the
way up, and her body prickled with awareness, her eyes
darkening and her nostrils flaring at the warm, spicy male
scent that rose from his unbuttoned jacket.

'Pierre tells me that your name is Eve.'

She nodded, her eyelashes fluttering nervously at his

towering proximity| Being short, she was used to men
looming over her, but she wasn't used to feeling such an
acute sense of feminine self-awareness.

Unlike Pierre, he didn't display even a flicker of scep-
ticism. 'How appropriate,' he said, capturing her hand and
raising her knuckles briefly to his lips. 'In that case you
can call me Adam.'

'Your name is Adam?' she repeated, jolted by the brush
of his warm mouth into forgetting that the last thing she
wanted to do was make an issue out of their names. Who
would have thought one innocuous kiss on the back of her
hand could feel so flagrantly erotic?

'One of them,' he smoothly conceded, stretching the coincidence. He lowered, but did not release her captive hand.
'So, here we are, Adam and Eve in a garden of de-
lights…and this time there's not a serpent in sight.'

No serpent, just a worm who had finally turned! thought
Regan, rescued from her confusion by a stirring of the
wicked sense of humour which had lately been all but
smothered out of existence.

'I'm sorry Cleo had to cancel,' she lied, sliding her tingling fingers slowly out of his hand, her fingernails scraping
deliberately across his relaxed palm, crossing the faint ridge
of a scar. 'I hope you aren't too disappointed.' She followed up her words by tilting her head so that her glossy
locks slipped against her soft cheek, and giving him what
she hoped was a brazen, woman-of-the-world smile.

A faintly arrested expression crossed his face. 'Every
cloud has a silver lining,' he murmured, looking from the
curve of her mouth to the glimpse of delicate earlobe, bare
of ornamentation, to the turbulent depths of her violet eyes,
shimmering with defiant excitement.

'And into every life a little rain must fall,' she responded
vaguely, distracted by the darts of electricity zinging along

her nerves into trotting out another of her mother's irritating maxims.

His lips quirked. 'Are you talking about Cleo's life, or mine?' His voice dropped to an insinuating growl. 'You're not planning to rain on my parade, are you, Eve?'

She wasn't quite sure of his meaning, but judging from his tone it had to be indecent. She touched her tongue to her upper lip. Witty sexual repartee was not exactly her forte.

She blundered on with the cryptic analogy. 'A man like you is always prepared for any eventuality. I'm sure you come equipped with your own umbrella.'

'A whole drawerful of them,' he agreed blandly. For some reason that made her remember what she had seen in the bathroom. No...surely they weren't talking about *contraception*?

Were they?

Whatever the topic of conversation, she was *not* going to ruin her image by blushing again!

'You look tired,' she blurted, seizing on the truth as the perfect diversionary tactic. She had noticed the faint blue tinge to the pale skin under his eyes, and the subtle tautness around his mouth and jaw that suggested a stern measure of control, and now she identified the lazy burr that had entered his tone. He was a man who concealed his fatigue well—as he probably instinctively hid any form of weakness.

'It's been a rough day. But don't worry, I'm rapidly getting my second wind,' he promised drily. He shot his cuff and glanced at his no-nonsense steel watch. 'I know it's late, and we may not get there for cocktails, but we can still make the banquet. If you'll just give me a few minutes to change...'

He had thought she was complaining! 'Oh, no—I didn't

mean—er Y-you don't have to rush—' she protested, laying a restraining hand on his elbow as he turned away.

All his former wariness had returned, and his smile was sharp with cynical understanding as he looked over his shoulder at her. 'Nonsense. You came here expecting to attend an elegant party at the most exclusive restaurant in town and I don't intend to deprive you of the pleasure,' he soothed.

Regan ignored his words in favour of his tone. He *was* tired, but he was resigned to going out because it was part of the unwritten bargain, and he was obviously a man who strictly honoured his obligations, however tiresome.

'I really don't mind if we go out to dinner or not,' she said, her hand tightening on the fabric of his suit.

'Really?' He turned back, but it was clear that he didn't believe her. He thought her a clone of the worldly Cleo—a selfish little cat who was out to milk their bargain for everything she could get.

'I'm not very hungry, anyway,' she told him, letting her hand drop. 'An expensive meal would be totally wasted on me. I think I ate too many of Pierre's wonderful canapés,' she explained ruefully.

There was a tiny pause as he studied her expression. 'So you would be quite content if I asked him to prepare a light meal for us here, instead,' he said slowly.

'I actually don't think I could manage anything at all,' she confessed, her earlier appetite having been swallowed up by the tension of meeting him. 'Whereas you probably need something substantial after your tough day…'

'But you're happy to keep me company while *I* eat…'

What did he think, that she would sulk and pout because he wanted to eat and she didn't? 'Of course.'

'And we'll join the party afterwards…'

'We don't have to do that, either, if you don't feel like going out. Unless, of course, there's some reason that you need to be seen making an appearance there,' she added hurriedly when his eyes narrowed, taking on a new and disturbing intensity.

'So…what you're suggesting is that we not leave the apartment at all?'

His soft-voiced drawl made Regan's knees go weak as she realised the full implications of her impulsive offer. If they didn't go out, then there would be nothing, and no one, to distract them from the *real* purpose of the evening. No way to hide from the consequences of her own actions.

'You're willing to forgo the excitement of a night on the town because *I've* had a rough day?' he continued in that same tone of silken curiosity.

She grasped her courage and opted for honesty. 'I expect that I'll have all the excitement I can handle right here,' she confessed, her wry words provoking him into a deep, purring laugh.

'Both kind *and* flattering—the perfect companion after a hard day at the office! I look forward to finding out how many other virtues you possess.'

Regan basked in an unexpected thrill of accomplishment. She had captivated his jaded interest—made him laugh. Maybe this was going to be easier than she had thought. After all, unlike her husband, this man *wanted* her to be sexy and seductive!

'If you were expecting a virtuous woman, you're going to be severely disappointed.' She flirted up at him through her lowered lashes.

He took her chin between his thumb and forefinger and tilted it until her eyelashes flew wide. 'No, I don't think so,' he mused, looking deep into her slumberous eyes. He brushed the pad of his thumb across her mouth, causing it to quiver and part, and then pressed firmly against her plump lower lip. She gave a little gasp as the tip of her tongue tasted the saltiness of his skin.

He misunderstood her tiny flinch. 'Don't worry, I'm not smearing your lipstick…it appears to have worn off.'

His tolerant humour made it obvious that he was used to women whose looks were their stock-in-trade.

Regan's eyebrows crumpled at the dent to her glamorous self-image. She had never thought to recheck her lipstick. 'It must have gone to garnish the canapés,' she laughed huskily, to disguise her chagrin. 'I'll put some more on while you're talking to Pierre about dinner—'

'No. Don't bother…' The pressure of his thumb stopped her words in her mouth. 'I like the nude look. I like the contrast between the sultry seduction of your elaborate eye make-up and the soft, pink innocence of your mouth.' And, as if that wasn't erotic enough to take her breath away, he added casually, 'Besides, I don't like the taste of lipstick.'

He took away his thumb and she swayed slightly, thinking that he was going to suit his actions to his words, but instead of following up his claim with a kiss he said indulgently, 'So how about fixing me a drink while I go and see Pierre about dinner? Whisky—on the rocks. The eight-year-old Scotch, if you please…'

Regan's hands were still trembling as she uncapped the Scotch and poured his drink, clashing the neck of the bottle against the squat crystal glass.

She ordered herself to calm down. They had the whole evening ahead of them…of course he didn't want to rush things. He was a highly civilised man. He wanted to unwind from his busy day first, to be amused and entertained in undemanding company. As Cleo had loudly insisted—this wasn't prostitution. And Adam had just proved her right with his willingness to do what his escort wanted rather than exercise his own preference. The message was that Regan was here to enjoy herself, not simply to provide raw sex on command…

When she turned from the bar her heart jumped to find

that Adam was already back, lounging on the couch, his long legs splayed, his head tipped back against the pale cushions, exposing his scarred throat as he gazed up at the ceiling. He must have moved as silently as a cat. He had shed his jacket and tie, the subtle sheen of his dark blue shirt catching the light where his arms stretched along the back of the couch. His collar was unbuttoned, and as she moved closer she could see a drift of dark hair revealed by the narrow V of his open shirt.

The ice cubes tinkled against the glass in her hand and he rolled his head to one side and lazily watched her approach. In spite of the relaxation of his big body, Regan wasn't fooled into thinking that his brain was clouded by his fatigue. His eyes, though heavy-lidded, weren't in the least bit drowsy as she offered him his drink.

He shifted his torso, dropping his right hand to rest near his hip, but made no attempt to reach for the glass. After a moment of dithering uncertainty she stepped between his splayed knees to bend over and place his drink directly into his hand.

His fingers flexed around the glass, momentarily trapping hers against the slippery surface, and when she lifted her head enquiringly she saw that his eyes weren't on her face. They were level with the plunging front of her dress, where her small, unconfined breasts, rounded almost to voluptuousness by gravity, crowded up against the edge of the deeply scooped neckline.

Trapped in her provocative pose, Regan was shocked to feel her nipples tighten and begin to rub against the material with every indrawn breath, as if beckoning his attention.

'You're not wearing a bra.' He voiced his intimate discovery, lifting his other hand to languidly trace a finger around her curving neckline, careful not to touch the creamy swells of flesh, only the seam of fabric against which they strained. He took a sip of his drink as he did so, allowing her captured fingers to slip away from the glass.

Deprived of the excuse to flaunt her modest charms in his face, Regan had to force herself to move. All he'd had to do, she thought, was tuck his finger into that edge and he would have been stroking her aching breasts...

'I—I'm so small I don't usually have to,' she said, her head throbbing with blood as she straightened reluctantly within the corral of his strong thighs.

'The best things come in small packages,' he murmured, letting his fingers trail down her bare arm, and then drift lightly over her hip and flank to the sensitive back of her knee, which he had earlier caressed with such electrifying effect.

'Stockings or pantyhose?' he wondered, plucking gently at the silky sheer black nylon.

Regan's tongue felt thick in her mouth. 'Stockings.'

Since she'd been widowed she had discovered a simple economy: it was cheaper to mix and match pairs of stockings than to buy pantyhose that might have to be discarded because of a ladder in one leg. But tonight it hadn't been economy dictating her choice of underwear.

'And, let me guess...black lace suspenders?'

She blushed at his gentle mockery. It seemed like such a ridiculous cliché, and yet the garter belt had made her feel wickedly sexy when she had been clipping it onto her silky stockings. She had bought the lacy black underwear on her second wedding anniversary, in a vain attempt to inject some excitement into her marriage bed. Of course, she hadn't known at the time that Michael's excitement was reserved for his busty blonde mistress!

Holding her rosy-cheeked gaze, Adam smoothed his spread hand slowly back up over the hem of her skirt and across the front of her thigh until he encountered the betraying outline of her suspender, pressing lightly to imprint it on his palm.

'Anything else?'

All her attention was concentrated on his hand on her leg.

'I beg your pardon?'

He took another swallow of whisky, watching her over the silvery rim. 'I asked if you were wearing anything else?'

She licked her lips. 'You mean a-apart from my dress?' she said huskily.

'I mean *under* your dress,' he clarified, removing his hand, but leaving behind its heated brand on her thigh.

Her eyes widened and she nodded jerkily. What kind of woman didn't wear panties when she went out, for goodness' sake? What if she got knocked over in the street, or was ambushed by a freak gust of wind? The potential for embarrassment was enormous. Even Lisa, who was an ardent minimalist, wore tanga briefs to cover the bare essentials!

'Black lace?'

She nodded again, riveted by the breathtaking boldness of that pantherish stare. He sipped his whisky and she had a strong premonition that what he was planning to say next was in the nature of a challenge.

'Would you take them off for me, if I asked you to?'

The air was sucked from her lungs and a molten wave of heat scorched through her veins.

'Y-You mean…here? *Now?*'

He tilted his head. 'Have I shocked you?'

Senseless.

Regan was furious. She'd thought she had been doing so well! And now he had flung down this outrageous gauntlet.

There was a faint smile on his face as he waited to see what she would do next, and to Regan the hint of mocking detachment in his regard was an added insult. She had a lowering suspicion that he wouldn't be surprised if she melted in a puddle of stammering embarrassment—that he had seen through her sophisticated charade to the nervous little mouse beneath.

No! She wasn't going to be shocked by his indecent proposal. Wasn't this precisely why she had come here— to play adult games, to experiment, to explore beyond the limits of her own experience? To celebrate her freedom from the tyranny of lies by flinging open the doors on her sequestered sexuality?

Aware of the danger she was courting, Regan was gripped by a powerful urge to shake up that infuriating masculine self-assurance…to pay him back, shock for shock. It struck her quite forcibly that, in spite of the explicit sexual threat that Adam represented, she was less afraid now than she had been all evening.

So… Adam wanted to see how far she could be pushed, did he? Well, now was the time to show him that she was more than equal to his game. Maybe if she had been more keen to indulge in sexual role-playing during their marriage then her husband would have been less keen to stray— except that Michael had never encouraged his loving wife to be anything other than strictly conventional in bed.

Conventional and boring!

Without a word Regan reached up under her skirt and hooked her shaking thumbs into the high-cut sides of her bikini panties.

Adam's face was suddenly wiped clean of all expression and he moved with lightning swiftness, his thighs tensing as he leaned abruptly forward to clamp a preventive hand on her forearm.

'I'm sorry…I was teasing you. I apologise for my lack of finesse,' he said, coolly snatching his gauntlet back out of her reckless grasp. 'I'd hate to spoil our evening by rushing pleasures that are better savoured. I'm afraid the potent combination of a sensuous woman and an excellent Scotch temporarily overwhelmed my self-control—not to mention my good manners,' he added, with just the right touch of rueful self-derision. He settled back with his whisky, looking up at her with carefully modified solemnity.

Smooth-talking devil! He might have been only teasing, but he had been in full control of all his faculties. He had been testing her compliance.

Pumped for action, Regan was tempted to ignore his glib apology and go ahead with her daring act of defiance. However, he had just referred to her as a sensuous woman, and for that delicious compliment she was almost willing to forgive him. If he had called her beautiful she wouldn't have believed him, but to be sensuous a woman didn't have to have model-girl looks. Beauty was only skin-deep, whereas sensuality was innate—and therefore infinitely more desirable as far as Regan was concerned.

She reluctantly removed her hands and ran them slowly up and down the side-seams of her dress, deliberately wiggling her hips as she smoothed the rumpled fabric back into place. It felt wild and wanton, stroking herself like this in front of him, but it was the kind of thing that a sensuous woman *would* do—inviting a man to share her feminine appreciation of her own body.

He watched, his face softening with a return of his former amusement, but this time it was laced with a measure of wry respect.

'Why don't you join me?' he murmured, intrigued by the hint of shy excitement in her slinky self-absorption.

'Thank you, I will…' she purred, caught up in her performance, her eyes glowing with smug triumph as she sank onto the empty cushions beside him. The couch was long enough to take his full length—and wide enough for an orgy, she thought, nervously.

'I meant in a drink,' he explained, toasting her with his glass.

'Oh…' Her sultry look dissolved. 'I did have a vodka and tonic around here somewhere…' She frowned vaguely about.

'Forget it. Just go ahead and help yourself to another,' Adam advised with the careless ease of a man who never had to worry about a budget—for alcohol or anything else. Lounging at his ease, he obviously expected her to play hostess while Pierre was occupied in the kitchen.

She thought she had probably infused enough alcohol into her system as it was, but a drink would give her some occupation for her nervous hands.

She stood up, ultra-conscious of her lack of grace as her narrow heels tilted awkwardly into the thick pile of the carpet and almost tipped her sideways into his lap. 'Shall I freshen yours, too?' she asked, to distract him from her clumsiness.

'No, it's fine,' he said, swirling the contents of his glass. 'You pour a mean Scotch.'

Regan shrugged with her hands. 'My father was a big whisky-drinker—' She bit her lip as she turned away, annoyed at her slip. She knew the cheap rot-gut that had killed her father by the time she was ten had little in common with the smooth, expensive, aromatic spirit that Adam savoured.

'And your husband? What about him?'

Her body stiffened as she swung back to face his grating accusation.

'My what?'

He caught at her left hand, lifting it to the light so that they both could see the faint band of pale skin on her ring finger. He immediately let it drop, as if contaminated by her touch.

'Are you married?' he demanded harshly.

She hesitated. Just what kind of man was she dealing with? 'What if I said yes?'

The light grey eyes hardened to cold steel. 'Then I'd politely show you the door. And Derek would cease to be part of my acquaintance. He knows my opinion on the subject: I don't sleep with other men's wives. And I despise cheating and deception—*No-one* gets a second chance to breach my trust. So if you *are* married tell me now, before this goes any further, because I make a very bad enemy…'

Regan was stunned by the ruthless force behind his pronouncement. He possessed the will, the wealth and the power to protect his personal honour, and wouldn't hesitate to use those weapons to threaten and punish anyone who sought to compromise it in pursuit of their own interests.

'I'm not married,' she declared huskily, her curiosity more than satisfied.

Unfortunately, his suspicion was too sharp to be easily blunted by the belated admission.

'But you *were*,' he rapped out. 'Divorced?'

If she hadn't been so naive for so long she might have been able to say yes with dignity. As things stood, there was little honour in being Michael's widow.

She shook her head and looked down, disturbed to find herself twisting the non-existent ring on her finger.

'Widowed. Mi—my husband was killed in a car crash.'

There was a brief, splintering silence.

'I'm sorry.'

Her chin jerked up at the deep gentleness of his tone, her cheeks stinging as if he had reached out and slapped her. The cold steel had gone from his eyes, to be replaced by a smoky speculation that made her angry heart burn. She didn't want tenderness, dammit! All she wanted from him was one night of simple, uncomplicated lust.

'Don't be.'

His eyes narrowed at the clipped command.

'Like that, was it?' he mused, still with that threatening undertone of softness.

She raked her fingers through her hair, and flicked the ends over her shoulder in a gesture half-nervous, half-defiant. 'You can't begin to imagine what it was like,' she said with a tight smile. 'And I'd rather you didn't bother.'

'How long ago did it happen?'

She tossed him a frustrated look. She could guess what he was thinking—he was wondering whether she was acting out some psychological trauma associated with her marriage.

With a vengeance!

Her eyes flashed. 'Long enough.'

Eight months. Long enough for her to have found out why Michael had insisted on handling all their joint finances. He had spent their savings, run up credit card debts, mortgaged the house and taken out loans for which, as his next of kin and inheritor of his estate, she was liable. The absence of a will had compounded the legal problems, and only after months of trying to straighten out the chaotic financial tangle her lawyer had informed her that there was little left to inherit.

And two weeks ago she had finally discovered why.

Two weeks ago she had received a tearful visit from Michael's long-term mistress, the earthy, voluptuous Cindy...and his three-and-a-half-year-old son.

Her last remaining shred of respect for Michael had vanished as she had been forced to face the degrading truth that for the entire duration of their marriage her husband had been living an expensive double life. One that she, all unknowingly, had helped finance!

Well, tonight she would have her revenge.

Tonight she wasn't going to be the sweet, understanding little woman, bravely swallowing her pride and doing what was expected of her.

Tonight *she* was going to be the ruthless user, the unrepentant sinner…

CHAPTER FOUR

'SO YOU don't miss having a husband?'

Like a hole in the head, Regan wanted to snap. Instead, she channelled her anger into another emotion.

'I miss...*certain things* about being married...' She tossed Adam a suggestive smile and swung back over to the bar. Conscious of his eyes levelled on her back, she relaxed her shoulders and moved with an exaggerated sway of her hips, the way she had seen Lisa move on the catwalk.

Drink in hand, she strolled back with that same, slinky roll and crossed her legs as she sat down, letting her skirt ride up above her knees as far as it liked.

'Would you like me to do that for you?' she offered, as he eased a hand across the back of his neck, digging his fingers into the tense muscle.

'You do massage?'

'I'm not a qualified masseur or anything,' she said innocently, 'but I'm sure I could give you a rub that would ease some of your tension.'

'I think having your hands on my body is more likely to increase rather than decrease my tension,' he said, with the faint smile that turned her insides to marshmallow.

She cleared her throat of a tiny obstruction. In the background she was vaguely aware of Pierre, moving to and fro from the kitchen to the table. 'So...what sort of things do you normally do to unwind after a hard day at the office?' she asked.

From his bland expression she knew he was going to tease her again. 'Well...I find flirting with a warmly receptive woman very relaxing.'

'Then you should soon be a positive puddle of content-ment,' she responded, equally bland.

His quick grin was white and wolfish. 'I already feel myself melting. And what do you like to do to relax, Eve?'

'Oh, read, sew, cook…' she said demurely. She lowered her lashes and slowly lifted them again. 'Make love…'

'Interesting. I usually find that the act of sex has the opposite effect,' he murmured, topping her with stunning ease. 'I don't feel in the least relaxed when I'm inside a woman's body. I'm all edgy and agitated, and every muscle feels explosively hot and tight with urgency…' He paused to take a swallow of whisky, enjoying the way her violet eyes widened and the pulse at the base of her bare throat kicked up a storm. 'But perhaps the feelings are very different for a woman…'

Regan hoped not! She mastered the impulse to throw herself on top of him and demand that he demonstrate right there and then.

She gave a blasé shrug of her slender shoulders instead. 'Men and women aren't so very different—'

'Honey, if you think that, then you must have skipped human biology in high school,' he interrupted drolly.

In fact her mother *had* removed her from class whenever there had been a danger she might be contaminated by sex education disguised as legitimate learning.

'I took Classics rather than Sciences,' she retaliated. 'But I meant in terms of having equal sexual needs and desires.'

'Equal but different,' he agreed. 'I don't suppose my sexual fantasies are the same as yours.'

He sounded so smugly certain she immediately wanted to take him down a peg or two. 'Which is not to say yours are any better than mine!'

He almost choked on the dregs of his whisky as a chuckle rumbled up from his chest. 'If I show you mine will you show me yours?'

Her blank response prompted him to continue. 'Didn't you ever play doctors and nurses as a kid?'

'I was an only child.'

'And? Surely there was some chubby little charmer in the neighbourhood who suggested disappearing into the nearest wardrobe with his play-stethoscope and handy torch?'

'If he had, he'd have found himself without a head.'

'So you were an aggressive, assertive little girl?' he speculated, looking deeply intrigued.

'I was very biddable and angelic,' she said primly, using a straight face to imply that her truth was actually an outrageous lie. 'But my mother was extremely vigilant where the seven deadly sins were concerned.'

'Thereby not giving you much of a chance to be anything else,' he guessed with uncomfortably swift perception.

'I'm sure I still have my trusty halo here somewhere,' she said, delicately patting her fingertips down the side of her dress.

'Somewhat tarnished by now, I suppose?' he drawled, his gaze following the taunting trail.

'Oh, I take it out every now and then and give it a good polish,' she said, exhilarated by her newfound ability to hold her own against his quick wit.

'And groom your golden wings?'

'No wings,' she dimpled, 'but I do have a pitchfork in my other dress.'

'Ahh…a woman of dangerous contradictions. I see my first act should not have been to kiss your hand but to pat you down for concealed weapons.'

She spread her arms in graceful offering. 'Feel free to do so now; I won't hold it against you.'

'Not even if I beg?' As a laugh gurgled in her throat his eyes flicked across to the elevated dining area, where Pierre was placing a bottle of Krug champagne into a silver ice-bucket on the table, next to a covered chafing dish. He drained his glass and set it down. 'It looks as if Pierre has served up. Shall we?'

Two elegant place-settings were angled next to each other at the head of the oval table; the overhead down-lights were dimmed, and the dancing flame of a slender candle was dully reflected in the burnished surface of the wood. A sheaf of the palest pink roses in a fan-shaped hand-blown vase complemented the oval white place-mats gleaming with silver and crystal.

Adam politely said something about washing his hands, and followed Pierre briefly into the kitchen. When he returned Regan was still standing behind the chair at the head of the oval table, her hands balled by her sides, her face mantled with a light flush that made him eye her thoughtfully. As he approached she drew back the chair and invited him to be seated with a tilt of her head.

'Usurping my gentlemanly duties?' he murmured, accepting the courtesy with a lazy smile, and Regan picked up the white damask napkin from beside his plate and snapped out the starched folds to drape it across his lap. 'When I told Pierre that we wouldn't need him for the rest of the evening, I envisaged that *I* would be waiting on *you*,' he added.

'I thought you might feel in the mood to be pampered,' said Regan, unfolding her fist and casually laying another item on top of his napkin.

He glanced down, and she was elated to see the ripple of shock glaze his features. His eyelids drooped and the hard jaw slackened and it was several exhilarating heartbeats before he regained sufficient mastery of his expression to hike up a mocking eyebrow.

'Misplaced something, Eve?' He lifted the wisp of black lace above the level of the table, dangling it from his crooked finger.

'Not at all,' she drawled. His eyes were irresistibly drawn to the outline of her hips and she made the most of it, sliding her bottom onto the padded chair with provocative slowness and squirming to make herself comfortable.

'Tease!' His soft accusation was redolent with masculine appreciation as he watched the performance.

Her dress slid against her bare skin and the slight coolness between her legs made her feel dangerously vulnerable, especially when her knee brushed his under the table. She pressed her quivering thighs together, excited by her daring. It felt so good to be so thoroughly bad that she wondered why she hadn't tried it years ago.

He danced the swatch of lace on his crooked finger. 'Then what's this? Some form of nouvelle cuisine appetiser designed to stimulate my jaded palate?'

It was her turn to look glazed as he dropped the skimpy black panties onto his gold-rimmed white plate and picked up his fork to lightly stir the frothy lace.

'I must admit, they do look good enough to eat.' He twirled the fork into the silky fabric, winding it up as if it was an exotic form of pasta.

'Adam—*no*!' she squeaked, clapping her hands to her mouth to contain her appalled laughter. She hadn't expected such an obvious sophisticate to possess such a mischievous sense of humour.

He paused, looking wickedly crestfallen. 'You don't wear edible panties?' he asked.

She had seen them in novelty gift shops and thought them embarrassingly tacky. 'Certainly not!'

Her scandalised denial made his mouth twitch. 'Then I suppose I'll have to settle for whatever Pierre has rustled up,' he said, calmly plucking the panties off his fork and tucking them casually into his breast pocket. He lifted the domed lid of the chafing dish to reveal a fragrant pile of steaming stir-fried vegetables burnished with a sesame-flecked sauce. 'Will you have some?'

Regan tore her eyes away from the lace frothing out of his pocket. 'No, I don't think so…' She watched him heap a generous serving of the vegetables onto his plate. 'Are you a vegetarian?'

He shook his head as he poured Krug into two long-stemmed glasses of Edinburgh lead-crystal. 'I asked Pierre to prepare something that would digest easily. I know a meal is considered the conventional prelude to seduction, but I don't think one should make love on an overly full stomach. Do you?'

The glass of champagne he handed her nearly slipped through her fingers. 'I—I never really thought about it…'

'You mean you usually just act on your natural instincts—I like that in a woman.' His approving look was transferred to his food as he savoured it with all his senses. 'Mmm….this is good. Here. Try a taste.' He held out a piece of glazed carrot on his fork and Regan automatically leaned forward to take it in her mouth.

'Good?' he asked, tempting her with another offering, this time of succulently crisp green pepper.

The sticky sauce was sweet, yet tart, and hotly spicy on the tongue. 'Scrumptious,' she admitted, her eyes half closing with bliss as he trailed the tines of his fork from her moisture-glossed lower lip. The gentle scraping against the soft pad of flesh sent a little shiver down her spine.

'Are you sure you won't have some?'

'Well…maybe a little.' She yielded to his culinary seduction, deciding that tonight no temptation was worth resisting.

As they ate Adam kept the conversation to light, entertaining subjects that rarely threatened to get too personal, but the look in his eyes was extremely personal and with every bite Regan was made more aware of the fact that he was a man and she was a woman—and that he had her panties in his pocket. Her daring tease had had the desired effect, and Adam was making no secret of his gently simmering arousal. He watched her mouth as she ate and her eyes as she sipped at her champagne; he watched the way her small hands balanced the solid silver cutlery and how her throat rippled when she swallowed; he seemed to find special fascination in the delicate skin that stretched across her collarbone and the movement of her breasts against her dress as she gestured and spoke.

Unused to being the focus of such concentrated masculine attention, Regan found herself increasingly responsive to the charged atmosphere created by his cool wit and hot, knowing looks. Just looking at him was like plugging directly into an electrical circuit—her whole body hummed with a pleasurable buzz of nervous anticipation. She noticed the easy flexibility in his strong wrists as his scarred hands tipped the heavy champagne bottle, the sexy lines that amusement carved in his taut cheeks and the muscle that jumped in his jaw when he mentally withdrew to brood on some private thought.

She was so caught up in her heightened self-awareness that when Adam finally pressed his napkin against his mouth all she could think of was how it would feel if he pressed *her* to those firm lips...

She found out when he suddenly threw the rumpled napkin down on his empty plate and with a rough sound of impatience reached over to jerk her out of her chair, tumbling her across his lap.

'And now you can make good on that promise,' he growled, supporting her slender back with one powerful arm as his other hand cupped her squirming hip, forcing her soft bottom against the bunched muscles of his thighs.

Her startled cry of alarm had made her breathless. 'What promise?' she gasped, her head falling back against his shoulder as she recognised she was helpless against his strength, even had she wanted to struggle...

'This one,' he rasped, silking his hand up under her dress, over the tops of her stockings, to stroke the satiny skin of her inner thighs, his fingertips drifting so close to the core of her feminine heat that she felt the fierce electrical jolt of his imaginary penetration.

Regan instinctively snapped her legs together, her squeak of shock smothered by his mouth coming hard down on hers, plundering her senses with a ruthless expertise that left her weak and panting.

He kissed her until she thought that her head was going to explode and her heart accelerate out of her chest. This was no coy flirtation—his forceful kisses were in brazen earnest. And after a slightly clumsy start Regan abandoned herself to his miraculous passion, splinters of delight cascading through her senses. His tongue slid in and out of her mouth, deftly stroking her in ways that made her twist feverishly in his lap, seeking even more intimate contact, sliding her arms around his neck and running her fingers up the back of his scalp to sift through his luxuriant dark hair, tugging at it in her eagerness to experience everything he had to offer.

But it still wasn't enough—he was too controlled and she needed more, much more—so she leaned hungrily into his devouring kisses, using her teeth and tongue to encourage him to stop holding back, to be rougher, more reckless...

He refused to co-operate, and she ran a hand down the side of his face, over his gritty jaw and down his flawed throat to his open collar, where she ripped blindly at the buttons to gain access to that tantalising strip of hairroughened chest. Under the dark mat of hair his skin felt smooth and hot to her fingertips, and she curled her nails into the resilient wall of flesh, revelling in the way his muscles bunched and rippled at the warning prick of five tiny daggers.

He grunted, his knuckles digging into her soft flesh as he flexed the hand trapped between her clenched thighs, forcing it gradually higher until his thumb brushed against the soft nest of hair protecting her femininity.

He broke the kiss and her head fell back against his shoulder. He bit at her exposed throat and then suckled at the glowing red marks. 'You're so incredibly hot for me,' he rasped as her sultry need irradiated the torrid, enclosed space between her thighs, misting the tip of his thumb. 'So ready for me…'

Had there been an odd note of surprise in his gloating words? 'Isn't that what you wanted?' she managed threadily.

'What I want from a woman and what I get are not always the same thing,' he murmured, moving his thumb the infinitesimal distance to final contact and watching her violet eyes bloom with colour so vibrant and intense that it was beyond the palette of any artist. 'But you may be unique in that respect. You're not going to have to fake a thing with me, are you, Eve?' This time his purring voice was purely triumphant.

'You're hot for me, too,' she countered, flattening her hand over his steamy chest.

He bent and licked her mouth. 'Hot and hard,' he conceded in an inflammatory whisper, moving his hips so that she felt the explicit truth of his words rubbing against her bottom.

He continued to kiss her with the same, slow, teasing rhythm with which he controlled the delicate movements of his thumb. Only when he felt her quivering thighs relax and her hips begin to lift towards his tantalising touch did he withdraw his hand to cup her breast, his fingers finding and moulding the stiff nipple through the fine fabric, drawing it out to an exquisite peak of sensitivity.

'Adam…' Regan's protest was a soft moan as she squeezed her thighs together, trying to ease the burning ache created by the loss of his vital touch at the core of her femininity.

'Eve…' He said something else that she didn't hear over the thunderous roar of her blood, and when his arms braced, gently yet inexorably easing her away from his body, a brief battle ensued that left him smouldering with sensual amusement.

'I said…I think it's time we adjourned to the bedroom while we can both still walk,' Adam said, his hands firm on her narrow waist as he rose with her struggling figure and set her squarely on her feet. 'I'd prefer to finish this in the luxury and comfort of a well-sprung bed…wouldn't you?'

His smile was mildly taunting, as if he sensed how close she had been to ravishing him right there in his chair.

Finish this? What if she didn't want to finish it? What if she never wanted to relinquish this glorious feeling of voluptuous well-being?

'Shall we…?' He turned her gently in the direction of the bedroom and invited her company with a spurring little pat on the bottom that ended in a lingering caress.

In spite of her turmoil Regan remembered to snatch up her beaded bag as they passed the couch, hugging it to her fast-beating heart as she walked down the wide hall and into the big bedroom which she had found so intimidating. Someone had already been in to turn on the recessed lights and fold back the corner of the dark bedcover to display an inviting expanse of lustrous black silk. Pierre, setting up the final scene for seduction, thought Regan as she noticed how some of the lights were angled to pool on the bed, making it appear to float above the pale carpet.

Adam was emptying his trouser pockets, placing the contents on the top of a tall dresser. He flicked open the remaining buttons of his shirt and reached for a nearby switch on the wall, illuminating an adjoining bathroom that Regan had failed to notice earlier, so intent had she been on the bed.

'You won't mind if I take a shower first, to rinse off the grime of the day?' He stripped his shirt down his arms and tossed it onto a chair by the wall, her lacy panties still decorating the pocket.

He stretched unselfconsciously, enjoying the freedom of his own skin, and Regan lost any chance of making a polite reply.

His nipples were dark brown against the lightness of his skin, mounted on slabs of muscle which were covered by a thicket of dark silky hair flecked here and there with rare strands of silver. The scars that marked his throat ended in a shiny swirl just below his collarbone, the rest of him—as far as she could see—was well nigh perfect. His belly was flat, with hints of corrugated muscle that flexed and rippled along his front and sides when he lifted his arms. The hair on his chest formed an inverted triangle, narrowing abruptly to a thin, downy line that ended well above his indented navel. In the huge mirror on the far wall Regan could see the reflection of his long, lean, unblemished back. He had already started to unbuckle his plain black leather belt and her eyes dipped helplessly to the obvious thrust of his arousal against the expensive black fabric of his trousers.

He saw her looking and prowled over to cup her jaw. 'I'd ask you to join me, but one stroke of your soapy hands and I'm afraid I'd go off like a rocket,' he admitted frankly, 'and I have a rather more extended form of foreplay in mind. Besides—' he lowered his head to graze his mouth and nose along her cheek '—you already smell delicious…that perfume you're wearing is the perfect aphrodisiac.' He nipped at her tender earlobe, making her shiver. 'If you like to play games in the water, how about we have a Jacuzzi together later…?' He padded towards the open bathroom door, pausing to tease her with an uplifted eyebrow. 'Wait for me?'

As if there could be any doubt that she would! thought Regan shakily, listening to the sound of a shower being turned on and the low buzz of a razor soon superseded by the intermittent splash of water hitting a solid object. A very solid, masculine column of flesh.

Regan hovered in the centre of the floor, wondering what to do. Should she undress…or would he want to do that? Did he expect her to be lying naked in bed when he returned, or did his notion of 'extended foreplay' require her to be perched on the covers in a provocative pose? She blinked dizzily at the thought and looked hastily around for a distraction, hesitating as she caught sight of herself in the mirror. Was that really her?

Her black dress looked somehow tighter, the neck lower and the hem higher, than it had at home. Her black satin hair was in tousled disorder, her mouth reddened and her eyes as dark as bruises in her flushed face. She put a hand to her throat and ran it down the front of the dress, over her taut breasts and down to the bottom of her skirt. She inched it up until the top of her stocking showed, and then a strip of bare thigh. She bent her knee and looked sideways at herself. No sign of a victim now—she was all vamp. She had never looked nor felt so brazenly sexy in her life.

She let her hem fall and wandered over to the dresser, trying not to strain her ears for noises from the bathroom. Along with the heap of items from Adam's pocket—a scatter of small change, a set of keys, a slim crocodile-skin wallet—there was a silver-backed male brush and comb set lying next to a small black leather case, the open zip of which displayed a manicure kit. The only other item of a possibly personal nature was a long, narrow navy blue jeweller's box.

Her *reward*...?

The shower was still splashing erratically.

Regan put down her bag and picked up the velvet box. The lid was stiff and her fingers sweaty with nervous guilt as she forced it back on its hinges.

She sucked in a sharp breath. The thin tennis bracelet was lying on a bed of blue velvet, the tiny diamond chips a blaze of white ice under the overhead light. God knows how much such a thing had cost!

Regan snapped the box shut and hastily replaced it exactly as she had found it. If that was what Adam planned to give his lady of the evening, she didn't want him to know that she had been snooping. But...oh, God, how flattering to be considered worthy of such loveliness. She went soft inside at the thought of those strong, scarred hands fastening the delicate strand of diamonds around her wrist.

Except for her wedding and engagement rings Michael had never given her any jewellery. His birthday gifts to her had usually been small household appliances and her most romantic anniversary present had been a cookbook.

But there was nothing romantic about the receipt of this first gift of jewellery, either, Regan reminded herself fiercely. She mustn't fall into the trap of thinking there was anything personal involved. Just because the bracelet was beautiful that didn't make it in any way *meaningful*, to either herself or Adam. It wasn't the gift of a lover; it was hard, cold evidence of their transaction, that was all. The bracelet hadn't been bought with her specifically in mind—nor, probably, had Adam even selected it himself.

She picked up her evening purse and unzipped it, determined to bring herself firmly back to earth. Pushing aside the condom packet, which showed a distressing tendency to stick to her damp fingers, she drew out the little square box she was searching for and opened it. The elegant gold cufflinks inset with darkly grained New Zealand jade stared accusingly back at her. They had been extremely costly, but Regan had been frugal with the housekeeping money for a long time in order to secretly save up for something special for Michael's twenty-eighth birthday. But he had been killed a week before she could give them to him, and in the emotional turmoil that followed the cufflinks had lain forgotten in the pocket of a rarely worn jacket until she had rediscovered them a few days ago.

She *had* intended to sell them, but tonight it had seemed like poetic justice to use the pathetic evidence of her wasted love to buy her way out of any pangs of conscience about her sexual fling.

'What are you doing?'

Regan stuffed the box back into her bag and whirled around, suddenly registering the lack of sound from the bathroom behind her.

Her mouth went dry. Adam wasn't quite naked but the towel wrapped around his lean hips rode drastically low, and the end tucked into the folds over his right hip-bone seemed tantalisingly insecure. Here and there on his skin was a faint beading of moisture, as if he had been in too much of a hurry to dry himself properly, and the hair on his chest glistened as if the strands had been individually polished. As he walked towards her the towel parted on his right thigh with every stride, showing her a lithe strip of hair-dusted muscle.

'I—I was just getting these,' she improvised, holding up the packet of condoms as she pushed her bag onto the dresser.

He wrapped his hand around hers and plucked the packet from her fingers, tossing it on top of her purse, not taking his eyes off her flustered face. 'You won't need them.'

Her eyes widened as the breath swooped from her lungs, the clean, soapy scent of him clogging her nostrils. The light gleamed on his cheek, making his freshly shaven jaw look as smooth as polished silk.

'But you— But I—' She couldn't believe he would risk either a sexually transmitted disease or a pregnancy from their encounter—so what kind of sexual activity *did* he have in mind?

His mouth kinked in amusement at her nervous stutter. 'I mean, I prefer to use my own,' he explained.

'Oh.' Her relief was writ large in her eyes before a frown wrinkled her fringe. 'You don't trust me? What do you think—that I've been at them with a pin?'

'It has been known to happen,' he said mildly, and she realised that it wasn't her he mistrusted, but women in general...perhaps even *people* in general.

That made the insult a little easier to take—but not much. He had no way of knowing that she was the last woman to want to trap him into any extended responsibility for their one-night stand.

'You must have a very pessimistic outlook on life,' she told him.

'Well, right at this moment I'm extremely *op*timistic about the immediate future,' he said, fingering the strap of her dress as he looked down into her eyes. 'For instance...I have complete confidence in your ability to arouse me...' He pushed the strap off her shoulder and bent to nuzzle the tender crease where her arm met the upper swell of her breast.

There was a soft rustle and she felt his towel brush against her calf as it fell to the floor. He was now stark naked, and only inches away from her electrified body. Apart from Michael, Regan had never seen a naked adult male in the flesh...let alone aroused. She let her eyes fall to the level of his chest as he toyed with her other strap.

She didn't dare look down any further, in case she completely lost her nerve.

She lifted her hands and laid them tentatively against his chest and he gave a shuddering sigh, his breath hot against her smooth shoulder.

'Oh, yes…that's right…touch me—show me how good you are with your hands.…' He kissed the side of her throat and put his hands over hers, stroking them up and down his chest. She could feel his heart thudding and her palms grew hot with the friction from the thick growth of hair. When he let her hands go to cup her head and angle her mouth up to his she let her fingers settle on either side of his flat waist, gripping hard as he shifted his stance, making her vividly conscious of a blunt force nudging against the front of her skirt.

He kissed her as he had before, with a deep thoroughness that made her knees turn to water. Drowning in sensation, she closed her eyes and dug her fingernails into his waist and he laughed into her mouth.

'Little cat…'

His hands slipped down the slender line of her back and suddenly she could feel them warmly cupping her bare bottom under the rucked up skirt, stroking the downy plumpness, tracing the sensitive crease in a way that made her automatically clench her buttocks. He growled with approval, his hands tightening as he squeezed and kneaded, lifting her hips hard against him so that she couldn't avoid the thick roll of flesh thrusting into her belly, and bending his head to string a sting of moist kisses into her plunging neckline. Her eyes flew open and she could feel the heat pulse between her legs at the sight of his dark head moving against her breasts and the feel of his teeth through the snug fabric.

He backed her trembling legs towards the bed, and as he angled them across the room she glimpsed their reflection in the mirror and gasped—the side-on view of a big, naked man in a passionate embrace with a partly clad female was like a scene from an erotic movie, her bared bottom starkly pale against the folds of her black dress, his hands positioned with an explicit sexual intent that gave her a sharp thrill of anticipation.

He had paused in his uneven progress, following her mesmerised gaze.

'Do you like what you see, little Eve?' One hand drifted down her buttocks and they both watched it burrow between her thighs. 'Mmm, I see that you do,' he said, testing with a lingering finger as the woman in the mirror quivered and arched her back.

He spun her around so that she could no longer see the mirrored wall. 'But for now I want you to concentrate on *me*, not on *him*...'

For a sickening instant she thought that he was referring to Michael, then she realised that he was teasing her again. She had never been taught that sex could be fun.

'You can't be jealous of yourself!' she sparkled.

'Can't I?' he said, in the tone of a man who could be whatever the hell he wanted. 'You can't have us both, honey—it's him or me.'

'But he's such a hunk!' she pouted, pretending to peep around his elbow at his reflection.

His eyes narrowed warningly above his silky smile. 'You think so...?'

'Well...he's in much better shape than you are,' she said, walking her fingers daintily up his chest. She had reached a nipple and stopped to explore. 'He has much bigger muscles.'

'Bigger than this?' he growled, grabbing her dancing fingers and pulling them down to his groin. She gave a little squeak as he folded her hand around himself, stunned by the feel of the rigid shaft stroking against her palm as he undulated his hips. He felt as hard as steel, yet satiny soft and smooth as he slipped through her fingers, so hot that she could feel sympathetic perspiration breaking out all over her body. Her fingers felt too swollen for her skin, stiff and clumsy as she tried to be gentle, knowing from her self-defence classes that men were extremely sensitive to pressure in that part of their anatomy. To the sharp scent of soap was now added the potent, musky aroma of male desire.

'Too much for you to handle, Eve?' he taunted, hardening further under her featherlight fumbling. He picked up her other hand and enfolded snugly it around the base of his shaft. 'Here, why not use both hands…? And no need to treat me like spun glass—I won't break.'

She gulped, looking helplessly down at his captive manhood framed by her cupped hands, and the thick cloud of hair in his groin. All that throbbing power in her fragile grasp, she wondered…all that magnificent masculinity hers to command…

She contracted her fingers, unconsciously licking her lips, and a groan ripped from his chest. He gripped her by the shoulders, pulling her close so that her hands were crushed between them and the tips of her breasts scraped against his chest.

'Well, do you think I measure up?' he asked harshly as his body threatened to career out of his control.

'To what—the Empire State Building?' she said, striving to match his banter.

She felt his jolting laugh clear to the precious heaviness nestling hotly in her hands.

'I'm flattered you even mention us in the same breath, Honey, but speaking about comparing measurements…'

He reached around her back and she felt her zip give all the way down her spine and instinctively reached up to clutch at the loosening fabric over her breasts.

His groan of explicit regret as she released him made her blush, and she babbled defensively, 'I hope you're not expecting the pyramids here—I'm not very big…'

'So you told me earlier,' he murmured, tugging away her folded arms so that the dress slithered to her hips. 'Small and perfectly proportioned for your size,' he approved, as her rosy round breasts came into view, the pert nipples trembling with each shallow rise and fall of her ribcage. 'A very tempting little mouthful…'

And so it proved as he bent her back over his arm and cupped her breast, lifting it to his mouth so that he could lick at the dark pink crown, circling and flicking at it with his tongue until it ripened into a plum-red berry that he could nibble and suck with lusty pleasure before transferring his attention to its neglected twin. Wave after wave of delight crested through Regan's body as her dress slipped to the floor and was impatiently kicked away.

She wasn't even aware of moving, but the backs of her knees hit the side of the bed and she felt him dip and wrench away the covers with one hand an instant before she sprawled backwards onto the cool sheets, taking him with her. She squirmed underneath his heavy weight and he laughed exultantly, rolling with her into the middle of the wide bed, his thighs pushing heavily between hers as he pinned her to the slippery silk. He ran his hands down her stockinged legs and crouched back on his knees to flip off her dainty shoes before manacling her ankles and wrapping them around his lean flanks as he came back down on top of her, crushing his arousal against the moist thicket in the V of her body, shuddering with tension as he braced himself on bended elbows above her panting body.

'You're so beautifully responsive that you drive me wild,' he said hoarsely, cupping her head in his scarred hands. 'Look at me—I can't control myself. So much for my fine boasts about foreplay…'

Her violet eyes drank in the glorious sight of him—the dominant male, helpless in the grip of the passion that *she* had generated…

'Oh, Adam…' She knew then that the real gift she was taking away tonight was far more valuable than diamonds. This wonderful, sexy stranger had given her the confidence to be a woman again.

She arched her hips in an age-old invitation and raised her arms to pull him down to her hungry mouth. 'It's you I want, not your clinical expertise,' she told him in a sultry husk that carried the warm ring of truth. 'I'd rather have honest lust than a textbook demonstration of the Kama Sutra…'

His heavy-lidded eyes gleamed with richly sensual amusement as he succumbed to her steamy challenge, reaching down between them to where their bodies almost joined. 'Then, Eve, shall we open the gates of paradise…? And maybe what we find there will enable me to rise to the occasion and give you *both*…'

CHAPTER FIVE

'WELL, Lass, it won't be long now.'

Regan glanced in amusement at her employer, who was fidgeting in his eagerness to get to their destination.

'Next on the right!' The bullhorn bark belied his benign, roly-poly appearance, and she swiftly returned her attention to her driving.

Two months ago she wouldn't have had the confidence to chauffeur the big, expensive Jaguar, but since *That Night* she had discovered an adventurous spirit within herself which had encouraged her to believe that she could conquer *all* her problems if she just had the courage to try.

That Night.

It stood in capitalised italics in her memory. Her deliciously guilty secret. Her infamous one-night stand.

She had forbidden herself to think about it during the day, although there was no keeping Adam out of her nighttime fantasies—which was exactly where he belonged, she told herself sternly. She had never heard another peep out of Cleo about that evening, and her chief feeling was one of ardent relief that she had got away with her reckless stunt. But one tiny, primitive part of her couldn't help harbouring a brooding disappointment that Adam obviously hadn't asked Derek for a return visit from the non-existent 'Eve'. It would almost be worth having her cover blown to have him affirm that he had enjoyed their night of unbridled passion so much that he wanted to repeat the experience.

But, given the way that she had left, sneaking out before dawn while he was still asleep, and her parting gesture, she knew she should count herself lucky that there had been no embarrassing repercussions.

'Here! Turn here! Now! Now!' A stubby freckled finger stabbed in front of her nose.

'Yes, I can see the sign,' she said mildly.

Sir Frank gave a wry chuckle as they flashed past the huge billboard advertising the Palm Cove condominium and marina development and turned off the main highway onto the wide, winding road which cut across the narrow, hilly peninsula of land jutting out into the waters of the Hauraki Gulf.

'Sorry, it's just that I'm looking forward to seeing Hazel's face when I tell her that all her worries are over.' He beamed smugly as he envisaged his sister-in-law's gratitude.

Since his doctor had diagnosed his heart condition Sir Frank had been trying to cut back on his stress levels, with mixed success. He had given up driving, fatty foods and smoking his beloved cigars, but he had found it harder to relinquish his habit of command. Selling the large development company which he had expanded from the single soft furnishings store he had inherited from his father was proving a wrench, even though it was staying more or less in the family—bought by a corporation headed by the man who was on the verge of marrying Hazel's orphaned granddaughter.

At sixty-six, Sir Frank complained that he was too young to stagnate, but even when he had handed responsibility for Harriman Developments over to Carolyn's new husband and retired to the family property adjoining the Palm Cove marina, Regan suspected he wouldn't be idle. He would just nose around until he found something else to engage his restless energies.

'Not quite over,' Regan said. 'I don't know how much help I'm going to be—I've never organised a big wedding before.' She and Michael had been married in a register office.

He waved a dismissive hand. 'Hazel knows what has to be done; she just needs a sympathetic someone to do all the running around until she's fit on her feet again. And you're a relative—she knows you, so she can't complain I'm foisting a total stranger on her...'

'Only a very distant relative. I still think you should have warned her I was coming,' said Regan uneasily. 'She might have rather have help from someone closer in the family—'

Sir Frank shuddered. 'The *last* thing she wants is any of that bossy lot moving in for the duration—they'd try to take over and ruin it for Hazel. No children of her own left to fuss over, y'see, and Carolyn's her only grandchild, so this'll be the last wedding she gets to play an important part in...I just want to make sure she doesn't overdo it.'

Regan could feel his frown fill the car. 'At her age a sprained ankle and broken wrist are nothing to be sneezed at,' he added darkly. 'She's lucky she didn't break her neck rolling down that hill. Old ladies' bones can snap like dry twigs, you know—I asked my doctor about it.'

Browbeat it out of him, more like.

Knowing that Hazel Harriman was only two years older than Sir Frank—who would howl if anyone called him an old man—Regan bit her tongue. She suspected that the crusty bachelor carried a torch for his elder brother's widow, and by dragooning Regan into helping with the run-up to Carolyn's wedding—now a bare month away—he hoped to bask in her good graces.

'I *told* her she should use a golf cart instead of trudging up and down all those gullies,' he grumped. 'Trouble is, she's too damned thrifty to rent one, no matter that John left her as rich as Croesus! Well, I shall just have to *buy* her one myself, that's all. I could get it done up in snazzy colours…maybe with her name painted on it. D'you think she'd like that?'

Regan had only met Hazel Harriman twice, but had recognised her at first sight as a lady of countrified elegance and good breeding. 'Uh, I think something a little more discreet might be preferable, Sir Frank,' she advised.

'I know you insisted it be *Sir* Frank at head office, but you don't have to ''Sir'' me everywhere else, too.' He tripped off on another tangent. 'Your mother would turn in her grave to hear you calling me by a silly title…'

Regan swallowed a chuckle 'My mother's not dead,' she pointed out.

She took another well-signposted fork at the top of a hill which gave her a temporary view of both sides of the peninsula. The gentle north-facing slopes were crowded with modern houses, motels and holiday homes leading down to flat, white sandy beaches lapped by a clear blue-green sea, while on the less fashionable southerly side the housing was more old-fashioned and rocky cliffs descended to small, pebbly inlets and the deep natural harbour where fishermen and yachties moored their boats.

'Might as well be!' Sir Frank replied with his customary contempt for tact. 'Buried in that compound with all those religious loonies. Never did hold with cults. Look what they brainwashed Joanne into doing—abandoning her only child and emigrating to the middle of the Australian desert!'

'It was hardly abandonment; I *was* eighteen,' said Regan. If anything, it had been a relief to wave goodbye to her mother at the airport. Joanne Baker had grown ever more narrow-minded and unpleasant to live with in the years following her husband's death, especially when her daughter had refused to embrace her apocalyptic beliefs.

Her companion hurrumphed. 'She should have at least made sure you were settled in at university—and kept in touch.'

'She *did* write to you about me before she left,' Regan felt constrained to remind him.

At first she had been horribly embarrassed that her mother had taken advantage of such a tenuous connection. The Harrimans were only very distant cousins of her mother, and Regan had been taken aback when she had received a letter from Sir Frank expressing interest in her plans for a law degree and offering her work in Harriman Developments' legal department during the holiday breaks in her course. The job would pay for her law school costs, accommodation fees for the university hostel, and allow her to save a little.

'Good thing she did, too—because you never would have looked us up, would you? You need to be brash to get on in this world. Like that husband of yours! Michael wasn't slow about approaching me for a job—very up-front about it, he was...telling me that he wanted to be able to afford to make a good home for his wife and family.'

'Yes, I know.' Regan couldn't help the clipped tone of her voice.

She had been careful never to act like an encroaching poor relation, but soon after they'd been married Michael had announced his discontent with his real estate job and had persuaded her that it was selfish to deny him the chance to fast-track his sales career through her family contacts. So she had got him an appointment with Sir Frank and he had talked himself into a job with the marketing team being set up for the Palm Cove condominiums, at that time still in the initial planning stages.

Michael had always been very glib.

'Now, now—I didn't meant to bring up unhappy memories.' Sir Frank patted her arm vigorously, with a dangerous disregard for her steering. 'I know you're still finding it difficult to carry on without him. Maybe staying at Palm Cove for a few weeks is just the tonic you need.'

Regan managed a strained smile at his heavy-handed sympathy. His kindness made her feel guiltier than ever about her ulterior motive for agreeing to assist in his timely—for her—family crisis.

'I'm sure it will,' she muttered.

'You could have come to us after he died, you know,' he added, piling on the coals of fire. 'Hazel would have known how to look after you. She had a bad time of it herself when m'brother died!'

'I needed to know that I could make my own way,' Regan defended herself awkwardly.

'I know, I know—you're touchy about your independence. Still, I could have given you some advice about the house. It was a bad time to sell—with the market in a slump.'

Unfortunately, Regan hadn't had any choice in the matter.

'It was far too big for one person.'

Sir Frank believed she was comfortably situated financially, and she preferred to leave it that way.

'If you didn't want to stay at the house we could have put you into one of the show condos—it's only an hour's drive from Auckland; you could still have commuted to your job...'

'I might not have a job when the new boss takes over,' said Regan lightly, her fingers tightening on the wheel at the thought of the new regime that was poised to send in the auditors before the final purchase agreement was signed.

'Oh, Wade's a shrewd judge of character—he's tough, he's demanding, but he's honourable and fair—he'll look at your record and realise it's not just nepotism that got you the job!'

Regan had never heard of Carolyn's fiancé, an Auckland businessman with worldwide connections, but Sir Frank had assured her that Joshua Wade was highly respected in financial circles. 'Fred tells me you're one of the best legal aides he's ever had—meticulous to a fault! He thinks you've got big potential—'

He broke off, and Regan's knuckles whitened further as she guessed what he was thinking. Sir Frank had curbed his disappointment when she had notified him that she was dropping out, assuming that she was suffering from an understandable excess of grief and that when it passed she would regain her enthusiasm for law. In the meantime, he had had Fred Stevenson in the legal office to take her on as a full-time employee.

'He was very miffed when I said that I was going to steal you away for few weeks for a roving assignment.' Sir Frank regained his bounce. 'But I told him it was one of the privileges of rank and since I wouldn't have the rank for much longer he should cut me some slack.'

'I did offer to take part of it as my holiday entitlement—' began Regan.

'Nonsense—we can't have you paying for the privilege of helping us out!' he huffed. 'Besides, you offered to work in the Palm Cove site office in your spare time, so that'll square things up with the books.'

It was an unfortunate choice of phrase, but Regan certainly hoped so!

'Ahh, home James!'

They had reached almost to the nature reserve at the tip of promontory, the road dividing into two—one route leading to the reserve carpark, the other passing between the gates of a massive drystone wall emblazoned with the Palm Cove name and logo in solid brass, glowing in the late-afternoon sun.

'Impressive, isn't it? Michael never brought you up here, did he?'

She shook her head. 'No, although I've seen the publicity

brochures and newspaper ads.' Michael had been extremely careful to keep her well away from anything to do with his work at Palm Cove.

On the other side of the wall the rolling green fields of a massive new subdivision stretched before them. The roads which snaked through the pegged-out sites were broad and palm-lined, and the numerous houses already under construction looked hugely palatial. Beyond, marching down towards the glittering sea, were the fully completed parts of the project—the country club with its eighteen-hole golf course and the triple tower of condominiums rising from the banks of the canal that formed the man-made marina. She knew from the photos that when they got closer they would see the multi-level paved terraces that surrounded the cafés, bars and shops at the base of the towers, and, flanking the canal moorings on both sides, blocks of two-storeyed condominiums stretching right down to the sea, so that true boating fanatics could walk straight out of their expensive living rooms onto their expensive yachts.

Regan turned up the narrow private road indicated by Sir Frank, following it through the thicket of mature native bush which fringed the edge of the new subdivision, completely screening it from sight of the adjoining property. The road wound out of the trees again and a house came into view—a huge, sprawling, double-storeyed white wooden villa, a graceful old lady from a bygone era surrounded by a crinoline of verandahs and set in what seemed like acres of ground—a mixture of formal plantings and rambling natural wilderness. The back of the house had a clear view to the sea, the front was a welcoming smile of curved flowerbeds, bursting with late summer roses.

Regan drew up where directed, around the side of the house, in front of a six-door garage which looked as if it might have been converted from stables.

She stretched the kinks in her legs as she got out of the

car, glad she had worn an uncrushable camel skirt with her cool leaf-green summer blouse, but when she tried to get her bags out of the car boot, Sir Frank hustled her away.

'Beatson will get those and put the car away—Steve's our caretaker and odd-job man—chauffeur, too, if you need him.'

Regan was staring at something around the back of the house. 'Is that gazebo on an *island*?'

Sir Frank chuckled at her astounded expression. 'Hazel's idea—thought it would be a romantic place to go for al fresco lunches. Had to have a brute of bulldozers in to dig the lake and divert a stream to feed it.' His blue eyes twinkled brightly in his plump red face. 'Why don't I go and break the good news about your arrival while you take a stroll in the fresh air…?'

Since Regan would sooner not be around when Sir Frank broke his 'good news' to his sister-in-law, in case it fell badly flat, she accepted his suggestion with alacrity.

The small oval lake was a marvel of engineering, and she wandered out onto the small wooden jetty where two small rowboats were moored and looked across the narrow divide of water at the latticed gazebo, guessing that the huge spreading oak that dappled the grass on one end of the little island had been there long before the bulldozers had moved it, probably as long as the main house itself.

The hot afternoon sun beat down on her unprotected head and she was drawn across the wide, luxuriant lawn to walk in the cool shade of the wild wood which grew along one side of the house. The undergrowth to the mature canopy of deciduous and evergreen trees was a mingling of native and exotic shrubs and seedlings, and Regan idly plucked a large, glossy leaf as she turned to view the building from this new aspect.

A movement at one of the ground-floor windows caught her eye and she saw the figure of a man talking on the telephone, pacing restlessly back and forth past the open sash. She was at least a hundred metres away, and at first all she registered was that he was dressed in a suit and that he was tall and dark-haired, but then he halted by the window, glancing up from the sheaf of papers in his hand, and she got a good look at him full-face.

A thrill of dumbfounded horror turned her blood to ice. *Adam!*

The leaf fluttered to the grass as her hand flew to her mouth.

He noticed her at the very instant of her appalled recognition, and for a moment they were both motionless, staring at each other.

Even at a hundred metres she could read his body language. His back stiffened in surprise and then his torso tilted forward in puzzlement. He moved right up to the open window and she began to edge backwards into the undergrowth, praying that he wouldn't realise who it was that he was seeing. Surely in her summery skirt, short-sleeved blouse and simple flat shoes she was a far cry from the sophisticated Eve whom he had tumbled in his bed.

The phone still plastered to the side of his head, he suddenly thrust his shoulders out of the window.

'Hey—you!'

Regan's body jerked. She took another step back. No—this nightmare couldn't be happening. Not here—not now!

'Hey! Don't go!' To her horror he dropped the phone from his ear and put one long leg over the windowsill. 'Eve?'

Oh, *God*!

'Eve, is that you?'

He was already out on the verandah, striding along to the wooden steps. Regan whirled around and blindly fled, crashing through the shrubbery in a desperate attempt to put as much space between them as possible before those long, powerful legs hit the grass running. Even in full business-kit, with a one hundred-metre handicap, he could probably still sprint her down on a flat track.

Fortunately she was small enough to scuttle through chinks in the tangled undergrowth that would have snagged larger bodies, but as she got deeper into the trees she could still hear him thrashing somewhere behind her, hoarsely yelling at her to stop, pausing now and then in his pursuit to gauge her direction.

When she almost ran slap-bang into the sturdy trunk of an old macrocarpa pine, top-heavy with needle-like green foliage, she let instinct take hold and shinned up the untrimmed branches until she reached a high fork into which she could safely wedge herself, out of sight of the ground.

None too soon. She clutched at her perch, the rough bark pricking her cheek and bare forearms as she flattened herself against the trunk, holding her breath as dried pine needles crunched under the pounding feet below.

'Eve? Dammit—answer me—is that you?'

To her dismay he halted almost directly beneath her, breathing heavily. Thank God she wasn't wearing anything bright that might give her away if he thought to look up. She felt dizzy, and suddenly remembered to breathe. She didn't want to faint and flatten him with the proof of her presence.

'What the hell…!' he muttered to himself. 'Look—whoever you are, you're not in trouble for trespassing, if that's what you're worried about!' he called, his voice rasping with controlled impatience. 'Come on out—I'm not going to hurt you…'

He fell silent until the hush of leaves stirring in the gentle seaward breeze was shattered by the muffled shrill of a cellphone. An angry curse floated up into the boughs as he ripped the phone out of the inside pocket of his buttoned jacket.

'Yes! What…? No—I put down the phone and got distracted for a moment… No, no, of course it's not—you're right; we need to get this settled now…' Her eyes hunted for the sight of him as he wheeled in a half-circle one last time and then began retracing his steps. 'Sorry…we'll pick up at the clause we left off and go through it point by point…just let me put my hands on that contract again—'

Regan remained frozen for a few minutes after she had listened to his retreat. When she was certain that his words weren't just a cunning ruse to flush her out, she uncramped her limbs and began to climb down with a great deal more care than she had tackled the ascension, thankful that her skirt was cut on an A-line rather than tight around her knees and that she had no pantyhose to snag.

She hit the ground with a groan of relief and bent to brush the bark and twigs off her clothes and legs, and straighten the seams of her skirt. She was retucking her blouse into her waistband when a prickle on the back of her neck made her swing around, her heart pattering like that of a baby bird who'd fallen out of its nest.

A thin, gangly youth, with hair the colour of used rope straggling to his shoulders and round, wire-framed glasses that accentuated the boniness of his face, stood watching her from the bushes.

Regan nervously flicked her hair behind her ears and pinned on a reassuring smile. 'Hello. Where did you come from?'

And more importantly—how long had he been there? She bit her lip. Had Adam grabbed a handy accomplice for the chase?

He didn't smile back at her, his brown eyes unnervingly intense. 'Hi.'

'Do you live here?' she asked brightly, scraping at the sticky residue of pine-sap on her reddened palms.

He pushed his hands into the pockets of his baggy khaki

shorts, hunching his thin shoulders under the plain white T-shirt. 'Nah.'

He looked at the scratches on her legs. 'What were you doing up that tree?'

Her mind went blank. 'I…thought I saw an interesting bird,' she improvised. Heavens, how low she had sunk—now she was even lying to children! Although judging from the squeak and scrape of his breaking voice he wasn't really a child any more. In his early teens, she estimated.

'What kind of bird?'

'Uh, I don't know…that's why I wanted to get a closer look.' She tried another smile.

'Didn't you know someone was calling for you?'

'No—were they?' She rounded her eyes innocently. 'I must be hard of hearing. Who was it—do you know?' she asked, hoping she might find out enough to plan herself a disaster strategy.

His light brown eyes looked innocently back. 'Big or small?'

'I beg your pardon?'

'The bird you saw, was it big or small?' he wanted to know.

'Big,' she said firmly.

'What colour was it?'

'Well…brown, I suppose.'

'Light brown or dark brown?'

'Both,' she said desperately. 'Sort of speckled.'

'Flying or perching?'

'It flew and landed in the tree, then it perched,' she said through clenched teeth.

'What colour legs did it have?'

She looked at him incredulously. 'Who do you think you are, James Bond?' she joked.

'Are you talking about the ornithologist or the spy named

after him?' he responded, and suddenly she knew that the weedy adolescent look was extremely deceptive.

She had tossed him a condescending comment, expecting its subtlety to be totally over his head, and he had fielded it with precocious dexterity. He knew very well she had been stringing him a line because he had been the one spinning it into a noose!

She folded her arms defensively across her chest. 'I'm surprised anyone of your generation knows where Ian Fleming got the idea for his character's name.'

He shifted his weight, sifting his battered sneakers amongst the fallen leaves. 'I read a lot.'

'So did I at your age, except I wasn't allowed to read Ian Fleming,' she said wryly.

'How old do you think I am?'

'Is this another guessing game?' She sighed at his steady stare. 'Fourteen,' she said, adding a year to her best estimate for the sake of his young male ego.

'Fifteen,' he corrected gloomily.

'Oh...well, what I said actually still goes,' she consoled him. 'My mother thought the Bible was the only book worth reading. Novels were a big no-no in our house.'

His thin face took on an expression of sheer horror. 'You weren't allowed to read any fiction at all?'

She shrugged. 'Not at home. I used to keep a stash in my locker at school, though.'

'But that's censorship! You should have told her that she couldn't violate your rights like that,' he said, showing he was a true child of the modern age. 'I'm allowed to read anything I like.'

'Lucky you. I guess your mother must be a real liberal, huh?'

'I don't know. Clare lives in America. My parents divorced when I was born, and I stayed with Dad.'

'Oh, I'm sorry.'

'Why?'

She was taken aback. 'Well…I'm sorry because you didn't have your mother there when you were a baby,' she said, stepping gingerly.

'Why? Don't you think that men can single-parent as well as women?'

Regan rolled her eyes. She had a feeling that this gangly youth might well best her in a debate. A question seemed to be his favourite form of reply.

'Look, I really have to go.' She couldn't believe she had stood here chatting when Adam might already be back on the prowl. She had to find out what he was doing here and whether it was going to be possible to avoid him. If he was just a visitor maybe she could keep out of the way long enough for him to think he had made a mistake…

'Sir Frank and Mrs Harriman are probably wondering where I am.' She hesitated, looking around.

'The house is back that way.' He pulled his hand from his pocket and pointed over her left shoulder.

'Thanks.' She still hesitated.

'If you turn right when you get to the bark track behind that tree big fern you'll come out of the bush by the front flower garden,' he added.

She gave him a sharp look, but his thin face was telling her nothing. If he was willing to help her, he surely couldn't be in league with Adam.

'OK—thanks again. Bye…'

'See you around,' came the laconic reply.

She paused, looking over her shoulder. 'Will you?'

'Probably.' He shrugged. 'I'm Ryan.'

She wondered what test she'd passed that he was willing to honour her with the information so far stubbornly with-held. 'I'm Regan. I'm here to help Mrs Harriman organise her granddaughter's wedding.'

Something flickered in his eyes, but he didn't respond and she offered him a cheerful wave and went on her way.

She discovered that her trust in him was justified, and five minutes later she was politely greeting Hazel Harriman in the drawing room at the front of the house and apologising for the state of her hands.

'You look as if you've been pulled through a hedge backwards, lass!' Sir Frank said, when she'd explained that she had strayed off the path amongst the trees and tripped over some creepers.

'Trust you to be blunt to the point of rudeness, Frank,' said the tall, thin, elegantly dressed woman on the Victorian sofa. Her strapped right ankle was propped on a footstool and a lightweight fibreglass cast covered her left arm from the base of her fingers to her elbow. A single crutch was propped against the arm of the sofa and an open *Brides* magazine lay on the polished mahogany occasional table beside her knee, along with the remains of her afternoon tea.

She turned a coolly gracious smile up to Regan, her dark brown eyes compassionate for her obvious embarrassment.

'Take no notice, my dear. I designed these grounds specifically to tempt people to explore rather than just to stand and stare.' She tilted her beautifully coiffured ash-blonde head. 'Won't you sit down? I'll ask Mrs Beatson to bring you a refreshing cool drink or cup of tea.'

'Tea, please,' elected Sir Frank. 'And scones. With cream and some of that homemade kiwi fruit jam of yours.'

His sister-in-law gave him a quelling look. 'Plain tea and biscuits is all you'll get from Alice,' she said firmly. 'The doctor sent her your diet sheet.'

'I think I may have ended up with some tree sap on my skirt as well,' said Regan, declining to besmirch any of the antique cream and white striped armchairs. Her nerves were on full alert as she tried to pay full attention to her hostess while also keeping one wary eye on the door for Adam, half expecting him to burst in and denounce her for a wanton harlot. 'Perhaps it would be better if I changed first...'

'Of course, and you might like a shower after your hot drive, too. Why don't I get Alice to show you to your room? Although you'll forgive us if the bed isn't made up yet, since we weren't expecting any more guests today.' She slanted a look at her brother-in-law which made him scowl sheepishly.

'I'm sorry. I quite understand, Mrs Harriman. I don't want to be a burden—I can make up the bed myself if someone shows me where the linen cupboard is,' said Regan. Whatever discussion had gone on between them before she'd arrived, it was evident that Sir Frank's steamroller generosity had paid off, but that Hazel Harriman was gracefully making him aware of her displeasure.

The smile in the soft brown eyes shifted from one of politeness to genuine warmth. 'Now *I'm* the one embarrassing you, Regan—forgive me, but I couldn't resist that little dig at Frank. You don't have to feel awkward—I know exactly what he's like. This idea of his was probably sprung on you with much the same lack of notice as he gave me. He calls my side of the family bossy, but he really takes the cake!'

'Cake, huh!' Sir Frank rumbled. 'Tea and biscuits is all I get around here!'

'And please do call me Hazel,' the other woman went on, as if he hadn't spoken, 'because we want to be comfortable with each other if we're going to be working side by side for the next few weeks. Much as I hate to admit it, I *do* need someone to help—I'm left-handed and I have endless letters and lists still to deal with. And Carolyn is in such a mental tizzy that she can't seem to concentrate on anything at the moment...'

One of the tight knots of tension loosened in Regan's

chest at the rueful admission of relief. At least now, on top of her other worries, she needn't fear that she was leeching off a reluctant hostess.

'Now, why don't you go upstairs with Alice and settle in?' Hazel ordered briskly. 'And later she can show you around the house, so you can get your bearings. We can leave our little get-to-know-you chat until later. Meanwhile, I suppose I should see how the meal will stretch to two extra...I think Alice told me she was doing a stuffed salmon...'

Oh, God, was she going to have to face Adam across a formal table?

'You said you weren't expecting *any more* guests?' Regan blurted. 'Does that mean you have some staying here already?'

She held her breath until Hazel shook her head, her soft-set curls shimmering. 'Not staying, no—except for Carolyn, of course, and she often flits back to Auckland to stay overnight at her flat. No, by "guests" I meant that Carolyn's having a little impromptu party here later this evening for some of our local friends. It'll be a nice, informal introduction for you.

'And we do have plenty of visitors popping in and out during the course of the day. Joshua's staying down at Palm Court, and he regularly drops by to see Carolyn, and there's Christopher, of course—that's Joshua's brother.'

Thinking about it later in her room Regan, pondered the uneasy look that Hazel had exchanged with Sir Frank when she'd mentioned Christopher Wade and then hurriedly changed the subject—thwarting any further casual enquiry about male visitors. Was the fiancé's brother considered some kind of problem? Could *he* be her Adam?

If so, she didn't run into him when the stoic Alice Beatson finally winkled her out of her room for a nerve-wracking tour of the house. The room in which she had seen him proved to be a blessedly empty library, and dinner turned out to be a straightforward foursome with the Harrimans. Carolyn, whom she'd never met before, seemed perfectly pleasant when introduced, but rather disconcertingly edgy when she learned the purpose for Regan's visit. Beneath the superficial gloss of sophistication often provided by inherited wealth she seemed rather young for her twenty-two years, and Regan had misgivings about the wilful curve to her lovely mouth and the highly-strung quality to her darting conversation. She had a beautiful figure and long, natural blonde hair which she kept twitching over her shoulder, and there was a hectic glitter in her golden-brown eyes as she bubbled excitedly about Joshua, whom she called her Darling Jay, and the people Regan was likely to meet later that night.

A good percentage of them were male, and as Regan ventured down later to join the party she was deeply fatalistic, determined that whatever happened she would brazen things out. Now that she had calmed down she had reasoned that a confrontation with Adam might be highly embarrassing but it wasn't the end of the world. Plenty of women had to endure the social awkwardness of running into inconvenient ex-lovers. And Adam was a sophisticated man, unlikely to want a public fuss any more than she did.

The 'little' impromptu party had the house bulging at the seams already, and after Hazel had introduced her without incident to several bunches of friendly, relaxed people Regan felt confident enough to grab a glass of non-alcoholic punch and wing it on her own. In her black flip skirt and plain white silk camisole she knew she looked more subdued than most of the younger women present, and that suited her perfectly.

'Hi, sweetie—you're definitely a new face around here.' As she moved away from the punch bowl she was accosted by a handsome, dark-haired young man with a cocky smile and to-die-for blue eyes who fell into step beside her. 'Now, you can't be a friend of Caro's or we would have met before—are you part of the local gentry?'

'I'm Regan Frances. I'm a house-guest here.' That was the unfussy label Hazel had used in her introductions.

'Are you indeed? Lucky thing! My name is Chris.'

She stopped by the French doors to the glass conservatory. 'Christopher Wade?'

He leaned his hand on the doorframe above her head and raised his eyebrows in a wicked leer. 'Ah, I see my fame has preceded me. What have you heard? How brilliant I am? How witty and good-looking? It's all true, I tell you!'

She laughed. 'I can see that.'

'A woman of exquisite discernment.' He grinned, and for the next few minutes elicited a string of giggles with his nonsense.

Regan was so busy enjoying the performance that she wasn't aware of her danger until a masculine arm suddenly shot into her line of vision, holding out another full glass of beverage.

'You appear to have run out of punch, *Mrs Frances*— why don't you take mine? It seems my brother is too intent on flirting to do his duty as a gentleman.'

Regan stared, not at the glass in the manicured hand, but at the stud securing the French cuff of the dazzling white sleeve—a solid gold cufflink inset with New Zealand jade. Her gaze slowly travelled up the length of the white arm to collide with a pair of murderous steel-grey eyes.

'Y-your brother?' she stuttered, not noticing the young man had stiffened at her side.

He knew her name. He must have asked about her. The cat was well and truly out of the bag.

His smile was lethally unamused. Her eyes shifted to Carolyn, clinging to his other elbow, and to the huge diamond flashing on her finger. Shock punched her in the stomach as her brain clicked back into gear and worked through all the clues she'd stupidly missed.

Owns a corporation—therefore must be quite a bit older than Carolyn; well-respected in financial circles—meaning millionaire; corporate-apartment-type rich; 'Darling Jay…'

Jay…JA…Joshua Adam.

Joshua Adam Wade.

Oh, God—she had slept with her employer's grand-niece's fiancé! The passionate fantasy lover who had told her he despised people who cheated on their partners was the very man whose wedding she was here to help arrange!

CHAPTER SIX

'How long have you been engaged?' Regan croaked, sipping on her fresh glass of punch.

'Nearly two months,' preened Carolyn, looking adoringly up at the man at her side. In a pink taffeta shift overlaid with a black satin and lace Empire-line dress she looked the perfect accessory to her fiancé's monochrome white shirt and black trousers. As a woman who had never had to work—and probably never would—she had plenty of time to devote to her appearance. 'We got engaged in the second week of February, didn't we, Jay Darling? Up here—on St Valentine's Day!'

Regan choked, spluttering liquid back into her glass. That was only two days after her own encounter with 'Adam'!

'Sorry, a piece of fruit pulp must have gone down the wrong way,' she said, as Chris gave her a light tap on the back.

At least Joshua hadn't been engaged when he had 'engaged' himself to be entertained by one of Derek's 'friends'!

But he hadn't just decided he wanted to get married and hunted out a wife within the space of two days. And if he had already been involved with Carolyn why hadn't he looked to *her* to satisfy his libido instead of seeking casual sex with a stranger…or did he come from that chauvinistic school which divided the whole of womankind into only two types: those you slept with and those you married?

But, no—looking at the golden-blonde's flushed cheeks, and the way she was leaning her breasts into Joshua's side, her eyes avidly darting between the two males, Regan got the strong impression that in spite of her dewy, debutante looks Carolyn was no innocent virgin. And, anyway— Joshua was surely too intelligent to subscribe to such an outrageous double standard!

When she dared look at his face she found that he was staring down at her with a blistering contempt that caught her on the raw. She squared her shoulders and lifted her chin, proudly rejecting his disdain. Did he think she had come here *expecting* to run into him? Her eyes were violet pools of reflective scorn as she glared back at him. As a betrayed wife herself, she hated that he had forced her into a position where she felt like the iniquitous 'other woman'.

'OK now?' asked Chris, solicitously rubbing her rigid spine.

Joshua's nostrils flared at the sight of his brother's petting hand.

'Do you usually allow yourself to be pawed by men you've only just met, Mrs Frances?' he drawled, his joking smile undercut by the venomous tone which suggested that she was in the habit of allowing liberties a great deal more obscene.

Regan's drink trembled in her hand, and even Carolyn stopped preening long enough to look startled at his smiling ferocity.

Chris bristled, his hand dropping to clench by his side, as if he was contemplating planting it in Joshua's cynical face. 'Her name is Regan.'

'I know what she calls herself.' The drawl was even more mocking. 'Mrs Frances and I are old acquaintances.'

Now old enemies, it seemed! Regan compressed her lips, bewildered by the depth of his anger.

'That's right,' she agreed, smiling with sweet falsity, 'but in spite of what he seems to want you to infer, Chris, as an "old acquaintance" *Mr Wade* knows full well that I'm not currently married—my husband died nearly a year ago.'

She was guiltily aware that it wasn't the first time today she had used her status as a widow to invite the pity she had previously always shunned.

Only one other person recognised the ploy. 'Ten months, actually, if my memory serves me correctly,' said Joshua. He looked her slowly up and down. 'From your outfit I take it that you're still not sure whether you're half in mourning or half out of it…'

Carolyn gave a high-pitched nervous giggle as Regan struggled not to throw her drink in his insulting face. His eyes glittered, and she knew he almost wanted her to do it. Didn't he care that his thinly veiled hostility was bound to raise questions about their former relationship?

'God, when did you become such an insensitive bastard!' Chris swore, his arm curving protectively around Regan's waist. 'I'd have thought you, of *all* people, would know better than to taunt anyone about the tragedy in their life.' He turned to Regan and fired out rapidly in a low voice, 'Maybe you should know that my parents—Joshua's father and stepmother—died in an arson attack on our house when Josh was seventeen. He got badly hurt saving my twin sisters and me, and then had to give up the career he'd planned to fight for custody of us kids, against our father's scavenging relatives and business partners who wanted to plunder our inheritance. I guess he feels that all that gives him the monopoly on suffering, so that he can sneer at those who can't match him for sheer angst—'

'I haven't asked you to apologise for me,' grated Joshua. 'Or speculate on my motives. You don't have to dredge up every last detail of my personal history—'

'I wasn't apologising—you can damned well do that for yourself,' Chris shot back, raking back a lock of dark-brown hair that had fallen over his forehead. 'I was just letting you see what it feels like to have someone violate your privacy in public. It's about time someone gave you a taste of your own medicine.'

Regan sensed unknown cross-currents and realised that while she might have been the catalyst for this confrontation she wasn't the sole cause.

A muscle flickered in Joshua's hard jaw. 'Back off, Chris.'

'Or what? You'll cut off my allowance? I'm not a little boy any more, to be bribed into living my life the way *you* think I should. I'm ten years older than *you* were when you took over our father's company. I'm a qualified doctor now, pal, and I earn my own damned living.'

A doctor? Somehow Regan hadn't pictured the cocky young man in his designer white suit as anything but a frivolous playboy.

Perversely, as Chris heated up Joshua cooled down, withdrawing behind a rigid barrier of self-control. 'I said, back off. This isn't the time or place.'

Chris threw his hands up, palms out, in a gesture of contemptuous surrender. 'Sure. Anything you say, *bro*. After all, you're the boss. The head of the family. The man who makes all the decisions on behalf of the rest of us—purely for our own good, of course—and takes it for granted that we'll fall in with his plans—'

'Don't, Chris!' Surprisingly it was Carolyn who put the brake on the runaway tension. Her eyes were sparkling with suspicious moisture, her lower lip trembling. 'This is supposed to be a party—I want everyone to be *happy*. Please, please don't spoil it for me…'

Very effective, thought Regan as she watched both men fold like limp handkerchiefs to dry out the little-girl tears. She wondered if Carolyn practised that look in the mirror, then told herself not to be catty.

'Maybe Regan and I will just take ourselves outside for

a stroll,' said Chris, grabbing her hand without even glancing at her for permission. 'Or maybe we'll take a row across the lake and I'll show her what the gazebo is like in the moonlight.'

Regan decided that Joshua wasn't the only one in the Wade family who took things for granted. She knew that whatever was going on, she didn't want to be involved.

She wriggled her fingers free. 'Thanks, but I get seasick in small boats.'

There was a tiny, startled silence, engulfed in the swirl of partying around them, then Joshua said smoothly, 'I'm sure the good doctor can find some medication somewhere so that you won't vomit on his romantic pretensions.'

Regan seethed. If he thought to push her into Chris's arms to neutralise the threat she clearly presented, he had another think coming!

'I prefer not to rely on chemicals to maintain my equilibrium.'

'You don't say?' His eyebrows shot up in taunting disbelief and Regan fought not to blush as she was forcibly reminded of the alcohol that had been flowing in her bloodstream the night that they had spent in bed together, making love for hours on end...

She hadn't been concerned about her equilibrium then; she had purely revelled in the explosive reaction of their mingled body chemistries. And they hadn't just made love on the bed...there had been the chair, the floor, the bath: the cold, shiny surface of the big mirror slamming against her back and buttocks, frosted by the heat from her steamy, straining body as he knelt between her legs, so that when he pulled her down to mount him she was faced with a fleeting, graphic imprint of herself fading mistily against the glass...

She lost the battle against the wave of heat that swept through her body, clenching her hands around her glass as she felt her soft nipples peak against the white silk. She just hoped anyone who noticed would put it down to the chill of the punch sliding down her throat.

'The lake's as calm as a millpond,' Chris was protesting. 'And it only takes a few minutes to get across.'

'Oh, come on, Chris, leave it alone.' Carolyn unexpectedly came to Regan's rescue. 'Can't you see she's trying to let you down politely?'

'And was succeeding, too, until you stuck your oar in,' he sniped back.

'So why aren't you taking your rejection gracefully?'

'Because maybe she was just leaving herself open to persuasion. Some women like their *men* to do the wooing.'

Carolyn stopped leaning on Joshua's arm and put her hands on her hips. 'I guess it all depends on what your definition of a *man* is. I'd say a *real* man is one who's willing to respect that a woman is capable of saying exactly what she means,' she struck back, leading Regan to revise her opinion of her as a total lightweight.

She threw back her head, her long hair shimmering like a veil over her shoulders. 'It's not as if you really wanted to row over there, anyway. You were just trying to get at Jay and me…'

Chris's handsome face darkened at her carelessly provocative stance. 'Don't presume to tell me what I was trying to do—'

'Maybe it's you two who should step outside,' murmured Joshua, but they didn't appear to hear him as they continued their crackling exchange, and he turned to Regan, effectively cutting her off from the other two.

'When Frank pointed you out from across the room and ordered Carolyn to introduce us he suggested I get to know you—since you're apparently going to be spending some of your time in the site office at Palm Cove while I'm familiarising myself with the operation there.' Regan's hands went clammy with dismay as he continued smoothly, 'So, tell me…how does a university drop-out with no qualifications keep herself such a cushy job in the legal department of a company than runs such a lean, mean operation?'

'I didn't sleep my way there, if that's what you're implying!' she flared.

'Trading favours? But you do it so well…' he taunted, lifting a hand to rub his jaw.

Regan caught her breath as the gold and jade winked mockingly in the light.

'What's the matter?' He tilted his strong wrist, looking down at it in mock surprise. 'Ahh, you're admiring my cufflinks—attractive, aren't they? And, as far as my investigations show, definitely a one-off.'

The hair rose on the back of Regan's neck. *Investigations?*

'Also unique is the fact that they were given to me by a woman,' he murmured. 'Except for my sisters, women rarely give me gifts, and never expensive jewellery. As a wealthy man it's considered my prerogative to give rather than to receive.'

Had he no shame?

'How you can have the gall to wear them around Carolyn, I don't know,' she whispered raggedly.

He shrugged, seemingly unconcerned at their proximity to his fiancée. 'But then you don't know me at all, do you? I didn't keep my family together against all the odds, and fight off the wolves that almost tore my father's corporation to pieces by being sweet-natured, mild and forgiving. As it happens, I was running late tonight and in a hurry to dress. I just scooped up the first things that came to hand…'

In spite of his logic she still didn't entirely believe him. 'You knew I might be here tonight,' she accused him.

His cynical eyes hooded. 'Let's say I thought it too much

of a coincidence that you should be sneaking around the property, spying on me, if you didn't intend to make some kind of contact.'

Shades of Ryan and his James Bond!

'I wasn't *spying* on you. I was just taking an innocent stroll in the gardens! If you think I was pleased to see you, you must be crazy!' she choked.

His mouth thinned. 'If it was so innocent why did you run? That's the second time you've disappeared on me, but now that I know who and what you are, you won't find it so easy to elude me in future. I'm sure Frank will prove even more informative if I flatter him about his charming protégée. A distant relative, I think he said…?'

'Yes, and when you marry Carolyn that means you and I will also be relations,' she pointed out with sweet relish.

But he turned even that point against her. 'You and I have already established our *relations*. You obviously think that entitles you to special consideration.'

'Do I?' Regan fenced, uncertain of his meaning.

He flicked at finger at her glass. 'You're running on empty again. Shall we revisit the bar together?' He cupped her elbow in his hand and turned his sleek head. 'Regan and I are going to get another drink. Shall I get you a glass of something, Carolyn?'

'Preferably water or punch,' Chris tacked on sharply.

Carolyn paused to give him a fierce look before she tossed Joshua a glittering smile. 'I'd rather have a glass of champagne.'

'That is *so* typical! Go ahead, then. Put your own selfish desires first, just as you always do—'

'I think you really should have something non-alcoholic,' interrupted Joshua, with a gentleness that sent tingles up and down Regan's spine. On this subject at least the two men seemed united in their opinion. She looked curiously at Carolyn, wondering if that high-strung air indicated an addictive personality.

'Oh, all right,' she was saying, with a pretty pout in his direction. 'If *you* say I should, Jay Darling…'

'No need to overdo it,' sniped Chris, and they were off again, arguing the point.

The clamp on Regan's elbow tightened and she found herself thrust reluctantly into motion.

'But I don't want anything else to drink,' she protested, dragging her steps as he manoeuvred through the crowd.

'You can keep me company.'

She tried to look back over her shoulder. 'Aren't you afraid to leave them alone together without someone to play referee—they might kill each other or something?'

A whimsical smile touched his lips. 'Or something.'

He didn't seem very worried. Stupid to think that anyone would be allowed to steal anything from *this* man.

That was why it was imperative that Regan get access to the Palm Cove advertising accounts before his auditors did. Bad enough that Michael had stolen from his employer through a fictitious printing company, but Regan had no desire to be tarred with the same dishonest brush if she was discovered trying to repay the money he had embezzled all those months ago.

She had believed Cindy when the other woman had sobbed that she hadn't known about the thefts. Cindy had willingly helped him cheat on his wife but she hadn't known—or evidently been bright enough to ask—how he had managed to finance his dual lifestyle. She had been horrified when, a few weeks ago, she had stumbled on the evidence of his activities, along with a stash of money, hidden in her garage. Afraid of the consequences to herself and her son if she went to the police, she had flung herself on the mercy of Michael's 'clever' wife, who knew the ins and outs of the law and surely wouldn't want to endure a public scandal, or condemn her husband's natural child to grow up in poverty, under the shadow of his father's crime…?

The child that should have been Regan's…

She was sick with shame at the way that Michael had abused Sir Frank's personal and professional trust. He would never have been in a position to do either if Regan hadn't introduced the two men. Sir Frank put great stock in his reputation for integrity and honest dealing, and she knew what a deleterious effect the belated discovery of embezzlement would have on his pride, not to mention his pocket, if it was uncovered by a close audit during the sale of his company. Determined that would never happen, Regan had used the information on the hidden disk to tot up the exact amount of Michael's theft and worked out a way to pay it back, hopefully without anyone ever knowing it had been gone. It had taken all the cash that Cindy had found, plus every spare cent that Regan could rake up from the sale of her former home and possessions, to get enough to square the accounts. All she needed now was the time and opportunity to put her plan into action.

'This isn't the bar!' she said, suddenly realising that Joshua had opened a door and was dragging her into an empty room.

A lamp shone on the desk, and twin pendant lights hanging from the high ceiling revealed the button-backed leather chairs and walls of bookshelves of the library.

She spun around as Joshua backed against the door, closing it with a definitive click. 'What do you think you're doing?'

'I thought you might like a little more privacy for this discussion.'

'Then you thought wrong! We have nothing more to discuss.'

'On the contrary. We have a great deal to settle.' He

folded his arms across his chest. 'First up, you can stop flirting with my brother.'

Her jaw dropped. 'I was not flirting!'

'I can read body language as well as the next man…you were leaning into him as he talked, giving him a close-up of those sultry little smiles and big violet eyes—'

'We were having a *conversation*. It was difficult to hear him over the music. Anyway, I didn't know he was your brother—'

'Ignorance is no defence in law, as you should know better than most. Stay away from Chris. Second: how much?'

'I beg your pardon?'

'How much were you going to demand from me to keep your mouth shut?'

'I don't know what you're talking about! You're being deliberately insulting—'

'And you're being deliberately obtuse. It won't work. You're a very bright lady, as Frank was at such pains to point out to me. Keen to make the most of your abilities. An eager opportunist. So…how much?'

Her slender bosom heaved. 'You think I'm here to *blackmail* you?'

His eyes flickered down to the rippling white silk and back up to her blazing eyes. 'It's a reasonable assumption. You found out who I was—who I'm engaged to—and figured that you were in a perfect position to threaten to disrupt my wedding plans unless I agreed to pay you soothing amounts of cash.'

That was the height of irony, considering what she had come up here to do, but she couldn't help the guilty blush that stained her throat and cheeks as she launched on the offensive.

'What a very active imagination you must have!' she

scoffed. 'I suppose you think that I somehow pushed Hazel down that hill in order to get myself invited up here...'

He tilted his head against the door, exposing the scars above his Nehru collar. 'You know exactly how imaginative I can be, Eve,' he drawled in a rusty voice that scratched at her frayed nerves. 'But, no, I don't think you were behind Hazel's accident. As I said, you're an opportunist—you take an existing situation and turn it to your advantage.'

'Well, I'm sorry to disappoint your paranoid fantasies, but I had no idea who you were until a few minutes ago,' she gritted. 'And now that I do know it makes not one iota of difference to me. I have no interest in you either as Adam *or* as Joshua Wade.'

To her fury, he grinned. 'You were interested in me every which way that night in the apartment...'

'I treat all my one-night stands like that!'

'That must make for an extremely exhausting social life...and an extremely expensive one.' He unfolded his arms to lightly adjust his cufflinks, one after the other, watching her pupils contract nervously. 'You left a gift on my pillow but you didn't take mine to you. Was it your intention to make me feel like a toyboy?'

She felt a wicked surge of angry satisfaction and sleeked her hair back behind her ears like a fastidious little cat. 'Oh, dear, how demeaning for you,' she sympathised.

His eyes slitted. 'Actually, I found the thought rather...stimulating.' He pushed off the door and came softly towards her. 'Didn't you like the bracelet? I know you looked at it while I was in the shower.'

If it was a guess then her expression as she backed away from him on unsteady legs would have been all he needed to confirm its accuracy. Her brief burst of triumph dwindled to renewed panic as he continued.

'Because that's my problem with all this, you see. What

you did doesn't quite jell with the image of you as a greedy, blackmailing opportunist, does it?' He prowled around the desk after her. 'You had those lovely baubles within your grasp and you deliberately let them slip through your fingers. Why, instead of waiting to accept your due reward, did you creep out and leave me to wake up alone? Apart from anything else, it's extremely bad manners.'

Regan backed into a swivel chair and nearly fell over. 'I'm sorry if I offended your sense of etiquette.'

'I don't think so. I think it was some kind of planned strategy on your part.' He steadied the swinging chair with his hands as she retreated behind it. 'After all, you didn't conjure those cufflinks out of thin air.'

'Will you stop *stalking* me?' she shrilled, almost at the end of her tether.

He was relentless. 'If you'll tell me exactly what's going on?'

'Nothing's *going on*,' she denied hectically. 'This is all just an unfortunate coincidence.' She glanced towards the door.

'Don't bother. You wouldn't make it,' he warned her.

Her hip bumped the corner of the desk and she winced, rubbing at her bruised thigh. 'How dare you harass me like this? If you don't open that door people are going to wonder what we're doing in here—'

'No one saw us come in, and given the crowd out there I doubt if we'll be missed.'

'Even by Carolyn?' She drew herself up to her full height, deciding the only remaining defence was attack. 'It's not as if you're in any position to criticise *my* motives. What about *your* behaviour? You wouldn't have any reason to fear blackmail if you didn't know you'd done something utterly reprehensible.' A mist of red covered her vision as she got to the crux of her inner anger. 'You virtually bounced out of bed with me to rush up here and propose to *her*!'

His grey eyes went dark. 'I owed Carolyn no sexual fidelity on the night that you and I slept together,' he said grimly.

'Don't play with semantics!' she cried. 'What about emotional fidelity? You must have been *intending* to ask her—'

His mouth twisted. 'Actually, no. I had not in the least thought of getting married again when I drove up here that day…'

Her feet suddenly felt nailed to the spot. 'Again? You've been married before?'

'I'm thirty-six. It would be more surprising if I *hadn't* had a previous serious relationship, wouldn't it?' he queried, taking advantage of her stunned expression to move closer.

This new facet of him threw all her previous assumptions into disarray. 'What did you do? Dump her when you discovered she'd married you purely for your money?' she said, using deliberate cruelty to distance herself from the odd feeling of melancholy that invaded her bones.

The twist of his mouth turned into a cold smile. 'Actually, yes. And it was worth every cent it took to pay her off!'

She swallowed. On top of all the other blows Chris had mentioned, Joshua had taken a king-hit to his pride—if not his heart.

'That must have been difficult for you?'

'She was the loser, not I. I was a rich man then, but I've become a lot richer in the last fifteen years.'

'But money doesn't necessarily buy you happiness,' protested Regan.

He looked at her, his eyes full of silvery satisfaction. 'What makes you think I was talking about money?'

'I—well, you're wealthy, and—I just assumed…'

Her voice tailed off and he said silkily, 'It's dangerous to make assumptions when you don't have all the facts. You seem to make a habit of it.

'The fact is that I *do* have some experience of courtship,' he said, when she failed to respond. 'And I assure you I wasn't even *close* to courting Carolyn when I took you to bed.' His tone became even silkier as he echoed her earlier thoughts. 'Or rather, when we took each other in all those assorted places…'

'Are you saying you proposed on the spur of the moment? I don't believe you!' she said coldly, trying to freeze out the hot flood of excitement his words had provoked. 'You don't strike me as a man who ever does anything on impulse.'

'I'm not—that's what makes the impulse I'm having right now all the more disturbing,' he mused darkly, making her suddenly aware that all the time they had been talking he had been drifting inexorably closer.

His brooding expression looked faintly murderous, and Regan clutched her hands to her vulnerable throat as he loomed over her. 'What impulse?'

He lifted a hand and she flinched, but all he did was stroke his finger down one dark wing of glossy hair where it swept behind her delicate ear.

'You don't really want to know.' His finger lingered in the crease just behind her naked earlobe. He seemed to have a perfect genius for homing in on the most sensitive points on her body, thought Regan shakily—ones that even she hadn't known were sensitive until he roused them to glorious life.

'Most women deck themselves in jewellery when they dress up—you don't seem to wear any…'

'I'm allergic to gold,' she said flippantly, thinking that lying was beginning to become second nature.

His eyebrows lifted over disbelieving eyes. 'As well as diamonds?' he mocked. 'You don't even wear a watch.'

'It broke— I haven't got round to replacing it yet.' Even a cheap time-piece took second place to digging herself out of a mountain of debt.

The door to the library suddenly swung open and Regan jerked guiltily away from Joshua's touch.

'Hello, what are you two doing in here?' Hazel Harriman's head ducked around the door, her innocent brown eyes travelling from one face to the other.

'Checking on the silver, Hazel?' grinned Joshua easily.

'Well, you know what Frank's like about his blessed first editions! He should have locked the door if he didn't want anyone coming in here, but he thinks that would be implying he can't trust his neighbours.' She opened the door wider and came further into the room, a picture of grace and dignity in her powder-blue chiffon and pearls, in spite of the wooden crutch propped under her right arm.

'Are you talking about the wedding? I hope you're not going to interfere as well, Joshua. I already have enough on my plate with Frank poking his nose in!'

'I wouldn't dream of it. I'm very happy to leave it all in your gracious hands,' he replied. 'Would you like to sit down and rest that leg?'

'No, thanks, I've been sitting down all night. A little exercise is good for me—whatever Frank has to say!'

Joshua smiled. 'He suggested that Regan and I get to know each other, but it turns out that we've met before…'

Hazel's eyes brightened with enquiry. 'Oh, really? Where?'

Joshua opened his mouth, and Regan didn't trust the bland look on his face. Was he about to conduct some advance damage control?

'It was only just the once—and not at all memorable,' she cut in quickly. 'Which is why Joshua's name didn't ring a bell when Sir Frank mentioned who Carolyn was going to marry.'

'Oh, well, at least you're not total strangers, so that makes everything much more cosy for all of us,' Hazel approved complacently.

'Indeed.' Joshua's blandness was even more pronounced.

'Frank is very keen for Regan to feel at home. I know he feels guilty that he didn't do more for you when Michael was killed—'

Regan was agonisingly conscious of Joshua's sharpened interest. 'Oh, really—he did *more* than enough for us when Michael was alive.'

But Hazel was unstoppable. 'It's such a tragic waste when people die with so much of life ahead of them,' she sighed.

'How long were you married?'

In front of Hazel, Regan couldn't flatly refuse to satisfy Joshua's curiosity, as he very well knew! 'Just over four years.'

'You must have married young?'

'I was twenty,' she admitted, with the thin end of her patience.

'The same age that I was when I married the first time,' he commented. 'How old was your husband?'

'Four years older than me. How old was your wife?' Regan retaliated, before realising that it was hardly a polite question to ask in front of his future mother-in-law.

'Twenty-four.' He tipped his head in acknowledgment of her slight blink of shock. 'I wonder how many other uncanny coincidences lurk in our pasts. Children?'

Her flinch was barely perceptible, except to a hawkish gaze. 'No.'

'A mutual decision?' he murmured.

'Isn't that what marriage is about?' she snapped.

Hazel's forehead wrinkled. 'I remember Michael telling

me one day when he dropped in here with Frank after showing some buyers around the site that he definitely didn't want to be tied down with children until you were both well established in your respective careers. He felt very strongly about it. And, of course, he was so very keen for you to graduate as soon as ever you could, Regan. He joked that he wanted a wife to be proud of, one that he could boast about at the country club!'

It had been no joke. Image had been everything to Michael. And the demands of her full-time study, her part-time job and the chores around the house with which he was always too busy to assist had ensured she rarely had the time to keep tabs on his whereabouts. Even though she had begun to yearn for a baby, Michael had flatly refused to even discuss it.

'And what did he envisage *you* doing while he was busy boasting about you in the bar of the country club?' asked Joshua with painfully acute perception.

'If you don't mind I'd rather not talk about it,' she said, casting a bleak look at Hazel, who instantly leapt to her aid.

'Of course you don't want to, dear,' she said, patting her hand. 'No sense in dwelling on what can't be changed. It's time to put the past behind you and think of the future. Speaking of which, Joshua—do you know where Carolyn is? I need to consult her about supper but I haven't been able to track her down—not that that's so very surprising in this crush! The naughty girl didn't tell me she'd been so casual with the invitations.'

'I believe she was with Chris, near the conservatory.'

'Oh.' Hazel's beringed fingers moved up to play restlessly with her string of pearls, her smile dimming. 'I didn't realise he was going to be here—I thought he was on duty this weekend.'

'He apparently swapped with someone else. He's staying the night with me at Palm Cove.'

'I'll go and look for Carolyn, if you like,' offered Regan, seizing on the excuse to escape her forced interrogation.

'We'll all go,' Joshua was swift to respond, and as he gently shepherded the women before him he leaned close to the back of Regan's head and whispered, 'I meant what I said: stay away from my brother; he needs no encouragement to flirt. If you do stir up any trouble, you'll have me to deal with…'

It was easier said than done. In the huge house and grounds it should have been easy to avoid someone, but Christopher Wade seemed to have developed a built-in radar that had him gravitating towards Regan with dismaying regularity—usually when Joshua and Carolyn were somewhere in the vicinity—combined with a thick-skinned good humour that refused to allow her to politely shake him off.

Later, when the guests were beginning to thin out, Regan sought her hostess out and asked if she could help with any of the clearing up before she slipped away to bed.

'Oh, heavens, no. The caterers will deal with most of the debris and Alice has an army of helpers coming in in the morning to help tidy up the house and gardens. You go off and have a good rest. And don't worry about getting up too early in the morning—we usually have breakfast at nine on a Saturday, but tomorrow I've told Alice to give us a brunch at eleven so we can all have a good lie-in.'

But when she tried to fade up the stairs Chris was there, dogging her heels.

'I'll walk you to your room.'

'I'm not likely to get lost!'

'No, but you could be waylaid by a gang of ghostly bandits. A creaking old rabbit warren like this could harbour all sorts of nefarious characters lurking amongst the shadows.'

'Yes, and I think I'm looking at one of them right now,' said Regan wryly as they walked along the hall, their footsteps muffled on the runner which ran the length of the polished floorboards. With his white suit glowing brighter every time they passed one of the glass wall-lamps, he made a very stylish ghost.

'I'll have you know that as a doctor I have an impac— an *impeccable* character,' he enunciated carefully.

'You've also had too much to drink,' she realised, as they came to a halt beside her door.

He laid his right hand on his heart. 'Alas, it's true. I cannot tell a lie. I'm tanked to the gills.' He used his other hand to open her door with a flourish. 'Would you like me to come in and check for bogeymen under your bed?'

'I wouldn't like you to get your nice suit dirty,' she said, stepping over the threshold to switch on the light, and turning with her body square in the door to prevent him following.

'I could take it off.' He began to unbutton the jacket.

'Good*night,* Chris.'

'Yes, push off, Chris. You've gone as far as either of you intend to go,' came a midnight-dark voice from behind him. 'So cut the clowning and take a hike back down the stairs where you belong. They're serving coffee on the back terrace. You might want a cup or three.'

Chris turned with a fat chuckle. 'Well, surprise, surprise! Look who's here. Keeping tabs on me, bro?'

Joshua's gaze was steely and calm, his stance relaxed and yet also finely balanced. 'Always.'

Chris snickered, even as he obeyed the silent command. 'Night, Regan.' He gave her a sloppy salute as he turned away. ''Ware the bogeyman!'

Regan watched him go with puzzled eyes, wondering what he was so smug about, what it was he thought he had achieved. She cast a fleeting look at Joshua, not quite meeting his eyes.

'Well…goodnight.'

She closed the door in his face, but she had only a few seconds to savour her small victory before it flew open again, and Joshua strolled in with an arrogance that immediately made her vibrate with outrage.

'You could have knocked!'

'Why? We both know you wouldn't have opened it.' He walked around the room, looking at the white flounced cover on the single bed, the half-open wardrobe displaying her small collection of clothes on hangers, the array of toiletries neatly arranged on the mirrored dressing table.

'Perhaps because I didn't want to let you in,' she said with withering sarcasm, watching his profile as he picked up a paperback from beside the bed. 'Would you mind not handling my things?'

He turned the book over with careful deliberation, stroking his fingers across the covers, touching every inch of the available surface before he just as deliberately set it down, satisfied he had delivered his silent message. He would handle whatever he liked, whenever he liked…

Including her? Regan felt a quiver of guilty excitement.

'I did warn you not to flirt with Chris. It seems that you chose to deal with the consequences…'

'You also said he didn't need encouragement!' she pointed out tartly. 'I didn't invite him up here, you know—he followed me. And in spite of everything Hazel said, I'm virtually a paid employee—I can't start off my first day by insulting the brother of the groom—'

He spun around on his heel and rapped out, 'You're a little ahead of yourself. I'm not actually a bridegroom until my wedding day.'

He was playing with words again. She bravely stood her ground as he invaded her personal space. 'He was very persistent. I couldn't get rid of him without being rude. What was I supposed to do?'

'Be rude…be very, very rude…' His hand came up to cup the side of her throat, his thumb extending under the point of her chin. 'I don't like him touching you. I find I really—don't like it an extraordinary amount…'

She swallowed, feeling the pressure of the ball of his thumb against her larynx and the heavy throb of blood at her pulse-point. 'You shouldn't be here,' she murmured thickly, her voice vibrating in the cup of his palm. 'The door is open…anyone could look in.'

'We're not doing anything wrong…'

Yet.

The unspoken qualification lingered in the air.

His eyes dropped to her mouth. Her lips parted. His head sank, his breath a hot streak of sensation across her cheek.

'Say my name…'

'What?'

He inhaled the scent of her skin. 'I want to hear you say my name…'

'Joshua.' It was a mere sough of wind across her tingling lips.

His head sank further, the pressure on her throat increased and her mouth tilted up like a flower to the brilliant incandescence of the sun, and he groaned.

'Damn and blast!' His lips were hard against her forehead for a fleeting instant before his hands were gripping her shoulders, setting her firmly away. 'No! We're not going to do this.' There was a sheen of perspiration on his forehead and upper lip as he stared down into her dazed violet eyes and ground out savagely, 'You're a complication I really don't need right now!'

Stricken, she writhed out of his implacably gentle grip and lifted the shield of her pride. 'Join the club, buster!'

There was a rustle from the hallway and they looked across just in time to see Carolyn drooping wearily past.

'Carolyn?' Joshua was at the door with startling speed.

She halted, her golden eyes curiously blank, not even seeming to register that her fiancé was coming out of another woman's bedroom. 'What?'

His voice gentled to a note that caused Regan physical pain. 'Are you all right?'

'No, I'm not all right.' Her pouty mouth turned down sullenly. 'I'm tired. I'm going to bed.'

'But not all your guests have left—'

'God, you sound just like Granny!' she snapped. Then she put a hand on her flat stomach. 'I don't feel very well, OK?'

'Do you think you're going to be sick?'

'Of course I'm not going to be sick!' Two patches of pink stood out on her cheeks. 'Tomorrow, when I get up in the morning, *that's* when I'll probably be sick, and I'll feel rotten for half the day.' Her eyes glittered with tears, this time genuine, and her voice was shrill. 'Oh, God, I hate this—it's all such a ghastly mess! If there were any justice in the world *men* would have to go through this, too!'

She dashed away down the hall towards her room at the far end, and when Regan would have gone after her she found a strong arm barring her way.

'No, let her go. She'll probably throw herself on the bed, have a good cry, and feel the better for it.'

After his tender tone, it seemed awfully callous. 'But she says she doesn't feel well.' She remembered her earlier suspicions. 'Perhaps she's had too much to drink—in which case she might need someone there.'

'She's not ill and she's not drunk.'

'Not ill? But—' Suddenly it hit her, nearly knocking her to the floor. She clutched at the door handle for balance and stared up at him as her mind made the conscious leap from instinct to understanding. That Empire-line dress and the many-layered look Carolyn had worn to dinner would cover a multitude of sins!

'My God!' Her voice cracked. '*That's* why you two are in such a rush to get married! Carolyn's pregnant, isn't she? *Isn't she?*'

His face was like granite, his voice tight with the effort of control as he lowered his voice. 'Yes, she's pregnant, but Hazel doesn't know about it yet...that's the way Carolyn wants it. So, for her sake, promise me you'll keep quiet?'

'You weren't *courting* her, and you didn't owe her fidelity, but you *did* go to bed with her—unless you're going to claim it's a virgin birth! You heartless, hypocritical, lying, lascivious beast!'

This time when she slammed the door thunderously in his face it stayed shut.

CHAPTER SEVEN

AT ELEVEN o'clock the next morning it was an unpleasant surprise to walk into the dining room and find the lying, lascivious beast laughing and chatting with Hazel and Sir Frank as Alice Beatson served him up a large plate of scrambled eggs and salmon cakes.

'Good morning, Regan,' carolled Hazel from her position at the head of the long refectory table. 'Look who's dropped in for brunch!'

While Sir Frank grunted and waved his marmalade-covered knife in greeting, Joshua had risen to his feet and rounded the table to pull out the chair squarely opposite his own.

Damning his manners, Regan sat down, giving him a stiff nod.

'Thank you.' Now she would have to suffer being directly in his sight-line all through the meal. In a straw-coloured casual linen jacket over an open-necked beige shirt and trousers he looked too damnably attractive for her unsettled state of mind.

'Good morning, Regan,' he chided her softly, stooping over her shoulder in the process of pushing in her chair, his open jacket brushing the short sleeve of her cherry-red shift dress.

She clenched her teeth on a smile. 'Good morning,' she parroted. She accepted Alice's offer of freshly squeezed orange juice and a dish of sliced fresh fruit in yogurt and looked around the table.

She had been so preoccupied with her effort not to react to Joshua that she had barely registered anyone else in the room, and now she felt a shock of recognition as she stared into a pair of familiar light brown eyes, gazing at her from across the table over the top of a tall stack of buttermilk pancakes.

He smirked at her surprise. 'Hi.'

'Hello, Ryan,' she blurted. 'Were you at the party last night? I didn't see you.'

'Nah—I have exams starting on Monday, I had to swot.'

In the act of reseating himself beside the youth, Joshua snapped up his head. 'You two know each other?'

'Sort of,' hedged Regan, praying that the sly humour that had entered the young man's eyes didn't mean he was going to rat on her for the pleasure of seeing an adult squirm. Today he had his hair slicked back into a neat ponytail and was wearing a brown T-shirt that made him look even more like a beanpole.

'We ran into each other yesterday and had a bit of a chat, didn't we, Ryan?' Her eyes silently begged him to play it casual.

'So, did you see any more of those birds?' he said loudly.

Sir Frank frowned. 'There's no need to shout, lad, we're not deaf.'

'Sorry, but I thought Regan was hard of hearing.' Ryan's eyes were owlishly innocent behind his wire glasses.

The wretch! Regan gave him a speaking look which he returned with a pious grin as he stuffed another pancake in his mouth.

'Why on earth should you think that?' asked Hazel.

Ryan moved his thin shoulders up and down, pointing to his bulging cheeks to explain why he couldn't answer.

'He must have misunderstood something I said,' Regan supplied hurriedly, 'We were bird-watching, so we were whispering—'

'*Bird*-watching?' Joshua's eyebrows shot up. He looked sceptically at the young man munching innocently at his side. 'Since when have you taken up such a tame hobby, Ryan? I thought Cyberspace ruled your life. Although I suppose staring at native flora and fauna could be considered an advance on staring at a computer screen all day. At least it gets you out in the fresh air.'

'Nothing's tame to a young, enquiring mind,' Regan objected at his disparaging sarcasm. If he was going to be a father he needed to buck his ideas up. 'I think children should always be encouraged to find *everything* interesting and not be stuck with labels that inhibit them from wanting to learn…'

Ryan gulped down his pancake to protest. 'I'm not a child.'

'I was speaking generally. Whether you're five, fifteen or fifty, you're still *someone's* child,' she countered, dipping her spoon into her fruit.

'Yes, but not *a* child. A child is someone between the ages of birth and puberty,' he argued.

She recalled his water-dripping-on-stone technique of wearing her down from the previous day.

'According to the dictionary, a child is also a human offspring—' she persisted.

'But not in the *first* meaning of the word,' he interrupted stubbornly. 'I bet if you looked it up you'd find my meaning listed before yours.'

'Don't take that bet,' came Joshua's dry advice.

'I wasn't going to,' dismissed Regan. 'OK,' she told Ryan, finding it amazingly easy to sink to his level, 'you win—you're far too boringly pedantic to be a mere *child*. You have to be at least ninety before you get to drive other people crazy by arguing endlessly over such irritating trivia with such single-minded intensity.' She smiled at him sweetly. 'I guess that puts you somewhere in your *second* childhood.'

Ryan thought about that for a moment, his eyes narrowing behind the round rims of his glasses in a way that struck a faint chord of uncomfortable resonance in Regan's brain.

'You kept arguing, too...'

'That's because I was right, but I showed my maturity by letting *you* win in deference to your mental age. When *I* was a child, I was taught to respect my elders...'

She tilted up her nose at him and he grinned, attacking his pancakes again. 'You didn't *let* me win.'

'If you say so, dear,' she said, in the indulgent, forgiving tone that she knew men—both young and old—hated to hear.

Ryan opened his mouth.

'Give it up, Son. Women are genetically programmed to have the last word. They can never bear to allow a man to feel that he's won an argument.'

'But, Dad...you told me never to give up on a fight when I believe I'm in the right!'

Son? *Dad?*

Regan's spoon clattered to her plate, splattering fruitjuice and yoghurt over the pale yellow tablecloth.

'He— You— You're father and son?' she said stupidly, dabbing at the tablecloth with her napkin in order to disguise her shaking hands.

Her eyes darted from face to face, suddenly seeing the echo of the boy in the man and the foreshadowing of the man in the boy...the similar angle of their cheekbones, the narrow, intelligent temples, the strong line of their noses.

Joshua's eyes narrowed, exactly as his son's had a few moments earlier. She must have been blind not to have seen it before!

'I thought you said that you and Ryan had talked?'

'Yes, but not about *you*!' He had been the single subject she had been desperate to *avoid*.

An unholy amusement filtered across his face as enlightenment dawned. 'Let me guess...you didn't realise who he

was because you never got around to exchanging sur-
names? Seems to be a habit of yours...'

Regan seethed as he picked up his cup of black coffee
and took a leisurely sip.

'You mean it's just what happened when you and Regan
met the first time?' chuckled Hazel, who had been following the conversation with lively interest. 'A case of like
father, like son!'

Flustered violet eyes clashed with thunderstruck grey as
they shared a moment of mutual consternation. Visions of
their torrid sexual encounter danced between them.

'God, I hope not,' muttered Joshua fervently, and Regan
knew that she was going to blush as Ryan sat up in his
chair, his precocious antennae twitching at the silent inter-
action. She quickly cast around for an innocuous change of
subject.

'So...where's Chris this morning?' she asked.

Bad choice. Hazel's eyes lowered as she thoughtfully
stirred a lump of sugar into her tea and Sir Frank stared
out of the window and made a gruff remark on the blustery
day.

'Still sleeping off last night,' said Joshua. 'Why? Were
you hoping to see him?'

'No—oh, no...I just wondered, that's all.' In her haste
to disassociate herself from the question she allowed Alice
to persuade her to a salmon cake she didn't really want. 'If
he's a doctor I suppose he must work very hard...' She
trailed off, seeing that she had only compounded her error
as Joshua's expression hardened.

'Works hard and plays hard. He's not sleeping because
he's tired; he's sleeping because he behaved like a total
idiot.'

'Uncle Chris fell into the canal coming home last night,'
supplied Ryan. At least her diversion had worked on *one*
level. 'I saw him from my window, splashing and yelling.

Dad told him to stop whining for help, that he had two choices: sink or swim. So he swam to the boardwalk and Dad hauled him out.'

'Goodness!' Hazel covered her mouth, and Regan couldn't decide whether she was concealing a gasp of horror or a smile.

'Serves the young fool right!' pronounced Sir Frank.

'But he could have drowned!' Regan thought she was the only one showing any compassion. 'Particularly in his state.'

'You mean drunk,' said Joshua.

'Why didn't you help him straight away?' Regan chastised, her eyes flashing. 'Instead of standing there taunting him.'

'Because I believe in tough love,' he said laconically. 'He'd got himself into a jam and there was no reason he shouldn't at least *try* to get himself out of it. Besides...I didn't want to risk ruining my clothes,' he drawled with a baiting smile. 'I was wearing some recently acquired items of great sentimental value.'

'It was OK, really—Uncle Chris used to be a champion swimmer at his school,' offered Ryan, torn between his natural loyalty and the delightful novelty of seeing his father being sternly lectured on behaviour by a slip of a woman. 'And Dad did throw him a lifebelt from the dock.'

'How kind of you,' Regan bit out at the mocking face across the table, fuming over the veiled reference to his cufflinks. Whatever sentiments he attached to them, she knew they wouldn't be the tender ones that he was implying!

'I was aiming for his head,' he said succinctly, and suddenly she couldn't help the quiver of a smile escaping her control. She chewed it off her lips, totally bewildered by her reaction. How could he make her feel like laughing when she was so *angry* with him?

'I wonder what's keeping Carolyn? She did know you were coming, didn't she, Joshua?' interrupted Hazel, squinting at the exquisite diamond watch whose face was a trifle too dainty for her aging eyes.

'I don't think I specified an exact time. I know she was planning on going yachting with the Watsons this afternoon, but I'm afraid some work has come up…'

'On a Saturday?'

'Money never sleeps, Hazel,' Sir Frank trotted out. 'Wade can't afford to be out of touch with what the market's doing. You can use the library again if you need it, Joshua.'

'Thanks, but I have everything back on-line at the condo again—thanks to Ryan's genius for electronics. If I get time I might even call in and see how things are going in the sales office.'

Hazel was looking unimpressed. 'Oh, dear, Carolyn will be disappointed.'

'Maybe she'll change her mind about going sailing once she sees how windy it is,' said Regan. She would have thought that the last thing anyone suffering from the nausea of early pregnancy would enjoy would be a ride on a rocking boat. How far along was she? Three months? Four? Obviously not long enough for her body to have stabilised to the added flow of hormones raging through her increased volume of blood.

'No, she won't—the girl loves a good blow! Got a great pair of sea legs,' beamed Sir Frank.

'I wonder if I ought to go and wake her?' Hazel was pondering dubiously. She had quietly divulged to Regan over last evening's sherry that Carolyn had been unpredictable in her moods of late, and extremely touchy about her privacy. From which Regan had deduced that she was disappointed that her daughter's daughter, whom she had brought up from babyhood after her parents were killed in a plane crash, was not co-operating wholeheartedly on the home front.

'I suppose it's all part of her growing up and preparing to move out into her own separate life, but it makes it a bit difficult when I'm trying to work out what she wants for the wedding,' she had admitted. 'She's so inconsistent—one minute she's madly enthusiastic; the next minute she's yawning with boredom. One day she seems happy; the next everything's a tragedy. Perhaps it'll be good for her to have another young woman in the house who can relate to something of what she's going through...'

'Would you like me to nip up and see if she's up and about—and let her know that Joshua's here?' asked Regan now.

'Not if you haven't finished your own breakfast, dear,' demurred Hazel.

'But I have.' She smiled, pushing back from the table and trying not to look too eager to escape. 'I don't usually have a great appetite in the mornings—'

'You save it all up for the evenings?' murmured Joshua, rising to his feet in unison with his son as she stood up. Whatever else kind of father he was, he had made the effort to teach his offspring old-fashioned manners. The top of Ryan's dirty-blond head only reached Joshua's eyes, but he was obviously still growing, and Regan guessed that one day he would be even taller than his father. There also seemed to be a mutual respect and easy affection between them that spoke volumes about their relationship.

'Well, it was nice meeting you again, Ryan,' she said, concentrating on the safer of the two. 'Good luck with your exams.'

'Luck should have nothing to do with it,' his father answered for him. 'But don't make it sound as if you're saying goodbye, Regan. Didn't anyone tell you that the condominium I'm living in at Palm Court is the one I bought as my personal investment in the project?' He paused a moment to let her sense the axe that was hovering over her head. 'And my visit here is proving so...fruitful and enlightening...that I've decided to stay on at the condo while Frank and I sort out the fine print on our deal. I can commute down to Auckland whenever I need to touch personal base with my staff, and Ryan's school holidays start in another week, so he only has to commute daily until his exams are over, then he has two weeks of freedom.'

Weeks! Regan's face paled slightly above the cherry-red dress as fresh panic fluttered in her chest. She had thought that it was only the weekend she would have to endure. Joshua lurking around for two *days* taunting her with his veiled threats and stalking suspicions was bad enough, but now he was talking about *weeks* of having to cope with him breathing down her neck, monitoring her behaviour and possibly thwarting her attempts to put her plan into action. Not to mention arousing forbidden desires!

'Dad says I can fly down and back in the company helicopter every day,' Ryan informed her.

'Won't that be rather expensive?' she said faintly.

'Perhaps, but I can afford it,' said Joshua. 'I look after my own, and I don't consider it extravagant when you consider what I'm getting in return.'

'And what would that be?' she braved.

'Peace of mind.'

'And of course you'll be able to spend much more time with Carolyn,' chirped Hazel.

'There is that,' Joshua replied gravely.

'I'll just go and see what's keeping her,' said Regan, and fled.

I look after my own.

Regan wasn't one of his own. She was an outsider, a threat to his established order, and it seemed he was prepared to go to any lengths to neutralise her as a possible source of trouble.

There was no answer to her brisk tap on the door, but when she tentatively poked her head into the bedroom she found Carolyn lying on her back in bed, wide awake. She had propped herself up on her elbows as the door opened.

'Oh, it's you,' she said, letting herself collapse back against the heap of pillows.

'Your grandmother just wondered if you were coming down to breakfast,' said Regan, taking that as an invitation to enter. The bedroom was twice as big as her own, with a prime view over the lake from the bed itself, and furnished in feminine but unfussy style in eggshell-blue and white.

'I'm not hungry,' said Carolyn listlessly. In her white batiste nightdress with her hair in a single plait she looked girlishly young, emphasising a natural beauty that didn't depend on cosmetics. She probably never woke with sleep-creases on her face or an embarrassing crust in the corners of her eyes, thought Regan enviously.

'You should eat something. Perhaps it might make you feel better...'

'*Nothing* can make me feel better!' was the vehement declaration.

'Maybe I could slip down to the kitchen and bring you up a piece of toast, and perhaps a cup of tea—'

Carolyn looked at her suspiciously. 'Why should you?'

Regan offered her a friendly smile. 'Well, if you're feeling nauseous, it might help to settle your stomach...'

Carolyn's lightly tanned face had gone from pale and wan to glowing pink in the space of a few seconds. 'What makes you think I'm feeling sick?'

'Uh...last night—you said you might be.'

Carolyn swore: a very unattractive, unladylike phrase. 'He told you, didn't he?' She thumped an angry fist against the bedclothes. 'It was supposed to be a secret and he told *you*!'

'No—'

'Oh, don't bother to lie!' she cried shrilly. 'I saw you two huddling together. He told you! And he has the nerve to call *me* immature and vindictive! He gave away an intimate detail of my life to someone he doesn't know from *Adam*!'

Her emphasis gave Regan a nasty jolt. 'Honestly, Carolyn, he didn't give away anything—I guessed. In the circumstances…and after the way you were talking about feeling sick for half the day… I just jumped to the obvious conclusion. Joshua didn't tell me anything I hadn't already guessed.'

'Joshua?' Carolyn looked disconcerted, the flags of temper in her cheeks fading.

'Yes, who did you think I meant? I didn't think anyone else knew…'

Carolyn smoothed her manicured nails over her rumpled covers. 'No one does…that is, only Chris—'

'Oh, is he your doctor?'

'No, of course not!' Carolyn looked horrified at the idea. 'He's still doing his residency. He wants to be a cardiac surgeon.'

'Nothing as lowly as wanting to specialise in caring for the mothers of our species, huh?' joked Regan.

Carolyn's reluctant laugh was tinged with bitterness. 'You're not kidding!'

'So, is your own doctor up here or in Auckland?'

Carolyn picked at the batiste ruffle on the scooped neck of her nightgown. 'I'm not sure yet who I want to use…'

Regan was shocked. She sat down on the side of the bed. 'You mean you haven't been seeing a doctor?'

Carolyn's eyes flashed. 'There's no need to yet. I know I can't be more than three months along—'

'But you must have had a pregnancy test?'

Her lips tightened. 'The test was positive; I'm going to have a baby. There's nothing any doctor can do about *that*!'

They both knew that there was. 'So you—you never contemplated not going ahead with the baby…?'

'Of course not!' said Carolyn fiercely, her hand going to her stomach. 'Why do you think I'm in this mess? If I'd gone quietly along and got rid of it I suppose everyone would have been much happier…'

By 'everyone' Regan assumed that she meant Joshua, and by 'mess' she meant her precipitous marriage.

'I don't believe that, and I'm sure neither do you,' she said firmly. 'You only have to look at Joshua with his son to know that he doesn't think of fatherhood as a chore. He strikes me as a man who deeply values his family. How do you get on with Ryan?'

'He's OK.' Carolyn's shrug was as off-hand as her tone. 'A bit of a know-it-all sometimes, but most of the time he's pretty mature for his age. He has a genius IQ, you know— three years ahead of himself at his school, and Jay says he'll probably be going to university next year…'

'It sounds as if he'd make a pretty good big brother.'

'I guess.' Carolyn didn't sound very enthusiastic.

Regan took a deep breath. 'As long as you and Joshua love each other,' she said steadily, 'surely that's all that *really* matters…?'

Her little fishing expedition failed. Carolyn looked broodingly out of the window. 'Jay has been great,' she sighed. Her lips compressed. 'Do you know that he married his first wife because she was pregnant?'

Regan's hands clenched in the folds of her red skirt. 'No, I didn't know.'

'She did it deliberately. Chris was only ten and the twins were eleven, and she knew that Jay didn't want to get involved in any heavy relationships until they were older, so she got pregnant, knowing that his over-developed sense of responsibility wouldn't allow his baby to be born illegitimately. According to Chris she was a stupid bitch who began pushing for the kids to be sent to boarding school as soon as she got the wedding ring on her finger, and when Jay argued with her about all the money she was spending she let it slip that if he hadn't been rich she wouldn't have wanted his brat. Jay didn't say anything, but the day after Ryan was born he had Clare served with divorce papers right there in the hospital.'

'My God!' For sheer ruthlessness that took some beating. 'She must have been shattered.'

'I don't think so. Chris says she split for the States a few weeks later and never raised a squawk about custody, so I guess Jay must have bought himself out of a fight.'

It was precisely what he *had* done, on his own admission, but Regan wondered if there had not also been an element of threat involved. Even at twenty Joshua Wade would have been a formidable force, with the tragedy and hardship that had shaped and toughened his character already behind him.

'But that's nothing like your situation, is it?' she said delicately. 'I mean, it's not as if you deliberately fell pregnant…'

'No, it's not!' Carolyn looked fierce. 'It's not my fault, and I don't see why I should be expected to act as if it is!'

Regan frowned. 'You're not being coerced into anything, are you? Joshua might have had strong views on illegitimacy back when Ryan was born, but social attitudes have changed quite a bit since then. You don't *have* to get married if you don't want to. I'm sure your grandmother would understand—'

Carolyn's golden eyes flared with alarm. 'You're not going to tell her!'

'No, of course not. But I think *you* should…before the wedding.'

'I was just hoping things might all sort themselves out,' Carolyn said moodily. 'She'll be hurt when she finds out what I've done—that I might besmirch the Harriman name…'

'Rubbish!' said Regan, who already knew that Hazel wasn't a snob. 'I think in the long run she's more likely to be hurt if she thinks that you were afraid to tell her the truth. It's not your marriage, it's *your* happiness that's important to her…'

Carolyn heaved another great sigh. 'I thought you were here to help with the wedding, not to try and sabotage it!' she joked morosely.

Regan recoiled. 'I would never do that!' But she uneasily acknowledged that she wasn't exactly an objective bystander.

'No—I suppose you'd have no reason to, would you?' said Carolyn, in all innocence.

God, what if she casually mentioned this little discussion to Joshua? He was sure to believe the worst!

'I'm just pointing out that you do have options,' she said hastily, getting up from the bed. 'Whatever you decide, you're the one who has to live with the consequences, so make sure you know exactly what they are and what it is you really want.'

A surprisingly militant expression crossed Carolyn's face, replacing the wistful indecision. 'Oh, I know exactly what I want.' She sat up. 'You know, I think I feel a bit better.'

'Then maybe you'd like to come downstairs. Joshua's here with Ryan—that's why Hazel sent me to see if you were awake.'

Carolyn threw the bedclothes down the bed and got up,

stretching lethargically. 'I suppose I could. Did Chris come with them?'

Regan told her about the canal and she laughed maliciously and seemed to perk up, throwing open her huge double closet to view the crowded contents.

'Serve him right!' she said, unconsciously echoing her great-uncle's sentiments.

She hummed as she selected white cotton shorts and a loose, flowing candy-striped cotton top and threw them onto the bed.

'I'll just have a quick shower—tell Jay I'll be down in about thirty minutes.'

Regan wondered how Joshua would feel about kicking his heels for that long. Perhaps he was used to her blowing hot and cold.

'I think he said something about having to do some work today,' she felt obliged to warn her. 'I don't think he's going to be able to go sailing...'

'Oh, well, I'll just have to find something else to do to amuse myself, won't I?' Carolyn showed no sign of the predicted disappointment. 'Maybe you could come over to the marina with me later, and we could stroll around the shops and look at the boats, maybe have a cappuccino at one of the cafés. Joshua's got his corporate launch moored down there, ready to take clients on junkets to next week's regatta out in the gulf, so maybe we could stop by for a drink on the deck...'

'Maybe...' said Regan, suddenly foreseeing the pitfalls that could result from becoming too friendly with Carolyn.

Joshua was on his cellphone when she went back down, and Regan was able to avoid any further barbed encounters by allowing Hazel to bear her off to 'what I call my GHQ' to show her the volume of work that awaited her on Monday— 'Because you've worked hard all week and we can't expect you to labour on weekends as well'.

'GHQ' turned out to be a large sewing room on the sunny side of the house, containing an impressive array of electronic machinery on a sewing table that Hazel sheepishly admitted she hardly ever used, a large overstuffed floral sofa and comfy chair and a vast roll-topped desk, its numerous cubbyholes crammed higgledy-piggledy with piles of letters, bills, papers, jotted lists, magazine cuttings and cards.

'It looks a lot worse than it actually is,' said Hazel, sitting down gratefully in the padded swivel chair that Regan hurriedly trundled forward and pointing to a second chair with her crutch. Regan obediently sat down and dubiously eyed what she thought looked like a bomb site as Hazel went on, 'Frank laughs at me, but I do have a system and it works very well when I have two hands to do my filing.'

She proceeded to prove it as she showed Regan how each cubbyhole pertained to one aspect of the wedding—the invitations, the gift list, the marriage celebrant and order of service, the marquee hire and catering, the wedding and bridesmaids' dresses, the flowers, the wine and the musicians, the photographer and accommodation for out-of-town guests.

Since the mid-afternoon wedding ceremony and evening reception were being held on the grounds there would be a lot of hustle and bustle around the house on the days leading up to the wedding.

Hazel showed Regan a sketch which positioned an enormous marquee by the lake. The aisle the bride would walk down was the narrow path of crushed shells leading down to the dock, flanked by hundreds of pots of standard roses, with rows of seating for the guests extending on either side. Should the May weather prove inclement, the whole area could be covered by another huge, open-sided marquee. Hazel explained that a string quartet would play the wed-

ding music from a covered barge moored a few metres out
on the lake, followed later by a disco.

'We're only inviting a couple of hundred because
Carolyn wants to keep it small and reasonably intimate and
informal. We did think of having the actual ceremony in
the gazebo itself, but we decided that would be too much
of a hassle, having to ferry so many people back and forth,
especially if it rains. Whereas like this, if the weather fore-
cast isn't good, we can make other arrangements.'

'It sounds marvellous. Especially since you've done it all
in only a couple of months.' Regan picked up a piece of
green parchment. 'This is your invitation list? Have you
got a folder of the acceptances?'

A tiny twitch crimped Hazel's small mouth. 'Well…we
haven't actually received any yet—formal ones, that is.
There was a horrendous problem at the printers where we
had the invitations done, I'm afraid.'

'They were late going out?'

'Actually, we haven't sent them yet,' said Hazel weakly.
'Joshua has taken the whole wretched mess in hand and we
hope to have them next week.'

Regan's eyes rounded. That was a huge clunker! 'I
thought invitations had to go out a couple of months before
the wedding to give everyone time to reply?'

'Yes, but it can't be helped, and since the guest list is
limited to mostly family and very close friends I've been
able to warn most of the people we're inviting, particularly
those from overseas—Chris's sisters are coming out from
England with their husbands and families, you know…'

'*Chris's* sisters?'

'Did I say Chris?' Hazel patted her ash-blonde hair, looking discomfited. 'I meant to say Joshua's…although they
are Chris's too, of course, all of them being from the same
family. Did I mention that Ryan is going to be best man?'

'No, you didn't. I would have thought Joshua might have

asked his brother to stand up with him,' Regan couldn't resist murmuring and she watched Hazel's smooth, barely lined cheeks flush a betraying pink. 'I take it he has got *some* kind of official duty—as an usher, perhaps?' she prodded.

'I'm not sure…the groom handles all that side of things.' Hazel waved a vague hand, her eyes brightening with relief as her granddaughter flitted across the doorway and enquired if Regan was interested in going shopping now, because Joshua was offering them a lift, and to buy them lunch later in the afternoon.

'Of course she is! Off you go, Regan, now, and enjoy yourself.' Hazel's enthusiasm made it little short of an order.

'I don't like to intrude,' said Regan, frantically trying to think of a polite excuse. 'Perhaps I could just look around the shops and walk back while you go on to lunch with Joshua—'

'We wouldn't dream of abandoning you to your own devices,' purred Joshua, appearing like a dark shadow behind his golden fiancée. 'If you're going to be as intimately involved in our affairs as you obviously plan to be, the least we can do is to ensure you're kept well entertained while you're here.'

For 'well entertained' Regan mentally substituted 'well under surveillance'. Joshua Wade was letting it be known that he had no intention of letting her enjoy the freedom of Palm Cove.

From now on she would have to step extremely carefully if she wanted to escape with her honour intact!

CHAPTER EIGHT

'WHAT are you doing?'

Regan jumped, her sweaty fingers skittering over the computer keyboard.

'God, Ryan, you shouldn't sneak up on me like that. You nearly gave me a heart attack,' she said as he rolled up beside her in one of the secretarial chairs. She quickly closed the file she was working on and opened another.

Ryan raked his long hair out of his eyes. 'Sorry, did you think I was Dad?'

'Why should I?' But Regan couldn't help a quick glance around the plush, open-plan office, decorated with photographs, sketches and models of the Palm Cove development.

The sales team operated out of the ground floor of the main condominium block, and with the influx of ocean-going yachts and tourists at the marina from the previous weekend's regatta, and the continuing sweltering weather, they were working at full stretch showing potential buyers and interested parties around the development. So much so they had welcomed an extra pair of hands to help with the filing and paperwork in the afternoons.

'Because whenever you turn up here, so does he,' said Ryan. As soon as he had finished his exams, he had wasted no time inventing a job for himself—creating a Palm Cove Internet website, spending hours at the office hunched over a spare terminal, becoming something of a mascot to staff eager to curry favour with the new boss. For Regan that had meant *two* Wades she had to try to avoid, for Ryan's insatiable curiosity posed as much of a threat as that of his father.

The first week of her stay had been every bit as bad as she'd feared, with Joshua so attentive to his fiancée and her family that Carolyn had begun to look more highly-strung than ever. Even Hazel had got a little exasperated when he'd chosen to invade her precious GHQ. While she had welcomed his problem-solving acumen, and the news that he would arrange for the belated invitations to be urgently hand-delivered, Hazel had protested that he was showing more interest than the bride and eventually succeeded in shooing him away.

But to Regan's horror she *had* taken him up on his offer to chauffeur the women around to check the progress of the various local craftspeople who were providing the hand-made decorations for marquee and house. Carolyn's febrile restlessness meant that she had little patience with such petty errands, and usually found something more pressing to attend to in her social calendar, and Regan found that Hazel—insulated by her delight in the million and one details that divided her attention—was little protection against Joshua's overwhelming presence. Regan had to fight not only a war of words, but also against the insidious attraction that seemed to thrive and grow at every meeting, in spite of their mutual distrust.

'In fact, he seems to know where you are even when nobody else does. Freaky, huh? It's almost like he has you bugged.' Ryan jolted her out of her fretting with a grin that reminded her of the way they had first met. 'Maybe you should check out that watch he gave you.'

Regan flushed. She had been mortified at dinner the second night, when Joshua had casually produced a beautiful platinum man's Swiss watch and fastened it on her wrist over her strenuous protests.

'Don't make such a fuss—it's not as if I'm trying to seduce you with jewellery,' he had said, amusing everyone but Regan with his apparent joke. 'This is a loan, not a gift. It's an old one of mine—I just had the jeweller at Palm

Cove whip out a few links so that the band would fit a smaller wrist. Hazel is a stickler for being on time for appointments, and you won't come up to scratch if you don't carry a reliable timepiece.'

Regan had been forced to act pleased and thank him nicely.

'It's fully waterproof and shockproof, so you can safely forget you've got it on,' he'd told her. 'You can even wear it washing your hair in the shower, if you like, though perhaps you're the kind of woman who prefers to do it in the bath.'

He had stood smiling at her blandly while Regan's eyes had spat violet fire, her composure almost destroyed by the vivid mental video of Joshua as he had been *That Night*, his tapered torso slick with soapy water as he'd braced his shoulders against the curving back of the marble bath and lifted her astride him with dripping arms, bringing her hard down on his up-thrust hips, churning up the waves until a tsunami of sensation had almost drowned them both!

His eyes had flickered to the band on her wrist and she'd felt it like a mark of his possession as he goaded softly, 'How fortunate that you don't appear to be as allergic to platinum as you are to gold...'

'You've left footprints all over the place, you know.'

'What?' Regan wrenched herself from her memories to find Ryan edging closer to her terminal. 'Where?' She automatically looked down at the carpet.

'On those files you've just been altering...you're leaving a trail that any competent hacker could follow.'

'What on earth are you talking about?' she said hollowly.

'It's just a clumsy way of doing it, that's all. I mean, I think the actual *idea* is clever,' Ryan said kindly. 'You have a printing company that in the process of long, legal winding-up has discovered a breach of its former contract with Palm Cove Developments that invokes a lump-sum penalty repayment clause. It's just that if the data and dates don't match up in all those files by the time the bank cheque arrives, your tampering is going to look pretty obvious to an expert...'

Regan was speechless.

'I could do it, you know!' Ryan's eyes shone with enthusiasm. 'I could hack in and manipulate the software to completely obliterate any sign you'd been in there. Or, I could use a very specific virus that would corrupt the data if anyone tried to call up the original file on that contract—'

'*No!* Ryan—you don't know what you're *saying*!'

'Yes, I do. I've been hacking around in the system and tracking what everyone's doing for days,' he confided. 'The security here really sucks and the passwords are a joke.' He grinned at her. 'You're trying to put money back into the system, aren't you? Sort of like Robin Hood in reverse—'

'*Nothing* like Robin Hood!' Regan was horrified by his admiration. 'For goodness' sake, Ryan, what I'm doing is *dishonest*!' She bit her lip; she hadn't meant to admit anything.

'Yeah, but for a good cause—you didn't steal it, right?' he stated, with an absolute confidence that she found unbearably touching. 'You're obviously just covering for someone else. Those files you were extracting were originally created with a password held by Michael Frances—I checked. Hey, I hope you haven't forgotten there'll be back-up files somewhere, too...'

Regan propped her head on her hand and closed her eyes, appalled that her sins had found her out before she had barely even begun. 'No, I haven't forgotten—that was the first thing I did, because the back-ups are kept at the legal office, where I work. Michael was my husband,' she sighed. 'Before he died he skimmed off the money by awarding contracts for printing posters and sales brochures to a fictitious firm, while he actually had the job done at a cheaper price.'

'Cool!'

Her head jerked up. 'No, it is not cool, Ryan!' she hissed furiously, surreptitiously checking that there was no one else in the vicinity. 'It's outright theft. It's totally immoral and wrong. And what I'm doing is wrong, too. It's nothing to be proud of!'

'So why're you doing it?'

She shook her head helplessly. How could she explain the reckless anger that had driven her to act so out of character?

His bony, tanned hand slid over the top of her twisting fingers. 'Hey, look it's OK. I'm not going to squeal. I know if I help you we can make this work, with a few modifications—'

She wouldn't let herself even contemplate it. Help him cheat and lie and deceive the one he loved? The way that Michael had?

'No—I don't want you involved in any way.'

'But I already *am* involved!'

That was undeniable. Shared knowledge made them co-conspirators. 'The correct thing for you to do would be to go straight to someone of authority in the company and tell them what I've done,' she forced herself to say. 'Or at least tell your father,' she said, flinging herself on her sword.

'Tell Dad? Are you crazy! Why would I want to tell him anything? Let Dad find his own fun!'

Fun? Regan looked at him as though he was an alien being. It must be the generation gap, she thought. He might be an intellectual genius, but physically and emotionally he was still a teenager, super-charged on his surging hormones. In contrast she felt as jaded as an old hag.

'I'm glad you feel that way, Ryan, because that's exactly what I intend doing.'

Regan's jaded feeling vanished in the instant it took for the deep voice to reach down inside her chest and caress her heart into violent action. Her swivel chair was spun on its pedestal and braked to a stop with one immaculate, custom-made Italian leather shoe.

Joshua crooked his finger at her. 'Come on. It's quitting time, and you and I are going for a little ride.'

It sounded like something a Mafia Don would say to a double-crossing Capo. Just how much had he overheard?

'I— I've never had anything to do with horses,' she said, feebly resisting the inevitable. 'I wouldn't know how to ride.'

His eyelids drooped. 'Oh, I wouldn't say that. Riding a horse is just like staying on top of any other form of mount—you grip with your thighs and allow your body to follow through with the motion of your hips. I'm sure you'd be a natural...' As she crimsoned he continued smoothly, 'But actually I was talking about a boat ride.' He turned to his son. 'We're going on a short cruise out into the gulf, and, since Carolyn has frequently reminded me that Regan hasn't yet had a sail, I'm taking her with us. I presume you can amuse yourself here for another hour or so, since there seem to be a few others working late—otherwise you can use your key to the condo...'

Ryan couldn't help his eyes darting triumphantly to Regan. 'Sure!' he said, bounding to his feet.

'I'll just have a word with the office manager before we go. WadeCo has someone coming in to look at the books next week as part of the discovery process, and I just want to make sure that he's happy with the arrangements...'

As soon as Joshua was out of earshot Regan stumbled out of her chair and grabbed Ryan by the sleeve of his T-shirt. 'Promise you won't do anything stupid about my—' she dropped her voice even lower '—my *problem* while I'm gone!'

He squinted down at her anxious face, thoughtfully chewing his lip.

'I mean it, Ryan.' She made her voice as stern as possible, considering that she had nothing with which to back up her threat. 'No dumb and misguided attempts at chivalry. Promise?'

He nodded slowly, something like relief shimmering behind the glasses. 'OK, I can certainly promise that.'

She released him and smoothed his wrinkled T-shirt back into place. 'Sorry, but I don't want you getting in trouble on my account. This isn't a game, understand?'

'Sure.' He pushed his glasses up his nose. 'I understand.'

She was too busy worrying about Joshua's motives to hear the lilt of resolution in the breaking voice. 'You notice he didn't *ask* me if I wanted to go on a cruise. I wonder who else is going to be on board?' she wondered nervously. So far she had managed to keep away from the twenty-five-metre luxury motor vessel. On board, she felt Joshua would have a home territory advantage.

'Well, there'll be the crew for a start—that's at least five. It's really cool, Regan, and has a spa pool and sauna. Uncle Chris and Carolyn used to say it was better than a posh hotel and they were going to use it for their honeymoon cruise!'

Regan frowned at him. 'You mean *your father* and Carolyn—'

'No, I mean when Uncle Chris and Carolyn were like…you know—together…'

'When they were *what*?'

He blinked at her vehemence. 'Uh—didn't you know?' he said, speculation rife in his face. 'Carolyn was Uncle Chris's girlfriend for ages. They even got engaged, but a couple of months ago there was this big blow-up between them and then suddenly it was *Dad* she was marrying…'

The tense atmosphere between the brothers, Carolyn's attitude and the Harrimans' odd manner whenever Chris was mentioned—all were suddenly explained…

Regan emerged from the coolness of the office into the dazzle of the hot, late-afternoon sun in a zombie-like mental fog. She trotted alongside Joshua's tall, striding figure as they crossed the cobbled paving, weaving around the clover-leaf arrangement of shops and cafés on the graduated series of curving terraces which descended to the edge of the circular head of the canal. Most of the bars and cafés had outdoor tables, shaded by umbrellas, and were doing a good business from the tanned boaties and residents and sunburned tourists who were starting to wind down, or up, from their day's activities.

Joshua led Regan along the wide wooden boardwalk past the first few berths to where the *Sara Wade* lay snoozing at her moorings. She was sleek and white, her streamlined cabins rising two storeys above the main deck, the roof bristling with antennae and electronic gadgetry.

'Sara was my stepmother's name,' explained Joshua, as he motioned her ahead of him up the short gangplank. He had slipped off his jacket and pocketed his yellow knitted silk tie as they walked, opening his collar and rolling up the sleeves of his white linen shirt to look the epitome of laid-back style.

'What about your real mother?' murmured Regan, still grappling with the impact of Ryan's words.

'She died when I was two—of breast cancer. I don't remember much about her. Dad married Sara when I was five. Careful.'

Regan had tripped on a wooden slat on the gangplank. 'I don't think I'm dressed for boating,' she said, looking down at her high-heeled sandals. The trim, lightweight tailored navy suit she was wearing was also more suited to an office than a quarter-deck. Regan hoped she wouldn't feel out of place amongst a crowd of people in smart-but-casual nautical gear.

'You can slip into something more comfortable on board.' She slanted him a suspicious look over her shoulder and he chuckled. 'We have lots of non-skid boat shoes on board in most sizes. There's sure to be a pair to fit you.'

His manner seemed so relaxed and unthreatening now that they were on board that Regan felt even more disorientated. Where was the implacable sense of urgency that she had sensed when he had swooped down on her at the office?

A fit, grey-headed, middle-aged man dressed in white shorts and short-sleeved shirt stood stiffly at the top of the gangplank, a white yachting cap tucked under his arm.

'Welcome aboard, sir—ma'am.'

'It's all right, Grey, she's a friend, not a client—we don't have to make an impression,' said Joshua drily.

The man's shoulders relaxed and he grinned, his teeth white in his weather-beaten face as he replaced his black-brimmed cap. 'What a shame. I've been practising my snappy salute.'

'This is Regan. I believe she gets seasick in small boats,' Joshua supplied wickedly.

'Then you won't have a problem with *Sara Wade*,' Grey told her kindly. 'She's as solid as a rock.'

'Don't rocks usually sink?' said Regan.

'Not a rock with this much horsepower,' he smiled. 'This baby could raise the *Titanic*.'

'Don't get him started,' said Joshua. 'It really *is* his baby. Grey has captained her since she was commissioned. You can cast off whenever you like, Grey—we'll be down on the aft deck, but I might bring Regan up later to show her the view from the bridge.'

'Aye, aye, sir.' This time Grey did salute, a careless, irreverent flick of his brim which made Regan smile.

'Let's go the long way round, so you can see where everything is,' said Joshua, opening the door to the main cabin and discarding his jacket and tie on the nearest chair.

The polished mahogany walls, maple floors and plush white and gold furnishings of the huge lounge were sumptuous, and the dining table in the next room looked as if it would easily seat twenty under the glittering modern chandelier. The U-shaped galley further forward was bigger and better equipped than some restaurant kitchens Regan had seen. Down a companionway there were four large double cabins with *en suite* bathrooms, the main bathroom and a sauna. Distracted by the confusion in her mind and the proximity of her guide, Regan was nonetheless stunned by the opulence of the gold-plated fixtures and fittings and co-ordinated furniture and fabrics.

Beneath their feet was an almost imperceptible vibration as a powerful engine purred into life, and when she murmured something about conspicuous consumption Joshua said, 'We bought it from an American billionaire who fell on hard times. We use it mainly for corporate entertaining, here and overseas—for events like the America's Cup—or charter it to visiting business-people who don't like to stay in hotels.'

Following him back up the companionway, Regan guessed that the weekly charter fees would cost more than the average New Zealander earned in a year!

While they'd been below the boat had left the slips, and as they stepped onto the aft deck Regan could see the marina terraces recede behind a forest of masts as they cruised around the first curve in the broad canal. But it was what she *didn't* see that concerned her. 'Where are the others?'

'Others?' Joshua leaned sideways on the brass rail, plucking a pair of sunglasses from the breast pocket of his shirt and sliding them on his face.

'You said, ''*We're* going on a short cruise—'''

'And so we are. Grey has had some minor adjustments done on the satellite navigation system and he just wanted to give her a brief shake-down run—'

'But you mentioned Carolyn, and I assumed...' She trailed off at his sardonic smile. He hitched up the knee of his black trousers and rested his foot on the lower rail.

'I've told you about the danger of making assumptions where I'm concerned.'

'You deliberately led me to think that you were taking a bunch of people out,' she accused huskily.

He turned aside the challenge with a lazy smile. 'You seem to be rather stressed-out lately. I thought you might appreciate the chance to get away from all the cares of the world for an hour or two.'

Since he was a major source of her stress, that seemed unlikely. 'What if I want to go back?'

'We can't ever turn back the clock…so forward seems the only logical place for us to go.' He shifted his stance, casually crossing his long legs at the ankle as he rested his elbow on the rail. 'What were you and my son talking so earnestly about when I found you?'

She stiffened. She couldn't see his eyes, but the stillness of his face suggested a penetrating watchfulness. She moved up to press her stomach against the rail, using the excuse of leaning over to study the boats they were passing to show him a delicate, unrevealing profile.

Now was her chance to do the honourable thing. To forestall any future trouble for Ryan with a full and frank confession. She would have to trust to Joshua's strong sense of justice, and the compassion she now knew he possessed, and hope that he would appreciate the honesty of her intentions…

'He has a crush on you, you know.'

Her head whipped around, as he had known it would, the glossy hair flaring out from her skull in a blue-black spray.

'Ryan? Don't be ridiculous!' spilled out of her lips.

'The more attention you pay him, the more likely he is to presume that you mean something by it,' he told her.

She lifted her chin. 'I do: it means I like him.'

'In spite of him being *my* son?' he guessed, putting a finger on her dilemma.

'He's a very nice boy,' she sniffed.

'He wouldn't thank you for calling him a boy. He's a young man, filled with a young man's passions...'

And foolish ideals.

Regan bit her lip and he turned to join her at the rail, his shoulder brushing against her navy sleeve as he bent to lean on both elbows, looking down into their lightly churning wake. 'Ryan loves complexity and finds any sort of mystery irresistible. You can't blame him for being intrigued, you're probably the most complex woman he's ever encountered. Add big violet eyes and a sleek little body to the equation and you have a perfect recipe for infatuation. He may think his intellect will protect him from emotional harm, but he doesn't realise that some emotions are not always answerable to reason...'

That was cutting too close to the bone. She looked at his bowed head, noting the way the breeze ruffled his hair, and the silky black growth on his muscled forearm. 'I really think you're overreacting—I'm just a novelty—'

'He watches you when he thinks you aren't looking...'

She tore her yearning gaze away from his averted head. 'So? You have no idea what's going on inside his brain.'

'I know how males think. And I know Ryan better than most men know their sons.'

'I just don't think he thinks about me that way,' she said feebly. 'You make it sound as if I'm some kind of *femme fatale*...'

He straightened up, removing his sunglasses, and she immediately wished he would put them back on. His eyes made her stomach lurch. Then she realised there was a physical reason for her reaction; they were moving out of the mouth of the canal into the light chop of the channel which extended from a half-melon of sandy beach—dotted with family groups taking advantage of the school holidays—to the open gulf.

'And you make it sound as if you don't believe you're

innately attractive to men. That unless you set out to entice a man he'll simply ignore your femininity. Why, I wonder?'

Regan's fingers automatically moved to twist her absent wedding ring. 'I'm not here for psychoanalysis,' she rasped.

'You sound a little dry,' he said gently. 'Would you like something to lubricate your throat while we argue the point?' He signalled to someone out of Regan's sight-line, and she completely lost her train of thought when she saw who it was bringing forward the silver tray.

'Champagne cocktail or tropical crush, Mam'selle Eve?'

She blushed furiously at the sight of his ugly face, pruned into a wrinkled smile. 'Hello, Pierre,' she said faintly, grabbing the nearest drink without caring what it contained.

'Actually, her name is Regan,' Joshua told his man, accepting a stemmed glass of straw-coloured liquid containing a hulled strawberry. 'She prefers to reserve Evangeline for those occasions when she's incognito.'

Regan jerked around to remonstrate, and fruit juice spilled out of her glass down the lapel of her jacket.

'Ah, *Mam'selle*, let me sponge that out for you before it stains.' The glass was taken out of her hand and her jacket removed and borne away into the air-conditioned depths of the vessel before she could do much more than stutter a protest.

'I think you might be safer with the champagne,' said Joshua, handing her one of the tall cocktails, his eyes flicking over the white singlet top she had worn under her navy suit.

'How did you find out my middle name?' she demanded.

Joshua toasted her with his glass. 'I asked around.'

She knew what that meant for a man of his wealth and power.

'You mean you had me investigated,' she snapped.

'Do you blame me?'

No, that was the problem. It was what she would have done were their circumstances reversed.

'I hope you got your money's worth,' she gritted.

The prow of the boat eased higher in the water as a low grumble signalled a surge of power from the throttle, and as Regan listed on the wooden decking in a belated attempt to find her sea legs Joshua reached out to steady her, his fingers firm on her waist. The breeze became a tugging wind as the vessel cut through the water with smoothly accelerating speed and the airstream flowed around the sleekly aerodynamic body to flute invisibly above the turbulent wake.

'Not yet.' His steadying hand dropped away. 'I'm only getting my reports in dribs and drabs. And it's mostly raw facts, not feelings. Care to fill in the blanks?'

He waited, and when she said nothing he continued with surgical precision.

'With such a fanatically religious mother and a passive alcoholic as a father you were bound to grow up sexually repressed and hungry for praise and affection—you must have been a sitting duck for a manipulative, smooth-talking bastard like Frances. He found out about your connection with Sir Frank and deliberately set out to recreate himself in the image of your ideal husband. But he never intended to be faithful to the image, did he?'

Regan sucked in a sharp breath. Laid out in his stark words the truth seemed even more ugly. 'You have no right—'

'I've been there myself,' he said quietly. 'I know how it feels to realise that your loyalty has been secured by a lie. You blame yourself for not seeing it from the beginning.'

'I don't want to talk about him.'

'Fine. Then let's talk about us.'

She set her untasted drink sharply down on the glass table which held the silver drinks tray. 'There is no *us*!'

He set his glass beside hers and shadowed her back to the rail. 'Tell me, why did you come to the apartment that night?'

'Why don't you ask your informant?' she said bitterly.

'What happened that night was not part of his brief,' he said with dangerous softness. 'But that could change with one phone call…'

She blanched. 'My flatmate's cousin is Cleo—she was the one who was supposed to meet you that night, but she was sick. I took her place, but I didn't tell anyone. No one knew—not even Derek.'

'That explains how, but not *why*,' he said, his eyes narrowed intently on her face. 'It's so out of character with everything else I've found out about you.'

'Maybe I was wild with grief,' she said sardonically.

But he was implacable. 'A kind of grief, perhaps. Was it anything to do with Cindy Carson visiting your flat? You never knew your husband had had a mistress, did you? Not until she confronted you.'

Regan thought that she would have preferred being interrogated about her attempt to fiddle the books to this painful emotional plunder!

'How did you feel when you found out that he had been unfaithful to you for years?' he goaded. 'How did you feel when you discovered that he had chosen to have a child with *her*, rather than you?'

The old, volcanic rage erupted through the thin crust of her self-control. 'How do you *think* I felt?' she burst out.

His eyes flamed with deep satisfaction as he taunted, 'Heartbroken?'

She tossed her head defiantly, the wind whipping the hair around her stinging cheeks. 'No—heart-*whole*! Cured of any lingering doubt that I was a fool for having loved him at all! Sick. Angry. *Furious!*

'You want to know what I was looking for that night I slept with you—I'll tell you: *Revenge!*' She gave a wild, triumphant laugh at his shaken expression. 'I did it purely for revenge, OK? To show Michael that he wasn't going to control me from the grave, to prove that I was as much a sexual being as his flashy mistress. *He* had an affair so *I* went out and had one, too!'

'You slept with me to get revenge on a dead man?'

He sounded incredulous. She hoped that knocked his male ego for a six.

'Not *you*. A *man*. Any man would have done. Being promiscuous means you're not choosy about your sex partners.'

'But you didn't get any man,' he said roughly. 'Lucky for you, you reckless little fool, you got *me*...'

She put her hands on her hips, her torso tilted aggressively forward as she snarled, '*Lucky?* I'd call it ironic that I chose to have my sexual fling with a man who was as dishonourable as my late, unlamented husband!'

The insult visibly struck him to the core. 'What in the hell do you mean by that?' he snarled back, closing the gap between them until the heat generated by their two bodies met and mingled.

She had him on the back foot; now it was her turn to shove, and shove until he tripped over his own lies. 'You seduced your brother's fiancée! Don't bother to deny it. Ryan told me that Carolyn and Chris were an item long before *you* came on the scene.'

He cursed rawly. 'Ryan might be a genius but that doesn't make him infallible.'

'You mean it isn't true? That Carolyn wasn't engaged to Chris when you slept with her and got her pregnant—?'

'Ryan couldn't have told you *that*!' he interrupted savagely.

'No, but it's so obvious when you look at the timing. This wedding should have been Chris and Carolyn's, shouldn't it?' She had noticed that some of the early quotes Hazel had stuffed in her desk dated back further than a couple of months, but had dismissed them as examples of her hopeful anticipation. '*You* must have been the reason they had their row and broke the engagement.'

'Must I? You don't think that, considering what you know of my character, you might have drawn another, less obvious conclusion—one more favourable to my honour?'

She felt the pain of his deep offence like a quiet shudder in her soul. He was truly outraged that she was calling his personal integrity into question. 'What do you mean? What other conclusion is there?'

The muscle flickered in his clenched jaw. 'Nothing. None. It doesn't matter.'

She didn't believe him. It had mattered enough to him to cause his tight-lipped control to falter. And if it mattered to *him*, of *course* it mattered to her, more than anything…

Joshua wasn't like Michael. Michael would never have rushed into a burning building to save other people's lives at a serious risk to his own. Michael had never faced up to his responsibilities—even in death he had evaded making any provision for his son's future. But Joshua behaved honourably even when it was dangerous to do so, even when it was difficult, or interfered with his own pleasures.

As the boat creamed over the glittering open sea, a clear shaft of light seemed to shine down from the blue vault of heaven and illuminate the answer in her heart.

But how to break down that wall of steely self-control and make him admit it?

'So…if you weren't sleeping with Carolyn *before* the big fight, then it must have happened after. After her horrible row with Chris she came running to his big brother for comfort, and instead you took ruthless advantage of her vulnerability—is that the scenario you expect me to believe?'

He picked up his glass again and took a long swallow. 'I don't expect anything of you.'

Now he was lying!

'Is it your baby—or Chris's? Or are the dates that you both slept with her so entwined that neither of you know *which* one of you is the father?'

His head jerked back at her slicing scorn. 'It's a Wade. That's all that's important.'

'And you don't mind marrying your brother's discards?'

He finished the drink, his knuckles white around the glass. 'Leave it, Regan.'

She was beginning to get an even stronger inkling of the way his mind worked. 'What's the matter? Don't you like it when the tables are turned and *I'm* the one asking all the intrusive questions?' she said recklessly. 'Maybe you three had a slightly incestuous *ménage à trois* going...does it turn you on to share a woman in bed with your brother?'

'Be very—very, careful what you say next,' he said thickly. 'In fact, it would be an extremely good idea if you shut up altogether!'

Adrenaline raced through her veins. 'Or what? You'll throw me to the sharks? What price your honour then? Oh, I forgot...you don't *have* any! So maybe Carolyn wasn't a willing party in this fascinating scenario of yours at all. Maybe it wasn't seduction on your part, but *rape*—'

'I've never even *touched* her—!' he roared, and broke off, his eyes blazing with silver wrath.

'But you're going to marry her all the same.' She was breathless in horrified awe. 'You're going to marry a woman you don't love, and who doesn't love you, in order to give your brother's baby the family name, because for some reason he's baulking at marriage and unplanned fatherhood. What you can't force *him* to do you're going to do yourself. My God, that's positively Gothic! Don't you think that's carrying your sense of honour to a ridiculous extreme—?'

She squeaked as she was snatched off her feet, dangling by her upper arms between two iron fists.

'I told you to shut up!'

'But you didn't tell me what would happen if I didn't,' she said breathlessly, pushing her hands against his chest and pointing her sandalled toes in a vain attempt to touch the deck.

He began to slowly lower her towards him, the muscles in his neck and shoulders bulging with the effort. 'It wouldn't have mattered if I had. You *wanted* me to lose control. I would have taken apart a man for saying those things—'

'But I'm a woman.' The smouldering acknowledgement flared in his eyes and her voice went abruptly and embarrassingly husky. 'B-besides, violence never really solves anything—'

'The hell it doesn't,' he growled, and kissed her—a hot, savage clash of mouths that made her go up in flames as he hooked his arm under her knees and swung her up into his arms, carrying her from the bright sunlight through the cool luxury of the lounge and down the narrow companionway into the dim depths of his cabin.

'You said we weren't going to do this,' she gasped, kicking off her shoes as he set her lightly on her feet and peeled his still buttoned shirt over his head.

He cupped her face, and drew her mouth under his.

'God forgive me, I lied...'

CHAPTER NINE

REGAN smoothed her trembling hands over his bare chest, skimming her palms over his rippling shoulders and down across the silky pelt of hair to the ridged muscles of his abdomen, thrilling to her rediscovery of his masculine beauty.

Joshua broke his mouth from hers and threw his head back, closing his eyes as he licensed her hands to rove caressingly against his skin, offering himself up like a sacrificial victim to the spearing pleasure of her touch.

'You remembered how much I liked that...' he groaned as her fingertips slid through the tangle of curls and nudged against the flat discs of his nipples. 'Yes...do that again...' His muscles contracted and his chest rose, pushing against her exploring fingers as she obeyed. He shuddered, his nostrils flaring at the scent of his own arousal. 'God, what you do to me...'

She could see it in the taut planes of his face, hear it in the harsh sound of his indrawn breath and feel it in the electric tension of his body, and it excited her unbearably to know that he was so violently responsive to her touch that even the lightest stroke could make his desire strain savagely on the leash. It had been the same that night in the apartment...his hunger for her so wonderfully intense that she had felt like the most beautiful and alluring woman in the world...the *only* woman who existed for him, the focus of all his dreams and the answer to all his desires.

He opened his eyes and smiled slowly at the sight of her flushed face, parted lips and smugly sensuous eyes.

'Little tyrant, you like having me at your mercy, don't

147

you?' he accused, but his deep tone was one of smoky approval. His hands stroked up her arms and spread around her back, massaging the soft cotton fabric of her top against her slender form. 'You like knowing that you have the power to drive me beyond the bounds of common sense, of decency...'

In a twisted way she did. It satisfied a deep-seated need in her to be the primal source of his actions.

'*I'm* the one who should be begging for mercy,' she said, drawing her nails delicately across his chest. 'I'm the one who was kidnapped by a pirate. Swept off my feet and carried down to the bowels of his ship—'

'—to be ravished from head to toe...' He cupped the side of her face with a scarred hand, his eyes darkening. 'But not entirely against your will...'

The taunting accusation of rape had wounded him, even if he had swiftly realised that it had merely been intended to goad him into revealing the truth. She turned her head, pressing her lips to the crease of his strong life line. 'Not at all against my will...'

Her husky confession made him shudder.

'I don't want to hurt you—' The tormented admission was dragged from him reluctantly, a concession to the impossible situation that existed outside the universe of the closed cabin. 'I've made a promise that I won't—*can't*—go back on...too much is at stake...'

She couldn't tell him that it was too late, that the hurt was already stored up in her heart against the day that she would no longer have any place in his life. She couldn't lay that burden on him, on top of the ones that he already bore on his broad shoulders. They both knew that what they were doing was wrong, but not as wrong as it would be tomorrow—or in a month's time, if and when he married Carolyn. Despicable as it might be, Regan wanted to snatch one more precious memory for herself before her conscience forever denied her the expression of her forbidden love.

It had taken months for her to be wooed around to the idea that she was in love with Michael, but with Joshua there had been no gradual awakening; the knowledge had come like a thunderbolt out of a clear blue sky—a violent, concussive shock exploding in her consciousness and accompanied by a strong whiff of sulphur. She hadn't been looking for love—quite the reverse—but it had stormed into her wary heart with a vengeance, and she found she could no more control the unruly emotion than she could the stars in their courses.

But, unlike her first, naive foray into love, this time the portents for a relationship were quite clearly disastrous, and she was prepared for the worst.

'I know...' she whispered reassuringly, loving him for his warning. 'I know you won't hurt me,' she added, her hands moving to his belt to unthread the buckle, 'because I already know what kind of lover you are...strong and virile, and incredibly generous.'

Her fingers went to his zip and he caught her wrists, using them to pull her up against him. His mouth came down on hers and he ravaged it with a forceful passion that triggered a gush of moist heat between her thighs. He angled his head, licking and nibbling at the soft, inner tissue of her mouth, drawing her tongue into his mouth and tugging on it with a rhythmic, erotic suction that made her yearn for an even more intimate intrusion into her moist interior.

His hands fisted in the thin, white cotton of her top, drawing the stretchy fabric tight across her breasts as he lifted his head to study the effect.

'I like knowing that you don't wear a bra,' he said thickly. 'The other night at the party I imagined I could see the shadow of your nipples against the white silk. I knew they'd be as dark as ripe cherries because they were so pointed and hard.'

'That was because of you,' she whispered, arching her back and tilting her head to give him a better view. 'Because your eyes on me made me want you, even though I pretended not to notice...'

He smoothed a hand across the small mounds, cupping and shaping them. 'They're hard now, too.' He found one stiff nub and fondled it gently, then more roughly as he watched her face register the sharp thrill, her eyelids sinking, her cheeks flushing, her damp mouth quivering in inarticulate pleasure.

One hand wrapped around her arched back and she clutched at his shoulders as he pushed the hem of the top up over her collarbone, framing her breasts for his admiration.

'Look, they're blushing...' he said, drawing a finger up one hot, swollen rise, tracing the blue veins that showed through the tight, translucent skin.

'I'm not surprised,' whispered Regan shakily. 'If you knew what I was thinking you'd be blushing, too...'

'What are you thinking about...this?' He replaced his finger with his hot, wet mouth, painting the entire surface of her breasts with slow, rasping strokes of his tongue, gradually narrowing his concentration to the glistening nipples. 'I remember how much you loved me doing this,' he said, his voice a whisper of sound against her creamy flesh, 'how you demanded I do it over and over again... I remember how I gave you an orgasm just by pushing my thigh tight between your legs while I sucked on your dainty nipples.'

And she remembered how he had used words as cleverly as he had used his mouth and his hands. Her knees melted, and on the way down he pulled the top over her head and threw it on top of his shirt, supporting her from hand to hand as he efficiently dealt with her trim skirt.

She was embarrassed at the plainness of her unadorned white panties, but he smiled as he hooked his fingers into the elastic.

'Prim little cottontail,' he teased as he stripped them down her thighs. 'Don't you know how erotic the contrast is between these and your own natural G-string of sexy black lace?' And he ruffled his fingers teasingly in the soft triangle of dark fur that the panties had concealed.

The throb of the boat's engine beneath her feet seemed to echo the thrumming of her heart as Joshua threw off the rest of his clothes with an enchanting, almost boyish eagerness. But there was nothing boyish about him when he pulled her back into his arms.

The wide double bunk was built into one corner of the cabin on a pedestal of drawers, its smooth, satiny, dark blue cover glowing under the strip of lights concealed in the bottom row of bookshelves on the wall above the bed, but when Joshua sat down on the edge and tried to draw her down on top of him, Regan resisted.

She sank to her knees between his legs, onto the thick, soft carpet, running her hands up the strong column of his thighs, gliding her thumbs into the sensitive patches of hairless skin on either side of his groin.

When she bent her head, he stilled, his hands cupping her shoulders. 'Regan—'

Her eyes lifted to his. 'I want to make love to you.' And, as his gaze moved hungrily down over her nude, submissive pose she reminded him huskily, 'The way you did to me…'

His nostrils flared as she closed her mouth over him and proceeded to pleasure him to the brink of madness with her soft tongue and throaty little sounds of seductive enjoyment. His back stiffened, the tendons in his neck cording as he arched his throat and gritted his teeth, fighting the approaching explosion in order to increase the deliciously excruciating torment of unsatisfied desire. He plunged his hands into her hair, guiding her beautifully eager mouth, and when he could bear it no more his iron muscles knotted and convulsed, and a harsh, guttural cry of groaning completion was torn from his heaving chest.

Only then did she allow him to pull her beside him on the rumpled cover and cuddle her up to his naked length.

'*You're* the incredibly generous lover...' he murmured, propping himself up on one elbow so that he might gauge her reaction to his languorous caresses. 'For all you know you might have just ruined your chances of being thoroughly bedded...'

She gave a small gurgle of sultry delight. 'I doubt it, if your previous performances are anything to go by...' Her breath ended on a little hiccup as his touch feathered dangerously low on her concave belly.

'Your husband didn't satisfy you in bed, did he?' He traced his way back up to her aroused breasts and bent over to softly moisten a rosy nipple.

She shivered. 'I thought he did...' she said huskily, '...until you... Then I knew. With him it never felt— I didn't— I never...'

His eyes were moon-silver as he combed her hair across the pillow. 'You never had an orgasm...' She blushed at his tone of gloating satisfaction and his soft laugh was tinged with triumphant pride. 'You were so delightfully frantic that first time—as if you didn't quite realise what was happening to you—but afterwards you were wildly uninhibited, and so eager to experiment I could hardly fail to oblige...'

He nuzzled at her mouth, deliberately abrading her cheeks with his soft whiskers, kissing her, stroking her until she was moving ceaselessly, restlessly, rubbing herself against him, becoming increasingly excited as she felt him hardening against her belly, and then he was reaching for her, rolling her under him.

'Miracle-worker...' he growled sexily as he pushed her thighs apart, settling himself firmly against the juncture of her body.

She felt the blunt force of him testing her readiness and suddenly stiffened. 'Are you—? Joshua, you're not wearing any protection—'

He froze and looked down at himself, stunned, then into the yearning violet eyes that were suddenly drenched with unexpressed sorrow.

'It isn't safe,' she told him shakily. 'I haven't used the pill since Michael died. He—he never wanted me to have his baby,' she whispered. She couldn't stop the words spilling out: how Cindy had confessed that Michael had thought her too brash, too poorly educated, too overtly sexy with her bleached hair and big breasts, to be groomed into a proper corporate wife, whereas Regan had been tailor-made for his ambitions. How, to please Michael, Regan had continued with her law studies, even when she'd realised she wasn't cut out to be a lawyer; how she'd increased the hours of her part-time job in order to help them afford the big, up-market house in a swanky suburb that he had insisted was essential to his image; how she had acted as his hostess whenever he'd wanted to show off his stable home life, and nobly respected his long hours of work and frequent absences from home.

'But whatever I did to please him, it never seemed to be enough. And I couldn't even make him want our child,' she said bleakly. 'He let *her* get pregnant, but he stood over *me* every morning until I'd taken my pill, to make sure I couldn't conceive...'

'Ah, Regan...' He drank from her trembling lips and rolled his forehead against hers. 'He was a worthless cheat.

Controlling your fertility was just another way for him to exert his domination over a wife whom he knew was his moral and intellectual superior. Don't be sad—be glad that your babies won't carry his genes.' He shaped her breast and stroked the tender peak. 'One day you'll suckle a baby at your breast, and I know you'll make a wonderful mother…'

But not with him…

He rolled off the bed and was back again before she could recover from his shattering words, donning the protection with deft movements that ensured she had little time to think before he was gathering her up again and moving smoothly between her thighs.

Sensing that only passion could banish her lingering *tristess*, he braced himself over her on locked arms and plunged inside her, each powerful, explosive thrust of his thighs and buttocks forcing her further up the bed. His pace didn't falter, the added tension in her tautly straining torso and her spreadeagled limbs exciting him to even more reckless heights. In the air-conditioned coolness the sweat glinted on his chest, forming droplets that pearled in the thick mat of hair and trickled down his rippling belly to add to the steamy moisture that slicked their thighs where their bodies met.

His face was hard and glazed, his eyes locked with hers, all his attention focused on her approaching climax as she jerked and shuddered under his rampant assault, uttering heated little whimpers and moans of encouragement that fed his lust to see her come totally apart before his own orgasm destroyed the last of his control.

Regan's vision began to fade around the edges, her mind disengaging as her senses drastically overloaded, unable to process the escalating bombardment of pleasure. Her eyes purpled as she rushed towards the abyss of ecstasy, exulting in Joshua's fiercely unrelenting possession, thrilling to the intrusion of his hard body, the hugeness of him filling her, loving her to the hilt, and the incredible feeling of swelling tightness that grew and grew until it exploded and she screamed with the agony of blissful release.

Then Joshua was wrenching and groaning and pouring himself into her, and their bodies eased into the sweet aftermath of mutual fulfilment that to Regan felt like the settling of her soul, like coming home...

She rolled over onto her side at the edge of the bed, facing away from him, trying to control the unruly emotions that threatened to spill out of her mouth. She stared, dry-eyed, across the cabin, trying to close herself off from the press of feelings, reaching inwards for the courage to accept what she couldn't change. Joshua wouldn't want tears and tantrums—he probably got enough of those from Carolyn. He would want her to be cool and sophisticated. He might even, God forbid, want them to remain *friends*...

'I'm sorry...' She heard the bittersweet remorse in his voice as she felt a finger slowly trace the bony centre line of her back from her nape to the hollow at the base of her spine.

'*I'm* not!' She widened her eyes fiercely, refusing to regret a moment of her glorious physical outpouring of love.

'No, not for what we've just done...' His finger stroked up again. 'But for the fact that I can't offer you any more than this...' She felt his lips against the wing of her shoulderblade. 'If I were a different sort of man and you were a different sort of woman we could remain lovers, but we both have too much pride and self-respect to sacrifice honour to a self-serving lie...'

She remembered that he had quoted her Shakespeare about her being a pearl, and now another quotation floated into her mind that summed up her understanding of Joshua Wade... '*Mine honour is my life; both grow in one; Take honour from me, and my life is done.*' She could not love him half so much if he were not a man of such unflinching principle.

'I know...'

She felt his hand spread out across her back as the breath came sighing from her lungs. 'Chris wanted a long engagement...he didn't want to lose Carolyn, but she refused to move in with him and he didn't feel quite ready for marriage. When she broke the news that she was pregnant they had a fight in which he accused her of trying to trap him and she accused him of wanting her to have an abortion. They both said some ugly things that neither seem willing to overlook—'

'You don't have to tell me this—' she began painfully, but he firmly overrode her.

'That morning after you left the apartment, Carolyn phoned me from here in hysterics, begging me to come up and help. She and Chris had been rowing for a week, and she was at the end of her tether. She isn't cut out to be a single mother; she's tough in some ways but emotionally fragile in others. She had given herself to my brother in good faith and he had turned his back on her when she most needed his support. I promised her that she wouldn't have to go through this on her own and I have to stand by that promise. I owe that to her—and to Frank and Hazel, for the way that they'd welcomed Chris into their home.

'Whatever her feelings for Chris, we agreed that if we married, then for the baby's sake it has to be a *real* marriage...not simply a temporary sham for the sake of convention. I'll be a faithful, protective husband and do my utmost to ensure that she's a contented wife. And the baby will grow up as Ryan's brother or sister.'

How noble of him. The acid words burned on the tip of her tongue as envy challenged her good intentions at the thought of another woman as the sole object of his cherishing. And yet it was balm to her heart to believe that the reason he had never tried to contact her again after their original tumble between the sheets might not have been because he hadn't been interested, but because his orderly world had suddenly exploded in emotional chaos and his strong sense of honour had relegated all women but Carolyn firmly into the past.

Only, where Regan was concerned, his past had come back to tempt him to dishonour...

She stiffened as there was a light tap of the door.

'Ahem...*monsieur*? *Excusez-moi*, but I thought you'd like to know that we've arrived back at the moorings. The captain is just backing into the slips...and your brother is waiting on the dock.'

'Chris?' Joshua swore in a low voice while Regan automatically yanked the edge of the satin cover over her nakedness. 'What in the hell is he doing here?' He lifted his voice. 'Thanks, Pierre—I'll be right up. Tell Grey not to lower the gangplank until he sees me on deck.'

He climbed lithely over Regan's prone body and began pulling on his discarded clothes.

'No—you stay here,' he commanded as she made a move to do the same, checking himself in the full-length mirror on the *en suite* bathroom door, raking his hair back with his fingers before buttoning the open collar of his shirt to hide the tell-tale red mark glowing on the skin on the unblemished side of his throat. 'He probably only wants to ask if he can stay the weekend in the condo. I'll be back as soon as I get rid of him.' He swooped and sealed his hastily made promise with a brief kiss on her dismayed mouth.

As soon as the door closed behind him Regan scrambled out of the bed and darted across to bolt the door. She picked up her clothes and shook them out. The skirt was a bit crumpled, but luckily the creases wouldn't show up on the dark fabric, and her cotton-knit top was uncrushable. She would have liked to have a shower, but didn't know whether the sound of the pipes would be audible above deck and instead contented herself with a quick sponge-down in the bathroom before hurriedly dressing.

She dashed warm water in her face from the marble basin and used a comb from the vanity to return her hair to silky smoothness. Her face looked naked without make-up, her lips pouty and swollen, and she could see whisker burns on her chin and throat. To her horror she remembered that she had put her handbag down somewhere in the lounge, when Joshua had been showing her around. Unfortunately the drawers in the vanity yielded strictly masculine toilet-ries, and without recourse to make-up she had to satisfy herself with a pat of male moisturiser and a dab of cologne.

Although the boat no longer felt as if it was moving, the engine still continued to hum, and even straining her ears she could detect no sound from above. The luxury interior fittings obviously included soundproofing.

However, for added safety, she closed the bathroom door and perched on the closed toilet seat to await her rescue. When fifteen minutes had passed by the tick of the excru-ciatingly accurate platinum watch on her wrist she paced back out into the cabin and peered out of the porthole, but all she could see was the stylish super-yacht parked in the next slip.

After twenty-five minutes she could bear it no longer. Perhaps Joshua had taken Chris across the boardwalk to his condominium. All the two-storeyed condominiums that edged the dock had electronically coded security gates that opened from the boardwalk into private courtyards, and it might be possible for her to slip off the boat without being seen, unless the two men were standing at one of the huge picture windows overlooking the canal.

She silently cracked open the cabin door and peeped down the empty corridor towards the companionway.

Everything was quiet. She decided that she would creep as far as the stairs and see if she could hear any conversation from the lounge. Her hand had just touched the smooth, polished stair-rail when there was a slight sound behind her.

'Looking for this?'

She spun around, hoping that Pierre had tidied up his accent.

Christopher Wade stood in the open doorway of one of the end cabins, her navy jacket dangling from a coat hanger on his finger.

He was looking very casual in white jeans and a striped T-shirt, and behind him an open suitcase lay on the three-quarter bed. Regan realised that whatever had brought him back to Palm Cove for the second consecutive weekend, he hadn't arrived expecting big brother to give him house-room. In view of the tension between them he had evidently chosen to stay on the boat.

'Yes, I was, thank you,' she said, hoping her voice didn't sound as nervously shrill to him as it did to her own ears. 'I spilled a drink on myself and Pierre was cleaning it for me.'

'He left it hanging on the shower door of the main bath-room. I found it when I went in to recharge my razor.' His gaze went from her slender figure to the cabin door she had foolishly left ajar. 'I knew it couldn't be Carolyn's—she never wears navy.'

She sustained his steady blue gaze with extreme diffi-culty as he slipped the jacket off the hanger and held it out to her. 'It seems to be cured of whatever befell it—do you want to put it back on?'

She cleared her throat. 'No, thanks—I'll just carry it; it's a bit warm.' She smiled as she took it from him, but his expression was uncharacteristically cool.

'You're going to have a fairly tender bruise there to-morrow,' he said quietly, and touched the soft skin at the outermost swell of her breast, where it was exposed by the cut-away armhole of her top. 'In fact, you're going to have quite a few by the looks of it,' he continued, his eyes moving over her bare throat and shoulders. 'And here I always thought Josh's bark was worse than his bite...'

Regan fell back a step, clutching her jacket to her chest, feeling worse than naked, her cheeks stinging hot.

'I— I—'

'I wondered why he seemed so unusually twitchy when I wanted to come down and settle in. He tried to convince me that I'd be better off at the condo—when we both know I'm the *last* person Carolyn would want around as a chaperon.'

'I'm sorry—' Regan's awkwardly expressed compassion caused a muscle to jump in his jaw, making him look markedly like his brother did when he was in a smouldering temper.

'Oh, so you're already in on that sordid family secret, are you?' he guessed bitterly. 'Josh is usually more discreet about his problems. I wouldn't have thought he was the type to indulge in careless pillow talk, but then neither did I think he regarded sex as a combat sport—'

'That's enough, Chris,' Joshua's voice crackled out as he came down the stairs two at a time, jumping the final distance and coming up behind Regan. 'There's no need to embarrass yourself more than you have already.'

'*I'm* not embarrassed.'

'Well, you should be. You're insulting a guest and I thought I'd taught you better manners. Come on, Regan, I'll give you a lift back to the house.'

'Why hustle her off in such a rush just because I've inconveniently turned up? Could it be *you're* the one embarrassed at being caught with your pants down?'

Joshua stepped in front of Regan, shielding her from his brother's crudity.

'You're asking for a punch in the mouth!'

'Why? Because I've found out the truth?' Chris said rawly. 'That you're not as lily-white as you like everyone to believe? I always knew you were a manipulative bastard, but to con Sir Frank into bringing your mistress up here so that you can flaunt your affair under Carolyn's unsuspecting nose—'

'I am not *flaunting* her, and she is *not* my mistress!'

'You're going to tell me you two were innocently playing checkers before I came on board? Don't make me laugh! Regan has your brand stamped all over her—God, she even *smells* of you.'

Regan went hot all over. She hoped he was talking about the expensive cologne!

'Dammit, Chris—'

'No—damn *you*! Don't you know how humiliated Caro would be if she knew? She *trusts* you, dammit!' His voice was thick with torment. 'She was so very quick to believe that *I* would let her down that she wouldn't listen to anything I said afterwards—but big Josh—oh, no, never! She really believes that *you're* the saint and *I'm* the sinner. And she *likes* Regan, she thinks of her as a friend...and all this time her new *friend* and her so-called fiancé have been—'

'*Don't* say it!' Joshua ground out as Chris teetered on the brink of obscenity.

His brother laughed harshly. 'I knew you were attracted to her, but I naively thought that—being such a stickler for men *doing the right thing* by their women—you'd merely suffer the tortures of the damned denying yourself.'

Instead of trying to douse the inflammatory situation with his cool reason, Joshua inexplicably chose to pour gasoline on the flames. 'Or, if I gave in to the attraction, that I'd feel compelled to confess all to Carolyn? Is that what you were *hoping* would happen, Chris? So that *you* could rush in and replay the big dramatic scene that you flubbed a couple of months ago, this time with *you* as the valiant saviour and me as the faithless villain? Forget it. You had your chance and blew it. As it happens, I've decided that Carolyn will make an ideal wife. There's a distinct commercial advantage in a businessman being associated with a beautiful, well-bred wife bouncing the evidence of his potent virility on her pretty knee...'

Regan felt Joshua's callous, careless taunt like a blow to her heart, but Chris looked utterly shattered. His young face was haggard as he looked at the brother he had idolised for so many years with an expression of pure loathing.

'You bastard. You think you're going to have it all, don't you? I won't let you do it! If you hurt Caro—'

'If you keep your mouth shut and mind your own business, she need never find out!' Joshua snapped. 'Get real, Chris—Carolyn may have been the embodiment of your boyish sexual fantasies, but, frankly, my tastes are a lot more mature. Now, if you don't mind, Regan and I will skip the rest of the moral lecture!'

Joshua was tight-lipped and broodingly morose on the way back to the house, and Regan made a coward of herself by pretending that she had a headache and ducking dinner. She had no wish to sit across the table from Carolyn and listen to her talk about her latest wedding dress fitting, or speculate feverishly on where Joshua might take her on their honeymoon.

But there was no avoiding the other woman early the next morning when she crashed into Regan's room just as she was finally managing to doze off after tossing and turning sleeplessly all night.

'What's the matter?' Regan asked blearily, struggling to sit up as Carolyn threw herself dramatically into the chair by the bed.

'I'm bleeding,' she moaned, and Regan's eyes snapped

wide, noticing the tear-tracks on Carolyn's normally flaw-less cheeks and her unnaturally pasty expression.

'My God, do you think you're having a miscarriage?' she said, leaping out of bed.

'No—I'm *bleeding*—I've got my *period*.' Carolyn wrung her slender hands and rocked to and fro in the chair. 'Oh, God, Regan—what am I going to *do*?'

'But—but—you're *pregnant*...' Regan squawked, and Carolyn shook her head.

'No—no, I'm not. It was a mistake—'

Regan collapsed on the side of the bed. 'A *mistake*? But you had a test...'

'It was wrong. It happens—not often, the doctor says, but it happens. I never went back for a physical examina-tion, you see. But I started feeling some cramps yesterday afternoon, and so I drove over to Granny's GP and...' her big golden-brown eyes filled with tears '...and she said she couldn't feel anything when she palpated me, so she sent me for another test and it came back negative...'

Regan's brain was reeling. 'But, how could that be...surely you had all the *symptoms*?'

'The doctor said sometimes a woman's body can mimic the early physical signs if she really believes that she's pregnant, and I did believe it—I did!' Carolyn's light con-tralto rose sharply, as if to convince herself of her own sincerity. 'My period didn't come and then I felt nauseous nearly all the time, and my breasts started to feel sore and I put on weight...of *course* I thought I was pregnant!' she shrilled.

'The doctor said part of it was probably only fluid reten-tion because my cycle was disturbed. I couldn't believe it—I didn't dare tell anyone in case it turned out to be another ghastly mistake. And then, when I woke up this morning...I found I had my period! There is no baby—there never was!' Her exultation held more than a hint of hysteria, and a volatile mixture of joy, misery, relief and despair. 'I need never have had that fight with Chris. Oh, God, he's never going to want me *now*. He'll hate me even more than he does already. I put us all through this torture for *nothing*!' She buried her head in her hands, her hair falling around her body like a golden veil. Then she wrenched her tragic face up again. 'And Granny—the wedding! Regan—please help me…what do you think I should *do*?'

Regan forced herself to be calm, not to choke on the throttling hope that threatened to close off her air supply. 'The first thing you have to do,' she said carefully, 'is tell Joshua.'

Carolyn looked white-eyed with panic. 'Oh, no, I can't tell Jay!'

'Why can't you?' asked Regan hollowly. Was Carolyn now going to proclaim she'd fallen out of love with Chris and in love with Joshua?

'I just can't,' she babbled, clutching the arms of the chair. 'Not after all he's done for me. He and Chris had never had a serious argument in their lives until I came along, and now, because Jay stood up for me and tried to help me, even knowing how much I love Chris— Oh, God, neither of them are going to forgive me…it's all going to be so *humiliating*…you just don't *understand*!'

Better a little humiliation now than a lifetime of unhappiness ahead, thought Regan acidly. How in the world had Carolyn thought she could be happy in a marriage that would have made her a sister to the man she still truly loved? How could even Joshua have been so arrogant as to believe he could *make* Carolyn content with such a situation? It was a recipe for emotional disaster whether or not the estrangement between the brothers remained permanent.

'No, I don't understand,' she said steadily. 'But I *do* know that you can't go through with the wedding with Joshua still thinking that you're going to have his brother's baby. You must know how he feels about honesty. Remember what happened last time he married a woman who tried to use a pregnancy to manipulate him? As a matter of honour—his *and* yours—you *have* to tell him.'

'He'll think I'm a moron—so will Chris!'

'Chris is a doctor, for goodness' sake—he should have considered the possibility of something like this and insisted you both reserve any decisions until you'd had a proper examination. Of course, that would have been the *rational* thing to do, and people in love aren't always rational.'

Carolyn's eyes suddenly went dreamy. 'No...that's true... I know I sprung it on him badly, when we were in the middle of a fight about something else, and he felt cornered—but so did I! Maybe I should tell *Chris* first. After all, it was supposed to be his baby—and *he* could tell Jay...'

Regan eyed her cynically. 'I don't think it's the sort of thing Joshua would appreciate hearing second-hand.'

All Regan's advice seemed to fall on deaf ears, and by the time she went downstairs she had a real headache, which suddenly got worse when Sir Frank greeted her in the breakfast room with cheerful congratulations on her excellent timing—because Joshua had just arrived and was waiting to see her in the library.

'I put him in there because he said it was business and he wanted somewhere you wouldn't be disturbed. I hope he's not going to try and poach you away from Harriman's before the takeover—but then, that would sort of be like poaching you away from himself, wouldn't it?'

His chuckle followed her down the hall, but Regan didn't feel at all like laughing. As soon as she walked into the library and saw Ryan standing slouched beside the desk, nervously pushing his glasses up his nose, her heart sank.

Joshua, standing behind the desk, threw a sheaf of computer printouts on the desk, scattering them like confetti.

'Perhaps you'd like to explain these?' Icicles dripped from every syllable.

Out of the corner of her eye Regan could see Ryan wince. Whatever he had done, against her express instructions, she knew she couldn't let him take any of the blame. 'I—what are they?'

Joshua's fist crashed down on top of the papers, the ice melting to reveal the molten volcano of temper beneath.

'Don't compound your lies by pretending innocence!' he roared. 'No *wonder* you were so eager to join me on the boat yesterday. It provided you with the perfect alibi!' He raked her with a look of searing contempt. 'You had my son back at the office doing your dirty work for you, while you kept me safely out of the way. I compliment you on your technique—suborn the son and seduce the father.'

Regan had done neither, but she could see he was in no mood to listen. She tentatively picked up one of the pieces of paper. 'But, surely, you must be able to see—'

He lunged forward and dashed it from her hands. 'I *see*, all right!' he erupted. 'I see that you *used* him…you used *my son*—' in his ungovernable outrage, his passionate protectiveness towards his family had never been more apparent '—to cover up a crime! You used his feelings for you to make him an accessory to fraud. When I found these in his room this morning I knew that *I* was the fool being taken for a ride yesterday.'

'But, Dad, I told you—Regan said she didn't want me to—'

'Be quiet, son, you're in deep enough trouble as it is! What Regan *says* and what she *means* are two different things.' He swung his attention back to her guilty white face. 'Was this a set-up right from the beginning—from that first night in my apartment?'

Regan rallied, as outraged as he by the notion. '*No!* You know it *couldn't* have been!'

'And you expect me to believe you?' he slashed sardonically, but seemed to accept that his accusation was incompatible with subsequent events as he went on, 'Serendipity, then, when you were given the chance to come to Palm Cove and realised that you might use our former...*liaison* to help create a smokescreen for your actions. Were those sexual tricks you performed on me yesterday supposed to be your version of a personal insurance policy? Designed to make me reluctant to summon the police in the event of your being found out—'

'*Joshua!*' she gasped in agonised protest, glancing meaningfully at Ryan, who was following the conversation back and forth with a deep, and noticeably unrepentant fascination.

Her concern seemed only to trigger an even greater fury. 'What? Do you think we might be corrupting his innocence? It's a little late to worry about that, isn't it? I think, for his own future protection, it's about time he learned the difference between an honest woman and a conniving little whore!'

CHAPTER TEN

'LEAVE? But you don't have to *leave*!'

Sir Frank's bluff response to her miserable confession made Regan feel marginally better. Her coruscating encounter with Joshua had ended shortly after his ugly outburst, when he had seemed to recognise that his inability to control his rising fury at her brave defence of her character rendered him unacceptably vulnerable in his son's eyes—and his own. He had stormed out of the house leaving a dozen menacing threats hanging in the air, with a stunned Ryan mouthing silent apologies and flapping cryptic hand-signals to Regan that she presumed were meant to be reassuring as he was frog-marched to the door.

It had all happened so fast that Regan had felt as if she had been the victim of a lightning razor attack—there had been no pain, only a numb shock as she'd contemplated her numerous slicing wounds. She had limped back to the dining room and summoned the presence of mind to make a clean breast about Michael's theft, and her failed efforts to replace the money, to an astonished Sir Frank and Hazel.

She hadn't mentioned Ryan, merely saying that Joshua had discovered what she was doing, and she had been staggered when, instead of accusing her of aiding and abetting her husband's crime, or condemning her stupidity, the Harrimans had rallied round with shocked support.

At her implacable insistence, Sir Frank had reluctantly accepted her resignation, but he was baulking at her proposal to immediately return to Auckland.

'Of course I do,' she said proudly. 'You trusted me and I've let you down.'

'Not you—that wretched bounder Michael!' Sir Frank growled in his quaintly old-fashioned terminology. 'If it's a matter of the money, don't you worry about it, lass. You know I'll see things right.'

She clung to the wreckage of her pride, devastated by the unexpected expression of faith. 'No...I have the bank cheque for the full repayment upstairs; I'll give it to you before I leave—'

'Now, Regan, you know we won't turn away from you just because you made a wrong choice under stress,' said Hazel gently. 'It's your intentions that count, and we understand that you were just trying to do what you thought was best. You've paid much too dearly for Michael's sins as it is, so you don't have to go on covering yourself in shame...'

Regan swallowed hard, overwhelmed by her kindness. She had thought that the Harrimans would be glad to see the back of her. And no doubt they would if they knew the true extent of her shame! As for the wedding—Regan didn't know what was going to happen on that score and was desperate not to care.

'I'm sorry...but I know Joshua won't agree with you. I realise I'm letting you down double-fold, but—'

'But nothing!' said Sir Frank. 'I'm sure Wade will come round once he cools down and hears all the mitigating factors.'

'He knows them already,' said Regan tightly, afraid she was going to burst into tears.

'Well, you've admitted everything and done everything in your power to put things right—that puts you on the side of the angels as far as I'm concerned, and I'll tell him so,' he gruffed.

'It's not just that.' She knew she was going to have to come up with a definitive argument. 'I'm afraid I've also fallen in love with Joshua,' she said flatly. 'It's very awkward and embarrassing, and I'm sorry to complicate matters, but I really think it would be better all round if I went home…'

Her honesty paid off. Sir Frank continued to bluster in a muted kind of way, but Hazel instantly empathised with the horror of an unrequited love. She hugged Regan, delivering a blizzard of sympathetic assurances that *of course* she understood her urgent desire to leave, and of course she could manage without her, especially now that she had discarded her crutch and was hobbling about on her rapidly improving ankle.

Regan packed and was gone within the hour, driven back to Auckland by Alice Beatson's lanky, monosyllabic husband Steve.

Fortunately, Lisa and Saleena were at work when he dropped her off at the flat, for, once inside, her fragile façade of dignity shattered and Regan indulged herself in a storm of weeping, the bitter culmination of months of pain and strain to which had now been added this wrenching new loss, greater than all the others added together.

When the fit of anguish was over her throat was raw, her face looked like soggy puff pastry and her bones ached as if she had been beaten all over with a baseball bat. Her throat was soothed with lemon and honey, and her face marginally improved with a cool wash, but she knew the ache wasn't really physical. Until the psychological bruising came out she knew she wouldn't feel much better, however much she cried, and there was no way that she knew to hurry the healing.

If she could have despised Joshua it would have been so much easier, but she understood him far too well. From his perspective he was perfectly justified in questioning her morals and suspecting her motives, and the fact that her actions had placed his son in jeopardy would be impossible for him to forgive. As he had once told her so forcefully, no one got a second chance to breach his trust.

The odds had been impossibly stacked against her from the very beginning. She had known that loving him was a one-way ticket to heartbreak...but, oh, the joy that she had experienced along the way was almost worth the price of arrival!

The next few days were spent compulsively trying not to think about anything or anyone connected with Palm Cove, which was next to impossible when she half expected a policeman to come knocking at the door...or for Joshua to come bursting in, a one-man posse on a quest for the modern version of frontier justice. He hadn't exactly ordered her not to leave town, but that had been the gist of his final threat as he had left the house. And when she had arrived home she had been horrified to realise that she was still wearing his expensive platinum watch—another crime for him to lay at her door! And this time he would be right, for she had deliberately done nothing about returning it. By now Sir Frank would have arranged for her cheque to be repaid into the company accounts, but she was afraid to hope that that would be the end of it, not if Joshua felt it incumbent on his honour to exact personal retribution.

Desperate to avoid having to deal with reality, she impressed on Lisa and Saleena she wasn't in to phone calls—from *anyone*—and whenever they went out she switched off the answer-machine and took the phone off the hook. She did, however, make one stilted call to Cindy, to tell her that the money had been repaid, and that whatever repercussions there might be from now on would stop with Regan. She had hung up on Cindy's hysterical thanks in the certain knowledge that she had finally closed the book on her failed marriage.

The following afternoon, on the fourth day of her emotional exile, her brittle shell was cracked by the last person she would have expected to bother to seek her out—Carolyn Harriman, floating on air after her final wedding gown fitting.

'Hi—you don't mind I got your address from Granny, do you?' she chirped to Regan, who *did* mind. She had refused to wonder if Carolyn had yet plucked up the courage to break the news of her phantom pregnancy, guiltily aware that she had fled without even saying goodbye—unwilling to risk any additional emotional trauma.

'I couldn't get through on the phone, but I figured you wouldn't have another job yet and thought you could probably do with some cheering up,' breezed Carolyn. 'Look—I bought Danish pastries to go with our afternoon coffee! Granny told me why you left—about the rotten thing your husband did to you. God, men can be utter pigs, can't they?'

Regan could detect no hint of falsity in her friendly attitude, and was forced to conclude that Chris must not have blabbed about what he had seen on board the *Sara Wade*.

It struck her that she had never seen the young woman looking more relaxed as she leant on the stove while Regan put the jug on to boil.

'You're still going ahead with it, then?' she said warily, when she learned where Carolyn had been.

Only Carolyn could simper without looking silly. 'Well, yes—sort of… Haven't you got a percolator?'

'No, we haven't. What do you mean, *sort* of?' Regan forced herself to ask.

'Uh…with a different groom.'

Regan's teaspoonful of instant coffee spilled all over the bench.

'*Chris?*'

'*Of course* Chris.' Carolyn sounded ludicrously offended that she should ask. At Regan's expression she offered up a sheepish smile and waggled the new ruby and diamond ring on her finger, 'Luckily he kept this when I threw it back in his face. We got re-engaged a couple of days ago.'

'And J-Joshua raised no objections?' Regan stuttered.

'Why should he?' said Carolyn smugly. 'It's what he expected all along. Why do you think he bribed the printer to muck up the invitations? He told me when he proposed that he doubted we'd have to actually marry each other. He said he knew that when it came to the crunch Chris loved me too much to let me marry anyone else!'

'How omniscient of him,' said Regan, shards of anger thrusting jaggedly up through a smothering blanket of pain. And he had had the nerve to rage at *her* for being conniving! She hadn't been the only one with a secret agenda!

'Well, he was *right*, wasn't he?' Carolyn defended. 'And if he *had* been wrong, then he *was* prepared to genuinely go through with it, for the baby's sake—and for that I'll always be grateful to him! It was really strange, though, because he's been in a really *filthy* mood about everything else in last few days, but he hardly reacted at all when I fronted up about not being pregnant. He acted like it wasn't even *important*. He just shrugged and suggested I tell Chris as soon as possible, so I did, and instead of rowing about it we talked and talked for hours, and admitted that we had both behaved immaturely and I cried and...' she almost managed a blush '...we ended up in bed.

'Oh, Regan, you should have heard what he said! He said that he'd been miserable without me and mad with jealousy when I turned to Jay, that's why he'd been so nasty! He said that he'd been forced to face up to the fact he hadn't been fair to me *or* to Jay. He said he'd have kidnapped me at the altar rather than let Jay have me!'

The idea of Joshua being humiliated in front of two hundred guests had a certain vicious appeal, thought Regan, even if it would have been partly at his own instigation!

She stuffed herself with fattening pastries as she masochistically encouraged Carolyn to happily twitter on, gleaning the fact that Joshua and Ryan were still staying at Palm Cove and that Hazel had conscripted a biddable niece of Alice's to be her letter-writer. Carolyn herself had made the trip down to her Auckland couturier in the WadeCo helicopter, and she gave Regan a nervous rash when she let slip that she had shared it with Joshua, who was expecting to stay overnight in the city and resume permanent residence in a matter of days.

As she departed, basking in her own happiness, Carolyn gave Regan a hand-addressed silver-gilt wedding invitation.

'Chris says you have to come,' she told her gaily. 'He told me to deliver it to you personally and tell you that he'll have something to say if you try to refuse!'

Regan gave her a sharp look, but Carolyn seemed to be unaware of any ulterior meaning to her words. The Wade brothers seemed to have a pretty similar line in ambiguous threats, thought Regan savagely as she closed the door and immediately picked up the telephone receiver and slammed it back on the hook. No more avoiding life!

It immediately began to ring, and she snatched it up with a belligerent snarl.

A startled silence. 'Hello…uh…is that Regan?'

She sucked in a wild breath. 'Yes, who is this?'

'Derek… You know—Derek Clarke.'

'Oh.' Her heart flip-flopped in her chest. 'Do you want Cleo? She's not here—'

'No, actually, I wanted to talk to you. A really weird thing just happened to me…'

Regan felt like snapping that a lot of weird things probably happened to sleaze-bags like himself.

'Oh, what was that?' she asked with immense restraint.

'Well…it's this guy I sometimes arrange dates for—he

just sent me an e-mail to say he wants me to set him up
with someone called Eve tonight…'

The furious roaring in Regan's ears made it difficult to
hear him as he went on, 'So of course I immediately zapped
him with the fact that I don't *know* any women called Eve
and—this is the weird part—he comes back on my instant
message system with *your* name. I told him that he had to
be mistaken, because I knew you weren't much of a
swinger, but he wasn't interested in anyone else. He was
real insistent that it had to be *you* and only you. He said
all he wanted me to do was give you the message that
Adam needs to meet you at the same time and place. No
other name or specifics—just Adam—and he said, to quote
him exactly here: "Tell Eve she can name her own terms."
So I thought, what the hell! I've got nothing to lose by
asking—'

'I'll do it!'

'After all, you can't very well slap my face over the—
What did you say?'

Regan firmed up her quavering voice. 'I said, I'll do it.
E-mail him back and tell *Adam* that he's got a deal!'

The marble foyer on the fourteenth floor was as coldly stark
as Regan remembered it, and the deep-set door just as intimidating, but this time when she rang the bell Regan
didn't hesitate.

She might be crazy to take this chance, but she would
be insane not to! Joshua had approached her through a neutral intermediary in a way that gave her the option of accepting or refusing to meet him. In the circumstances, she
supposed that using Derek might be considered an implicit
threat, but Regan didn't see it that way. She viewed the
offer through the optimistic eyes of love. Trying to dupli-
cate the exact conditions of their first meeting might be
Joshua's oblique way of saying that he wanted them to start

afresh, to rewrite their history together. It would be typical of that sophisticated, ironic sense of humour, tinged with unexpected mischief, with which she had fallen in love!

He had said Adam *needed* to see Eve, and that she could name her own terms—that didn't sound like someone aggressively seeking revenge. It sounded alluringly close to begging. Perhaps, for once in his life, Joshua was willing to entrust someone with a second chance...

She might be walking into a trap, but if there was *any* prospect, however small, of *any* kind of future relationship with the man she loved, Regan owed it to herself to find out.

As she waited for the doorbell to be answered she didn't allow herself any romantic fantasies. Now that he was an unencumbered bachelor again, it was highly likely that Joshua might just be on the prowl for some no-holds-barred, guilt-free sex from an occasional mistress...

Well, she hadn't found much security as a wife, thought Regan defiantly, maybe she'd be better off as a rich man's mistress!

She had her smile all ready for the man who opened the door.

'Hello, Pierre.'

'Mam'selle Regan!' His turtle-mouth gaped open and shut.

'Actually, it's Eve,' she teased. 'Do I have to produce a card this time—or are you just going to invite me in?'

'*Mam'selle!*' His voice crackled with reproach and she laughed, a soft, clear, lilting sound, tinged with excitement, that stole into the apartment ahead of her. Instead of responding, Pierre looked back over his shoulder, and Regan, impatient with the delay, took the opportunity to slip under his arm and stroll inside.

'Uh, *mam'selle*, you must wait to be announced—' Pierre let go of the door and darted across her path.

She laughed again. 'Oh, you mean you're not going to tell me he's delayed in some business meeting somewhere and ply me your fantastic canapés while I wait?'

He frowned. 'Really, Mam'selle R—Eve—I think you should let me—'

He was interrupted by a deep voice floating up around the glass-brick stairwell.

'Who is it, Pierre?

Joshua came springing casually up the steps in shirt-sleeves and the grey trousers of a suit, glancing over what looked like an architectural plan in his hand. When he looked up from what he was reading and caught sight of Regan he froze in mid-step. His face was unguarded for a split second during which Regan saw a shock of incredulity tauten the skin across the bones of his skull.

'Regan?'

She looked from his wary face to Pierre's uncharacteristically deadpan expression and it hit her, then, with humiliating force: both men were so stunned to see her that it was evident her arrival was totally unexpected.

That e-mail *hadn't* been an invitation, *or* a trap—because Joshua had obviously never sent it! And Regan had been so eager to believe that he wanted to see her again that she had never entertained the idea that it might have a cruel joke perpetrated by someone else entirely!

Oh, *God*!

Her confidence smashed into a million tiny pieces as Joshua's gaze dipped, his eyes suddenly narrowing with predatory sharpness as he recognised the combination of classic black sheath, black stockings and gold-heeled evening sandals. Even the bag she was carrying was the same one she had been carrying *That Night*.

'Regan?' This time his voice was redolent with heated speculation, and a hint of amusement.

A hot flood of embarrassment welled up in her soul as

she sought to extricate herself from her gross folly. She couldn't bear to be the object of his derision. 'I—I'm sorry, I—this is a mistake.'

Joshua was up the rest of steps in a flash, the sheet of paper he had been holding wafting unnoticed to the floor. 'What makes you say that?'

She tried to back away and stepped on Pierre's foot, ignoring his yelp. 'I—I must have come to the wrong door...' she invented absurdly.

Joshua looked at her provocative garb. 'Did you want the elderly grandmother to the left of me, or the gay art director on the right?' he asked gravely.

'Floor. I said the wrong *floor*,' she quickly corrected herself, putting her hand to her throat to cover the fluttering pulse on which he seemed to be fixated.

Another mistake. He saw the watch—*his* watch—still strapped to her wrist and smiled, as if he knew that she hadn't taken it off for even a second since the day he had given it—*lent* it—to her...as if he knew that she lay in bed each night with her hand tucked under her cheek, the almost inaudible ticking a lullaby that sang her into her dreams of the man to whom it—and she—belonged.

'Well, why don't we make the most of your Freudian slip?' he purred. 'Won't you come in and have a drink for old times' sake?'

She frantically shook her head, and he lowered his voice to a coaxing murmur.

'Please...' He held out a hand, palm up. 'Eve...one drink with me?'

Unable to trust herself to speak, Regan continued to shake her head, resisting the explicit invitation in his eyes and voice.

'To keep me company...' he appealed, and thrust his outstretched hand into his trouser pocket and produced a set of keys. 'Because Pierre was just going out—weren't you, Pierre?'

He tossed the keys through the air and Pierre fielded them in one hand. 'To be sure, *m'sieur*.'

'Have a good time, and don't forget to set the deadlock when you leave—I don't want anyone breaking in on me while you're gone...'

Pierre had already slipped out of the door before Regan realised the implications of the message that had been passed over her head. She grabbed at the heavy brass handle but it was too late; the door refused to even rattle on its hinge.

She closed her anguished eyes, raising her fist to rest it helplessly against the wood.

'You must see that now that you're here I can't let you go,' he said quietly.

'No, I don't see!' she cried. 'I told you, my being here is a mistake—'

'Dressed like that? I don't think so,' he said with that same awful, quiet certainty. 'You came here to see me, didn't you? And you came in the persona of Eve, because Eve isn't as vulnerable as Regan.'

She whirled around, her back flat against the barrier to her freedom. 'What do you know?' she scorned proudly.

But his eyes weren't gloating or triumphant, they were beautifully solemn. 'About you? Not enough, it seems. About me? Not as much as I thought I did. I thought I had everything under control, including myself. I was wrong. Quite spectacularly wrong.'

He approached her soft-footed, holding her captive with that hypnotic gaze. 'By the way, you might be interested to learn that I'm not marrying Carolyn.'

'I know, I saw her this morning—' She broke off, biting her lip as she saw his eyes light up at the nugget of information. Now he was *really* locking himself into the mind-set that she had come rushing over here to grovel for his attention.

'I'm a cynical swine,' he continued, on his original course. 'Experience has taught me that it's safer to expect the worst of people instead of trusting to the best—'

'Is this an apology?' Regan cut him off stonily. All she could think was: *He didn't invite you here.* He thought *she* had come crawling back to *him*.

He met her aggression with a soft answer. 'Oh, I think you'll find it's much more than that. Won't you come in and sit down? You may as well accept that I have no intention of unlocking that door—even if I did know where Pierre kept his keys.'

He held out his hand again, but she ignored it as she stalked past him down the stairs. He allowed her to evade him until they reached the level of the sunken lounge, then his fingers curled around her elbow as he turned her to face him.

She tried to jerk it away. 'Don't touch me!'

'I can't help it,' he said, cupping her other elbow and drawing her towards him. 'It's a compulsion. Since the first time I met you I can't be near you without wanting to have my hands on you. You churn me up, and in the beginning I wasn't sure I liked that; I wasn't prepared for it—it interfered with my plans. I wanted to be able to push what I felt for you aside until I was ready to deal with it. But do you know what I've found that I don't like even *more*, Regan...?'

What I feel for you? She shook her head, dazed with feverish apprehension, her eyes huge in her face, unable to believe that this was real and not just a figment of her reckless imagination.

'I don't like you being away from me. I don't like not having you around to churn me up—to intrigue me, infuriate me, comfort me, excite me and, yes—to enrage me.

Even when I'm furious with you I still want you near me…'

She began to tremble and he eased himself into contact, his trousers brushing her legs. 'I don't like knowing that I hurt you. That I prated on about family responsibility and honour and then failed to respect that you felt a duty to protect *yours*. I'm so used to people expecting *me* to handle their problems for them that I didn't know how to act when I ran up against someone who was so determined *not* to demand anything of me. I should have admired you for having the courage of your convictions and for your stubborn loyalty. Instead I was furious that you'd continued to squander it on that crooked bastard you married rather than transferring it to *me*, even though I'd done nothing to earn it! I knew I couldn't afford to make another mistake with you, so I've spent the last few days racking my brains to think of a logical reason I might use to persuade you to see me again.'

His fingers tightened and his voice roughened. 'But it isn't logic you want from me, is it, Regan? You can't imagine how I felt when I saw you just now, when I realised that you'd been willing to sacrifice your pride to reach out to me, even after the contemptible way I treated you, that your desire to be with me was so strong that it conquered all your fears—'

'Don't!' she choked, her fierce elation tempered by the knowledge she was a fraud.

His tender smile was a kiss upon her sight. 'You're going to stop me now? When I'm humbling myself for you?'

'It's not necessary—'

'But it is. For me, it is. You've done your bit, now it's my turn to do the risking.'

Much as she longed to let him do just that, she had to put him right before he went any further! 'Joshua—'

She turned her head, searching for the right words, and

suddenly caught sight of the frozen picture on the big-screen television behind him. 'What's that?'

Joshua let her go and quickly scooped up the video remote control from the arm of a chair, pointing it at the machine.

'Wait a minute.' Regan snatched it out of his hand as she looked at the freeze-frame. 'That's *me*!'

She moved around for a better look and swallowed a fuzzy feeling in her throat as she pressed the 'pause' button and her screen self began to move. 'That's the security video from the night I was here!' she whispered as she watched herself tentatively step out of the apartment building lift.

Joshua sighed. 'It's the only picture I have of you,' he said simply, and her eyes stung as he turned his brooding gaze back at the screen. 'You look a little nervous here, don't you?' he murmured. 'I've watched it over and over, and I definitely think the lady is having some second thoughts, but look there—see—she squares her shoulders and decides: What the hell! I'm going to go for it…'

He was watching the screen, but Regan was watching his softened face. She imagined him sitting here all alone, surrounded by every luxury money could buy, replaying those same few seconds of videotape over and over again, studying her every move and trying to analyse her thoughts, and her heart surrendered itself for ever into his keeping.

'Oh, *Josh*…' She wrapped her arms around him, wanting to protect him from ever being lonely again. Whatever he felt for her, she loved him enough for the both of them.

'Now you know how I recognised Ryan had a crush on you,' he said wryly, tipping her face up to meet his. 'I felt the same way—only mine was the fully-fledged adult version. After that first night I was going to find out who you really were, and make arrangements to see you again,' he confessed. 'But then Carolyn called and events overtook me. But you still haunted the back of my mind. So much so that I thought I was hallucinating when I first saw you out the window at Hazel's.'

She told him about Ryan and the tree, and he laughed. 'No wonder he took to you so quickly. Hide-and-go-seek used to be one of his favourite games.

'And speaking of favourite games...' He leaned forward and whispered teasingly into her ear, 'Are you wearing anything under that dress?'

Regan went utterly scarlet and he stilled, his eyes widening with stunned admiration as he realised the daring wickedness with which she had hoped to seduce him.

'You're *not*?' he guessed, erupting into more, very sexy laughter as she shook her head and hid her scalding face in the front of his silk shirt. His hand slid down to trace her shapely naked bottom through the dress. 'My God, you did come prepared for battle, didn't you, honey? I never stood a chance!'

She remembered what it was so important for her to make clear and lifted her hot face. 'It wasn't actually my idea to come here tonight,' she told him, her eyes daring him to take back anything he had said. She told him about Derek's call regarding the e-mail. 'Naturally, I thought it'd come from *you*,' she said, thinking that a sleaze-bag made a rather unlikely cupid. 'I thought *you* were making the first move.'

Joshua's response was a slight touch of colour on his hard cheekbones, but he was too smug at the serendipitous outcome and too intrigued by the puzzle to be truly embarrassed by his error—the supremely arrogant assumption that had prompted him to reveal his deepest emotions.

'If he was responding to my private Internet address then he would have presumed so, too. I don't know what's on there at the moment because I don't check my personal messages every day. Ryan's always on my back about—'

He broke off and backed out of her arms. 'Excuse me a minute!' He was a lot longer than a minute, but when he had finally hung up the phone and came back to her after his low-voiced conversation his eyes were glowing with dangerous amusement.

'My son's doing. It seems that Ryan suffers from a God complex.' His ruefulness was an irresistible temptation.

'I can't imagine where he got that from!' murmured Regan

He quelled her with the lift of an eyebrow. 'Apparently he cracked the password on my e-mail account some time back and decided to use it to set us up.'

'But—how could he know about—? Or that we called each other Adam and Eve?' she gulped.

He ran a hand through his hair and slanted her a look that was charmingly abashed. 'I had drink or three too many that night I lost my temper…after I found out you'd skipped out on me *again*,' he confessed. 'I got a little rowdy—and drunkenly maudlin, according to Ryan—in my lecture to him on the evils of doe-eyed women who lead men around by the uh—certain parts of their male anatomy. He says I mentioned that Derek Clarke had arranged for us to meet…and I also mentioned that we had jokingly appropriated our middle names…'

'You mentioned an awful lot to an impressionable fifteen-year-old-boy,' Regan said ominously.

'Yes, well…' Joshua shed his chagrin in a little spurt of paternal pride. 'I suppose his super-intelligence filled in most of the gaps and the rest just took a little research— for example, your full name is bound to be on the database at Harriman Developments, and as *you* well know my son doesn't see privacy laws as a barrier to his investigations. Give him a computer, a modem and enough time, and Ryan could well rule the world.'

'But *why*?' Regan said, not wanting to think that Ryan

had *intended* for her to be hurt and humiliated by his father. 'He *knew* that we parted on terrible terms.'

Joshua sighed. 'That was why. He thought it was his fault, and that, with Carolyn out of the picture, if he could just get us together, propinquity would do the rest—although he had a rather more basic term for it…'

Regan put her hands over her still warm cheeks. 'He must think I'm an awful tramp.'

He took pity on her mortification and took her back in his arms to kiss the tip of her pink nose. 'I think he thinks you're a very sexy woman whom his father is crazy about. He said to tell you, by the way, that he never broke his promise to you—what he did was *not* ''dumb and misguided''—it was extremely clever; it was keeping the hard copy evidence that did him in!'

'Still, what if you hadn't wanted to see me?' she worried.

His voice was warm with disbelief. 'Darling, the boy watched me skewer you with a knife and then listened to me prose on about you for hours while I ploughed my way through half a bottle of Scotch. I assure you, he was in no doubt as to what I was going to do when I got my hands on you again.'

'Throttle me?'

His hands tightened around her waist as his mouth came down on hers. 'Never let you go.'

'Oh…' Bliss was a warm mouth and a strong pair of arms.

'So, does that mean you're willing to accept my son?' he murmured against her throat.

'I've already accepted he's your son,' she replied, confused.

'No, I mean…as your own. I think all the children of one family should call the same person Mother.' He lifted his head as she stiffened in his encircling arms. 'Did you think I wasn't going to ask the woman I love to marry me?

Especially one as elusive as you—what kind of idiot do you take me for?'

Her small face was incandescent with joy. 'I think you're a pure genius. I guess that's why I love you.'

It was the first time she had said it out loud, but instead of the expected romantic response, Joshua raised a challenging eyebrow. 'Prove it.'

She laughed, and kicked off her shoes, and raced him into the bedroom. As she wrestled him playfully onto the bed he murmured, 'The last time I entertained Eve in here, she was too proud to accept anything from me. I hope this time will be different.'

'"Pride comes before a fall,"' quoted Regan.

He smiled. 'Don't I know it!' He traced her kiss-swollen mouth with a gentle finger. 'So…is your pride willing to be flexible for me tonight?'

'Have you still got that gorgeous tennis bracelet?' she teased.

His eyes glinted. 'You're not really allergic to gold, are you?' And when she shook her head he pulled out the bedside drawer and began dragging out boxes and shaking them open over her prone body—bracelets, necklaces, lockets, bangles, brooches falling in an extravagant rain over her black dress.

'Josh!' She sifted them through her fingers with a laughing protest.

'Not enough?' He produced more, until she was heaped with splendour and helpless with giggles.

'I bought them all because you don't have any jewellery and I wasn't sure what you'd like best,' he said with perfect seriousness. 'I want to give you everything, you see,' he said roughly. 'Me—life, love, babies galore…everything that it's in my power to give you.' Then he took out one last item, a folded piece of creased tissue paper, and carefully unwrapped it, and she sat up, shedding the expensive baubles, to look at the thin, old-gold band plainly set with a straight row of three extremely modest diamonds.

'It was my mother's engagement ring, and her mother's before her,' he said. 'Dad kept it for me after Mum died so I could give it in turn to my wife. But Clare thought it was too old-fashioned and the diamonds too small. And I never even considered showing it to Carolyn. For the last fifteen years, although I didn't know it, I've been keeping it for you...'

'It's beautiful,' said Regan shakily, imagining all the emotion invested in the cherished reminder of loves past.

He slid it on her slender finger. 'I knew it would suit you...'

'Small, plain and simple?' she taunted his ruthless pride.

'Dainty, rare and precious.' He tumbled her back on the bed and carelessly brushed away his lavish offerings in order to get down to the serious business of loving.

'Do you know, I think that you and I together have helped prove an old saying?' he said, lifting the hand bearing his ring to his lips.

'What's that?' she murmured dreamily as he bent his head to give her the most treasured gift of all.

'That revenge *is* deliciously, irresistibly sweet...'

THE FRENCHMAN'S
MISTRESS

KATHRYN ROSS

Kathryn Ross was born in Zambia, where her parents happened to live at that time. Educated in Ireland and England, she now lives in a village near Blackpool, Lancashire. Kathryn is a professional beauty therapist, but writing is her first love. As a child she wrote adventure stories and at thirteen was editor of her school magazine. Happily, ten writing years later, *Designed With Love* was accepted by Mills & Boon. A romantic Sagittarian, she loves travelling to exotic locations.

Look for Kathryn Ross's brilliant new Modern™ romance
Italian Marriage: In Name Only.
Available now from Mills & Boon!

CHAPTER ONE

WHEN Caitlin had told people that she was leaving England to start a new life in Provence it had sounded glamorous and exciting. Now, as she peered out through rain that seemed to be slanting in diagonal sheets across the windscreen of her car reality started to set in. *Was this it: her dream villa, her escape route from everything that had been wrong in her life?*

In her imagination the villa had been cradled in the lush green warmth of the French countryside, painted deep ochre to blend with the surroundings, green shutters closed to protect the perfectly proportioned rooms from the full glare of the Mediterranean sun. But the reality looked nothing like her dreams. Perhaps once it had been a quaint cottage, but now it looked sad and neglected and frankly rather bleak.

Maybe she had taken a wrong turning and this was not really her house? She picked up the maps, checking the route she had taken, and then glanced again at the papers she had been given at the solicitor's office. The directions had been fairly straightforward; she didn't think she had made a mistake, and there didn't seem to be another building for miles around.

Caitlin peered out at the dilapidated building again. Daylight was beginning to fade, before it went dark she was going to have to get out and investigate. Or she could turn her car around and head for the nearest village and book into a hotel. For a moment the thought of a hot shower, fine French food and cool cotton sheets was very tempting. She had set off driving from London at four-thirty this morning; it was now almost seven in the evening and she was exhausted. But she had come this far and, as tired as she was, she would not be able to rest easily until she knew for certain if this was Villa Mirabelle...her inheritance.

She switched off the car engine and the silence was filled with the rhythmic sound of rain hitting the roof so heavily it sounded like a distant roll of thunder. The world outside was lost in a dark watery haze as the wind-screen wipers stopped. Caitlin pulled up the hood of her raincoat and, taking the front door key she had been given and a torch from the glove compartment of the car, she took a deep breath and stepped out of the vehicle.

Her feet sank straight into the sodden, muddy ground making her progress towards the front door a bit like paddling through thick, syrupy treacle and her jeans beneath the blue raincoat were instantly soaked and splattered with mud. There were two steps up to the front door and she almost fell up them as the raindrops blurred her vision. In case she had the wrong place, she knocked on the wooden door and waited to hear any movement from within, but was aware of nothing except the drumming of the rain against her waterproof coat.

With slightly shaking hands she tried her key in the enormous lock. It slipped in easily but wouldn't turn. She almost laughed aloud in relief, but before taking it out tried again, this time turning it in the opposite direction. With a sinking heart she felt the soft click of the lock opening and knew then without a shadow of doubt that she had the right place.

Disappointment prickled inside her for just a second and then she quickly brushed it away as she reminded herself how kind it had been of Murdo to leave her the cottage. She would be forever grateful to him, especially as the bequest had come at a time in her life when she had most needed it. And it had been totally unexpected. It wasn't even as if she was related to him, she had merely been his nurse. There was no reason why he should have left her a single penny, let alone a property in France with all its land.

She pushed the door open and shone her torch into the thick blackness inside. The yellow beam of light played over what looked like a lot of white sheets and it took her a moment to realise that they were dustsheets over furniture. She stepped inside out of the rain and the floorboards creaked in protest as if no one had dared to step on them for a long time. There was a light switch next to the door and she flicked it on but wasn't surprised when nothing happened. The electricity was probably turned off…that was if the place still had electricity. Leaving the door open she stepped further into the room. It smelt vaguely of lavender mixed with the damp earth smell of somewhere that hadn't been aired for a long time.

On a sideboard there were a few silver-framed photographs of people Caitlin didn't recognise. They made her realise how little she knew about her former employer. He hadn't been a man given to revealing intimate insights of his life, indeed she had only known about his land in France because from time to time he had been visited by his ex next-door neighbour, a tall dark Frenchman called Ray Pascal.

As she ran a curious eye over the photographs she suddenly picked out the familiar face of Ray amongst all the strangers. She lifted the photo and blew the dust from it.

It was obviously his wedding photograph. There was a beautiful woman by his side in a long white dress; she had dark hair and laughing eyes. Caitlin guessed it had been taken about fifteen years ago because Ray looked as if he was in his early twenties. He had been good-looking back then, she thought as she studied the photograph intently, but he had matured into a formidably handsome man—if a somewhat disagreeable one. Her eyes flicked again to the woman he had married; apparently she had died in a car crash and Ray had never got over losing her.

She had only met Ray a few times but on each occasion there had been an underlying tension between them that had unnerved her completely. She wasn't used to men looking at her with such disapproval. In fairness she supposed they had got off to a bad start. The first day she had opened the door to him she had been wearing a pair of minuscule shorts and a T-shirt and he had looked at her with a raised eyebrow when she had casually told him she was Murdo's nurse.

'Aren't you a little scantily clad for work?' he had inquired dryly.

Now, at that point she probably should have explained that in fact it was her day off and she wouldn't have been there except for an urgent phone call from Murdo telling her that he needed her. Worried about him, she had rushed straight over only to find Murdo looking better than he had in ages, sitting in the lounge, telling her that there was someone coming whom he wanted her to meet.

Consequently she hadn't been in a very good mood when she had opened that door to Ray and the note of censure in his tone had been the last straw. 'What I wear for work is between my employer and me...' she had retorted coolly, and then with a toss of her long dark hair she had marched past him out of the door. 'He's in the lounge.' She had thrown the words casually back over her shoulder. 'And tell him never to ring me like that again.'

Murdo had been infuriating sometimes, she reflected wryly as she put the photo down. For some reason during the brief period of Ray's visit last summer he had got it into his head that she and Ray would make a good couple. It had been a crazy notion, not only because they didn't even like each other, but because Caitlin was with David—had in fact been living with David for three years.

After a couple of weeks of heavy innuendos Murdo had finally come out and asked her directly if she was attracted to Ray. She remembered she had blushed wildly when she had told him that she most definitely was not. Even now she didn't know why that question had made her so hot and bothered. Murdo had found her reaction amusing. He hadn't been a man given much to laughter, at least not in the two years Caitlin had known him, but he had laughed that day, a rich, warm chuckle that had even made her grin.

'I'm in love with David,' she reminded him when he continued to laugh.

'If you say so.' Murdo grinned.

'Yes I do say so, we're engaged to be married.' She waved her diamond ring in front of his eyes.

'You've been wearing that since you first worked for me,' Murdo said dismissively. 'And you've only just set a wedding date.'

She frowned. 'I know Ray is very good-looking, Murdo, but then so does he. He is arrogant and not my type at all.' Murdo's deep blue eyes twinkled in amusement and she thought maybe it was because she was protesting too much; then she realised that they were not alone. Ray was standing behind her in the doorway of the bedroom. If ever Caitlin wished the ground would open up and swallow her it was that day.

She attempted to apologise to him later, good manners forbidding her to just leave it. So she caught him when his visit with Murdo was over and he was heading for the front door.

'I'm really sorry about...before...you know...' She had tried not to be intimidated by the steady way his dark eyes held hers. 'Murdo was winding me up and... well...I shouldn't have risen to the bait.'

'You don't need to apologise,' he said and in contrast to her he sounded completely self-assured. His lips twisted in a half smile that was slightly mocking. 'The fact is, you're not my type either.'

Then he turned, leaving her wishing she hadn't bothered to apologise.

'Why didn't you warn me he was behind me?' she asked Murdo crossly a little later.

He grinned, not at all repentant. 'I don't have many pleasures left in this life but one of them is very definitely watching the sparks that fly between you and Ray.' Then the smile faded and suddenly he grew tired of the game and became cantankerous. 'I haven't taken my medicine yet... You know how I hate being even five minutes late with it...'

Murdo hadn't been the easiest of patients she reflected now, but she was going to miss him. There had been something almost endearing about him even at his most crotchety.

'Your house is a bit of a mess, Murdo.' She spoke aloud as she looked around, her voice sounding strange in the enclosed space. 'But I appreciate the thought nevertheless.'

'You know that talking to yourself is the first sign of madness.'

The voice from behind her was so unexpected that she jumped violently and spun around, her torch unsteadily wavering over the white sheets, her heart thundering against her breast.

A man stood silhouetted against the open door and for a crazy second she thought it was Murdo returning from the grave to answer her. But the outline in the doorway was that of a more powerfully built man, he was taller, the shoulders broader.

'I wondered when you'd turn up.' His French accent was dryly amused, not at all ghostly, and suddenly very familiar.

'Ray! You scared the life out of me!' She shone her torch onto him and he held a hand up to shield his eyes from the glare. The yellow beam glinted over the raindrops in his short dark hair and she noticed he wore a heavy oilskin jacket over jeans. It was a far cry from the way he had dressed when she'd seen him in England—back then he'd always worn smart suits. 'What on earth are you doing here?' she asked, lowering the beam of light from his face.

'I was on my way up to the house and saw your car.'

'Up to the house?' She was truly mystified.

'My house.' His voice was acerbic now. 'I live about six kilometres further on up this road.'

'Oh! I didn't know... Well, I knew you lived in France, of course...' She felt flustered and confused. 'But Murdo told me you had an apartment in Paris now, so I assumed you had moved from around here.'

'I do have an apartment in Paris—I use it for work—but my home is here in the south.'

There was an edge to those words that she didn't understand. Why did she always feel out of kilter when she was talking to him? Caitlin wondered. Why did he unnerve her so much? Was he telling her that she was on his territory and she wasn't welcome?

The rain seemed to be increasing outside and a bright flash of lightning lit the room, followed a few moments later by the distant rumble of thunder. And suddenly it didn't really matter that Ray's manner was unwelcoming; at least he was another human being, and in the unknown surroundings a familiar face was reassuring. 'Well, I'm glad I'll have a neighbour I know,' she said cheerfully. 'I'll be able to pop over if I run out of sugar. That's an unexpected bonus.'

'You are not thinking of staying here…are you?'

The shocked incredulity in his voice made Caitlin hesitate; she didn't honestly know what she was going to do. The plans she had made back in England now seemed absurd. She had dreamed of turning this place into a small guest-house. A vision she had unwisely shared with a few colleagues and friends who had all delightedly assured her they wanted to be the first to book themselves in.

Caitlin cringed as she imagined the expression on their faces if they could see this property. And when word travelled around the circle of their friends and David heard…he would probably laugh. The thought of David laughing at her was almost the last straw.

He had accused her of being too impulsive when she had finished with him and his tone had been patronising. He had honestly believed that she wouldn't call the wedding off. He'd thought that she would make a token visit to her mother down in London and then return to him, her common sense restored.

And then she had inherited this house and it had been like a lifeline...

Another flash of lightning lit the room and for a second Ray had a clear view of Caitlin, dark hair bedraggled around a face that looked far too pale and eyes that shimmered intensely green.

'I'll decide what I'm going to do once I can look at the place properly in the daylight.' She angled her chin up stubbornly; she wasn't going to give up on her dream that easily.

'But you can't stay here tonight,' he continued softly. The sudden gentleness of his tone took her aback.

'Well, I suppose I'll go down to the village and book into a hotel.'

'I don't think so.' He turned away and glanced out of the door. 'The roads further down the mountain will be flooded now. Plus I think you'll find it hard to go anywhere in your car.'

'What do you mean?' She crossed to stand beside him at the door. The sky was a forbidding shade of deep indigo lit every now and then with several jagged streaks of fork lightning that illuminated the trees on the hills with unnatural brilliance. Almost immediately the light was followed by a fierce crash of thunder that reverberated and echoed through the mountains like cannon fire.

'Flash floods come out of nowhere when the weather is like this,' Ray said matter-of-factly.

Caitlin could see for herself that water was now flowing like a river down the narrow winding road she had driven up.

'Plus you've parked your car off the road; the tyres will be stuck in the mud by now.'

Following his gaze towards her old estate car, she could see that he was right.

'I'll just have to stay here then.' She tried to sound undaunted, but truthfully the thought of staying in this house, in this storm was making her panic levels rise.

'Don't be absurd.'

The scornful remark chafed on raw nerves. 'Well, have you got a better suggestion?' She turned and looked up at him.

He didn't answer immediately and in the pause a brutal roar of thunder tore through the air again.

Then he shrugged. 'Well, I suppose you'll have to come home with me, won't you?'

It wasn't the most gracious of invitations and there was a part of Caitlin that instantly wanted to refuse out of pride and say, No, thanks, I'll be fine here. But she was too tired to pretend, so instead she inclined her head. 'Thanks, I'd appreciate that,' she said.

'And anyway, I suppose it will give us a chance to talk.'

'Talk about what?' She frowned.

For a second his features were illuminated by the lightning, the dark eyes were cool, and there was something about the rugged set of his square jaw that was unyielding.

'About Murdo leaving you this place, what else? Now let's get out of here before the roads are completely impassable and we're both stuck here for the night.'

That thought galvanised Caitlin into following him back out into the rain. Carefully she locked the door behind her and hurried down the steps.

Why did Ray want to talk about Murdo's will? she wondered as she trailed behind him. But no explanation came to mind and she pushed the question away under more pressing immediate problems. The rain was cold against her face and she realised she hadn't zipped her coat up again or put her hood up. She felt water striking straight through to her skin and dripping down her back. 'I'll just get some belongings out of my car,' she called after Ray, but he didn't seem to hear her.

As she struggled to find her overnight case in the dark amidst the chaos of her other belongings Caitlin suddenly thought about the warmth and security of her old life. The apartment she had rented with David had been in a trendy area of Manchester and they had put a lot of time and effort into the furnishings and the decoration. It had been a lovely home. Then she thought about her wedding dress, which still hung in the spare wardrobe. It had been her dream dress, yards of exquisite cream silk with tiny rosebuds around the neckline. In another couple of weeks' time she would have been Mrs Caitlin Cramer. A sudden knot formed in her throat.

Caitlin found her bag and tugged it out with some impatience. Marrying David would have been a huge mistake, she told herself fiercely. Their relationship was over and she had no regrets because he wasn't the man she had thought he was.

As she swung around she was surprised to find Ray standing behind her. He reached to take the bag from her. 'Be careful around here—it's treacherous underfoot.'

'Thanks.' She smiled at him hesitantly. She was glad he'd taken the bag from her but she wasn't going to take the hand he held out to help her. 'I'll manage…' The words were no sooner out of her mouth than she lost her balance in the mud and stumbled. Only for Ray's quick reflex action, his arm catching her around the waist, she would have been on the ground. She found herself held close against him, her body pressed against the powerful contours of his. The enforced intimacy was the strangest sensation. For a moment the cold rain beating down over them was forgotten and all she was aware of was his arm holding her securely and the warm, almost electric feeling that his closeness generated.

She extricated herself from him with a feeling of awkwardness. 'Sorry about that.' She felt breathless as she met his eyes, as if the air was knocked out of her body.

He smiled. 'I told you the ground was slippery.'

Caitlin looked away from the amused glint in his eyes. She hated it when people said I told you so. And why had she imagined it pleasurable to be close to him? He was the most irritating type of man you could wish to meet.

She walked ahead of him towards his car, picking her way with care, determined not to need any further assistance. The water on the road flooded over her shoes, penetrating inside to her feet, making them squelch as she stepped up onto the running board of his silver four-wheel drive.

'Is this really the sunny south of France?' she muttered once they were safely inside the car.

Ray smiled. 'When it rains here it usually does the job properly. That's why it's lush and beautiful.'

'Is it?' Caitlin stared out of the windscreen at the dark watery surroundings. 'I'll have to take your word for it.'

There was a certain feeling of security being inside this car, it was higher off the ground than Caitlin's and the leather interior was warm and comfortable. She watched as Ray engaged the gears before negotiating a steep turn in the road. Then as the narrow track widened their way was barred by a gate.

'This marks the boundary between your land and mine,' he said, stopping the vehicle.

'So to get to your property you have to drive through mine?' she asked frowning. 'Isn't that a bit unusual?'

'There are several entrances to my estate—this is just a back route—but I do have a right of way,' Ray muttered. 'However it is an inconvenience…and that is one of the reasons I wanted to buy Murdo's property from him last year. I made him a very generous offer, in fact, when I was visiting him in England. But then I suppose you already know all about that.'

'No.' Caitlin frowned. 'I had no idea.'

'Well, my offer was substantial, which was why I was very surprised when he turned it down and then left the place to you instead.'

Caitlin suddenly understood the barbed note in his tone. Ray had wanted Murdo's land. She shifted uncomfortably in her seat. 'His will came as a surprise to me as well.'

'Really.'

'Yes, really.' Caitlin frowned. 'I don't know what you are trying to imply but I don't much care for your tone, Ray.'

He made no reply to that, but instead got out of the car. She watched him in the beam from the headlights as he opened the five-bar gate that blocked their way.

Was he insinuating that she had somehow persuaded Murdo into leaving his house to her? The idea was abhorrent.

Caitlin didn't know why Murdo had left her his property. She had been stunned when the letter had arrived from the solicitor. But the fact that it had happened at a time when she had reached a crossroads in her life had

been like a pointer sent from above and she hadn't spent
a lot of time analysing it.

Yes, it was an overly generous gift, but she certainly
hadn't influenced him into giving her anything. The suggestion was insulting.

Ray got back into the car and drove on through the
gates. There was a tense silence between them as they
continued on up the long winding road, until suddenly
Caitlin couldn't stand it any longer. 'Look, I don't blame
you for being a bit miffed that Murdo left his land to
me instead of selling it to you. I know your friendship
with him goes back years and I'm a stranger by com-
parison, but I assure you that the decision had nothing
to do with me and I certainly didn't entice Murdo to
leave me anything.'

'I never said you did,' Ray said quietly. 'Although the
word entice is an interesting choice. And you were…
shall we say…rather unsuitably dressed for work when
I first saw you…'

Remembering the scanty top and shorts that she had
been wearing when she'd answered the door that day
made Caitlin's face flare with colour. 'You've completely misread the situation. That was my day off.'

'And you usually went around to Murdo's house on
your day off dressed like that…did you?'

The calm question sent Caitlin's temper soaring. 'No,
I did not! I was around there like that because I had
been summoned urgently and I thought it was an emergency. But in fact he'd only sent for me because you
were there.'

'Because I was there?' Ray sounded baffled.

'Well…yes… He had this weird idea that…' Caitlin
trailed off, too embarrassed to go any further.

'Weird idea about what?' Ray glanced over at her.

She shrugged. 'Well, you must have known…he thought that…you and I would make a good couple.'

'You're not serious!' There was silence for a moment and then Ray started to laugh. The warm sound of complete amusement grated on Caitlin's nerves.

'Yes, all right, Ray, we both know it's absurd. I don't much like you and you don't like me.'

'No, in fairness I have never disliked you, Caitlin,' Ray said, shaking his head. 'I've always thought you were very attractive, in fact…for a little gold-digger.'

'Right, that's it, turn the car around,' Caitlin demanded furiously.

'Why?'

The calm question made Caitlin fizz inside like a firecracker ready to explode. 'Why? Because I would rather spend the night in a rundown house with no electricity than one more moment with you in this car, let alone the night under your roof. You are rude and and… insensitive and I absolutely detest you. That's why.'

'I'm not turning the car around,' he said, without losing a shred of his cool detachment. 'So if you want to go back to Murdo's house you'll have to walk.'

Caitlin stared out at the dark wild night lit every now and then by the bright flicker of lightning and, as much as she didn't like Ray, she decided that walking wasn't an option. 'I'll phone for a taxi, then.'

'Please yourself. But no taxi will come up here in this weather. So I think you are stuck with me for tonight.'

Caitlin's hands curved into tight fists and she felt her nails digging into her skin. 'Well, I suppose I'll have to put up with you, then,' she muttered tightly.

'I suppose you will,' he said with a hint of amusement in his tone.

The drive turned and through the rain an impressive building came into view, its windows spilling welcoming light out into the darkness. It was the kind of château that you would see in the pages of glossy magazines, quintessentially French with fairy-tale turrets at either side of the long straight edifice. Caitlin couldn't help wondering why he was so bothered about the dilapidated house down the road when he owned this palatial spread.

He parked by the front door. 'I'll get your case. You run ahead, the door will be unlocked.'

Caitlin did as he asked and hurried through the rain, almost tumbling in through the front door as an almighty roar of thunder cracked the air. It was a relief to be out of that weather and away from the close proximity of Ray Pascal. How dared he suggest that she was some kind of gold-digger? She was still reeling with shock at the horrible accusation.

Apprehensively she glanced around at her surroundings. The house was as impressive inside as it had been outside. She was standing in a wide flagged entrance hall and through an archway she could see a stone fireplace where a log fire crackled invitingly. Drawn towards the warmth of the fire, she went into the room. It was like something out of a film set. Pale orange sofas were placed strategically at either side of the huge fireplace and a staircase led up to a wooden gallery that encircled the room. Caitlin walked over and stood with her back to the fire as she admired the antique furniture, the crystal lamps that sent out a delicate warm glow, the vases of fresh flowers, the writing bureau placed by the window.

It was a large house for one man to live in alone and Caitlin wondered fleetingly if there was a serious woman in his life. Murdo hadn't seemed to think so, but then

Murdo couldn't know everything. All right Ray had been widowed in his twenties, but he was about thirty-eight now she reckoned. It was a long time for a man to be on his own.

One thing was certain: Murdo had been absolutely crazy to think she and Ray were suited.

Ray came into the house carrying her case. She watched as he put it down to hang up his jacket, muscles rippling through the thin cotton of his shirt. She was willing to bet her last penny that there was no shortage of women falling into his arms or his bed...

'Have you eaten?' he asked, turning and catching her eye.

She shook her head.

'Okay, I'll show you up to your room and you can get out of those wet things while I rummage through the kitchen and see what is in the cupboards. Unfortunately my housekeeper is having some time off so you'll have to suffer my cooking.'

'I don't want anything to eat,' she said with stiff politeness. 'So if you don't mind I think I'll just turn in.'

'Of course you want something to eat. You must be starving.' He came closer. 'I'm sorry I said I thought you were a gold-digger, okay, so can we just drop the Ms Iceberg act now?'

The casual tone of his apology did little to cool her annoyance with him. 'No, it's not okay actually,' she said stonily. 'That was a very insulting remark.'

He shrugged. 'You know you can't blame me for thinking what I did. Murdo never stopped extolling your virtues and telling me how beautiful you were. I wanted to talk to him about business and all he could talk about was you. I thought he was in love with you.'

'He was sixty-five. I'm twenty-nine,' Caitlin said rigidly.

'Your point being?' Ray enquired lightly.

'That's disgusting.'

Ray shrugged. 'You wouldn't be the first twenty-nine year old to capture an older—rich—man's heart.'

'I was engaged to be married,' Caitlin said furiously.

'Murdo made no secret of the fact that he didn't like your fiancé.'

Caitlin's heart thumped uncomfortably against her chest. She had always thought Murdo's dislike of David had been irrational—after all, he'd hardly known the guy. But in light of recent discoveries it seemed Murdo had been right all along.

'You can't blame me for wondering what was going on,' Ray said.

'That's your suspicious mind; there was nothing going on!'

Ray shrugged. 'And then of course there was the time that I overheard you reassuring him that you weren't attracted to me...'

'I wasn't reassuring him!' Caitlin spluttered angrily. 'I was telling him in no uncertain terms how absurd his notion was about us.'

Ray grinned. 'With the benefit of hindsight I can see I might have got things wrong.'

'Not might... You definitely made a big mistake,' Caitlinsaid firmly.

Ray nodded. 'Absolutely. So, now we have that cleared up, how about I take you upstairs so you can freshen up before dinner?'

Caitlin shrugged. In truth she was a bit hungry and she was longing for a hot shower. And she supposed he had apologised... 'Okay.'

'Good.' He smiled and she noticed how his eyes were almost as dark as the raven-black of his hair; there was something intensely sensual about those eyes. 'I'm glad we have sorted that out.' He reached out and, to her consternation, stroked back a stray strand of wet hair from her face.

His touch was oddly tender and as she looked up into his eyes there was a crazy moment where she felt her stomach flip as a wild rush of pure physical attraction hit her. Hastily she stepped back from him. What the heck was wrong with her? she wondered frantically. She disliked Ray...disliked him intensely.

'So, tell me, where is your fiancé?'

The sudden question was almost as disconcerting as the feeling that had just struck her.

'He's back in Manchester.'

'Well, I gathered he wasn't here,' Ray said sardonically.

A heavy rumble of thunder filled the air and the electric lights flickered.

'The storm sounds like it's directly overhead,' Caitlin said nervously.

'Yes, seems like it.' Ray turned away. 'Come on, I'll show you up to your room.'

Relieved that the subject of David had been dropped, Caitlin followed him upstairs. Ray opened a door and led her through into a large bedroom decorated in a pale shade of lemon.

'There's an *en suite* bathroom through there.' Ray waved a hand towards the other end of the room. 'Just make yourself at home.'

'Thank you.'

He nodded, seemed about to turn away then paused.

'So…you didn't tell me… Is your fiancé following you out here?'

He seemed to be looking at her very closely and she realised that, as well as being incredibly sexy, his eyes could also be disturbingly intense, as if they could reach into her very soul and find all the secrets hidden there.

She intended to tell him that her engagement was off but instead she found herself saying something completely different. 'Yes. He's just too busy with work to come over at the moment.'

'I see.' Ray smiled and she wondered if he did see…if it was entirely obvious that David would never be joining her here. 'Well, I'll leave you to freshen up. Come down when you are ready.'

Caitlin stood where she was as the door closed quietly behind him. Why had she done that? she wondered. Why had she lied?

Maybe it was just that her pride wouldn't let her admit that she had made a mistake with David. Or maybe because she felt vulnerable around Ray Pascal. She didn't know what it was, but the guy fascinated her in some strange way. He seemed to have danger written all over him.

CHAPTER TWO

THE storm was still raging outside as Caitlin finished drying her hair. She stepped back to survey her appearance in the bedroom mirror. The mud-spattered jeans had been replaced by a clean faded blue pair and a black top with a scooped neckline, not particularly glamorous apparel but at least she looked human again. Her dark hair was shining and healthy-looking, and the shower had restored some colour to her cheeks.

Her eyes flicked towards her waistband. She had lost weight. Caitlin had always been slender but now her jeans hung slightly on her waist. It was stress, probably. She had always been the same—as soon as something worried her, weight just dropped off her. And the past few weeks had been amongst the worst of her life.

The strange thing was that there had been no hint of what was to come. Everything had seemed so settled…her wedding date fixed. Okay she'd had a few fleeting doubts about the marriage, but she had brushed them aside thinking they had just been the normal cold feet variety, the kind of uncertainties that faced most people before they made such a massive lifelong commitment.

Caitlin had thought she loved David… The only thing that had concerned her was the fact that he had never set her passions completely on fire. But as soon as those thoughts had entered her head she had always dismissed them, feeling guilty for even having given them space. Because David had seemed so easygoing and he'd made her laugh. He had been boyishly good-looking. Not as powerfully handsome as Ray, but attractive nevertheless with thick sandy-blond hair, grey eyes and a pleasing physique. Most of all she had felt safe with David. And after the disastrous relationship she'd had before him, that feeling of security had been important to her. She had been ready to start a family... Her thirtieth birthday was looming and she could feel her body clock starting to tick.

David had agreed that they would start trying for a baby straight after the wedding. Caitlin remembered how after that discussion he had pulled her into his arms and held her tight. 'I'll make you happy, Caitlin,' he had whispered. 'I promise I will.'

There had been something of the little boy about David, she thought now; something endearing. And like her he wasn't afraid of hard work. He had a high-flying career and all the glossy accessories that went with it; a top-of-the-range sports car, expensive clothes and a taste for the high life. They'd had a good time together, meals out, trips to the races with never more than a modest flutter, a good circle of friends. There had been nothing to suggest that he wasn't the respected and responsible man that he claimed to be.

Then a few months ago he had arrived home without his car. He'd told her it had been stolen and she'd had no reason to disbelieve that. At the time she had been too worried about Murdo to give it much thought anyway. His health had been deteriorating rapidly and she'd been spending most of her spare time with him. Then she had arrived home late one night and had thought they had been burgled. The TV had gone, so had the stereo and DVD player. In fact anything of any value had just been ripped out, including personal items of jewellery. She'd been alone in the flat and terrified. David had arrived just as she'd been phoning the police.

'You don't need to do that,' he said calmly, taking the phone from her and putting it down. 'It's all under control. They have already been around here.'

Caitlin believed him. She'd had no reason not to; she trusted him.

It wasn't until later in the week when she phoned the police to see how the investigation was going that she realised David had lied to her and something was very wrong, because the burglary had never been reported.

When she went in to see Murdo that day she didn't intend on saying anything, but he caught hold of her arm as she made to leave his bed.

'So what's the matter with you?' he asked gruffly.

'Nothing.'

He didn't let go of her and his grip was surprisingly strong. 'We've always been able to talk in the past.' He'd pulled her back towards the bed and she'd sat beside him.

'It's just this burglary... David didn't report it; at least, the police say there is no record of it being reported. And when I rang him at work to ask him about it he was furious with me, said the police had made a mistake and lost the report or something. He said he'd deal with it later and I wasn't to get involved.'

She remembered the look on Murdo's face. He was frail; his skin as grey as the colour of his hair, but in those few moments there was a glimpse of his former vitality in the sudden anger of his dark eyes. 'Do you believe him?'

Caitlin shrugged and looked away from him. 'Why would he lie?'

'David may not be all that he seems,' Murdo said

softly. 'I didn't tell you this, Caitlin. But a long time ago…about five months after you came to work for me, David came to collect you. There was some money sitting on the coffee table in the lounge. And when he'd gone…so had the money.' He noted the expression of horror on her face. 'I didn't tell you because I knew you'd look like that and, anyway, I'd no proof and I didn't want to risk you falling out with me.'

'How much money was it?' Caitlin asked distraught.

'The money doesn't matter.' Murdo was dismissive. 'It wasn't that much anyway… It's you I care about.' He squeezed her hand. 'If I'd had a child…a daughter…I'd have wanted her to be just like you; you know that, don't you? And I appreciate everything you have done for me—'

'Murdo, you don't need to say this,' she said tearfully.

'Yes, I do. Because the time we have together is growing short now. And I want you to know that I care about what happens to you and I want you to be happy. And, quite frankly, Caitlin, I don't think David is right for you.'

Just thinking about that conversation—one of the last conversations she'd had with Murdo—made her eyes fill with tears.

Hurriedly she brushed a hand underneath her eyes. It was strange how she and Murdo had bonded. There had been so many years between them and no blood ties, and yet when he had died it had been like losing a member of her family.

Murdo had been right about David. When she'd got back to the flat that night she had raided the cupboards and drawers to see if she could shed some light on what was going on. And that was when she had discovered the pawn tickets for their belongings and the joint credit cards that she knew nothing about. Cards with bills that she was jointly responsible for…

It had turned out that David had a serious gambling habit, although he didn't see it like that. When confronted, he had become almost violent towards her and the tone of his voice had frightened her. It had been as if he had become a stranger when he had informed her that he could do what he liked with his life, was just going through a bad patch, that if she left it to him he'd sort it out in a few weeks.

Even as she had walked out of the flat with her bags packed he had been telling her that he'd fix everything, and that she was being stupid…that it was a set-back and he'd had them before. And of course they would still get married.

If David was waiting for her to go back to him, he was going to have a very long wait.

But should she stay in France? The question churned inside her as she headed back downstairs.

Apart from the fire that still burned brightly in the stone fireplace, the lounge was in darkness.

'Ray?' Caitlin paused at the end of the stairs, wondering which way she should go.

There was no answer, only the roar of thunder and the bright flickering light of the storm illuminating the trees outside the lattice windows.

'Ray?' She wandered down the long hallway glancing through open doors at darkened rooms. Then as she rounded a corner she saw light at the end of the corridor and heard the low murmur of a radio.

'Ah, there you are.' He turned from the stove as she stepped through the doorway. 'You look better,' he said, his eyes sweeping over her.

'Well, it wasn't hard,' she said self-consciously. 'I looked dreadful before.'

'No, you didn't… You looked…' He paused, as if searching his perfect English for the exact word. 'Strained.'

'Well, I'd been driving since the early hours of this morning…and the house was a bit of a shock. Not to mention your…wild accusations—'

'Hey.' He caught hold of her arm as she walked towards him. 'I've apologised for that…so can't we just forget it?' He seemed to be looking very deeply into her eyes.

She shrugged, feeling uncomfortable again. 'Yes, I suppose so.'

'Good.' He smiled at her and she felt a surge of butterflies inside. What on earth was wrong with her? she wondered dazedly. She didn't like this man; he was arrogant, irritating and, anyway, she was off men, probably would be for the rest of her life.

Carefully she moved away from him and walked across to the stove. 'Can I do anything to help?'

'No, it's all done. I made pasta… I hope that's acceptable?'

'Very.'

'Okay, well, I'll lay the table in the dining room and we can move through.'

'Let's just eat in here, shall we?' Caitlin said quickly, not liking the thought of leaving the warmth of this kitchen for the darkened intimacy of a dining room. There was something reassuring about this friendly light space, the stylish country pine décor, the Aga, and the babble of the radio even if it was in French.

'If you like.' He shrugged.

'Shall I lay the table for you?' She pounced as he

opened a cutlery drawer. 'I may as well make myself useful.'

'Okay.' He stepped back. 'I'll open a bottle of wine.'

'That would be lovely.' Caitlin busied herself clearing the pine table, transferring the vase of daisies and some post over onto a sideboard.

They sat down opposite each other at the table. Caitlin glanced across at him apprehensively. She noticed that he had changed his clothing since they had arrived back and was wearing a dark shirt and dark trousers. The attire was more formal and made him appear even more intimidating for some reason.

What was it about Ray that unnerved her? Caitlin wondered as she watched him surreptitiously from beneath dark lashes. Was it the fact that he was able to wind her up with such insouciant ease? Or the fact that he was overwhelmingly handsome, or was it just the whole package? There was a latent power about him, a look that magnetically drew and held the senses. Everything about him was enthralling, from the way his clothes sat so easily on his broad-shouldered frame to the fact that he was French and spoke perfect English with an accent that sent shivers of sensuality racing down a woman's spine. Then there were his eyes... His most lethal weapon, dark and penetrating, they had a way of slicing through you that could disconcert and disarm all at the same time.

As if sensing her gaze, he turned those eyes on her now. The impact was intense. It had always been the same; on their first meeting just over a year ago he'd glanced at her and her senses had reeled into chaos. That one man should be able to exert so much power over her senses had scared her then... It still did now.

He smiled, a faint, almost imperceptible light of amusement in his eyes.

'Well, I'm sure Murdo would approve of us dining here together tonight,' he said. 'So maybe we should drink to absent friends?'

'Absent friends…' Caitlin raised her glass and touched it against his.

He smiled at her and she felt that same prickle of unease that told her she had to keep her wits very firmly about her.

Hastily she looked away.

There was silence between them filled with the drumming of rain against the window and the soft melody of a French song on the radio.

She looked at the bottle of wine and noticed it had a label with the name Pascal on it. 'Is this any relation to you?' she asked, tapping the label curiously.

'It's from this estate. But I have little to do with it now. My cousin is the local wine producer; I just rent him the land.'

'It's very good.'

'Not bad.' Ray nodded. 'So how long did it take you to drive here?' he asked, switching the subject.

'I broke the journey at my mother's place in London last night. Then set off at four-thirty this morning.'

'That's a long drive. You should have flown from Manchester.'

'I wanted to bring as much of my belongings as possible. Plus it gave me a chance to see my mum before leaving.' Caitlin remembered the horrified look on her mother's face when she had told her that her relationship with David was definitely over and that she was moving to France.

'Couldn't David have driven over later with your belongings?' Ray asked.

Caitlin tried to concentrate on what he was saying and shut out the image of her mother, who had tried to persuade her to stay on in London with her to think about things. 'Do you really want to finish with David?' she had asked in some distress. 'All the invitations are out. The wedding is only weeks away. Caitlin, you are probably just suffering from nerves.'

She hadn't wanted to tell her mother that the breakup was down to something far more serious than nerves. The truth would just have been too much for her to bear. It had been better to sound upbeat and positive, as if she had made the right decision and the split had been amicable.

'Caitlin?'

'Oh, sorry.' Aware that Ray was waiting for an answer, she quickly pulled herself together. 'I suppose he could have driven over later, but as I told you earlier he's pretty busy at work right now.'

'What does he do for a living?'

Caitlin toyed with her glass. Why did he keep asking her about David? she wondered irately. 'He's in advertising.' With a determined effort she fixed him with a direct look and changed the subject. 'What about you?' she asked. 'What do you do for a living?'

'I'm an architect.'

'Oh, yes, I remember Murdo telling me now.' She smiled. 'He said you were a rare combination of creative genius and hard-headed businessman, and that you could sometimes be a bit eccentric.'

'Coming from the king of eccentricity, I'll take that as a compliment,' Ray said easily.

'Well, he was an artist and I suppose they are allowed to be eccentric,' Caitlin reflected.

Ray smiled. 'I suppose they are,' he conceded. 'His paintings are fetching tremendous sums of money, I believe.'

'Yes, so I heard.'

'He left me two in his will as a matter of fact. I haven't received them yet—they are being crated up and shipped out to me next week.'

'That was kind of him.' She looked over at Ray hesitantly. 'He seemed very fond of you.'

'He was an old family friend.' Ray shrugged. 'Best man at my parents' wedding and later when my father died he helped my mother through a difficult time.'

'I didn't realise the bond was that close.' Caitlin toyed with her wineglass. 'And yet you didn't come to his funeral?' She had looked for him on that dreadful day, had been surprisingly disappointed not to see him at the graveside.

'I was in Paris on business. I didn't know he'd died until later that week; it was too late by then.'

'I see.'

'So what are you going to do about Murdo's house?' Ray changed the subject. 'I know that inheriting it was a shock, but I'm sure the state of the place was an even bigger one.'

'Yes. I don't know what I was expecting but it wasn't…that.'

'I did try to tell him that the place had fallen into a state of disrepair, but I don't think he was listening to me.'

'He was good at that.' Caitlin smiled. 'If he didn't want to hear something he'd just blank it completely. As my grandma would have said, he had selective hearing.'

Ray laughed. 'You're right, he did.'

'And he was as cantankerous as hell sometimes...' Caitlin smiled. 'But, strange thing is, I'm really going to miss him. We grew quite close in the two years I looked after him.' She looked up at him quickly. 'Well, when I say we grew close I mean...he was like a father figure to me,' she explained quickly.

'Relax, Caitlin,' Ray said with a shake of his head. 'I think we have established that.'

'Well...I suppose I still can't get over the fact that you thought Murdo was in love with me... It's just... wild.'

Ray shrugged. 'He always did have an eye for a pretty woman.'

'He was also very ill.'

'Not too ill to try a spot of matchmaking, though?'

'He had some very strange ideas sometimes,' she murmured.

'Yes, very strange,' Ray said wryly. 'I've been thinking about it and I suppose that's why he left you his house. It's a last-ditch attempt to throw us together.'

'No...I don't think so,' Caitlin said quickly.

Ray met her eyes steadily. 'Why not? It seems obvious now I think about it. Murdo always was stubbornly persistent when he got an idea into his head.'

'Even so, I don't think he would be that dogged.' Caitlin's voice was firm. She wanted to squash that suggestion in Ray's mind the way she had squashed it in her own. Even entertaining that idea for a moment was highly embarrassing. 'It's totally preposterous.'

'Totally.' Ray met her eyes and smiled. 'As is the thought of you living in that house. The place is uninhabitable and it will be hard work to put it right. Which is why I think it would be best all around if you sold it to me—'

'Now hold on a minute...' Caitlin cut across his sweeping statement, instantly on the defensive. 'I've only just arrived, Ray, and I'm hoping to keep the house. I like the idea of living in the French countryside and I'm no stranger to hard work.'

'I'm sure you are not. But you have to admit that the house would demand a lot of attention, you would have to organise builders and decorators and I bet neither you nor David speak French.'

'I speak some French.' She angled her chin up and met his eyes determinedly. It was one thing if she decided not to stay...quite another being told she was incapable of staying! 'And I'm very handy with a paintbrush.'

To her annoyance he seemed to find that remark amusing. 'I think you'll need a little more than a lick of paint to put that place right.'

'I'm not incapable.'

'Then there is the land...' Ray swept on as if she hadn't spoken. 'Over a hundred olive trees and a small vineyard—it all takes expertise and hard work.'

'I didn't know there was a vineyard.'

Ray nodded. 'Murdo didn't make the wine himself— he used to sell the grapes. It was a bit of a hobby for him, really.'

'I could do that,' Caitlin reflected thoughtfully.

'Now, come on, Caitlin.' Ray shook his head. 'You're not serious?'

'Why not?'

'Because, as I just said, looking after a place like that takes a certain amount of expertise.'

'I could learn.' She shrugged. 'I could do anything I set my mind to.'

'Maybe you could...' Ray said slowly, noticing the light of determination in her eyes. 'But why would you want to? You are a qualified nurse.'

'I feel like a change of direction.' She toyed with her glass of wine. Nursing had been rewarding, but recently she'd also found it exhausting both emotionally and physically. And after the trauma of her breakup with David she felt like a whole new start. 'Actually I was thinking that I could convert the...building into a small guest-house.'

For a moment Ray's eyes seemed to narrow on her. 'And what does David think about that idea?'

Caitlin frowned. Why did he keep bringing David into this? It really irritated her. 'Nothing is set in stone yet,' she said noncommittally. 'I'll have to take a closer look at the property in daylight.'

'You mean he's not too happy about it,' Ray said dryly.

She met his gaze frostily. 'This is my decision, not David's.'

'Call me old-fashioned, but I thought when you were engaged to be married you made joint decisions,' he said bluntly.

He watched the rise of colour in her cheeks and then reached to refill her wineglass. 'Sorry, it's none of my business.'

'You're right, it's not.'

For a moment Ray was silent. He ran one finger around the rim of his glass thoughtfully. 'It seems to me that the house is causing you problems already. And it's going to get worse. The place is a mess and it is certainly no place for a woman on her own.'

'You are very patronizing, do you know that?' she said quietly.

'Well, I'm sorry if you feel like that.' He looked up at her then, his eyes incisive and direct. 'But I'm just being honest. So let's cut to the bottom line, shall we? I want that land and the offer I made to Murdo is still open.'

'I haven't decided what I'm doing with the house yet, Ray. I haven't had time to think—'

'Well, let me help you think more clearly.' He cut across her impatiently and then named a sum of money that made her breath catch.

For a moment she didn't say anything, she was too stunned to make a reply.

He glanced over and met her eyes. 'It's a generous offer considering the condition of the place.'

'I'm sure it is,' she murmured, totally taken aback.

'Well, think about it.' His mouth twisted in a sudden grin. 'When you've taken a look at the place in daylight you can give me your answer.'

In other words he was quietly confident that once she had assessed the level of work needed she would take his money. Caitlin would have liked to toss her head defiantly, tell him she didn't need his money, that she was staying. She didn't like that smug attitude that said clearly that he didn't think she was up to the challenge, and she didn't like giving up so easily on her dream for a new life. But she had to be sensible. The mess of her relationship with David had left her savings sadly depleted and she didn't know if she could afford the renovations the house needed.

'Okay.' She inclined her head. 'I'll consider it. But I feel I should tell you that selling the house isn't a straightforward option.'

'Why not?'

Caitlin shrugged. 'Apparently Murdo put a few provisos in his will covering that possibility.'

'What kind of provisos?' Ray asked.

Caitlin noticed the sudden tensing of his attitude and had to smile. Ray obviously thought that throwing money about could solve any problem. But maybe he had reckoned without Murdo's steely determination. 'I don't honestly know.' She shrugged. 'I was so overwhelmed by Murdo's generous gift that I didn't pay much attention to the details. It was something about waiting six months. Or I had to live here for six months...' She shrugged. 'Something along those lines.'

Ray drummed his fingers impatiently against the table. 'Well, I suppose we'll get around all that. With the help of a good lawyer there are usually ways around most problems.'

'Maybe.' Caitlin sipped her wine and couldn't resist adding. 'But that's if I decide to sell.'

'Once you've looked at that place again I think you'll agree that I've offered a very fair price.' Ray lifted his glass in a salute.

Caitlin straightened her cutlery. She didn't feel like drinking to that toast. The thought of a new beginning in France had been all that had kept her going these past few weeks. It had been the one ray of hope in an otherwise bleak future. Going back to England didn't seem like something to feel overjoyed about.

'I haven't made any promises,' she said quietly. 'And I have to tell you I won't be rushing to find ways of breaking Murdo's will. I respected him too much for that.'

'You are obviously a woman of great integrity,' he said.

She glanced over at him, unsure if he was being facetious. 'For a gold-digger, you mean?'

His lips twisted wryly. 'I thought we'd bypassed that.'

'So did I. But your tone leaves me in some doubt.'

For a moment their eyes met across the table. There was something forceful about the way he looked at her, something that made her raise her chin slightly and defiantly. 'So as I said before…I'm not making any promises. I'm a woman who enjoys a challenge and that house might be just what I'm looking for.'

There was a flicker of some emotion in the darkness of his eyes and then a grin tugged at the sensual curve of his lips. 'I can suddenly see why Murdo might have thought that you and I would be well suited.'

'Can you?' Caitlin was taken aback by the observation. 'Why's that?'

'Because I also enjoy a challenge, Caitlin.'

Disconcerted, Caitlin looked away from him. She didn't know what to say to that.

Outside the thunder growled threateningly, filling the silence between them. The lights flickered.

Suddenly Caitlin felt as if she had endured enough for one day, she just wanted to escape to the sanctuary of her room. 'Anyway, I think I'll turn in now if you don't mind.'

'Not at all.' He picked up their empty plates and brought them over to the sink. 'Would you like a coffee before you retire?'

'No, thank you, I'm really tired.' She was just getting up from the table when her mobile phone rang. It was lying on the counter and Ray picked it up for her. 'You put it down when you were laying the table,' he said, and then glanced at the screen before handing it over. 'It's your fiancé.'

'Thanks.' She felt her heart thud with apprehension as she took the phone from him. Then as she turned from Ray's line of vision she clicked the disconnect button. There was no way she wanted to have a conversation with David tonight.

'We got cut off,' she said as Ray looked over at her inquiringly.

Before she could switch the phone off completely it rang again. 'I'll just take the call in the other room, if you don't mind.' Hastily she stepped out of the room and walked down the corridor, turning her phone's ring tone onto silent.

The lounge was still in darkness, the fire had almost burnt out—just a fragile orange glow remained. Caitlin sat down on the edge of the sofa and tried to pull herself together. Just the thought of talking to David made her feel sick inside. She couldn't face it… There was too much pain inside her…too much hurt altogether.

It was quiet in the room; the only sound was the rain against the windows. Back in her apartment in Manchester there was always a constant rumble of traffic despite the double glazing. Was that where David was sitting now as he tried to phone her? Did he regret his behaviour?

Although she was furious with him, there was a part of her that also felt sorry for him. He obviously needed help.

'Are you okay?' Ray's voice from the doorway made her strive very hurriedly to compose herself.

'Absolutely.' Her voice wobbled a little and she swallowed hard before continuing. 'Everything is fine.'

He switched on one of the lamps and looked at her, his dark eyes searching over her face.

'The weather is shocking in Manchester, apparently,' she lied cheerfully and forced herself to smile.

'I know you didn't speak to him, Caitlin,' he said calmly.

'Of course I spoke to him.' She sat ramrod straight and watched as he walked over to throw a log on the fire.

'No, you didn't, you hung up on him.' Ray stimulated the dying embers of the fire with a poker, prodding it back to life until the flames crackled greedily around the wood.

She met his eyes with a tinge of annoyance and decided to just sidestep the issue. She didn't want to talk about this and it was none of his damn business anyway. 'I don't know where you have got such strange ideas from. Now, thank you for dinner, I'm going to bed if you don't mind.'

Unfortunately as she headed for the stairs she had to walk past him and that was when he reached out and took hold of her left hand, halting her in her tracks.

'The strange ideas started when I noticed this.' She looked down and watched as he lightly traced his thumb over the white band of naked skin on her third finger. 'It's a bit of a give-away, Caitlin,' he said softly. 'I noticed it straight away over dinner. If you were my fiancé I wouldn't want you to walk away without the symbol of our betrothal visibly in place.'

She stared down at her finger, the finger that had worn David's ring for three years, and a shivery feeling raced through her, but strangely it wasn't caused by the thought of her broken engagement—it was caused by the way Ray was touching her and the strange intimacy of his tone.

She pulled away from him. 'How very observant of

you.' She tried to keep her voice brisk, but it had a quaver to it that wasn't normal. 'If you noticed it straight away, why did you keep asking me about David?'

'Because I thought it better you tell me about it in your own time.'

'Dear Abby eat your heart out,' Caitlin muttered sarcastically.

'Dear who?' One dark eyebrow rose. 'Who is this Dear Abby?'

'She's an agony aunt. I was being facetious.'

Ray's lips twisted wryly. 'You don't need to hide behind sarcasm, Caitlin, and you don't need an agony aunt.'

'I suppose you are going to tell me what I do need now,' Caitlin murmured.

Ray reached out and put a finger under her chin, tipping her face up so that she was forced to look at him. 'You need a good friend, and in the absence of Murdo and everyone else you've left behind in England... If you need to talk, I'm a good listener.'

'I don't need to talk.' She stepped back from him because the touch of his hand against her skin was starting to do crazy things to her senses. 'I'm fine... absolutely fine.'

'If you say so.'

'I do.'

'So Murdo was right all along. David wasn't the man for you.' The steady, serious way he looked at her made the shivery feeling inside her intensify.

She looked away from him in confusion. 'Well, maybe...'

'So you must just tell yourself that you have had a lucky escape.'

Caitlin thought about all the plans and dreams she'd

had for the future…about the wedding…the baby she had wanted. 'I don't feel very lucky,' she murmured huskily.

For just a second, the veil of composure slipped from Caitlin's expression and Ray saw a glimpse of vulnerability in the beautiful eyes that looked up at him. Then she pulled herself sharply up. 'Anyway, I'll wish you goodnight,' she continued on briskly.

'Goodnight, *chéri*.' His voice followed her as she moved away. 'Sweet dreams.'

CHAPTER THREE

DESPITE the fact that she was so tired, Caitlin couldn't sleep. She tossed and turned and her mind seemed to catapult from the life she had left behind to her strange new surroundings. She lay listening as the rain lashed against the window and thought about the house down the road with its crumbling walls and ramshackle rooms. Had she made a mistake coming to France?

When she finally fell asleep her dreams were a confused tangle of places and people. She could see David, his grey eyes glinting with amusement as he asked her if she really intended living in that house. 'Come home, Caitlin,' he whispered earnestly. 'Come home and we'll be married, this is madness.'

Then suddenly she was walking down a church aisle in her cream dress. She could see the scene vividly, could hear the organ playing, could even smell the scent of the roses in her bouquet. Her best friend Heidi smiled at her and waved. 'I knew it would all work out well in the end,' she whispered.

Her mother was wearing her new blue outfit with the matching wide-brimmed hat that she had searched the length and breadth of London for; she wiped a tear from her eyes as Caitlin passed. 'You look wonderful, darling; see, I told you it was just nerves.'

Then as she reached the top of the aisle she could see David waiting for her. He looked very handsome in his dark suit, hair glinting in a shaft of light shining down from one of the windows. He turned slowly and smiled at her. Only it wasn't David, it was Ray!

She woke up, her heart racing with shock, and sat up. The pretty room with its primrose-yellow walls and floral bedclothes was unfamiliar to her. Sunlight streamed through the open curtains, reflecting on the mirror of the dark wooden dressing table, and glinting into her sleep-filled eyes.

It took a moment before she realised where she was, another moment for her to realise that her heart was racing because of a dream. She lay back against the pillows and sighed. What an absurd thought! Marrying Ray indeed! Even if he were the marrying kind, which she strongly suspected he was not, he was definitely not her type.

She flung the bedclothes off and walked over to the window. The rain clouds had gone, replaced by a clear, freshly washed blue sky. A misty haze of heat shimmered over the undulating countryside criss-crossed by vineyards and lush green fields awash with crimson poppies. The scene was so beautiful that Caitlin could hardly wait to get outside. Her bad dream forgotten, she headed for the shower.

There seemed to be no one about downstairs. Caitlin went into the kitchen and put on the kettle, then stood at the kitchen sink looking across towards the purple mountains in the distance.

What would today bring? she wondered. She supposed she should ring her mother and tell her that all was well and she was safe. Where was her phone? she wondered suddenly. She didn't remember seeing it in her room this morning. Quickly she retraced her steps through to the lounge, wondering if she had left it in there last night. She was searching behind cushions when Ray came downstairs.

'Looking for this?' He held up her phone.

'Yes.' Caitlin straightened and watched as he walked across towards her.

Hell, but he was impossibly handsome, she thought. Like her, he was wearing jeans. They clung to his lithe hips and waist, and the light blue shirt he wore emphasised the breadth of his shoulders.

She tried to avoid touching him as she took the phone back. Why she didn't know…he just made her incredibly wary.

'So, did you sleep well?'

She looked up and met his gaze and felt herself dissolve at the impact of his dark eyes.

'Yes, thanks.' She tried not to think about her crazy dream.

'Good.' He smiled and she noticed the sensual curve of his lips. 'We'll have some breakfast and go and see about your car.' He turned towards the kitchen and then glanced back. 'By, the way you've missed two calls this morning.'

'Have I?' Caitlin looked down at her phone but there was no message to say she'd missed calls.

'Yes. One from your mother, lovely woman—we had a long conversation.'

'I beg your pardon!' Caitlin hurried after him towards the kitchen. 'You mean you answered my phone?'

'Yes…well, it was sitting next to me.'

'You've got no right to answer my phone.' Caitlin was furious. 'Whoever it was could have left a message with the answer service.'

'They did leave a message…with me.' Ray seemed totally oblivious to her rage. He took some croissants from a bag by the bread bin. 'Now. I know the English like their bacon and eggs—'

'I don't want anything to eat.'

'Now, Caitlin, I promised your mother that I would keep an eye on you and that involved making sure you ate something,' Ray said calmly.

'How dare you speak to my mother—'

Ray shook his head and glanced over at her. 'She's very worried about you, you know. She thinks you have gone far too thin.' His eyes flicked down over her. 'And actually I agree with her.'

Caitlin could feel heat seeping up under her skin and she felt as if she wanted to explode. 'That is my private phone and you shouldn't have touched it.'

'So, shall I rustle up some bacon and eggs or do you just want the croissants?'

'I don't want anything.'

'We'll have the croissants, then. I have some chocolate ones here and you can go heavy on the butter if you like... I know that is an English penchant.' The smell of them mingled with the coffee he had set on the stove.

He pulled out a stool at the breakfast bar. 'Sit down and relax, for heaven's sake. So I answered your phone...it was no big deal.'

Caitlin sat down. 'So who else rang?' she asked, her throat tight.

'Someone called...Heidi—yes, that's it, Heidi, like the book.'

Caitlin felt herself relax slightly. At least it hadn't been David. That would have been too awkward and embarrassing.

'Heidi is also worried about you. She seems like a very lovely young woman.'

'Yes.' Caitlin nodded. 'She's my best friend.'

Ray put the plate of croissants and a cup of espresso coffee in front of her.

'So what was the message?' she asked shortly.

'They both want you to phone them.'

Caitlin nodded. It could have been worse, at least her mother didn't know the circumstances of her breakup with David. If she had started to divulge the details it would have been mortifying. And Heidi was too discreet to have said anything.

'Okay...well, thanks,' she muttered grudgingly as she took a sip of her coffee. 'But don't answer my phone again.'

Ray pulled out the chair opposite her. 'Anyone would think you were in the secret service or something.'

'I just like my privacy respected, that's all.'

Ray nodded. 'Oh, and your mother wants to come out on a visit,' he added casually.

Caitlin almost dropped the coffee in shock. 'You are joking now, aren't you?' she asked hopefully.

Ray shook his head. 'I'm afraid I had to tell her about the sorry state of your house. She was most concerned.'

'You did what?' Caitlin put the coffee-cup down in the saucer with a clatter. 'Are you joking?'

'No. She's your mother, Caitlin, she asked me directly about your circumstances, so out of respect I had to tell her.'

Caitlin's eyes darkened with fury. 'You did that on purpose, didn't you?'

'I don't know what you mean.' Ray shrugged, but there was a gleam of humour in his dark eyes that said he knew exactly what he had done.

'Yes, you do. You told my mother how bad the house was in the hope she'd talk me into selling to you. That was below the belt, Ray.'

'Rubbish.' Ray shook his head. 'But, yes, I have to admit that I hope you will see sense about keeping that place.'

'Just how badly do you want that land?' she asked suddenly.

'Not badly enough to increase my offer, if that's what you mean,' he said succinctly.

Caitlin pushed the croissants away and stood up. 'Come on, then, let's go. The sooner you take me back to the house, the sooner I can decide what I'm going to do.'

Ray sipped his coffee and made no hurry to follow. 'You haven't finished your breakfast. Your mother would be most upset.'

'Well, my mother is not here, is she?'

'Not yet.' He grinned.

The drive back to her house was totally different from the journey last night. They had the windows of the car down and the breeze that blew through her hair was warm and scented with the fragrance of the eucalyptus trees that lined the tarmac road. The sky was a dazzling blue, the landscape dotted with wild flowers and as they pulled up at the front of her house even that looked different. Yesterday it had seemed sad and dilapidated, but this morning it seemed to have gained a certain look of charm. The terracotta roof glowed in the sunshine and the peeling yellow paint on the walls seemed almost quaint surrounded by the tangle of ivy and wisteria that curved around the windows.

'It needs a lot of work and money spending on it, doesn't it?' Ray said as she climbed out of the car.

'Actually I was just thinking that it doesn't look as bad as I'd thought.' She shaded her eyes to look up at it, and then slanted him a wry look over the bonnet of the car. 'In fact, I'd go so far as to say I'm pleasantly surprised. I really like it.'

Ray shook his head. 'It's up to you what you do, of course, but let me tell you, I know for a fact it needs a new roof, plus it is probably infested with woodworm.'

'No one would ever guess you don't want me to stay here,' she said with a grin.

'I didn't say that.' He smiled back at her. 'On the contrary, I was just trying to be helpful.'

Something about the way he looked at her made her senses swim. Hastily she looked away from him. 'Sure you were.'

She walked over towards her car. The mud around the wheels had dried into solid red soil. 'So, any suggestions on how I get my car out of this rut?' she asked lightly.

He didn't answer immediately, but when she glanced over at him she saw that he was taking a long-handled shovel from the back of the car.

'You are organised.'

'Prepare for any eventuality, that is my motto,' he said and met her eyes with a cool steady look. 'You'll have to remember that if you are going to stay around here.'

She watched as he rolled up his sleeves and then started to dig beside each wheel of the car. He made the work look effortless, but in the dazzling heat of the sun she doubted it was. As his huge shoulders heaved against the hard soil Caitlin wondered idly if he worked out in order to keep such a wonderful physique. There was a raw sexuality about him that despite all her best intentions, drew her attention...fascinated her. But then it had always been like that. From the moment she had opened Murdo's front door to him, she had been disconcertingly conscious of his sex appeal.

He turned. 'Do you want to get in and start the engine now, try and drive it out?'

'Yes, certainly.' Annoyed by the thoughts that had been going through her mind, she took her keys out of her bag and unlocked the car. Okay, he was a very handsome man, she told herself, but he had danger written all over him, she wasn't interested in him. The next man she got involved with was going to be safe and dependable, a true family man. She certainly didn't want any dizzying heights—it was too far to fall.

A wall of heat hit her as she opened the car door, along with the smell of burning vinyl. Gingerly she slid into the driving seat and started the engine. It spluttered into life and on Ray's instruction she eased it forward so that it climbed easily out of its hole and back onto the solid safety of the road.

Relief flooded through her. 'Thank you so much,' she said as she got out of the vehicle, this time leaving the windows down. 'You've been very kind and I'm totally in your debt,' she added impulsively.

'That's true.' He smiled at her, a teasing light in his eyes. 'So, what are you doing on Monday night?' he asked suddenly.

Her stomach seemed to go into free fall. 'Monday?' She stared at him blankly, the question catching her completely by surprise.

'Day after tomorrow,' he informed her, leaning back against the bonnet of her car and fixing her with that nonchalant dark-eyed stare that seemed to slice straight through to her bones.

She rubbed the palms of her hands against her jeans and found they were wet with a perspiration that had little to do with heat, and her mouth felt suddenly dry with panic.

He noted the sudden vulnerable light in the beauty of her green eyes, before she looked away from him.

'Well, if you are asking me out, Ray...I'm not really ready to start dating again.' Her heart hammered fiercely against her chest. She felt like a teenager who had never been asked out before.

'Relax.' In contrast to her he sounded totally cool. 'I'm not asking you out.'

'Oh!' Her glance skated back to meet with his and she could feel her cheeks going from orange to a shade of beetroot. 'What are you asking me, then?'

He grinned. 'I'm giving a dinner party for some business clients, and I could do with someone to assist me.'

'You want me to cook for you?' She was startled by the request, and to think she had imagined he was asking her out! Embarrassment mingled with annoyance now. Honestly, the cheek of the guy! she thought crossly.

'No, I don't want you to cook for me. I'm getting caterers in. All I really need is for you to act as hostess for the evening, just so things are kept flowing easily.'

'Oh!' She was momentarily puzzled. 'I'm not so sure about that,' she said cautiously. 'Isn't that something your girlfriend should be doing?'

'It's okay, you won't be treading on anyone's toes, I assure you,' he said with a smile, then added with a teasing gleam in his eye, 'I'm between lovers at the moment so you'd be doing me a big favour.'

'Well...' She wasn't quite sure what to say to that.

'Thanks, Caitlin.' He swept on decisively. 'Tell you what, I'll come back this afternoon to see how you are getting on here and we can make arrangements for the evening then.'

Before she had a chance to say anything else he had turned away and was heading back towards his car. She watched helplessly as he opened the boot and threw the shovel in, before driving off with a casual wave of his hand.

Caitlin shook her head and felt slightly bemused by the speed with which she had been railroaded into that! 'Honestly!' she muttered to herself as she opened her bag to get the key of the house. As if she didn't have enough to think about.

The front door squeaked in protest as she pushed it open and peered inside. If the outside of the building had suddenly acquired a charm of its own under the blaze of the Mediterranean sun, the same could not be said about the interior. It was just as dark and just as creepy as she had thought it was yesterday. The floorboards were uneven and the staircase looked as if a few of the steps were rotted through. Maybe Ray was right about the woodworm, she thought as she walked across the lounge area. Gingerly she felt around the casement of the window looking for the fastenings so that she could throw open the shutters.

When she finally found them sunlight flooded into the room, and for a moment all she could see were dust particles dancing in the air. Then slowly she took in her surroundings. It was a good-sized room with a huge stone fireplace at one end. Hastily she flicked the dust-sheets off the furniture. The blue sofa looked soft and comfortable. A large cream rug covered the centre of the room; it was covered in a grey layer of dust and had definitely seen better days. But she felt a stir of excitement inside her—the place had definite possibilities.

She walked through to the kitchen. It had a quaint old-fashioned charm, the units were dark wood and some of the doors were hanging off. But there was a large Belfast sink and what looked like an old wood-burning stove. A dining room led off to the left. But instead of walking through there, Caitlin unbolted the back door and walked outside. She found herself in a sunny court-yard with a crazy-paving path that led down through a small grove of almond and olive trees. She walked through the dappled shade down the path and as it turned a corner she found herself in a field criss-crossed with the stubbly growth of vines. Someone had tied a rope swing from an almond tree and she perched herself gingerly on the old wooden seat and looked back towards the house.

She could see that some of the red roof tiles were missing and one of the chimney pots looked as if it had a bush growing from it. The place definitely needed a lot of money spending on it, money she probably didn't have. But that didn't stop the pure burst of joy that assailed her. The house had definite potential and she loved it! Loved the red roof and the old shuttered windows, loved the blue irises that lined the path and the blossom on the almond trees. If it took every ounce of her energy and her last penny, she wanted this property.

When Ray returned it was late afternoon. The front door was open and he stood on the doorstep and called her name. There was no answer so he stepped inside. The strong odour of bleach hit him. The lounge was completely empty of furniture; the windows were open and the floors scrubbed to a deep honey yellow.

'Caitlin.' He raised his voice an octave but there was still no reply. Gingerly he made his way over the clean floor and into the kitchen. And that was where he found her. She was wearing a pair of denim shorts and a blue halter-neck top and she was on her hands and knees on the floor, scrubbing with an old wooden brush, singing tunelessly at the top of her voice as she worked. It took a moment for him to realise that she was listening to a Walkman because she had her back to him and he couldn't see the earphones. It was only as she turned slightly to rinse her brush in the bucket of water beside her that he saw the wire leading up under her dark hair and saw the blue machine clipped to the front of her belt.

She still hadn't seen him and he smiled to himself as he watched the way she was working. Her energy fascinated him, as did the wiggle of her very shapely bottom in the tight-fitting shorts.

She sang away to herself as she sat back on her heels to survey her work; stretching slightly as if her shoulders were stiff. Ray had a brief glimpse of her flat midriff and the up-tilted swell of generous breasts. And from nowhere he felt the heat of sexual attraction hit him hard.

'Caitlin.' Impatient with himself, he stepped forward into the periphery of her vision.

'Oh, gosh, you startled me!' Flustered, she pulled the headphones off her ears. Her hair fell glossy and fluid around her shoulders as she threw it back from her face to look at him. The sound of music, tinny and contorted through the wire, sang on for a second before she clicked a button off. 'How long have you been standing there?'

'Only a few minutes. I did call you several times but you were too busy singing.' He noticed with amusement that she blushed. He liked the way he was able to make her blush; it stirred up a feeling of devilment inside him, made him want to wind her up...see the soft swell of colour increase even further.

'You could enter for the Eurovision with a voice like that,' he added softly. 'Incredible!'

'Very funny.'

He smiled as he saw the soft pink glow spread over the top of her cheekbones. He wondered if she would blush like that if he kissed her...what she would look like with her hair spread out around her on white pillows, the flush of lovemaking still on her skin.

'I see you've been down to the village.' He transferred his attention to the basket of groceries that was sitting on the sideboard.

'No, I haven't ventured as far as that. I just went into the little shop a couple of miles down the road.' She got to her feet and lifted the bucket of water to throw it away. 'I was pleasantly surprised to find that they stock most things.'

'Ah, Madeline's shop.' He nodded. 'Yes, it's very convenient.'

'She's very friendly as well and spoke perfect English. She was telling me that her nephew is a builder. She is going to send him up to see me so that he can give me an estimate on work that I want doing.'

Ray's eyebrows rose. 'From that...and all the work you are doing here, am I to deduce that you have made up your mind to stay?'

'Yes.' She answered with her back towards him as she washed her hands under the cold-water tap. A necessity as the only hot water she had had been boiled on the stove. When he made no immediate reply she turned and met his gaze. 'Look, I know you think I'm mad and I know you want the land here...but I've decided to give it my best shot,' she told him honestly. 'So I'm sorry but I will have to turn down your...generous offer to buy the place.'

He frowned. 'I think you are making a mistake.'

His words irritated her; obviously he wanted rid of her. 'Yes, well, it's my mistake to make, isn't it?'

'Certainly.' He inclined his head. 'But at least wait until after the builders have given you their estimates before closing your mind completely to my offer.'

Caitlin shook her head. 'I want the house. I'm sorry, Ray. I've made my mind up—'

'And I'd advise you to get more than one estimate on the work that needs doing here,' he cut across her as if she hadn't spoken. 'Madeline's nephew, Patrick, is a willing worker but inexperienced.'

'Yes, I know how the game works. I get a few estimates and choose the best.'

He nodded. 'And remember the best doesn't always equal the cheapest.'

She glared at him. 'You think I'm a helpless female, don't you?'

'No.' He smiled to himself as he saw her eyes blaze. 'I'm just giving you some advice.'

'No, you're not. You're thinking, She's not going to last here… I'll give her two months and then offer her less for the land and by that time she will be so broke and so ready to leave that she'll take it.'

'Maybe I am.' He laughed at the look of outrage in her eyes. 'You don't know what you are taking on here, Caitlin—'

'Well, whatever I am taking on, I'm going to give it my best shot,' she said firmly. 'So, now that we've sorted that out, shall we have a coffee and discuss Monday night?'

Ray shrugged. 'Okay. We'll put the subject of you selling in abeyance. And we'll discuss it again when you've had the builders' reports.'

Caitlin ignored that. She didn't want to discuss the subject again, she desperately wanted to stay here and make it work. 'So what time do you want me to come over on Monday night?' she asked lightly instead as she filled a pan of water to put on the stove.

'About six-thirty, but don't worry, I'll call for you. Whereabouts will you be staying? There's a hotel in the village that's very good—'

'Hotel?' Caitlin frowned and looked over at him. 'Why would I stay in a hotel? I'm staying here.'

'You are not thinking of sleeping here tonight, are you?' He sounded shocked.

'Of course I am. This is going to be my home now.' She glanced around at him. 'Will dried milk do? As I have no fridge yet I didn't bother buying fresh.'

'I take my coffee black. But, Caitlin, you can't possibly stay in this house.' His dark eyes seemed to pierce right into hers with steady determination.

'Why not?'

'Well, for one thing, it's got no electricity.'

'I've already sorted that problem.' She reached into her shopping and held up a candle. 'I've been told it won't be possible to reconnect me for a few weeks. So unless I want to wander around in pitch-black these will suffice.'

He shook his head. 'I can't see how you can possibly contemplate sleeping here until you have a new staircase and a new roof.'

'I'm going to sleep downstairs in the dining room.' She took some mugs from a box. 'I'm afraid you'll have to have instant coffee. It will be a while before things start to get civilised around here.'

'You're not kidding.' Ray's voice was derisive. 'Look, you'd better stay with me up at the house, at least until you've got the electricity fixed.'

'That's a very kind offer, Ray, but honestly I'll be fine.'

'I don't think so.' He reached out and touched her lightly on the face. 'Come and stay with me, Caitlin, for a few days at least. I don't like to think of you here alone.'

The gentleness of his tone, the touch of his hand and the thought of spending even more time with him sent a mixture of panic and pleasure through her in wildly disconcerting waves.

The water in the pan started to bubble. A bit like her temperature around him, she thought wryly as she stepped back from him. 'That's very kind of you, Ray. But this place isn't as bad as you think.'

That statement met with silence. Hastily she turned away from him and made the coffee.

'Actually I made a great discovery as I was moving the furniture from the lounge. The sofa pulls out into a bed. So I'll be fine on that.'

There was a lot of incredulity on his face as she handed him his drink. 'The place is uninhabitable,' he said bluntly.

'No, it's not. I've got this great old stove.' She patted the bar on the cooker behind her. 'You can burn anything in it, and I found a load of old wood out the back so it should keep me going for ages.'

He still didn't look convinced so she put down her coffee. 'Downstairs is fine, Ray, and there is even a downstairs bathroom. Come on, I'll show you what I've done to the back room this morning.'

Ray followed her through a door at the far end of the kitchen into the dining room. It was a charming space with south-facing windows that looked out towards the olive grove and the purple mountains beyond. Like the other downstairs rooms, she had obviously scrubbed it out. There was a white tablecloth on the pine dining table and a white jug of blue irises. The sofa bed was under the window and was already made up with white linen, a colourful patchwork quilt and several scatter cushions. He had to admit that with a few womanly touches Caitlin had succeeded in making the place look comfortable and homely. Ray was impressed at what she had accomplished in such a short space of time and he felt he might have underestimated her; there seemed to be more to Caitlin than first met the eye.

'You see, this will be quite adequate for now,' she said defensively, then as she caught him looking up at the cracks in the ceiling added quickly, 'Obviously it still needs sorting out properly, but that will have to wait.'

Ray perched himself down on the arm of the sofa. 'I'll agree you've certainly made the place look a lot better.'

'I can sense the word "however" hovering on your lips,' she said wryly.

'Can you?' He looked over at her then and smiled. 'Maybe it is, but I won't say it...not just yet anyway. You are a very stubborn woman, Caitlin.'

She shrugged. There was a certain way he had of looking at her sometimes that made her feel almost light-headed. And she liked the way he said her name; it rolled from his tongue sometimes almost like a caress.

She tried to blot those thoughts out very firmly. Her name sounded attractive on his lips because of his accent. And he probably bestowed that look of teasing, sensual approval on a lot of women.

'So all I'll say instead is that if you have any problems you can phone me.' She watched as he put his coffee down on the window ledge and took a gold pen from the top pocket of his shirt. 'Have you got a piece of paper? I'll write down my mobile number for you.'

'I won't need to phone you, Ray,' she said determinedly, 'because I'm not going to have any problems; I've got everything under control.'

'I'm sure you have.' He grinned. 'But you never know, you might want to phone me anyway.' He reached out and caught hold of her hand. 'It doesn't matter about paper, this will do.'

She watched as he turned her wrist and proceeded to put his number on her arm in blue ink.

The touch of his hand and the cool firmness of the pen against her skin were unsettling. 'There, you can write it down somewhere safe later.' He smiled into her eyes and that was even more disquieting.

'Thanks.' Her heart was thumping against her chest in a most peculiar way. She pulled her hand away from his sharply and hastily took a step backwards. 'But as I said before I have everything under control, so you won't be getting any damsel-in-distress calls from me.'

'Well, maybe you'll change your mind and want me to rescue you when the old timbers begin to creak and the bullfrogs start their nightly chorus, or when you've had enough of playing house and waiting for builders.' He put the pen away and stood up.

'In your dreams,' she replied, her voice hardening. 'It will take more than a few frogs to make me run scared.' Now she wanted to scrub the number off her arm immediately. 'I will manage here,' she said quickly. 'Being alone doesn't bother me and, anyway, I'm expecting to have this place up and running as a bed and breakfast business by the end of the year. There are five good-sized bedrooms upstairs that will lend themselves very nicely to having *en suites* put in.'

'It's an ambitious project.'

'Maybe, but once I make my mind up to do something I usually see it through to completion.' She raised her chin slightly.

'That's something else we have in common, then.' Ray smiled and stood up. 'Well, you've got courage, Caitlin, I'll give you that.'

There it was again, that rolling, sexy emphasis on her name. No man had a right to sound that good as well as look that attractive. He should come with a health warning, she thought hazily. *Warning: this man could seriously affect your heartbeat.*

'So, anyway, I'll see you Monday night,' she said, hastily gathering her senses.

'Yes, I'll pick you up at six-thirty,' he said, heading towards the door.

'There's no need, I'll make my own way over,' she told him firmly as she followed him back through the house. Somehow it seemed important that she arrived under her own steam, maintained her complete independence.

She thought he was going to argue the point, but he didn't. 'Okay.' He stopped at the front doorway and looked back at her. 'And don't forget, ring if you need anything,' he said over his shoulder as he strode away towards his car.

She watched as he drove away, his vehicle crunching over the uneven surface of her drive. Then as he disappeared silence fell and darkness started to steal over the landscape.

Caitlin looked down at the number written so boldly on her arm and went inside to wash it off. But before she did, she found herself writing it down in her address book; why, she didn't know. She'd never ring him, she told herself sternly. *Never.* Then she returned her phone calls from that morning and tried to reassure her mother that she was fine.

As soon as Ray reached the château he headed for the phone and dialled his business partner in Paris. 'We've got more of a problem with plot twenty-seven than I had first thought. Yes, Murdo's property. One very determined lady is in residence and it looks like it's going to hold back the whole development.'

He tapped his fingers impatiently against the rosewood counter as he waited for the reply, and then grinned. 'Yes, she is, actually. No, I'll take care of it. It's a temporary hitch, I'm sure. Oh…and see if you can get hold of a copy of Murdo McCray's last will and testament.'

CHAPTER FOUR

CAITLIN had never lived alone before. At eighteen she
had got a job at a central London hospital and had
moved straight from living at home into the nurses' accommodation there. She had shared a room with two
other girls and it had been a very lively time. When they
hadn't been studying for exams or working they had
been out partying. There had never been a dull moment…or a quiet one.

That was when she had met Julian Darcy, a first year
intern, incredible-looking, and as sexy as hell. She had
fallen completely under his spell. For a full year they
had dated and Caitlin had honestly thought he was the
one…but unfortunately Caitlin hadn't been the only one
the suave doctor had been whispering sweet nothings to.

Julian was the reason she had moved away from her
job in London to work in Manchester. She had moved
into a flat up there with her best friend, Heidi, who was
also a nurse. And slowly she had recovered her confidence and her heart. The two of them had really enjoyed
sharing a flat. And again there had rarely been a time
when Caitlin had felt alone. They had made lots of
friends and gone out on lots of dates and then they had
both fallen in love, Heidi with Peter, Caitlin with David.
It had been during the run up to Heidi's wedding that
David had asked her to move in with him. She hadn't
said yes straight away; she hadn't been sure if it was the
right thing for her. But David had been persistent. He
had wooed her with bouquets of flowers, extravagant

gifts. And he had told her over and over again how much he loved her, how much he needed her…and how he wanted to be with her forever.

It was the forever bit that had finally won her around. Caitlin had witnessed her own parents' divorce when she was twelve, and she never wanted to go through anything like that. Commitment was important to her. So when she had moved her things in with David's she had honestly thought it was for the rest of her life.

They had got engaged a few months later and had intended to get married the following spring but somehow the date hadn't been set for another two years.

Murdo had sometimes remarked that David wasn't her soul mate, because if he were she wouldn't have kept putting off the wedding date.

She had dismissed the notion out of hand. Now she wondered if it was true. Maybe subconsciously she had known David wasn't right for her. Maybe she had even been on the rebound from Julian?

Lying alone on the sofa bed, in the darkness and deepest silence of the French night, Caitlin reflected on the past and tried to make sense of it. Maybe she was just destined to always fall for the wrong kind of man. She'd read articles about that—about women who kept making the same kind of mistakes. Trouble was, she had tried to play safe with David…had thought he was steady and reliable…

But when she had found out about his gambling debts all her trust in him had evaporated overnight. If he had lied to her about that, what else had he lied about? And worst of all David had refused to acknowledge that he had a problem. Suddenly their life together had seemed like a façade and she just hadn't been able to go through with the commitment of marriage. After deep contem-

plation in the weeks that had followed, Caitlin had contacted everyone to tell them the wedding was cancelled.
It was the hardest thing she had ever had to do.

At first light of dawn Caitlin got up. Work was the
best way of keeping her mind off her problems. And it
wasn't hard to keep busy. There was so much to do.
Sunday passed in a haze of hard exertion, and then on
Monday morning Patrick arrived.

He was a good-looking man in his late twenties with
tousled dark hair and serious eyes. He wandered around
her house with a worried look on his face, scratching his
head, making Caitlin feel as if she were waiting for a
life and death doctor's report.

'So what do you think, Patrick?' she asked finally
when she couldn't stand the suspense of waiting any
longer.

'I think,' he said in careful pidgin English, 'that the
house needs much work. First it needs to be rewired…
next it needs damp proof…and new stairs…new roof…'

'So how much money are we talking here? Don't forget I want new bathrooms.'

Patrick scratched his head again. 'The roof is a job
for my brother Raul. But I can do everything else. It will
probably take a few months. If you like you can pay me
by the week and buy the materials separately.'

'That sounds acceptable… So how much do you estimate it will cost?'

Patrick named a sum that was just within her budget
and a wave of relief rushed through her. However, the
feeling was short-lived because it was then that Patrick
delivered his bombshell.

'Unfortunately, that is not the end of the work that
needs to be done,' he said slowly. 'You see, you are not

connected to the main water supply here and that is something you should rectify.'

'But I've got water,' Caitlin said with a frown.

'That supply comes from a nearby well. You don't know how long it will last. Maybe a month…maybe six months…maybe six years…' Patrick shrugged. 'It is—how you say?—unreliable. You need to get connected to the mains.'

'And how much will that cost?'

'It's a big job, not one I can do,' Patrick said firmly. 'There is a lot of land here needing brand-new pipes. My cousin had a similar problem last year.'

'And how much did he pay to rectify the situation?'

Patrick shrugged and then went on to name a sum of money that, on top of all the other work that needed doing, sent her budget wildly in excess of anything she could afford.

As the sun started to fade and Caitlin got ready for her evening with Ray, she was still reeling from Patrick's assessment. If the water ran out she would be beaten here before she had even started. But if she fixed the water first she wouldn't be able to afford the structural work on the house. It was a catch-22 situation and a depressing thought. However, as she washed her hair in cold water and boiled pans of water in order to have the shallowest of baths she tried to convince herself that everything would be okay. Maybe the water would last six years. After all that rain the other day maybe sixteen years! Patrick wasn't an expert on the subject; he had admitted that, so she would look on the bright side.

Trying to forget about her financial problems, Caitlin stepped into her black dress and peered at her reflection in the small vanity mirror. The last time she had worn this dress had been to a cocktail party for David's work.

Back then it had been a snug fit over her hips; now it seemed to hang a little loose. However, in the soft glow of candlelight she looked presentable. The cold water seemed to have given her hair a luxuriant shine and her skin had a soft honey glow from two days of sunshine. But would she pass scrutiny under the blaze of electric light at Ray's residence? Caitlin felt a flutter of butterflies. Then, annoyed with herself, she stepped away from the mirror and picked up her bag. It didn't matter what she looked like; she wasn't trying to impress Ray, and this wasn't a date.

As she blew out the candles in the dining room and walked through to the lounge she heard a car drawing up outside. The sound was abnormally loud in the soft stillness of the night.

She peeped cautiously out from the front windows. Caitlin loved the solitude here during the days, but at night when darkness fell she had to admit to feeling a little nervous. A car door slammed and there was the sound of footsteps. Caitlin could see the dark silhouette of a man. Moonlight slanted over him, throwing a long shadow that made him appear exceptionally tall. It wasn't until he reached the top of the garden and looked up that she could see it was Ray. He was wearing a dark suit and his hair gleamed almost blue-black in the silver moonlight. Relieved that it was someone she knew, she went to open the door, swinging it wide before he had a chance to knock.

'Hi,' she said lightly. Now that she had discovered it wasn't a mad axe murderer who was making his way to her door, her heart rate should have decreased, but instead it seemed to increase wildly as her eyes connected with his. 'I thought we'd agreed that you wouldn't call for me.'

'I know.' He smiled. 'But I was passing anyway. So I thought if you were ready you might like a lift.'

'Thanks. Yes, I am ready, actually; you couldn't have timed it better. I'll just blow the candles out in here, won't be a moment.'

He stepped inside the door to wait for her and as she crossed towards the sideboard she was very conscious of the way his eyes followed her.

'You look very beautiful tonight, Caitlin,' he said softly.

'Thank you.' Her heart rocketed unsteadily, as if it were trying to escape. It was crazy to feel this nervous she told herself as she bent to extinguish the white church candles. He was just being polite; the fact that the compliment sounded dangerously provocative was just because his accent was so deliciously sexy.

'So how are things going with the house?' he asked as she made her way back towards him in darkness.

'Everything is going very well.' She made herself sound positive and upbeat; she wasn't going to admit she had problems already. 'Patrick is going to start work tomorrow.'

'I thought you were going to get a few quotes before you decided who to give the job to?'

'Yes, but I liked Patrick and he can start immediately, which is great. Time is money, after all, and the sooner I can get this place up and running, the sooner I will be recouping my expenses.'

'Sounds sensible.'

'Yes, I thought so.' Her instincts told her Patrick was a decent guy. The job would be fine. 'So how are the arrangements for dinner going?' she asked, swiftly moving on before Ray could throw any doubts on the situation.

'Everything is under control.'

Caitlin had the feeling that everything was always under control in Ray's life. He had that air of power about him.

He took hold of her arm as they walked outside. She could smell the tang of his aftershave; it was fresh and warm and immensely attractive. The touch of his fingers against the bare skin on her arm sent shooting little shivers of awareness rushing through her. It was extremely perturbing.

He opened the passenger door of his car and saw her safely inside before going around to the driver's side.

'So the catering staff have arrived, I take it?' she asked, trying to concentrate her thoughts back on the evening ahead.

Ray started the car engine. 'Yes, there was a delightful aroma of fresh herbs and roast lamb wafting through the house when I left. So you can rest assured your cooking skills will not be needed.'

'Just as well,' Caitlin said lightly. 'I had a weird dream last night that I burnt all the food for your dinner party and everyone shook their heads and said they had expected as much from *la cuisine anglaise.*'

Ray laughed at that. 'I don't know why you dreamt that. I did tell you I was getting staff in.'

'I know.' Caitlin shook her head and looked out at the dark blur of the passing landscape. She didn't tell him that in the dream Murdo had turned up at the table and demanded to know why they hadn't set their wedding date yet.

'I have been having the strangest dreams recently,' she murmured quietly.

'I'd have thought any nightmares you would have

would be centred on that house of yours,' Ray said lightly.

Caitlin frowned. 'The house will be fine, Ray. It's got loads of potential.'

'Yes and loads of drawbacks.' Ray flicked her an amused glance. 'Did Patrick tell you about the water problem?'

'You know about that?' She looked over at him in surprise.

'Of course I know about it. I kept telling Murdo that it needed sorting out.'

'Well, it's obviously been like that for years, so I don't see any reason to rush into fixing it just yet.'

'You must be joking. If you want my advice that's the first job you should do.'

'Yes, well, I've got Patrick's advice, thank you, and that's all I need at the moment.'

'He won't be able to fix the water problem, you'll have to get other contractors in for that, and in my opinion you should budget at least double what Patrick has told you it will cost.'

'Double?' Caitlin felt her heart bounce somewhere down into her shoes. 'That's crazy. With respect, Ray, I don't think you know what you are talking about.'

'I know that place is a money pit.' Ray shrugged.

'Maybe, but I've got my budget well planned out.' Caitlin angled her chin upwards defiantly. Ray's know-it-all attitude really was starting to irritate.

Ray glanced over at her and smiled to himself. 'So how much is your budget for the place?'

'That's really none of your business,' she muttered.

'Well, let's see…let me guess.' Ray pursed his lips thoughtfully, before naming the exact sum that she had discussed with Patrick.

Caitlin turned to look at him in astonishment. 'How on earth do you know that?'

He smiled. 'I've been in Madeline's shop,' he said pointedly. 'Patrick is Madeline's nephew.'

'Yes, I know that, but it doesn't give her the right to discuss my business.' Caitlin was furious.

Ray pulled the car to a standstill outside the château. Then he turned to look at her. 'She's just a concerned neighbour, Caitlin. The fact is that Murdo had that work priced years ago and it was twice the sum you are bandying about with Patrick now.'

'Well, maybe I'm more resourceful than Murdo.' Caitlin reached for the car handle. 'And I'm not going to worry about water because, let's face it, after that storm the other night water levels must be high.'

'This is early spring, Caitlin,' Ray said quietly.

'Ray, if you don't mind I don't want to discuss this a moment longer,' Caitlin said as she got out of the car.

Ray shook his head. He had to admit he liked her determination. It was almost a pity that she was going to fail.

There was an air of quiet sophistication about the house. The dining room looked resplendent, the polished table was laid with sparkling silver and cut-glass crystal and there were three members of staff in the kitchen who were going to serve the meal.

As Ray talked to the chef about the menu Caitlin tried not to dwell on their conversation in the car. She knew what Ray's game was. He wanted her land; it was in his interest to put her off staying here. Angrily she repositioned a vase of freshly cut dark red roses so that it didn't obscure anyone's view on the table. But apart from that there was nothing for her to do.

'I don't think you really needed me here tonight at all, Ray,' she said as the chef departed.

Ray didn't answer her immediately and she turned to find him leaning against the doorframe, watching her with a lazy, almost indolent stare.

'Now, you are not going to sulk all evening just because I'm right about your house, are you, *chéri?*' he asked softly, almost teasingly.

'You're not right about the house,' she retorted crisply. 'And I never sulk.'

He smiled at that. 'Good. Then how about a pre-dinner drink?' He moved to the sideboard.

'A glass of white wine would be nice,' she said.

Their hands touched briefly as she took the glass. 'Thanks.' She took a step backwards and searched for something to say to fill the silence that suddenly seemed to have opened between them.

She could feel his eyes moving over her in an assessing manner, as if he was taking in every detail about her dress and her hair.

'And in answer to your earlier question I really do appreciate you being here tonight,' he said softly.

She looked up and met the directness of his eyes and for some reason her heart seemed to give a nervous thud of anticipation. He looked extremely handsome in the dark suit, the pristine whiteness of his shirt throwing his olive skin and dark hair into sharp contrast. But there was also an air of danger about him, she thought warily. She couldn't explain it, but there was something about him that made her feel infinitely nervous. Maybe it was the predatory way he looked at her sometimes…or the sensual curve of his lips. Or that way he had of cutting straight through her defences just with his eyes, making her feel as if he could see straight into her soul.

'So…who is coming, this evening?' she asked briskly, trying to dismiss that notion.

'My business partner Philippe and his wife Sadie. Philippe runs our office in Paris so it's a chance for us to touch base. Also a new business client, Roger Delaware, with his partner Sharon, who I am hoping will put a lot of work our way over the next few months.'

'Sounds like quite an important evening for you.'

'Yes…I must admit I would like Roger to sign up with us. He's planning to build a new hotel in Cannes. It's just the type of development our company likes. So I'm hoping tonight will help swing things in our favour.'

'So the evening is more about business than pleasure.'

'Well, I'm hoping it's going to be about both.'

His dark eyes held with hers for a moment and then hastily she looked away before she could be sucked towards that magnetic, charismatic appeal. If captivating the opposite sex was an art form, Ray had the talent in spades, she thought warily. It seemed almost to come naturally to him. She wondered how many women had been passionately in love with him, only to have their hearts broken…probably hundreds. It would be a brave woman who took Ray on. 'So who usually acts as your hostess on these occasions?' she asked curiously, trying to concentrate on the golden liquid in her glass rather than on him.

'For the last few months a woman called Claudette. But things didn't work out between us.' He shrugged in that Gallic way of his. 'That's life.'

He didn't sound too upset, which led Caitlin to suspect that he'd been the one to finish it. 'You strike me as the kind of man who probably breaks a lot of hearts.' She spoke impulsively.

'Do I?' He looked amused. 'Why's that?'

'I don't know.' Her eyes moved over him contemplatively. 'Something about you.'

'Well, I enjoy the company of women and I am a red-blooded male, but I hope I don't break hearts. It certainly is not my intention—in fact I'm very careful about the women I choose to have relationships with. And I am always honest and up front about the fact that I have no wish to get married again.'

'You loved your wife very much, didn't you?' Caitlin reflected. She watched the way his eyes seemed to darken with some emotion she couldn't begin to analyse. 'Murdo told me,' she murmured hastily. 'And I'm sorry, I didn't mean to pry.'

'That's okay. You're right, I did love my wife...very much.'

Caitlin looked away from him, feeling sorry that she had intruded on something so intensely personal.

'So what about you? Do you break hearts, Caitlin?' he asked, changing the subject with that swift ease that never failed to disconcert her.

'I hope not.'

'But it must have been you who called the wedding off—no man in his right mind would have done that.'

'Thanks for the vote of confidence,' she said wryly, a little suspicious of the flattery. She hesitated. 'I did call it off...but it wasn't something I wanted to do...'

'You did it because you had no choice, because he hurt you.' It was a statement rather than a question, so she made no reply.

'You know, the best way to get over one man is to get involved with another.' He put a hand under her chin and tipped her face upwards so that she was forced to look at him again. 'Having a little fun helps clear the mind and heal the heart.'

The gentle touch of his hand against her skin seemed to burn like a branding iron. She really tried not to blush, but she could feel her skin heating up as if someone had lit a fire under her.

'Is that what you do?' She stepped back, trying to break the intimate spell that suddenly seemed to be swirling powerfully between them. 'Jump straight from one relationship into another?'

'I haven't got a broken heart,' he said lightly.

'I see.' She took a sip of her wine and gathered herself together. 'I'm afraid, Ray, that I've got some bad news for you.' She forced a lightly teasing note into her voice and met his eyes directly.

'Apart from not selling me your property, you mean?' He smiled.

'Oh, yes, apart from that.' She waved a hand in airy dismissal and angled her head to one side. 'The thing is, Ray…and brace yourself for this…the thing is that you are never going to make an agony aunt. Your advice is rubbish.'

He looked at her and his lips curved in a smile that also lit his eyes. Then he laughed, a warm, genuine laugh that somehow also seemed to set her pulses racing. 'I like you, Caitlin,' he said with a shake of his head. 'I have to tell you I like you very much…'

Their eyes met and for a moment she was tempted to say she liked him too. But it was a fleeting thought and one she immediately buried.

To her relief the shrill ring of the front doorbell interrupted them. 'That will probably be Philippe and Sadie.' Ray turned away. 'They said they would be early.'

Ray's business partner and his wife were both French. Philippe was about forty-five, slightly on the portly side, his dark hair greying at the temples. He had an air of sophistication; here was a shrewd man who was successful in business and very laid back about it. His wife Sadie was about ten years younger than him and stunning. Her dark hair was coiled into an attractive style high on her head, emphasising her delicate features, her high cheekbones and dark almond-shaped eyes. Her cream dress was obviously from a designer boutique in Paris, but even if it had been from a charity shop she would have looked good in it, because her figure was superb, voluptuous yet slender. She possessed the kind of chic style that seemed to come so naturally to continental women.

'It's lovely to meet you, Caitlin,' she said as she kissed the air at either side of Caitlin's cheeks. 'I've heard all about you.'

'Have you?' Caitlin looked over at Ray in surprise and he smiled. 'Oh, yes, I've told Philippe and Sadie all about my pesky neighbour who stubbornly refuses to sell out to me.'

'Are you still going on about that land, *chéri?*' Sadie stood on tiptoe to kiss Ray. Caitlin noticed that her scarlet lips made contact with Ray's skin, and her hands lingered on his arms as she drew back to look up at him playfully. 'Honestly, you own most of the countryside around here as it is.'

Caitlin noticed that Philippe sent her a warning look, as if she was being too outspoken, but Sadie seemed unconcerned. And so did Ray.

'I do,' he replied easily, a gleam in his eye. 'But that doesn't stop me wanting more. However, I've discovered my new neighbour has other assets so I'm content to leave things as they are…for now.'

'What do you mean, ''other assets''?' Caitlin asked

distractedly, unsure if she liked the direction of this conversation.

Ray gave her that lopsided grin that she was starting to recognise. 'I mean the pleasure of your company, of course.'

Caitlin shook her head. She wasn't going to allow herself to be affected by Ray's compliments. When the mood struck him he probably knew all the right things to say to make a woman feel special and get what he wanted. And of course he was a born flirt. She remembered the way he'd looked at her earlier. *You know, the best way to get over one man is to get involved with another...* He'd been teasing her, of course, and it didn't necessarily mean a thing, but if she were to let down her guard and take him seriously she'd be courting trouble.

Instead she turned her attention to Sadie as they moved into the lounge.

'Have you come all the way down from Paris for dinner tonight?'

Sadie smiled. 'Yes, we flew down to Nice and motored up. We often do that, and of course we have a potential new client joining us tonight so it's pretty important to secure that contract.'

'Let's hope his partner, Sharon, is in a better mood tonight than the last time we got together.' Philippe sighed. 'Good job you're here, Caitlin, otherwise we might never get this contract.'

'Why is that?' Caitlin asked in puzzlement.

'You mean Ray hasn't told you?' Sadie laughed. 'I'm afraid Sharon has a bad case of lust for Ray. It was quite embarrassing last time we got together. And we were worried it would make Roger back out of doing business with us altogether.'

'Oh, I see.' Caitlin smiled over at Ray. 'So much for the pleasure of my company.'

'I told you, Caitlin, you are quite an asset,' he said without a shade of remorse. Then he smiled that warm smile that seemed to light up his eyes.

The doorbell rang and Ray got up to answer it.

'He's incorrigible, isn't he?' Sadie laughed. 'And gorgeous—everyone falls in love with him. I have lost count of the beautiful women that have been on his arm. Is that not so, Philippe?'

'He just hasn't found the right person yet,' Philippe said, somewhat crossly. 'I don't think you should be giving Caitlin the wrong idea.'

Caitlin wanted to say that she didn't care and that she wasn't one of his many girlfriends, but she didn't get the chance because Ray entered the room with his remaining guests.

As the evening progressed Caitlin relaxed. Ray's friends were all very agreeable and he was certainly a charming and attentive host. She watched him surreptitiously during dinner and noted how the women hung on his every word. She also saw exactly what Sadie meant about the partner of their new business client. Sharon was definitely smitten by Ray. The woman was in her mid thirties, a rather glamorous blonde with a shapely figure and smouldering blue eyes. As the wine flowed she became more and more outrageously flirtatious, fluttering her eyelashes at Ray and making blatant references as to how attractive she found him.

Ray handled the situation with suave ease and Roger Delaware didn't look too perturbed by his partner's behaviour, but Caitlin agreed with Sadie: businesswise the situation did not bode well.

'So what do you do for a living, Caitlin?' Roger

Delaware asked suddenly as Sharon reached across the table to place a hand on Ray's in order to tell him how wonderful dinner had been.

Caitlin couldn't help feeling sorry for Roger. He seemed a pleasant guy, a lot older than Sharon—he could possibly have been in his early sixties—but very attractive.

'I have a small holding not far from here and I'm converting it into a bed and breakfast business,' she answered lightly.

'Really. How interesting. That's how I made my money, you know, in the hotel business back in the USA. Started in Texas and gradually worked my way through each state. Now I'm moving my attention to the continent. I'm hoping Ray is going to design a fine building for me.'

'I'm sure he will, I've heard Ray is very talented,' Caitlin said with a wry smile. She had often listened as Murdo had waxed lyrical about Ray's skill as an architect.

'Yes, he has an unrivalled reputation, I know that.' Roger nodded. 'But it comes at a price…' He shook his head.

'Roger, if you started out in Texas I'm sure you know that only the ropey ends of the meat trade are cheap, you have to pay prime money for prime steak.'

Roger laughed at that heartily. 'You've got a point, Caitlin, you've got a point.'

'Well, I don't know too much about Ray's business dealings,' Caitlin admitted, 'but I *do* know he's very much in demand. Anybody who is anybody wants Ray Pascal. I suppose it's like buying a Prada handbag or Jimmy Choo shoes—there is a certain chic about having them.'

'You think so…?' Roger nodded. 'Yes, I suppose you are right, and I have a certain image to maintain. My hotels are known for their style.'

Caitlin smiled back at him and reached to top up his wineglass.

'So tell me about your B&B.' Roger leaned a little closer.

'Well, it's small and I'm certainly not going to make a fortune out of it. But it will suit me. After years of living in cities it's nice to be out here in the fresh air of the countryside. And renovating the place is proving to be quite a challenge.'

'A challenge is putting it mildly,' Ray interjected as he removed his hand from under Sharon's for the second time. 'I think Caitlin must have the courage of a lion to take the place on.'

'I'm enjoying it.' Caitlin shrugged. 'But I have a lot to learn. There is a small vineyard that I would like to get up and running, and an olive grove that I'm sure I could make extra money out of. Only problem is my knowledge is pretty limited.'

'Are you living in Murdo's old place?' Philippe asked suddenly.

Caitlin nodded.

'Well, it's structurally unsound, isn't it?' Philippe glanced over towards Ray for clarification. 'Didn't you have surveyors go to look at it one time for Murdo?'

'I don't remember that, Philippe,' Ray said with an edge of impatience in his tone.

Caitlin wondered if it was her imagination, but she thought Philippe looked annoyed by Ray's reply.

'But I know if Caitlin doesn't get connected to the water mains she might be out of water there some time soon,' Ray continued with a shrug.

Caitlin fidgeted in her chair. She didn't want to talk about this. 'The place is fine; it just needs a bit of time and some TLC.'

'So how long have you and Ray been an item?' Sharon suddenly cut across all the talk of Caitlin's house, her tone bored. Then she fixed Caitlin with a direct look that was so forceful it was almost aggressive.

Suddenly Caitlin was conscious of everyone's eyes on her. She wanted to say categorically that she and Ray were not dating...but she knew very well Ray was hoping her presence here as his partner would encourage Roger to do business with them. So she didn't know how to answer. 'Well...I...'

Ray came to her rescue. 'Caitlin and I met last year through a mutual friend of ours. But it's only in the last few weeks that romance has blossomed, is that not so, *chéri?*' He leaned across and squeezed her hand gently as he spoke.

She met the challenging light in his dark eyes and knew very well that he was giving her the standpoint from which to back him up. 'Eh...yes. It's been an unexpected development...' She went along with him hesitantly and he smiled.

'Totally out of the blue,' he agreed. 'But that's the thing about the love bug—you never know when it will bite. I went over to Caitlin's one day and there she was singing away to herself looking extremely fetching and I just thought...she's perfect...the most beautiful woman I have ever seen...'

Caitlin pulled her hand away from his uncomfortably. He was going over the top now. 'Don't exaggerate, *darling,*' she warned him crisply.

His smile widened as if he found her embarrassment endearing.

'Let's move into the lounge and have coffee, shall we?' Caitlin pushed her chair back from the table, wanting to put an end to this very quickly.

'Good idea,' Ray agreed easily. 'Then maybe we can talk a little business, Roger.'

'Certainly.' Roger's tone was jovial. 'We will have to get things moving pretty quickly with this project, Ray. Pull out all the stops.'

Caitlin excused herself and headed for the kitchen. The catering staff had left over an hour ago but the place was spotless. She busied herself putting cups and saucers on a tray as she waited for the water to boil.

Ray followed her into the room a few minutes later.

'So which am I?' he inquired with a grin. 'The prime piece of meat or the designer accessory?'

She swung a glance around at him, humour dancing in her green eyes. 'Sorry, was I a bit over the top?'

'Hey, I'm not complaining. Whatever you've said to him it seems to have worked. He's no longer haggling over the price, it's when can I start.'

'I think that's probably down to the very impressive meal,' Caitlin said dismissively.

'And maybe the way you smiled at him,' Ray added softly.

She looked over at him.

'Thanks for helping me out in there.' Something about the way he said that, the way he met her eyes, sent little darts of awareness pulsating through her.

'That's okay.' She shrugged the feeling away and then laughed. 'You dug me out of a hole and I dug you out of one. We'll call it even shall we?'

'If you want.' He crossed to stand beside her.

'Did you really send a surveyor up to Murdo's property once?' She tried to concentrate on the conversation and not on the way he was watching her, with that intense, steady gaze.

'No, Philippe must have been confusing your house with somewhere else.'

'Thank heavens for that.' She gave a wry smile. 'At least the place isn't going to fall down before I can fix it.'

'No, it's not going to fall down.' He smiled and tucked a strand of her hair behind her ear so that he could see her face more clearly. 'You hide behind your hair sometimes, do you know that?'

'Do I?' Her voice wavered a little; the touch of his hand had sent volts of electricity through her like lightning through a conductor.

Desperately she searched for something to say... something that was light and distracting. 'Sharon was rather persistent, I thought.'

'Very, but you played the part of girlfriend perfectly. In fact, is there no end to your talents?' He lowered his voice provocatively.

He stepped even closer. She could smell the evocative tang of his aftershave; feel the heat of his body just a whisper away from hers.

As she tried to move away from him he put a detaining hand on her arm and then somehow she found herself facing him, looking up at him instead.

She noticed how his eyes were on her lips and her heart started to thump out of control. 'I suppose you should get back to your guests...' She made an attempt at sounding sensible but her voice had an unsteady, husky quality.

'Ray...?' It was Sharon's voice calling him from the hall, but neither of them moved. It was as if they were locked in their own private world.

'Ray, where are you?'

The voice came nearer.

'I think your prospective mistress is looking for you...' Caitlin tried to force her brain into some semblance of sanity.

'Not funny, Caitlin,' Ray admonished. He reached up and brushed his fingers softly over her high cheekbones, following the contours of her face gently down to the sensitive area at the side of her neck. The caress sent thrilling little shivers of sensation shooting through her. 'And, anyway, I've got someone else in mind for that position.'

Before she could even formulate a reply his head lowered closer to hers; she could feel the softness of his breath against her skin, see the flecks of deepest gold in his dark eyes.

'Ray...' Her breath came out in a rush as she whispered his name. He covered her lips with the warmth of his, then gently...slowly...tasted her, caressed her with lips that were dominantly masterful...yet tenderly possessive. The sensation was one of overwhelming eroticism; it was as if he were pulling every string of her consciousness, tugging deep inside her to find the sensual core of her womanhood.

Caitlin couldn't help herself responding. She moved her hands to rest against his shoulder, feeling his strength beneath her fingers as they curved into his shirt. Her lips trembled with need against his. Somehow reality faded away and all she was left with was a sense of need...an almost desperate hunger that was like a gnawing ache. She heard herself give a small, breathless whimper as he moved even closer, crushing her body against his.

She could feel the warmth of his chest burning through to the softness of her breast, and the sensation

made her tingle with pleasure. She wanted to be closer...
She wanted to immerse herself in him, feel the pleasure
of his hands against her naked skin.

'Sorry to interrupt.' Sharon's cool voice from the
doorway made them break apart.

'Sorry, Sharon, we didn't hear you come in.' Ray
sounded remarkably offhand. But Caitlin's emotions
were raging all over the place. She felt mortified at how
she had responded to him, and at the same time she was
angry with Sharon for interrupting, because she wanted
so much more...

'I did call a couple of times.' Sharon's eyes held
Caitlin's; there was venom in their blue depths. 'But you
obviously had other things on your mind.'

'Yes, we did.' Ray sounded completely unconcerned.
'So, what can we do for you, Sharon?'

'Claudette is on the phone for you,' Sharon answered
pointedly.

'Okay, I'm coming.' Ray flicked a glance at Caitlin
and smiled as he saw the glow of heat high on her cheekbones, the overbright sparkle in her green eyes. 'I'll
leave you to finish the coffee uninterrupted, Caitlin.'

'Good idea.' She turned away from him and reached
for the kettle.

Her hand shook a little as she poured boiling water
into the coffee pot. She was annoyed with herself for
feeling so shook up. Ray had kissed her because flirting
and seduction were just a game to him, and the fact
Sharon was around to witness their closeness was a bonus. She should shrug the moment off...forget about it.

'It's strange that Claudette should ring tonight, isn't
it?' Sharon remarked as she leaned against the kitchen
table and nonchalantly lit a cigarette.

'Is it...?' Caitlin swallowed and tried to steady her

voice. 'What's strange about it? She's just a friend of Ray's.'

'A bit more than that, Caitlin—she was Ray's hostess at the last dinner party he threw for us. And they looked very much a couple.' She blew out a long curl of smoke and regarded Caitlin through narrowed eyes. 'But then, as we all know, Ray's partners don't last very long.'

'Not until now, anyhow,' Caitlin replied coolly, infuriated by the enmity of the woman's words.

'Well, darling, only time will tell,' Sharon said, her voice almost gleeful. Then she turned and left the room.

What a bitch, Caitlin murmured to herself. But reluctantly she had to admit that, although she didn't like the woman, perhaps she had a point. Ray was a smooth operator.

She remembered her reaction to his kiss. It had been incredible. She couldn't understand why she had felt that way. Some kind of chemistry had flared between her and Ray from nowhere…and it was shocking. But what was even more shocking was the fact that no man had ever succeeded in turning her on like that before. Never had a kiss felt so explosive. The loss of control that she had experienced with Ray a few moments ago was a whole new experience and it scared her.

She took a moment to compose herself before going back through to join everyone.

Ray had just put the phone down as she stepped back into the lounge. 'Here, let me help you.' He moved to take the tray from her and as she passed it over their eyes met. Instantly flame flared inside her again. Her heart thumped unevenly against her chest, and hastily she looked away from him.

'We were just saying, Caitlin, that we would love to come and have a look at your house some time,' Roger

Delaware was saying cheerfully. 'Sharon and I are going to be in the area for a couple of days, so maybe we could come and visit.'

Caitlin swallowed her dismay. 'Well, yes…but not yet. The place isn't really ready for receiving visitors and it's going to be even more of a mess tomorrow. I've got builders coming in.'

Ray watched Caitlin as she passed Roger his coffee and he tried not to think too deeply about the way she had responded to him earlier… The heat of his desire was only just starting to fade. If he dwelt on how much he wanted to take her to bed right now he was liable to throw all the guests out into the night.

He liked the way she was able to handle herself so confidently. Roger Delaware hadn't taken any offence at the subtle way she had put him off visiting her.

She laughed at something Philippe had said, her eyes sparkling with merriment for a moment as she gave a quick and funny reply.

Ray smiled. Yes, Caitlin was good to have around…a terrific hostess, very appealing to the eye…and extraordinarily sexy.

And that was when he decided that business could be put on hold until he got to know this fascinating woman much more intimately.

CHAPTER FIVE

SUN streamed in through the windows of the dining room. It was warm on Caitlin's face and for a while she lay on the sofa bed between waking and sleeping, memories from last night's dinner party drifting lazily through her mind. At the end of the evening Ray had suggested she stayed overnight rather than make the journey home. The offer had sent warning signals into orbit and she had hastily refused. After the kiss they had shared she hadn't even wanted him to drive her home, saying she would get a taxi, but he had brushed the suggestion aside and insisted on escorting her. Short of being extremely rude, she'd had to accept.

All the way back he had kept up a light conversation but she had hardly been able to concentrate on what he'd been saying. All she'd been able to think about was how she would react if he were to kiss her again. Consequently as soon as the car had pulled up by her front door she'd jumped out and, with a cheery wave, she had rushed for the sanctuary of her house and had slammed the door tightly behind her.

Groaning at the memory, she flung back the sheets and stood up. She was annoyed with herself for allowing one kiss to spook her like that. It would have meant nothing to him at all and it should have been the same for her. So why had it kept her awake for hours last night?

The question tormented her and fiercely she tried to forget it. She didn't want to start thinking too deeply about it again today. There was too much to do. Besides, she had probably imagined the sensual intensity of the moment. Ray had just been fooling about in order to keep Sharon at a distance, and she'd had a couple of glasses of wine. The incident was best laughed off and forgotten.

She had just dressed in shorts and a T-shirt when Patrick arrived for work. Caitlin made him a cup of coffee and they chatted easily about which job to tackle first. They decided that it should be the staircase, and as Patrick unloaded his old pick-up truck and carried tools into the house to start ripping out the old set of steps Caitlin closed the doors through to the kitchen and dining room so that the dust couldn't reach her living quarters.

As work progressed in the house Caitlin went outside to try to restore some order to the overgrown garden.

The sun slowly climbed up into the azure-blue sky and by midday the heat shimmered with intense ferocity over the olive grove. Even though Caitlin was in the shade she was so hot that her throat felt raw with dryness. If the heat was like this in early spring she couldn't help but wonder what it would be like here in the summer. Hotter than Manchester, that was for sure, she thought with a grin as she took a swig of her bottled water and then climbed up a ladder that she had positioned in order to prune branches from a tree. It was hard work and she was still up the ladder an hour later with only a few branches cut when Ray arrived.

He stood at the base of the tree and admired the shapely length of her legs in the denim shorts. Her long dark hair was tied back in a pony-tail and it made her look about sixteen. For a moment he watched as she struggled on determinedly with a wayward branch that was obviously far too thick and heavy for her to cut. He noticed the small frown of concentration on her face, the way she bit her lip with pearly white teeth in vexation as the stubborn branch refused to break.

'Need any help?' he asked softly.

'Oh, hi, Ray.' She turned and looked down at him. 'I didn't expect to see you today.' She tried to make her voice light-hearted, but in truth as soon as she saw him her body seemed to tense. 'You seem to be making a habit of catching me off guard.'

'I do, don't I?' He grinned.

And suddenly she was remembering the way he had kissed her last night, the heat of his lips and the passion that had ignited so fiercely inside her.

'So, what can I do for you?' She turned her attention quickly back to her struggle with the branch, trying to saw through it with all her might.

Instead of answering her, Ray was watching what she was doing. 'You are making a mess of that,' he said.

'Am I? What am I doing wrong?'

'For a start you are using the wrong implement for the job.' He turned and searched through the old toolbox that she had found in one of the outbuildings. 'This is what you should be using.' He held up a lethal looking pair of shears.

Then to her surprise he climbed up the ladder behind her. He stood on the rung beneath her, his body pressed close behind hers. 'You see these branches here.' He leaned over her to point, his breath soft against the side of her face.

'Yes...' Desperately she tried to concentrate but his closeness was sending alarm bells ringing through her.

'They need to come out and you should always cut just about here.' He pointed to a joint in the branch, and then clipped neatly, so that the branch fell with one smooth action. In his hands the task seemed effortless. But Caitlin only vaguely registered what he was doing; all her senses were tuned in on the feeling of his body against hers, the scent of his cologne, the strength of his arms wrapped so tightly around her. The sensation was dangerously exhilarating.

'There, that should do it.' He pulled away from her and jumped down onto the ground, then held out a hand to help her down.

'Thanks.' She put her hand in his and felt as if explosive shivers raced straight from his fingers through her body.

Her feet connected with the ground but as she looked up at him she still felt as if she were falling. The world seemed to be at a crazy angle. It would be so easy to just sway closer into his arms. He was so sexy and the powerful memory of his kiss tantalised and tormented her.

Caitlin pulled away from him and mentally shook herself. She did not want to be one of Ray's conquests.

'So, what do you think of the rest of my handiwork?' she asked, looking around at the orchard and pretending to be deeply absorbed in the work she had done.

For a moment she didn't think he was going to answer her; he seemed to be studying her face very intently. 'I think...' he said carefully, slowly, 'that you have been working far too hard and should take a break and have some lunch with me.'

'I can't, Ray. I've got far too much to do.' She moved away from him, picking up branches to put them into a neat pile.

'Lunch doesn't take that long and you can't work in the heat of the day.' He leaned back against the stepladder and watched as she moved out from beneath the tree, dusting her hands against slender hips as she walked.

'I can.' Her hair was escaping from the confines of the pony-tail and she pulled it free impatiently so that it swung down around her shoulders.

Ray noticed that the dark chestnut colour had gold undertones in the sunlight. For a moment he found himself wondering how it would feel to run his hands through it as he brought her very gently and possessively to climax. 'You are in France now and you should learn to do things the French way…' he murmured distractedly.

'And what way is that?' she asked, flicking an edgy look around at him.

'The civilised way, of course.' He smiled.

She couldn't help but smile back at him.

'Anyway, I thought you would say no to lunch and that you'd tell me you were too busy. So I made a contingency plan.'

'What kind of contingency plan?'

'You'll see.' Without another word he disappeared around the side of the house.

Caitlin felt a jolt of disappointment that he was leaving. Then frowned and hurriedly continued to pick up the fallen branches. She'd done the right thing passing on lunch; she needed to keep her distance from that man.

To her surprise Ray arrived back a few moments later carrying an ice box and a blanket.

'Ray, what on earth are you doing?' she asked as he spread the blanket out under the dappled shade of the olive trees.

'What do you think I'm doing?' He glanced over at her wryly. 'If you won't go to the restaurant, then I've brought the restaurant to you. The chef at Chez Louis put together an interesting menu. I hope you'll approve.'

Caitlin walked a little closer, curiosity making her lean over to look in the cooler box. She watched as he brought out an ice bucket with a bottle of white wine. 'So what else have you got in there?'

'*Salade Niçoise,* which is a speciality of the region, followed by goats' cheese and a Mediterranean vegetable roulade, and then, to follow, a selection of fruit.'

'Sounds wonderful, but I won't be able to do any work this afternoon if I eat all that.'

Ray reached up and, catching her off balance, pulled her down onto the rug beside him. 'You know what you need, don't you?'

'No, what?' Breathlessly she watched as he poured a glass of white wine.

'You need to relax.' He pressed the glass into her hand and for a moment their eyes met across the rim.

'Well, thanks.' Quickly she looked away and held up the glass in salute. 'This is very kind of you.'

Caitlin took a sip of the wine; it had a honeyed undertone and was crisply cold. It was bliss after the busy morning in the orchard. Moving slightly so that her legs weren't touching his, she leaned back against the bark of the tree.

'Shouldn't you be working today?' she asked him.

'I always take time off for lunch.' He was unwrapping tin foil from some china plates, so she took the opportunity to study him. She noticed the muscle of his arms in the cream short-sleeved shirt, the stylish yet casual lightweight beige trousers. He looked incredibly stylish and yet there was such an air of strength about him. The pale colours he wore emphasised the dark tan of his skin and the almost blue-black hair.

He looked around, caught her watching him and smiled. 'How's the wine?'

'Delicious.'

'Try a little of this with it.' He held out a fork with some goats' cheese wrapped in crispy pastry.

After a moment's hesitation, she allowed him to feed it to her. There was something sensuous and intimate about allowing him to do that. She felt self-conscious but at the explosion of taste on her tongue she closed her eyes and gave herself up to the experience.

'What do you think?' he asked.

'Heaven...I'm sure it's the food of the gods.' She opened her eyes and smiled at him.

'Good.' He put the plates between them and some small bowls of black and green olives.

She was surprised at how hungry she was. Never had a meal tasted so amazing. Maybe it was because they were eating out of doors in the heat of the day, maybe it was the tranquil silence of the orchard, only broken by the occasional drone of a bee. Or maybe it was the company she was in. It seemed that just being around Ray sharpened all of her senses.

'The chef who put this together needs a gold medal,' she murmured as she leaned her head back against the tree and treated herself to another mouth-watering morsel. 'What did you say his name was?'

'Louis, he owns a bistro down in the village. I'll take you there for dinner one evening.'

The casual offer stirred up an anything-but-casual response inside Caitlin; she felt her stomach tighten with the kind of anticipation that had nothing to do with the thought of food.

'Well, thanks for the offer but I'm pretty busy at the moment.'

Her answer met with a moment of silence. She slanted a surreptitious glance over at him. He was lying on his side propped up on one elbow. 'You are very serious sometimes, you know,' he said lightly. 'Life is for living.'

'I know and I am living.' She grinned. 'I'm lying in my own orchard eating food prepared by a gourmet chef, a glass of wine in my hand and the heat of the sun beating down. I feel quite decadent, as a matter of fact, and more relaxed than I have in ages.'

'That's good.'

'It's just a pity I've got to get back to work.'

'Well, you are now your own boss so you could take the rest of the day off.'

'But then the garden will never get done.'

'If it makes you feel any better I have a lot of work to do this afternoon as well.'

'Do you work from home?'

He nodded. 'I have an office upstairs. I work three weeks here, one week in Paris.'

'Sounds like a good arrangement.'

'Yes, I like it.'

'I've never been to Paris.' She leaned her head back and looked up at the clear blue sky through the green tracery of branches. 'I saw the road signs for it on the drive down and was sorely tempted to make a quick detour into the centre, but I thought if I got in there I might not be able to find my way out onto the right road again.'

'You would have enjoyed the visit. It is a very beautiful city, especially at the moment with the horse-chestnut trees in bloom; the view along the Seine is magnificent.'

Caitlin took a sip of her wine. 'Well, maybe I'll go one day.'

'Come with me next week if you want. I have to go into the office most days but I'd still have time to show you the sights.'

If his invitation to dinner had caused a stir inside her, it was nothing to the reaction to this oh, so casual enticement. It caused a major landslide to her senses and the temptation to accept was powerfully strong.

When she didn't answer him immediately he shrugged. 'I suppose you are too busy working on this place.'

Something about the sardonic edge to his tone made her instantly defensive. 'Well, look at it, Ray. It needs all my attention.' She waved a hand towards the house.

'You know what they say about all work and no play?' he said lightly.

She looked away from him and swirled her wine around the glass, watching the way the sun made its contents gleam deeply gold. 'How many bedrooms has your apartment got?' She forced herself to ask the question and then glanced over at him uncertainly.

'Two. But it is not obligatory to use them both.' He watched the flush of tantalising colour over her cheekbones and smiled.

Caitlin held his gaze for a second too long and she knew without doubt that if she accepted his offer they definitely wouldn't be sleeping in separate beds and she didn't think she was ready for that. 'Yes, well, maybe I'll take you up on that some time in the future. But as I said earlier, I'm far too busy now.'

'Of course.' He smiled at her, a teasing half-smile that confused her.

'Why are you looking at me like that?'

'No reason.' He reached across and topped up her wineglass. 'I just think you are scared to relax around me. What is it, Caitlin? Are you afraid you might enjoy yourself?'

'I'm not afraid of anything.' Her heart pounded dramatically against her chest and her panic levels rose as he leaned a little closer. It made her distressingly aware that she was lying; she wasn't just scared, she was terrified. But she wasn't scared of him; she was scared of herself, of her own body's traitorous reaction to him. Because there was a wild part of her that wanted to throw caution away and say, Yes…take me out to dinner…take me to Paris…take me to bed. It was a crazy desire and the sane part of her fought it with every ounce of fortitude she could muster. Rebounding from one disastrous relationship to another was not what she needed right now.

'David and I were to be married next week.' She blurted the words out impulsively. 'And we were to honeymoon in Rome. So, you see, going to Paris with you…especially next week…just wouldn't be right.'

'Paris isn't Rome,' he said with a shrug. There was an uncomfortable silence. Then he looked at her with that penetrating gaze. 'Do you think your marriage would have worked out?'

The calm question made her frown. 'No, I don't suppose it would. But that doesn't stop the breakup hurting. We lived together for three years.'

'But he wasn't right for you, Caitlin, and when something isn't right you have to move on.' He reached out and stroked her hair back from her face so that he could see her more clearly. It was a tender gesture that brought a lump to her throat.

'How long have you been living apart?'

'Two months.' She had stormed out of the apartment on the day she had discovered the truth and had taken refuge at Heidi's house. It had been a tough few weeks, cancelling wedding arrangements, trying to untangle her finances from David's and grieving for Murdo. Caitlin took a sip of her wine and tried not think about it.

'What day should you have got married next week?' he asked casually as he started to pack away empty dishes into the basket.

'Saturday.'

'Well, if you don't want to come to Paris for the whole week, why don't you fly out towards the end of next week and join me...shall we say Friday? I'll meet you at De Gaulle airport and we can spend the weekend together, fly back together Sunday afternoon.' He turned and looked up at her. 'It will take your mind off what you would have been doing that weekend.'

It sure as hell would, she thought dazedly as she met his eyes. The thought of spending a weekend in Paris with him was like some kind of adrenalin drug that made her dizzy with confusion.

'I don't know, Ray, it's a bit soon for me to be having weekends away. But thanks for the offer.'

He grinned. 'The words "I don't know" suggest you haven't made up your mind yet. But the words "thanks for the offer" sound like a definite no. Which is it?'

'It's...' She hesitated as he moved even closer and her heart missed a beat as she noticed that his eyes were on the softness of her lips.

'So which is it?' he asked again.

'It's a definite...'

He reached over and took the glass of wine from her hands to put it down on the grass beside her and she found that she couldn't concentrate on what she was saying at all now, because he was leaning closer. 'You were saying?' He whispered the words against her ear.

'Ray, stop it...' But her tone was half-hearted and when he pulled her down to lie beside him on the rug she made barely a murmur of protest.

He smiled down at her. 'So...where were we?'

Her heart was thundering so fiercely now that she was sure he would feel it pounding against his chest as he leaned against her.

'Ray...' His lips silenced her and suddenly all coherent thought was gone. The kiss was tender and the hands that cupped her waist were gentle as he lifted her T-shirt and slid them beneath. His hands were cool against the heat of her naked skin. She could have pulled away but mortifyingly, she found she didn't have the inner strength. Instead she started to kiss him back and the sensations of wild need that raced through her body were forcefully compelling.

She longed for his hands to move higher, to touch her all over, but they remained at her waist, stroking her, tantalising her until she thought she would go out of her mind with wanting him.

His kisses were passionately sensational; it was as if he set alight some bonfire inside her that she hadn't even known existed.

He was the one to pull back and he smiled down at her lazily. 'Shall I take that as a definite yes?'

She hadn't wanted him to stop and a mixture of frustration and fury raced through her veins; frustration because she wanted to reach up and put her arms around him, tell him...no, beg him...to continue, and fury because he was so damned sure of himself.

'It was just a kiss, Ray,' she murmured gruffly. 'Don't get carried away.'

His eyes raked over her flushed countenance and the swollen softness of her lips and he grinned at that. 'I wasn't the only one who was getting carried away,' he reminded her teasingly.

She moved from him, furious with herself for responding. The guy was arrogant and overbearing and…she should have smacked him not kissed him back.

Trouble was, he was a good kisser… The shivery, delightful sensations he had stirred up inside her were still flowing around in her body now. She tried to ignore them, tried to ignore him as she stood up. But it was difficult because she was intensely aware of him.

Self-consciously, she adjusted her clothing.

'Okay, it was just a kiss…' He also got to his feet. 'But you've got to admit there is a certain chemistry between us.'

'Is there? I hadn't noticed…' Her voice trailed off huskily as he took a step closer.

'Care to put that to the test again?' He smiled as he saw the flicker of turmoil in her cat-green eyes. 'No? Well, that's a pity.'

'Stop teasing, Ray,' she muttered.

'I'm not teasing. I'm very serious. And I'm especially serious about our weekend together in Paris. In fact, to prove it to you I will offer to sleep in the spare room.' He spread his hands wide, a boyish look of contrition on his handsome features. 'Now I wouldn't do that for just anybody.'

She felt herself melt under that smile like an ice block put in the microwave.

'Yes…well, I'll think about it.' She added hastily. 'Now I'd better get inside and see how Patrick is progressing.' It was a relief to change the subject towards something mundane.

'Patrick went for lunch just as I arrived,' Ray informed her, and then added, 'He said to tell you that he would be back at four and you've got a problem with the floor.'

'What's wrong with the floor? I thought he was doing the staircase.' She shook her head.

'One problem usually begets another in these old properties, Caitlin. You'll learn that as you go along.'

'Thanks,' she grated dryly.

He grinned. 'Knowing you, you'll soon have the problem solved.' Then he glanced at his watch, picked up the picnic box and the rug. 'I've got to go. I'll speak to you later.'

'Yes...see you later.'

She watched as he disappeared around the side of the house, leaving her alone in the heat of the orchard wondering if she had just imagined the last hour.

CHAPTER SIX

'IF RAY is as attractive as you say, then I think you should go.' Heidi's voice was positive. 'What have you got to lose, Caitlin?'

Caitlin thought about the way Ray made her senses dissolve into chaos just with a smile. 'Apart from my self-control, you mean?' *And my heart,* a little voice whispered waywardly in her ear. Strenuously she ignored that. She didn't intend opening her heart again to anyone for a very long time.

'He has a weird effect on me, Heidi. I've never known anything like it. He touches me and I turn to jelly.'

'Well if some drop-dead gorgeous Frenchman wanted to whisk me off to Paris for the weekend I'd definitely go.'

'No, you wouldn't, you are happily married.'

Heidi laughed. 'Whoops, almost forgot that.'

Caitlin smiled; it was good to hear her friend's cheerful voice. She'd missed her.

'I'm just a bit wary, Heidi…'

'After what you've been through, that is understandable,' Heidi said sympathetically.

'He's not the type to want a serious relationship and that's fine… Part of me thinks it will just be a bit of fun and I should go for it. But there is another part of me that says I could get burned here. He's a smooth operator…'

'Mr Cool?' Heidi asked.

'Oh, yes, definitely Mr Cool. It's six days now since

he issued the invitation and I haven't had sight or sound of him in that time. In fact I think he is in Paris now. He said he was there this week on business, so for all I know he's changed his mind about the weekend anyway.'

'Well, you've got his mobile number, haven't you? Ring him and find out.'

Caitlin frowned. She was definitely against ringing him. Why, she didn't know; maybe it was that arrogant manner of his or that laid-back confidence that said he knew he could have any woman he wanted. Well, to hell with that—she had far too much spirit to give him the satisfaction of running after him. It wasn't her style at all.

'No, I don't think that is a good idea,' she murmured. 'Anyway I'm starting to go off the idea of Paris. After all, I should have been in church this Saturday exchanging vows with David. It's too much, too soon.'

'I wasn't sure if I should tell you this or not.' Heidi hesitated. 'But Peter and I went to China Town last Saturday night for a meal, and David was in the restaurant.'

'Really?' Caitlin frowned. 'On his own?'

There was a brief pause. 'No, he was with a voluptuous blonde. And she was all over him, Caitlin, like a bad rash.'

'Oh.' A cold, raw feeling swirled inside Caitlin.

'I shouldn't have told you, should I?' Heidi said apprehensively.

'No, I'm glad you did, because stupidly I've been worried about him.'

'You are joking! Why?'

Caitlin shrugged helplessly. She couldn't explain the complex feelings she had about David. 'There was a part of me that wondered if I should have stuck around to help him. He does have a problem, Heidi—'

'You're telling me.' Heidi's voice was brusque. 'Apart from the gambling, he's a thief as well as a liar. Remind me again… How much did it cost you to extricate yourself from the mess?'

'You know very well it was a big chunk of my savings.'

'And you're worried about him?' Heidi sounded angry now. 'You are far too soft-hearted. Let me tell you, Caitlin, he didn't look one bit worried about you on Saturday night. The guy is a user.'

'Maybe you're right but…I suppose he couldn't help himself. Gambling is a bit like alcoholism, isn't it?'

'I don't know but I think you are well out of it.'

'I suppose so. I'm a disaster when it comes to picking men, aren't I?' Caitlin said wryly.

'Ray sounds all right.'

'Well, at least he's honest and up front,' Caitlin agreed. 'He's been straight about the fact he's not looking for a serious commitment…and he's been brutally honest about this house.' She perched herself on the window ledge, her eyes moving over the shambles that had once been the lounge. There was a hole where the staircase had been and a bigger hole where part of the floor had once been.

'Well, grab him quick and have a fab time in Paris.'

There was a sound of a car drawing up outside and Caitlin looked out of the window wondering if it was Ray. Her heart sank a little as she saw it was a van. 'I've got to go, Heidi. Someone's coming to the door. And no, it's not him.'

'Pity.' Heidi laughed. 'Don't forget to send me a postcard.'

'I might not go,' Caitlin warned as she glanced outside and noticed the logo on the van. 'Gosh, I think it might be the electricity people here to connect me. Now this is a wonderful surprise—I'd been told they could be another three weeks.'

'You see, things are looking up.' Heidi laughed. 'The future is looking bright.'

Over an hour later golden light spilled through the house and Caitlin's fridge and immersion kicked into life. She was back to civilisation. Heidi was right, she thought as she filled up the ice tray for the freezer. The future was what mattered now and she wouldn't dwell on the past. A hot bath and then an ice-cold gin and tonic beckoned.

She was just running the bath when her mobile rang again. It was an unfamiliar number not keyed into her address book, so she answered it half expecting a wrong number.

'Hello, Caitlin.'

She recognised Ray's voice immediately and she was filled with surprise and pleasure. 'Oh, hi, where did you get my number?'

'I took a note of it when I had your phone in my possession. So, how are things going with the house?' he continued swiftly.

'They are progressing well.' She closed her mind to the mess in her lounge.

'Have they reconnected your electricity yet?' he enquired.

'Well, yes, as a matter of fact they have.' She smiled. 'You must be psychic; they've just been here.'

'I'm glad things are going well for you, Caitlin.' His voice held that note of relaxed humour that made her stomach dip.

She sat down on the edge of her bath. 'So, how are things going with you? Did you get the contract with Roger Delaware all signed up?'

'Yes. He was up at the house the other day. He asked me to pass on his regards to you.'

'That was nice.' She made her voice airily light. Was he ever going to mention Paris? she wondered. And if he did, what should she say?

'I think he really wanted to call to see you.' Ray laughed. It was a warm laugh to which every sinew of her body responded positively.

'I meant to come over to see you myself, but I haven't had a minute. Work has been chaotic.'

'And I thought you French had such a relaxed attitude to work. What about those long lunches with wine?'

'They have been sadly missing. But I've been in a Paris frame of mind recently…the big city always makes me much more driven.'

'Are you there now?' she asked.

'Yes, I'm phoning from my apartment. The weather has been lovely today, a bright, cloudless blue sky…not that I've seen much of it. I've been in the office since first light.'

'That's a shame.'

'Yes, well, hopefully I'll make up for it at the weekend.'

Caitlin felt her heartbeat increase. Here it was—he was going to ask her again.

'Have you got a pen handy?'

'A pen?' She was puzzled by the request.

'Yes, I want you to take down a number.'

'I've already got your phone number.'

'Haven't used it, though, have you?' He laughed. 'No, this is a different number.'

Hastily Caitlin got up to find her bag and root through it for a pen. 'Okay fire away,' she said as she poised with her diary and pen in one hand, the phone tucked under her chin.

He reeled off a number and she wrote down. 'So what is this?' she asked as he finished.

'It's the reference number of your flight on Friday. Now, you have to be at Nice airport at five-thirty, and you collect your ticket at the Air France desk. You'll need your passport to confirm your identity.'

'You've already booked me a seat?' She didn't know whether to be cross or flattered. 'But I haven't told you if I am coming yet!'

'Well, I got impatient waiting so I booked the flight anyway. I'll pick you up at the airport. Oh, and pack a few warm clothes—although the weather is good it is a few degrees cooler than the south. I've got to go, Caitlin, I've got a call coming through on my other line.'

Caitlin opened her mouth to speak, but he had already gone. Now what should she do? she wondered restlessly. It was very presumptuous of him to just book her flight like that. By rights she should just ignore it. It would probably be the sensible thing to do.

She sighed and then looked at her reflection in the bathroom mirror. Being sensible hadn't really got her very far up to now. Maybe it was time to take a risk, live dangerously and fly to Paris. Although her heart bounced very unevenly against her chest at the thought, there was also a wave of excitement that completely engulfed her. She reached for her gin and tonic and took a deep mouthful. Roll on Friday. Whatever would be would be and she wouldn't analyse the rights and wrongs of it. She deserved a fun time anyway, after the last few weeks. Murdo would definitely approve, she thought with a grin.

The flight from Nice to Paris was short. It seemed as if the jet was no sooner up in the air than it was preparing for landing. Caitlin's stomach seemed to flip wildly as they made the steep descent into De Gaulle but she wasn't sure if it was the air pockets they hit or the fact that she was here in Paris…and a whole weekend with Ray stretched before her.

Ray spotted her immediately amidst the crowds in the arrivals hall and he smiled to himself. It had been a calculated risk just booking her ticket and he had half expected her not to turn up.

Caitlin hadn't seen him yet, but, instead of walking over to her immediately, he stopped and took the opportunity to study her as she looked around for him. The long grey skirt and matching cropped jacket she wore were teamed with black high-heel boots and a red top. They skimmed her slender body in a stylish way, making her look taller than her five-feet four. Her long dark hair was loose around her shoulders; it curled slightly at the ends and gleamed chestnut gold under the overhead lights. She looked absolutely stunning. As if sensing his gaze on her, she turned and their eyes connected across the crowded concourse. He saw the smile of relief on her face.

'I thought for a moment that I had been stood up,' she said lightly as he reached her side.

'So did I.' He grinned. 'I half expected you not to come as a punishment for my impetuosity.'

'It crossed my mind,' she admitted.

'Well, I'm glad you are here.' He smiled.

She looked up into the warmth of his eyes and she

wanted to say, Me too. But the words wouldn't come out. 'Thanks for the ticket,' she said lightly instead. 'And of course I'll pay you for it—'

'Caitlin.' He cut across her firmly. 'Shut up, will you?' Then he leaned closer and suddenly she was enveloped in the warmth of his body as he kissed her lightly on each cheek. 'Welcome to Paris,' he said softly as he pulled back.

Her heart was racing so hard against her ribs that it was actually hurting her. She looked up at him wordlessly and, just as she thought he was going to pull away completely, suddenly his lips brushed against hers. It was just a light, almost teasing caress but it set clamouring fires of fierce desire instantly blazing inside her.

'So are you hungry?' he asked casually as he moved back and picked up her overnight case from beside her.

She wondered if their kisses didn't affect him as intensely as they affected her. Maybe he was used to that level of sensuality when he kissed…

Aware that he was waiting for her reply, she hastily pulled herself together. 'Eh, yes, starving, in fact,' she lied. The truth was that she was so wound up that eating was the last thing on her mind.

'Good. I know a great little bohemian restaurant on the Left Bank.'

He strode ahead of her, leaving her struggling to keep up. She noticed the way women looked at him as they wove their way through the crowds. There was open admiration in their eyes. It was no wonder they were attracted to him, she thought as he turned and waited for her by the doors. He was formidably handsome, and the dark suit he wore emphasised his stylish Parisian good looks.

They found his Mercedes in the car park and while

she settled herself in the comfortable leather seats he stored her case in the trunk.

'Is it okay with you if we go directly to eat or do you want to go back to my place first?' he enquired as he slid behind the driving wheel.

'Oh, let's go and eat,' she said hastily. She wanted to put off going to his place for as long as possible; just the thought of being alone with him there made her insides tighten with a weird kind of apprehension.

They travelled in silence. Caitlin watched his hands on the wheel of the car—capable, confident hands. She tried to think of something to say, something that would take her mind off the thought of those hands travelling with equal ease and confidence over her body. But nothing came to mind.

He changed gear and the sports car roared down wide tree-lined streets. It was dark now and the cobbled streets glistened under the beam of the powerful headlights.

'You seem to know Paris pretty well,' she managed weakly at last.

'I spend a lot of time here. And I suppose you could say it is my hometown, it's the place where I was brought up. My mother was a Parisian model who worked for some of the top fashion houses. And my father was a merchant banker here.'

'Are your parents still alive?' Caitlin probed lightly.

'No, my father died when I was sixteen and my mother ten years later. She made a disastrous second marriage which ended in an acrimonious divorce. Her health was never good after that.'

'I'm sorry, Ray, that must have been awful.'

'That's life, isn't it?' He pulled the car into a vacant parking space. 'I used to blame my stepfather for making her so unhappy. But looking back I realise it wasn't entirely his fault. My mother was desperately unhappy after my father died and I suppose she was on the rebound. She was looking to recapture what she once had and that can be a dangerous route.'

She followed Ray as he stepped out onto the pavement. The night air was cool, and the pavements glistened from an earlier shower.

She wondered if that reasoning was what kept Ray a single man. Maybe he felt he'd been lucky having one good marriage and didn't want to push his luck by getting involved again. Then, realising that she was analysing him, she pushed the thought to the back of her head. Ray was single because that was the way he wanted it, she told herself sharply. And it was none of her business.

'Careful on these cobbled surfaces, they can be slippery,' Ray said as he waited for her to walk around to join him. He took hold of her hand as they waited for a space in the traffic to cross the road.

She liked the touch of his hand, cool and firm against hers.

As they rounded a corner she could see the Seine, its silky dark surface reflecting the lights of the city, its banks lit with an amber necklace of light.

'That's where we are going.' Ray let go of her hand to point down at the amber light and she realised it was a terrace overlooking the river. 'There are great views of the river from there. And the food is very good.'

'Sounds wonderful.' She smiled. 'Is this where you bring all your latest conquests?' As soon as the words left her lips she regretted them. What on earth had made her say something as crass as that?

'I wasn't aware that you were a conquest.' His eyes moved over her face thoughtfully, and then he smiled. 'Yet...'

The gentle emphasis on that last word made her blush furiously.

'Well, when I said conquest I meant the fact that I'm here in Paris with you…not…anything else.' She tried desperately to extricate herself but with each word felt she was making it worse.

He laughed and took hold of her hand again. 'Come along, Caitlin, it doesn't do to think about anything too deeply on an empty stomach. You're here and that's all that matters.'

They walked down the slip road towards the restaurant in silence. Ray opened the door for her and then stepped back to allow her to enter the building first.

It was warm inside, despite the fact that the sliding doors were open onto the terrace. Maybe the heat was generated by the amount of people, because the place was full to overflowing; people were sitting and standing at the bar area and each candlelit table seemed to be occupied. Or maybe the huge bread ovens just visible through a stone archway generated the heat. The place had a wonderful lively atmosphere, with just the right mix of sophistication and informality; the French conversations swirled around Caitlin as they made their way to the bar.

'Do you think we will get a table?' Caitlin asked. 'It's very busy.'

Before Ray could answer he was greeted by a man behind the bar who came around and embraced Ray warmly with much back-slapping approval.

For a moment they spoke in French. Caitlin was fascinated to listen to Ray speaking in his own language. If his English sounded sexy, it was nothing to the wonderful melodious tones of his native tongue.

Ray introduced her briefly to the man, who was called

Henri, and he kissed her on each cheek before steering them towards the only vacant table in the place, which was strategically placed for a good view of the floodlit terrace and the river.

'You were saying?' Ray asked with a grin as the man disappeared and a waitress immediately arrived to hand them a menu.

'You've obviously got friends in high places, haven't you?' She smiled. 'Not only have you got us a table, but I think it's the best in the house.'

'Yes, well, Henri and I go back a long way. We were at school together.'

'He's the owner of this establishment, I take it?'

Ray nodded. 'He operates a system of first come, first served; you can't book a table—'

'Unless you are an old school friend,' Caitlin finished with a smile.

'Exactly.' Ray glanced down at the menu. 'So what would you like to eat?'

She looked down at the selection. It was all in French but she could make out most of it. 'What's this?' She leaned over and pointed at something she just couldn't decipher.

'Venison with sweet potatoes. Why don't you try the escargot to start with?'

'Snails?' She pulled a face and then, glancing over at him, realised that he was deliberately teasing her.

'I don't even like to look at snails in the garden, never mind eat them.'

Ray laughed. 'Then predictably I take it your choice is that most English of dishes, *Rosbif?*'

She laughed as well. 'But I'll take French mustard with it.'

'You are extraordinarily beautiful when you laugh, do you know that, Caitlin?' he said softly.

The compliment caught her off guard. There was a part of her that wanted to make a glib remark, shrug it off as nothing more than his smooth tongue. She glanced across and met his eyes; they looked dark and intensely serious and for a moment she was completely tongue-tied. It was as much as she could manage to just say the words, 'Thank you.'

He watched the flicker of uncertainty and vulnerability in her green eyes. 'David did quite a job on you, didn't he?' he remarked suddenly.

'I don't know what you mean,' she said, clearing her throat nervously.

'I mean he hurt you a great deal…took away some of that radiant confidence that sparkles naturally in your eyes and your laughter…'

She swallowed hard. 'It's been a tough few months,' she admitted lightly. 'But I'm fine now, Ray.'

He nodded. 'Well, at least being here for the weekend will take your mind off things, so we will change the subject…hmm?'

'Yes, good idea.' She smiled brightly and looked away from him pretending to study the menu in great detail. But in truth her heart was thumping erratically and it wasn't because he had mentioned David, it was the way he looked at her…the way he complimented her, the way he talked with such sincerity, as if her well-being mattered to him. It was all probably a very smooth act. But it was a wonderful one.

The waitress arrived to take their order. Self-consciously aware of Ray watching her, Caitlin ordered in French and hoped her accent sounded all right. Then

Ray took over, smoothly ordering his meal and some wine.

'So how was my French pronunciation?' she asked as they were left alone again.

'You sounded fine.'

'I just wondered.' She shrugged. 'When you French speak English it sounds deliciously attractive...I wondered if the same could be said of the reverse.'

'Let me hear you again.' He rested one hand under his chin and leaned forward as if ready to catch every nuance of her tone, amusement sparkling in his eyes.

She wished now that she hadn't asked him, as with embarrassment she repeated her order.

'Hard to tell with a food order...' he murmured thoughtfully. 'Say something else.'

'What should I say?'

He grinned and pretended to think for a moment. 'You could say, Ray, I'm so pleased to be here in Paris with you... Where have you been all my life?'

'Idiot.' She grinned back at him.

'You don't care for that? Okay, let me think of something else.'

Behind them on a small stage a female guitarist started to play a French love song. Its haunting melody silenced a lot of the conversations around them, and a few people got up to dance on the small dance floor outside on the terrace.

'Ah, I know,' Ray said gently. 'You could say, Please dance with me. I want to be held close in your arms.'

She knew he was only teasing, but even so she felt her skin heat up as he waited for her to speak. Caitlin glanced towards the couples on the dance floor; they weren't so much dancing as smooching and the thought of being that close to Ray made her blood pressure increase dramatically.

'Let me help you,' Ray murmured with a smile, before repeating the words again in French. Then he stood up and held out a hand.

She had no alternative but to put her hand in his and allow him to lead the way. The floor was packed with couples so, even if she had wanted to, she couldn't have kept a distance from him. Wordlessly she allowed him to pull her close into his arms. The familiar tang of his cologne assailed her senses. She closed her eyes and leaned her head against his chest. The dangerous intensity of pleasure that ricocheted through her was terrifying in one way, and yet pure bliss in another.

One of his hands rested at her waist, the other on her back; she had never been more acutely aware of a man's touch before, or of the powerful body against hers. And suddenly it was as if they were alone in the room, as if time stood still. She wanted this dance to go on forever, to stay wrapped in the warm cocoon of his arms and never—ever—come back down to earth again.

As the music changed they continued to dance. Ray murmured something against her ear in French; the sound of his voice and the touch of his breath against her skin sent tingling shivers racing through her.

'I have something to tell you…my Caitlin,' he said gently in his native language.

The possessive way he used her name made her raise her head to look up at him.

He hesitated and then smiled. 'I don't know how I am going to keep my hands off you tonight,' he said slowly.

Although her French wasn't good she knew exactly what he had said. She tried to pretend she didn't, tried to just give a shrug of incomprehension. But the truth was she understood exactly what he meant…and, worse, she felt exactly the same way. She wanted him so much that it hurt inside.

'And something else,' he added in English, a warm, teasing glow in his eyes. 'You made Moules Mariniére sound like the sexiest food on the planet,' he assured her solemnly.

She laughed at that, loving him for being able to lighten the sexual intensity of the moment in such a silly, light-hearted way.

'You are crazy, you know that, don't you?' she said huskily.

'Crazy about you,' he said softly, looking deep into her eyes.

Caitlin decided to accept that remark as just light-hearted flirting, but even so it sent a tremor of delight rushing through her.

'Come on, let's go and sit down… Our food has arrived.' He pulled away from her and, keeping a light hold on her hand, led her back to the table.

As she took her seat opposite him her heart was still pounding erratically. Ray, on the other hand, seemed totally at ease. He smiled across at her and leaned over to pour her a glass of wine.

'So tell me,' he invited easily. 'How is the house *really* progressing?'

She should have been relieved that he had returned the conversation to the safety zone, but perversely her house was the last thing she wanted to talk about now. Caitlin reached for her glass and took a cooling sip of the white wine.

'The staircase is almost in.' She forced herself to concentrate. 'Patrick has been working really hard.'

'He's a decent guy.'

Caitlin nodded. 'I think he's very trustworthy. I left keys with him because he said he might come and do some work over the weekend.' She played with the food on her plate for a moment. 'There are no hard feelings, are there, Ray…about my not selling to you?'

She didn't know what made her ask that, but suddenly it seemed important.

He thought about that for a moment and wondered what Caitlin would say if he told her that her property was holding back a major development of luxury *gîtes*. And that every week that passed she was costing his company thousands of Euros. Philippe was getting very annoyed and impatient about it.

She frowned when he didn't answer her immediately and leaned forward. 'It's just that I love that house, Ray.' She spoke with passion, her eyes shining. 'It has such char n and I just know it's going to look fantastic when it's f nished.'

H r infatuation with the project made him smile. 'You sour l like me when I'm working on a new design,' he said 'But if I can give you some advice, Caitlin… Never fall 1 love with a business project. You should be objecti e and unemotional at all times otherwise it could end up costing you more money than it is really worth.'

'And are you objective and unemotional at all times?' he asked meeting his eyes steadily.

'I've always tried to be in the past,' he said quietly.

Something about the serious light in his eyes, the in-nation in his voice, made her wonder what was going n in his mind.

She shrugged. 'Well, I think there are more important hings than money, a sense of achievement being one. And something that brings pleasure, two…' She trailed off self-consciously as she felt his eyes moving with searing intensity over her features. 'You think I'm incredibly naïve, don't you?'

He smiled at that. 'I think you are incredibly lovely,' he said easily. 'And in answer to your earlier question: no, there are no hard feelings.'

The waitress arrived to clear their table and ask if they'd like anything else.

Ray looked across at Caitlin. 'Would you like a coffee and cognac here, or shall we have them back at my place?'

The nonchalant question set Caitlin's adrenalin racing. 'Let's go back to your place,' she said softly.

CHAPTER SEVEN

IT WAS cool outside after the warmth of the bistro and Caitlin shivered slightly.

Ray put an arm around her shoulders and all of a sudden there was a different explanation for her shivers. 'Are you okay?' he asked gently.

'I'm fine.' She allowed herself to lean close to him. 'It's not really cold, is it?' she said lightly. 'It must be old age.'

'Old age?' He laughed at that. 'You are only twenty-nine.'

'What time is it?' Caitlin asked.

Ray glanced at his watch. 'Quarter past midnight.'

'Then I'm no longer twenty-nine,' she said with a sigh. 'I'm thirty. And it's damned depressing.'

'It's your birthday!' Ray stopped walking and looked down at her. 'You were going to get married on your birthday?'

She nodded. 'When I was planning it, it seemed like a mature and sensible thing to do. Thirty felt like a good age to settle down, make a commitment…'

'Not if it's to the wrong person,' Ray said gently.

'Well, with the benefit of hindsight I can see that,' she said huskily.

Ray looked down at her and wished he could see the expression on her face, but it was in shadow. He stroked a hand through her hair. 'Happy birthday, Caitlin.'

'Thank you.' She swallowed on a sudden lump in her throat. Being here with him suddenly seemed so right…as if she had come on a long and perilous journey, taken lots of wrong turnings and by sheer fluke ended up in exactly the right place. It was the strangest feeling and she couldn't really understand it. She was here for the shallowest of reasons: a bit of fun…to take her mind off things…

He reached down and then his lips met with hers and the fireworks started inside her again, and as she kissed him back all those shallow reasons for being here seemed like the thinnest tissue of lies. There was nothing superficial about her feelings for Ray. As the thoughts tried to unfold in her mind she stopped them. She wasn't going to analyse this, she told herself fiercely. This was just a light-hearted dalliance and if she tried to make it into something serious then she risked getting hurt.

It started to rain, a light, squally shower that took them both by surprise. They broke apart, laughing, and then they held hands and ran for the sanctuary of the car, but by the time they reached it the rain had passed.

Paris looked wonderful by night. They drove down wide boulevards passing floodlit fountains and impressive squares. The Arc de Triomphe looked white against the night sky, and statues of magnificent winged horses almost real as if they might fly at any moment up into the starry night. Then they were passing the Eiffel Tower, which shimmered with gold light, sending ripples of gold reflection over the Seine.

'This city is so beautiful,' Caitlin murmured.

'Yes, I think so.' Ray smiled. 'I've made a detour to get back to my place so you could see some of it. But tomorrow I'll show you around properly. And hopefully it won't rain.' He added, softly. 'Although I can't promise anything—it is April in Paris.'

Caitlin looked across at him and smiled. 'That sounds wonderful.'

He parked the car on a quiet, leafy road. 'My apartment is just down here.' He indicated an elegant row of terrace houses. Caitlin admired their wrought-iron balconies, the intricate detail around the curve of their windows. She could just catch a glimpse of the sophisticated interiors lit by softly shaded lamps.

'Come on.' He opened the door of the car. 'Let's get inside.'

The words and the fact that she was here at his place made tension suddenly escalate inside her.

Firmly she tried to keep her mind away from the intimacy of being alone with him in his apartment. 'I half expected your city pad to be in an ultra-modern glass tower,' she said, trying to keep the conversation going in a light vein.

'I guess I'm just a traditionalist at heart.' Ray laughed. 'In fact I draw a lot of inspiration for my designs from the grandeur of bygone days. I hope you are not disappointed.'

'On the contrary, I think that's something we've got in common. I like older properties; I suppose it's one of the reasons I love Murdo's house. Restoring it almost seems like an honour.' She watched as he took her weekend case from the boot of the car. 'So you see I'm a bit of a traditionalist myself.'

The words had a hollow ring inside her. It was true; she was almost old-fashioned when it came to certain things…but she wasn't just talking about her love of period properties. For instance, she had never had a one-night stand or a casual liaison. Her relationships had all been with people she had loved…and people who she had believed loved her.

So what was she doing here? she wondered, apprehension uncoiling fully like a serpent ready to bite. Was she about to throw her rule book in the Seine and fall into bed with Ray Pascal? And if so, was she making a huge mistake?

They walked up some steps and into a wide hallway lit by a chandelier. She watched as he collected some post from a line of five boxes in the wall. He flicked through the contents briefly, before leading the way across the white tiled floor towards the lifts. The doors were open and they stepped inside.

Ray pressed the button for the top floor. The overhead lights were bright and she noticed the way rain still sparkled in the darkness of his hair, and suddenly she was filled with the urge to reach out and brush her hand lightly over the dampness, smooth it away. The temptation startled her almost as much as the sudden rain shower had done a little while ago. It sent vibrant heat flooding through her.

He glanced over and met her eyes. Their dark, sensual power made the heat increase even more, and that made her even more nervous.

She cleared her throat. 'I take it you haven't been home today?' she asked, indicating the mail in his hand.

'No, I headed straight from the office to pick you up at the airport.'

'You must be tired.' It was just something to say, but as soon as the words left her lips she regretted them, especially as she saw the gleam of amusement in his dark eyes.

'Not really,' he assured her wryly.

'Well, it's been a long day for both of us.' She brushed at an imaginary crease in her grey skirt and studied the black leather of her boots as the lift slid smoothly to a halt.

She felt like a gauche teenager on a first date… This was ridiculous, she told herself crossly.

The doors opened and she followed him out of the close, confined space with a degree of relief. At least the lighting along the hallway was more subdued. He unlocked a door and led the way inside.

The apartment was elegant and spacious. The floors a highly polished maple and the leather sofas a squashy vanilla cream; in fact everything about his home spoke of style, sophistication and money.

'It's a beautiful apartment.' She crossed to the French windows to look out. There was a small roof-top garden outside. Ray flicked a switch and the space was lit with the twinkle of subdued lighting, illuminating the flower pots and the wrought-iron table and chairs. In the background the city of Paris glittered like a million priceless diamonds. 'You have a wonderful view as well.'

'Yes, I just don't get much time to admire it.' Ray tossed his post down onto an antique sideboard as he crossed to switch on a few more lamps around the sides of the room. 'Would you like to freshen up while I get us a drink?' he asked.

'Yes, okay.'

'I've put you in my room. I thought you would be more comfortable in there.'

Caitlin turned from the window and their eyes met. She wondered what it would be like to share that room with him…to lie in his arms, drown in his kisses. Urgently she tried to ignore the electric feeling of desire that sizzled inside her. She shouldn't have come here an insistent voice warned her. Maybe she should leave while she still had some semblance of sanity. 'I feel very guilty turning you out of your bedroom, Ray, especially as you've had such a busy day.' Her words came out in a rush. 'You know, I can still go to a hotel... There must be hundreds around here.'

'Hundreds.' He agreed. He leaned back against the sideboard and regarded her with a lazily amused grin. 'But the agreement was that you stayed here and, as I am a man of my word, I wouldn't hear of you disappearing off to a hotel.'

'Thank you.' There was little else she could say, but deep down she wondered if she should still have insisted on going to a hotel anyway. Ray probably was a man of his word, but it was her own strength of spirit that worried her. One look from him and she felt her self-control melting...one kiss and her mind started to wander.

'The bedroom is this way.' Ray turned and led her down a small corridor and up some steps. The room he showed her into was very luxurious; a massive bed dominated the centre. It was probably the biggest bed Caitlin had ever seen and it was covered in plain cream linen that echoed the colour of the curtains and the carpet.

'Bathroom is through there.' Ray put her bag down and indicated a door at the far end of the room. 'We'll have a coffee and cognac out on the terrace if it's still dry.'

'Thanks.' As soon as the door closed behind him she sank down onto the bed. She should have told him she didn't want a drink... In fact the safest thing would be to hide in here and not come out until it was time for her flight on Sunday.

She smiled to herself. 'Coward,' she mocked herself silently. And then, annoyed with herself, she got up from the bed and took her cosmetic bag into the bathroom.

Her reflection stared back at her from several mirrors over the basin and the bath. She looked a little pale and her green eyes seemed to swamp her small face. 'Just have a drink with him and then retire for the night,' she told herself sensibly. 'You've never had any difficulty saying no to a man before, why should Ray be any different?' But deep down she knew that, whatever the reason, Ray was different and she didn't want to say no. Certainly David had never swept her senses into such tumultuous turmoil.

She wondered what David would be doing today… Would he think about the fact that this should have been their wedding day? Maybe not, maybe he would be too busy enjoying himself with the mysterious blonde Heidi had seen him with. She hoped sincerely that, whoever he was with, and whatever he was doing, he had taken her advice and sought counselling for his addiction.

Hastily she refreshed her make-up, brightened her lipstick and ran a comb through her hair. After the rain it was curling more and she gently teased the ends so that they were soft and loose around her face.

There, that was better. She stepped back and looked at herself, then smiled. She was going to just relax and enjoy herself and not think too deeply about anything.

There was music playing in the lounge when she went back through. But Ray wasn't in the room. She glanced out onto the terrace. It was raining again, fat drops of water were bouncing on the table.

'I'm in here,' Ray's voice called her from a room off the lounge. She followed the sound and found him in his office, sitting on the edge of a writing bureau, reading through some of his mail. There were two glasses of brandy sitting next to him. 'Sorry.' He picked a glass up and held it out to her as she came in. 'I got sidetracked. I'll make coffee now.'

'No, that's okay.' She came closer and took the drink. 'I'm happy with just the brandy.' She glanced at the in-tray next to him, which was full to the brim. 'You look like you've got a lot of correspondence to get through.'

'A week's worth of faxes. It's always the same when I'm back here—I spend all my time catching up on the correspondence I've missed. A lot of it is junk, of course, but I have to wade through it just in case.'

'You could do with a secretary.' Caitlin perched next to him on the desk and sipped her drink.

Ray was still perusing the letter in his hand. 'Yes…I have one at the office, of course.' Despite the fact that he answered her, she knew he was only half listening.

Caitlin glanced around the room. Although this was a place of work, it had a cosy feel to it with its book-lined walls at one side and subdued soft lighting. There was a daybed in one corner and above it some beautiful paintings of Paris.

She wandered over to have a look at them. 'These are impressive.' She glanced over at him but he barely looked up.

'And it's a lovely office,' she commented, sitting down on the daybed. 'You could use it as a spare bed-room.'

She had his attention now. He put the letter down and looked over at her with a grin. 'I'm going to tonight. That's unless I get a better offer, of course,' he added roguishly.

'Oh…I see!'

Ray watched as her skin coloured slightly and he smiled.

'It's quite a comfortable bed,' Caitlin continued hastily, trying to cover her embarrassment.

'You think so?' he asked, one dark eyebrow raised wryly.

'Definitely.' She bounced slightly as she tested the mattress. 'I'll trade with you if you want and you can have your own bedroom back.'

He shook his head. 'That wasn't the kind of offer I had in mind,' he said softly.

The words sent a tremor of awareness shooting through her. She glanced over at him and met the teasing gleam of his eye. 'You are one smooth operator, Ray Pascal,' she said lightly.

'Now what makes you say that?' He laughed.

'Because you just are.' She stood up from the bed and walked back towards the desk. 'And I've been warned about you.'

'Who by?' he asked with amusement.

'Sharon, for one.' She stopped a few feet away from him.

'Now what would Sharon know about anything?' Ray reached and took hold of her arm and pulled her closer, then he took her glass and put it down beside his on the desk.

'Well, she was able to tell me all about the rapid turnover of women in your life and she knew who Claudette was.'

'All Sharon knows is that I've never taken her to bed—nor would I ever want to.'

Caitlin grinned. 'She would be devastated if she heard you—'

'Well, I'm not going to lose any sleep over that,' he said gently. 'This is how it is,' he said solemnly, looking into her eyes. 'Claudette is in the past, David is in the past and at the present it's just you and me and one very uncomfortable daybed.'

She smiled tremulously, her heart starting to race as he pulled her even closer.

'That's all right, then,' she whispered huskily. 'Because the present is all I'm interested in right now.' Then she leaned forward and to her surprise she found herself making the first move, touching her lips against his in a tentatively gentle caress. He didn't respond immediately and she moved closer, her hands resting on his shoulders as she deepened the kiss provocatively.

For a little while Ray allowed Caitlin to dictate the pace; he returned her kisses with restraint, reining himself back with supreme control.

Caitlin's lips became more and more persuasive, her hands moving to thread their way through the darkness of his hair. She wanted him so much, longed for his kisses to deepen the way they had before.

Then suddenly he started to return her kisses more forcefully, his lips demanding and hungry against hers. She revelled in the feeling, her whole body tingling with need. But as she slipped further and further into the whirlpool of pleasure he suddenly pulled back from her. 'Are you sure about this?' he asked huskily. 'It's just if we carry on like this I'm not going to be able to pull back. I've only got so much self-control, Caitlin.'

Her heart quivered unsteadily. From the moment she had leaned over and kissed him the fires had started inside her and they refused to be dampened now. 'So have I,' she admitted softly. 'Make love to me, Ray.'

He smiled and she saw the sudden flare of triumph in his dark eyes. Then he reached and started to unbutton her red top, his fingers brushing lightly against her skin making her tremble inside with chaotic need.

'What about all those strong words,' he murmured playfully as he looked into her eyes, 'about sleeping in separate beds...hmm?' As he spoke the red top was pulled off.

'They were strong words...weren't they?' Caitlin murmured, her eyes closing on a wave of ecstasy as his hands moved over the lace of her bra, his fingers touching lightly against the hardened peaks of her breasts. 'And they got me here, didn't they?'

He found the fastener at the front of the black bra and toyed with it provocatively. 'So no more talk of separate beds, then?'

'Not for now...' She was desperately anxious for him to just carry on caressing her. She didn't want to talk. He was sitting on the desk and she was held between his knees; they tightened against her thighs.

'That's not a good answer,' he drawled teasingly. 'You should have said, No more talk of separate beds, I promise, Ray.'

'You are just a tease, Monsieur Pascal,' she murmured, half annoyed, half amused by his demands.

'It takes one to know one,' he said with a smile, his fingers moving to the zip at the back of her skirt. He unfastened it and pulled the skirt down, letting it fall to the floor, so that now she stood before him in only her underwear, black boots and lace top stockings.

'Nice outfit,' he murmured, his eyes moving boldly over her.

The possessive way he looked at her made her senses race; it was almost as if she could feel his eyes touching her. 'So am I the only one getting undressed here?' she murmured huskily and reached to start unbuttoning his shirt. As it opened she slid her hands beneath the material, stroking over the powerful contours of his chest.

He leaned forward and kissed her; it was a kiss that was so passionate it made her body dissolve with need. She wound her arms tightly around his shoulders and kissed him back wildly. The next moment he was lifting her up and turning her so that she was the one sitting on the desk. He swept the papers and the glasses roughly to one side and some of the paperwork tumbled to the floor but neither of them even noticed the chaos around them, they were entangled in an embrace that shut everything else out.

Caitlin was only vaguely aware of the cool surface of the desk against her back as she lay against it. All she could think about was the bliss of his hands against her skin, the heat of his lips as he kissed the sensitive areas of her neck and then her shoulders.

He unfastened her bra and then his lips moved downwards to tease the rosy hard peaks of her breasts. She gasped with pleasure as she felt his hand moving the delicate lace of her panties so that he could explore her more thoroughly.

'Ray, I want you so much.' She murmured the words almost incoherently, desperate now with a longing that was tearing into her with searing intensity.

He lifted her up from the desk as if she were a mere doll and she wrapped her legs around his waist as he carried her over to the bed in the corner.

'We may as well make ourselves a little more comfortable,' he said as he placed her down gently against the satin cushions.

She watched as he took his shirt off and then hastily she unzipped her boots and rolled down her stockings. When she looked up she found he was watching her, a gleam of naked desire in his dark eyes.

'God, you are so gorgeous, Caitlin.'

He stroked his hands along the shapely length of her legs as she leaned back against the cushions. He was gorgeous too, she thought hazily. He had an incredibly beautiful body, wide shoulders, lithe hips, a flat stomach and an arousal that made her heart start hammering with even more force.

The only item of clothing she wore now was her lacy black panties and he played with the delicate string of material for a moment before pulling them firmly down, then he moved to kneel over her. His eyes raked over her, taking in the way her hair spilled over the gold cushions behind her head, the flush of heat on her skin, the soft pout of her lips, then moved lower, examining her curves as if committing them to memory.

He touched her breasts softly, exploring the full roundness, his thumb rasping slightly against the sensitive hardness of her nipples. She shivered and closed her eyes on a wave of ecstasy. Waiting for him was like a pleasurable kind of torture; every nerve, every inch of her skin was aching. She reached up and put her hands on his shoulders, urging him silently to come closer.

And then she felt the full force of his arousal pressing against her and suddenly he was inside her. The feelings of pleasure were so vehemently intense that she gasped.

'Are you okay?' he murmured, stroking her hair tenderly back from her face, his movements gentle.

'I'm more than okay.' She smiled up at him, loving his tenderness. Then she moved her hips provocatively and drew him closer. She felt greedy with need; it was eating her alive. She wanted him with an impatience she had never known before. Ray grinned and bent down to nuzzle his lips in against her neck and her ear.

'Patience, my sweet…' he whispered softly and then spoke in French. His words were teasingly provocative as he skilfully brought her again and again to the brink of climax. She clung to him, pressing her lips against the warmth of his skin, moaning with pleasure, wanting the joy to go on and on forever and yet at the same time desperate for the ultimate sensation of release.

Ray was a skilful lover. He knew exactly how to please a woman. He teased and tormented her, showing her the dizzying heights of passion, his lips ravishing her body, his hands caressing her with the smooth ability of experience. Then just when she thought she could stand it no longer he took full possession again and brought her to the wild heights of a bliss that splintered inside her in wave after wonderful wave of fulfilment.

She clung to him afterwards, wrapped in the warmth of his arms, so exhausted she couldn't even think coherently, never mind talk. He soothed her tenderly as if she were a babe in his arms and whispered sweet nothings against her ear.

Caitlin cuddled closer. She felt as if she could never get close enough to him, as if she wanted to melt into his very skin. She had never known the ache of such a longing...or the wonder of such sweet content.

Then his lips found hers and he kissed her again, this time without the fierceness of hunger and with all the tenderness of a sated lover...

Caitlin groaned and wound her arms around his shoulders. She wanted to tell him how much she loved him...how desperately she wanted him...that she would do anything for him. The thoughts tumbled through her mind in wild confusion before exhaustion took her over and she fell into the peaceful oblivion of a deep sleep.

CHAPTER EIGHT

WHEN Caitlin woke she was disorientated. She was wrapped in a tangle of white sheets. Across from her on the opposite wall she could see bookshelves; everything was unfamiliar to her sleep-blurred eyes. She stretched and every part of her body felt stiff. Then suddenly the memories from last night unfurled in her mind in a red-hot reel of Technicolor. The way she had almost pleaded with Ray to make love to her, the way he had undressed her at his desk...the way he had lazily and skilfully brought her to climax amidst the cushions of this bed.

Then she remembered the way he had woken her in the night to take her again, and the way she had met his demands with fiery acquiescence, loving the hotly possessive touch of his lips and hands against her body. Her stomach muscles tightened as a wave of renewed hunger hit her.

But the memory that disturbed her most was of the feelings that had accompanied the wild, reckless love-making...the emotions that had driven her, the words that she hadn't dared speak... She frowned and pushed a trembling hand through her hair... At least she hoped she hadn't spoken them. It was disturbing enough that all her inhibitions had been totally stripped—and that Ray knew her body was completely his for the taking—without letting him know that her heart had also some-how been thrown in with the package.

She stared up at the ceiling and told herself in very angry terms that her feelings of love had been a mistake…an illusion. Last night was about having fun—two consensual adults letting their hair down. If Ray thought for one moment that she was attaching more importance than that to it, he'd be horrified. And she wasn't, she told herself fiercely. She didn't know where those mad thoughts had come from. Maybe it was because no man had ever made her feel so wonderful…so wanton, so pleasured…and she was confusing mind-blowing sex with love… That could explain it, she told herself with conviction.

The sound of a drawer closing made Caitlin aware suddenly that she wasn't alone in the room. She sat up slightly and looked down towards Ray's desk.

Early morning sun slanted through the slatted blinds. It fell over the discarded clothes on the floor. Her skirt was in a heap at the foot of his desk, her bra was sitting in the in-tray…her lacy pants were in the middle of the floor. Embarrassment ate through her.

Then the chair behind the desk swivelled around as Ray turned from the filing cabinets. He was wearing a thick white towelling robe, his dark hair was tousled and there was the beginning of dark designer stubble on his square jaw.

Their eyes met and he smiled. 'Good morning, sleepyhead,' he said tenderly and at the sound of his voice and the sexy glint in his dark eyes she felt all her strong words melt into confusion… She couldn't ever remember feeling so overwhelmed by a man before; he was just sensational.

'Morning.' She smiled back at him. 'What time is it?'

'Seven forty-five.'

'Gosh, so early!' She stretched again and sat up further, taking care to keep the sheets firmly in place so that her nakedness was covered. 'What are you doing?' she asked.

'We made a bit of a mess of my paperwork last night.' He glanced across at her again and grinned as he noticed the blaze of heat on her cheekbones. 'So I thought I'd sort it out and do a bit of work while I'm at it. Then we can go out and enjoy the day.'

'Sounds like a good plan.'

She wanted to get out of bed but she was embarrassed by her nakedness... Absurd, considering the fact that he had seen and sampled every naked inch of her body last night, but she couldn't help it—in the cool light of day she was suddenly shy again.

'I think I might go and have a shower,' she said hesitantly.

'Mmm, good idea. I'll follow you once I've finished here.'

Did he mean he intended to follow her into the shower itself? she wondered heatedly. Or did he just mean that he was allowing her to use the bathroom first?

Caitlin wasn't used to being in such close quarters with a man she knew so little about. All right, she knew his body very well now...and she had been as intimate with him last night as it was possible to get. But apart from the fact that she knew he found her attractive and that they were sexually compatible, she didn't know what else was going on in his mind. It made her feel awkwardly inept as to how to handle this situation. It made her almost wish that she had more experience in casual affairs.

Gathering her courage, she wrapped the sheet around her toga-style and stepped out of the bed. She could hardly dash from the room while all her clothes were scattered about the place in wild abandonment, so she stooped to pick up a few things. Her panties and stockings from the floor were first to be snatched up. Then she approached his desk and picked up her skirt and the bra from his in-tray.

She didn't dare look at him as she did this, but she was aware of him watching her. Then as she made to turn away from the desk he reached out and caught hold of her arm.

'Don't I get a good morning kiss?' he asked gruffly.

Her stomach turned over as she met his eyes, and she allowed him to steer her around the side of his desk where he pulled her down onto his lap.

'There, that's better.' He smiled, his eyes on her lips. 'Last night was very enjoyable.'

'Yes...' She felt breathlessly helpless. All she wanted was for him to fold her into his arms again and do exactly what he had done to her last night. The lack of all control scared her. She needed to be careful around him; her emotions were all over the place. The wild feelings of love last night worried her especially. She was still raw from her breakup with David and she couldn't trust her feelings.

He noticed the flicker of uncertainty and vulnerability in her green eyes and then as she tried to avert her gaze his finger firmly lifted her chin so that she was forced to look at him.

'You are an incredibly sexy woman,' he murmured. Then his lips met with hers in a warmly seductive kiss and the fire ignited inside her with such ferocity that it swept her mind away all over again. He laced his hands through her hair, holding her still while his mouth explored hers with compelling sensuality, then his hands moved to the sheet that covered her, pulling it away so that his hands were free to move over the smooth velvet nakedness that lay beneath. His fingers found her breasts, caressing and toying with her as his lips trailed a heated path down her neck and lower. The slight rasp of his skin against the softness of hers was somehow incredibly sexy, adding to the intense desire welling up inside her.

As his lips found the sensitized warmth of her breast she gasped and closed her eyes, the clothes that she had gathered from the floor slipping from her fingers as her hands moved to rake through the darkness of his hair. She buried her face into its softness, breathing in the scent of him, the tang of cologne and soap.

The sudden shrill ring of the phone behind them made him stop abruptly. Her heart was thundering against her chest; she wanted to tell him not to answer it, but to carry on. Her eyes met with his, wide and silently pleading for more of his kisses…much more of his caresses.

And for a moment she thought he was going to oblige and that he was as impatient to continue as she was. Then the answer machine came on. 'Hi, Ray, it's Sadie…I need to speak to you.' She spoke in French, her voice huskily attractive. 'Can I see you today or is that not convenient? It's just…' Anything else she was saying was cut off abruptly as Ray swung the chair around and picked up the receiver.

'Hello, Sadie.' As he spoke he watched Caitlin gather the sheet around her body. 'No, today isn't suitable… Yes, that's why I left the office early yesterday.'

Caitlin slipped from his knee and bent to pick her clothes up again. Their eyes met as she stood up. 'I'm going to go have that shower,' she mouthed.

He nodded.

As Caitlin left the room his conversation continued. She closed the door behind her and told herself that it was just as well they had been interrupted; it gave her time to gather her senses. The words fought valiantly with the red-hot need that still swirled inside her, refusing to be extinguished.

She made her way back to her bedroom and threw her clothes down on a chair. The massive bed, still pristinely untouched, seemed to mock her. So much for hiding in here all night, she thought wryly, so much for being in control of the situation.

Leaving the sheet on the floor, she went through to the bathroom and turned the shower on full. Standing under the razor-sharp jets of hot water, she washed her hair and soaped her body with hard, vigorous strokes in the vain attempt to rid herself of the need that was still rampaging through her.

Caitlin didn't like the feeling of being out of control. It was important that she took stock of things now; emotionally distanced herself from the heat Ray stirred up inside her.

Then the shower door opened and Ray stepped in beside her and suddenly the thought of distancing herself was the furthest thing on her mind.

'Now where were we?' he murmured with a grin as he took her firmly into his arms.

Hours later as they wandered along the Champs-Elysées, gazing into designer boutiques, Caitlin was still trying to close her mind on the steamy hot passion they had shared together earlier. But it seemed to colour the whole day. It was there in the heat of the sun that shone down on them, it was there in the white intensity of the blossom on the trees, in the swirling silky darkness of the Seine. And it was fiercely present every time Ray looked at her or smiled, or touched her. The emotions she so wanted to suppress were out of control, and as much as she tried, she couldn't seem to get them back into the neat little compartment where she could shut the lid on them.

Was she on the rebound? she wondered as Ray insisted on dragging her into a jewellery shop to look at a necklace she had admired in the window.

Maybe…she was…

'You must try it on.' Ray cut through her thoughts as he lifted the amber necklace from its velvet case.

'No, really, Ray. I think it's very pretty but—'

'Lift your hair up,' he cut across her with a smile. 'And I'll fasten it for you.'

She found herself doing as he asked. Even the touch of his fingers against her skin as he fastened the gold chain made her senses swim.

'So what do you think?' he asked as the assistant brought a mirror so Caitlin could see herself.

She released her hair and glanced at herself. The necklace looked fantastic against her skin, its amber colour reflecting the amber lights in her hair and bringing out the green-gold of her eyes.

'It's looks wonderful, doesn't it?' Ray said softly. He leaned forward and kissed her cheek and for a moment they were both reflected in the oval mirror. Caitlin couldn't help thinking that they looked right together somehow. The thought was crazy and she moved away from him slightly and reached to unfasten the necklace.

'You should keep it on.' He caught hold of her hand before she could find the catch. 'It complements the black trouser suit you are wearing perfectly.' He nodded at the assistant who took the mirror away. And then the next moment Ray was passing a credit card across the counter.

'No, Ray, I can't let you buy it!' Caitlin was horrified. She had been so busy daydreaming earlier that she hadn't been fully aware of the price of the piece. 'It's far too expensive.'

'You like it. Don't you?' he asked nonchalantly.

'Well, I love it, but—'

Ray was already signing on the dotted line. 'It's a birthday present,' he said. 'And I want you to have it.'

The sales assistant gave him his receipt and smiled at them both. Caitlin noticed how she particularly smiled at Ray…but then it was the same everywhere they went—women just seemed to fall over themselves for him.

'Thank you, Ray, but you shouldn't have done that,' she told him as they made their way back outside. 'It's far too generous a gift.'

'No, it's not.' He caught hold of her hand and smiled at her. 'Besides, I have an ulterior motive.'

'You have?' She looked over at him uncertainly.

'Yes.' He leaned closer and kissed her softly on the lips. 'I want you to undress for me later and wear it as I make mad, passionate love to you.'

The wild rush of adrenalin inside her seemed to scorch through her skin. 'I think that could be arranged,' she said huskily, and there was part of her that wanted to ask if they could go back to his apartment right now.

'Good.' He pulled a strand of her hair playfully. 'But now I think we should go and have something to eat.' He raised a hand to flag down a taxi.

Ray took her to a small restaurant in a lovely old square and they sat at a table outside and sipped some wine as they perused the menu.

He glanced across at her and smiled and her heart seemed to do an alarming somersault. If she was on the rebound, then how come these emotions were so much more intense than they had been with David the first time around? The question snaked its way into her thoughts. No one had ever made her feel like this before.

'So have you decided?' he asked as a waitress came out to take their order.

She glanced quickly back down at the menu. She had decided, she reminded herself firmly, not to think about anything too deeply any more.

After the waitress took their order they sat in companionable silence. It was interesting watching the people walking across the square; some were obviously tourists because they posed for photographs outside the small chapel opposite. Some were Parisians, smartly dressed going about their daily business, and others were lovers strolling hand in hand in the sunshine.

For a moment Caitlin found herself thinking about her wedding and she glanced at her watch. It was almost three. She would have been arriving at the church now.

And it probably would have been the worst mistake of your life, a little voice reminded her sharply.

Watching her, Ray noticed how she looked at her watch and how her skin suddenly blanched. Was she thinking about the wedding and David? he wondered.

'Are you okay?' he asked softly.

She glanced across at him and smiled, and suddenly the pain inside her started to subside.

'I'm absolutely fine,' she told him sincerely.

It was late by the time they got back to his apartment. They had sailed down the Seine on the Bateaux Mouches, admiring the fine architecture of the city. They had taken the lift to the top of the Eiffel Tower and they had sat at a pavement café at Montmartre as darkness had stolen over the city.

The plan had been to shower and change and go out for dinner. But once in the privacy of the apartment the plans were somehow forgotten as they ended up tumbling into bed, to make wild, passionate love.

At ten-thirty they awoke in the darkened apartment and both were ravenously hungry. So Ray phoned for a take-away and opened a bottle of champagne. They picnicked on the roof terrace, admiring the twinkle of the Parisian lights.

'Life is strange, isn't it?' Caitlin reflected as she sipped the champagne. 'If someone had told me a few months ago that I would be spending my birthday in Paris with you, I wouldn't have believed them.'

Ray grinned. 'What is it they say…? Life is what happens when you are busy making other plans.'

'That's very true.' Caitlin sipped her champagne and the bubbles went up her nose.

'What happened between you and David?'

The quietly voiced question took her by surprise.

Ray watched her silently for a moment and noticed the flicker of vulnerability in her wide green eyes. Then she looked away from him.

When they had got out of bed she had thrown on a white silk blouse and a pair of jeans. Her hair was tousled around her face and very sexy; her skin still had a glow across her cheekbones that a moment ago had been due to the wild heat of their lovemaking… And now probably was down to the fact that she was uncomfortable with his questions.

'It just didn't work out, Ray,' she said lightly.

'Was there another woman?'

'No!' Her skin held even more heat now. 'I think maybe I could have coped with that better,' she added impulsively. 'At least I could have hated him for that…' She shrugged and then added huskily, 'Instead there is this horrible feeling that I failed him…because I wasn't able to help him.' She looked over at Ray and her eyes shimmered with a different raw emotion for a moment. 'But how can you help someone when they won't admit they have a problem, when they refuse to even talk about it in terms of a problem? He had a serious gambling addiction, but he refused to see it that way.'

'I see,' Ray said quietly. 'A lot of addicts are like that and if they are not ready to accept help there is very little you can do.'

Caitlin shook her head. 'I probably didn't handle it very well. When I found out I was shocked and angry and I moved out. But afterwards when I'd calmed down I tried to talk to him. I got all the leaflets, you know, about places to call and counselling services, but he was furious with me for even suggesting it. He thought we should just go on as if it didn't matter—it was just a hobby, he said.' Caitlin toyed with her glass. 'Taking my engagement ring off was a last resort...but even then he thought I was the one in the wrong.'

'You still care about him a lot, don't you?' Ray said softly.

'Of course I care about him, and I'm worried about him. We were together for three years, and it's hard to switch off from that...' She trailed off huskily. Then she glanced over at him and their eyes met and a red-hot wash of emotion swept through her. Although it was true, she did care about David, it was nothing to the explosive feelings that Ray could stir up inside her.

The acknowledgement sent shock waves through her and hastily she took another sip of her drink. She wasn't thinking straight, she told herself fiercely.

'So, anyway, that's the sorry state of my romantic entanglements.' She forced a light note to her voice and gave him a half-smile. 'What about you?'

He shrugged. 'Since Hélène died I have found it easier to avoid entanglements. I've kept my relationships light and my workload heavy.'

'And that's what you recommend for a broken heart, is it?' It was difficult to sound detached. She knew that her time here with him was just a casual fling, but she didn't like it pointed out in such cool terms.

'No, I wouldn't recommend that...' For a moment he was silent. She glanced over at him and noticed how his eyes seemed shadowed with sadness. 'I can't say that it has helped heal the pain of losing her.'

She swallowed hard, suddenly ashamed that she had made such a flippant remark. 'I'm sorry, Ray.'

He shook his head. 'I've come to terms with Hélène's death...I've had to. But I still miss her.'

Caitlin drew her legs up onto the chair and hugged her knees close in against her chest. 'Tell me about her,' she invited softly.

'What do you want to know?' He looked amused for a moment.

Caitlin shrugged. 'Where did you meet? What was she like?'

She rested her chin on her knees and watched him as he spoke.

'We met in Provence at the château. My mother had relocated down there after my father died and she was having the place redecorated. I had just graduated from university and was only there for a short visit before starting a new job in Paris. Then Hélène walked in with her team of decorators in tow. She looked incredible with her dark hair billowing around her face, like something from a pre-Raphaelite painting. Dark eyes, pouting soft lips that were quick to smile, she oozed life and vitality. My four-day break stretched into a two-week stay. I only just made it back in time to start my job. Then two weeks later I had persuaded her to give up her interior design job and move up to Paris to live with me.'

'Wow,' Caitlin said softly. 'It must have been love at first sight.'

Ray nodded. 'I had never been a great believer in that before. But yes it was like a bolt of lightning…*coup de foudre*…I can still see her very clearly in my mind just as she was that day when she walked into the château, still remember the feelings she stirred up inside me. We were married two months later. There were a few raised eyebrows that everything was happening so quickly.' He shrugged. 'But we just knew it was right, and I'm glad now that we didn't waste time…'

'How long were you together?' Caitlin asked softly.

'Seven years, and they were good years.' He shrugged. 'So that is something to be happy about. I went into partnership with Philippe and as the business took off we were able to spend more and more time down in Provence. Hélène always loved it down there, it was home for her. At first we were just there for the month of August when everything shut down in Paris. But then later, after my mother died and I inherited the château we would spend longer there.'

He fell silent for a long moment. 'And that was where she died, down in Provence where it all started… She lost control of her car on one of the hairpin bends going down to the village.'

'I'm sorry, Ray…'

For a moment he looked as if he hadn't heard her, then he glanced over at her and shrugged. 'Life goes on, doesn't it Caitlin? And you learn to just get on with things.' His voice seemed hard suddenly.

Caitlin reached across and covered his hand with hers. She didn't know what to say to him; words somehow seemed so inadequate.

He smiled at her. 'Anyway, enough of this maudlin talk,' he said, his mood lightening in an instant as he pulled away from her touch and refilled her champagne glass.

'Let's drink to the future, shall we?' He raised his glass.

She had just taken a sip of the sparkling wine when the sound of the phone ringing in the apartment disturbed them.

'I won't be a moment.' Ray lifted his glass and brought it inside with him, leaving Caitlin to gaze out over the city and reflect on his words.

Her breakup with David had been raw and difficult but next to Ray's loss it seemed to pale into insignificance.

It was obvious that Ray was still deeply in love with his late wife; it was there in his voice, in his eyes.

A cool breeze whispered over the terrace, sending the wind chimes ringing. Caitlin shivered a little and then decided to clear the table.

As she came back out of the kitchen she could hear the deep, melodious tone of Ray's voice as he spoke in French. On impulse she went and stood by the office door to look in at him.

He was sitting in his chair behind the desk, but he didn't see her because it was swivelled sideways as he riffled through some papers he was taking from a filing cabinet. The phone was balanced between his ear and shoulder as he spoke. It was clearly a business call.

I've kept my relationships light and my workload heavy. Ray's words echoed inside her mind and she felt a tinge of pain as she thought of them. Then hastily she turned away from the door. She needed to do the same thing, she told herself sternly.

Out of the corner of his eye Ray glimpsed Caitlin as she moved away from the door. He raked a hand through his hair impatiently. 'Look, Philippe, it is nearly midnight and I don't want to talk about this now. For one thing I have Caitlin here with me. Let's leave it at least until Monday.'

'Time is money, Ray. We need to sort this out as soon as possible.' His business partner's voice was insistent. 'The solicitor faxed me a copy of Murdo's will this morning. It makes interesting reading.'

'Yes, Sadie rang to tell me all that this morning—'

'But I've had my solicitor look through it since then,' Philippe cut across him swiftly. 'And there is a way around the problem of Caitlin not being allowed to sell the place for six months.'

'Go on.' Ray leaned his head back against his chair resignedly.

'You could marry her.'

The softly spoken words made Ray sit up as if he had been shot. 'You are joking, Philippe!'

'No, I'm deadly serious. Murdo has made special provisions for it, even named you in the will. If you marry Caitlin the property will be yours straight away, lock, stock and barrel, as they say, and he has even placed some money in trust as a wedding present for you both. I'm telling you, Ray, if you marry Caitlin there would be nothing to stop us bringing in the bulldozers the next day and levelling the place. And, what's more, you would make a handsome profit from the wedding gift. All right, I know that once you marry her then half of everything you own will be hers, but you could get around that with a pre-nuptial. My solicitor is red-hot on things like that.'

Ray swore lightly under his breath. 'That is the most preposterous thing I have ever heard. And what makes you think Caitlin would want to go along with a crazy scheme like that?'

'Come on, Ray, you could sweet-talk her around if you really wanted to.'

'This is Caitlin we are talking about,' Ray reminded him. 'She loves the house and doesn't want to sell it...and what is more she is probably still in love with her ex-fiancé.'

'Great, so catch her on the rebound,' Philippe said jovially. 'This makes good business sense for both of you. I know you like her, Ray. I saw the way you looked at her when we all had dinner that night. And you've obviously taken her to bed.'

'That is none of your damn business, Philippe,' Ray cut across him furiously.

'Look, all I'm saying is consider it. As I see it you've got nothing to lose and everything to gain; a beautiful woman in your bed and a healthy profit. And if you don't like being married to her you can always divorce her and it probably won't cost you as much as losing out on this land deal—'

'You know something, Philippe,' Ray cut across him heavily. 'You've got a disgustingly mercenary mind.'

Far from being outraged, Philippe laughed. 'Just think about it, that's all I am saying. Anyhow, have you received that copy of Murdo's will that I faxed you earlier?'

'Yes, it is here on my desk, but I'm not interested, Philippe, and you are going too far.' Ray's voice was tight with anger.

'Well, you should at least look at it. And I don't wish to be too intrusive or mercenary, Ray, but remember these were Murdo's last wishes and should be respected. Anyway, I'll talk to you Monday… Oh, and by the way, Sadie thought the idea was great. She said it was about time you took the matrimonial plunge again, even if it is only for six months.'

Ray put the phone down in disgust. Then he sat still for a moment, Philippe's words thumping through his mind, before pushing his chair back and going in search of Caitlin.

He found her outside on the patio; she was leaning against the wrought-iron railing looking down at the street below.

'Everything okay?' She turned and looked at him as he came to stand next to her and she was surprised to see a glitter of anger in his eyes.

'Yes, everything is just fine.'

It didn't sound as if it was, but she didn't press him. Instead she said gently, 'You know, I think you are right about throwing yourself into work. It does help take your mind off things. I feel a lot better when I'm busy.'

His eyes moved over her contemplatively. The breeze was ruffling her hair back from her face. She had a beautiful bone structure, high cheekbones, perfectly proportioned lips that were full and sensuous, a small button nose and eyes that shimmered with beauty. All in all she was a very desirable package.

Aware that he seemed to be watching her very closely, she felt her heart start to speed up with a mixture of desire and uncertainty. Desperately she sought to keep her mind away from the longing he could fire up in her. 'And I've been giving Murdo's house a bit of thought,' she said.

'Well, it is your favourite subject.'

Caitlin decided it was best to ignore the wry comment and continued swiftly. 'I was wondering if I should take the wall down between the dining room and the lounge and put in an archway. What do you think?'

There was a flicker of amusement in his gaze now. 'Why are you asking me?'

'Because you are an architect and I wanted a professional opinion,' she said, a small frown playing between her eyes.

'Well, you know what I think,' he said softly. 'I think the place should be demolished.'

'Ray, that is not funny.' She put one hand on her hip and glared at him. 'That is Murdo's house you are talking about!'

'It's your house,' he corrected her softly. 'To do with as you see fit.'

'Yes, and I see fit to restore it lovingly to its former glory.'

'I know.' Ray put one hand under her chin, tipping her face so that she was forced to meet his gaze. 'Tell me, Caitlin, did you ever see Murdo's will?' He watched her face, searching for any flicker of emotion that might tell him she knew the terms Murdo had laid down.

Caitlin frowned, the question taking her very much by surprise. 'Well, no...of course not. I got a letter from the solicitor telling me of my inheritance. And I saw him briefly in his office to collect the keys. But I didn't actually see the will.' She shrugged. 'Why? Should I have done?'

'No. I just wondered what you knew about the conditions of sale, that's all.'

'All he said was that I've got to live there for six months before I can sell it. And he told me that there were a few special conditions attached to the will regarding that. I didn't pay much attention to that part of things, to be honest, because I was just so thrilled to be inheriting a house, selling it was the last thing on my mind. Oh, and he told me to get back in touch with him if my marital status was going to change.' She grimaced slightly. 'I told him there was no chance of that.'

Ray nodded. It was quite clear to him that Caitlin had no inkling of Murdo's final wishes.

'Why are you asking, anyway?' She looked up at him, puzzled by the questions. 'You are not still obsessed with buying the place, are you, Ray? I thought we'd agreed to forget that.'

'You were the one who brought up the subject of the house,' he reminded her with a grin.

'Yes, well, I'm sorry I did now. That joke about bulldozing the place wasn't funny.'

He smiled and leaned a little closer. 'Caitlin,' he said softly, 'it's just a house, let's forget it and move on to more interesting subjects.'

'Like what?' she asked breathlessly as his lips hovered a fraction from hers.

'Like this, of course…' And then he kissed her with deeply searing, purposeful kisses. And suddenly Caitlin forgot all about the house…all about Ray's love for Hélène…and all about David.

CHAPTER NINE

IT WAS early Sunday morning. Caitlin cuddled closer to
Ray in the deep comfort of the double bed and listened
to the sound of church bells drifting on the air. She
wished that time would stand still and they could lie
entwined in each other's arms like this forever. But unfortunately their flight home was at twelve-thirty this
afternoon...so time was running out.

She glanced up at Ray, studying the lean, handsome
features as he slept. His lashes were dark and thick
against his cheek. He had eyelashes that any woman
would be proud of, she thought hazily, and his mouth
was softly sensuous. Remembering the heat of his kisses
last night made her go hot all over and stirred a feeling
of renewed need inside her. She stretched up and kissed
him softly on his lips. His arms tightened around her
waist and he returned the kiss sleepily, his eyes flicking
open.

'Mmm, that is a nice way to wake up,' he murmured
lazily.

'I was just thinking the same myself.' She rolled over
and leaned against his chest, looking down at him with
a smile. This close, his eyes were a gorgeous shade of
deep molasses honey.

He reached up and stroked his hands through her hair,
then, cupping her face, he kissed her tenderly.

The phone cut through the silence of the morning.

Caitlin groaned and wound her arms around his neck.

'Does your phone never stop ringing? Just ignore it,' she murmured.

Ray continued to kiss her back and she thought he was going to do just that, but then suddenly he was pulling away from her. 'I've just remembered that Philippe said he'd phone me this morning,' he said, sliding out from under her.

Caitlin watched with disappointment as he walked away from her to pick up his robe from the chair. She had a brief glimpse of his powerful body before he had put the robe on and disappeared out of the bedroom door.

Caitlin wished he wasn't able to switch quite so easily from thinking about passion to business. It sent a small feeling of disquiet through her. Surely he could have let the answer machine take that call? After all, it was Sunday morning.

With a sigh she climbed out of bed and reached for her dressing gown. She was being selfish, she told herself firmly. Trouble was, she couldn't seem to help herself.

Tying the belt of her gown firmly around her waist, she walked through to the kitchen and put the kettle on.

'Bad news, I'm afraid,' Ray said as he joined her a few moments later. 'I'm not going to be able to fly back to Provence with you today. That was Philippe and some problems have cropped up that I'm going to have to take care of at the office. I'll drop you out at the airport first, though.'

'There is no need, Ray,' she said quickly. 'I can take a taxi to the airport.'

'Always so independent,' he mocked her lightly, and then as she made to move away from him he caught hold of her hand and pulled her back. 'Okay, but I'll only allow you to take a taxi to the airport if you will have dinner with me on Wednesday night?'

She pretended to think about it for a moment. 'All right, you've got a deal, but come over to my place and I'll cook for you.'

'Sounds wonderful.' He pressed a kiss against her lips. 'You can impress me with your *cuisine anglaise*,' he murmured teasingly.

She smiled up into his eyes. 'And you can impress me with your architectural skills and give me your opinion on that wall that I'm thinking of taking out...'

'I thought you wanted to cook for me and all along you've got an ulterior motive.' He shook his head. 'I can see I've met my match with you, Caitlin Palmer.'

'You've caught me red-handed,' she said with a smile.

He kissed her softly on the lips again. 'Wednesday it is, then,' he said gently as he moved back. 'Now I've got to shower and leave you, I'm afraid, but I'll ring that taxi for you before I go.'

It seemed strange being left alone in Ray's apartment. Caitlin showered and changed and packed up her bag. Then she wandered around and tidied up while she waited for the taxi. Her steps led her into the office and she collected the champagne glass Ray had left on the desk last night. As she did her glance fell on the papers neatly stacked by the phone and Murdo's name caught her attention.

She moved the papers slightly and they slid down onto the floor. Hastily she bent to pick them up and that was when she realised that what she was looking at was a copy of Murdo's last will and testament.

Caitlin frowned as she remembered the way Ray had questioned her last night about Murdo's will. Why had he questioned her about it when he already had a copy?

Why did he even have a copy? The answer to that was easy: *he hadn't given up on buying her house.*

Frowning, she leafed through the papers. Pinned to the will there was a note from Philippe. It was in French and she had difficulty in understanding it…something about marriage being a solution, which didn't make any sense. Caitlin sat down in Ray's chair and leafed further through the papers. There were some plans folded at the back and she spread them out across the desk. At first she didn't know what she was looking at, then she realised that Ray's château was marked on the map, and Murdo's house and behind it several other houses.

But there were no other houses behind Murdo's. She frowned and flicked back to the note Philippe had sent, and wished her French were better. Why was marriage the solution…and a solution to what?

The sound of the front door slamming made her jump nervously.

'Hi, Caitlin, it is only me,' Ray's voice called out from the lounge. 'I forgot some documents that I need.'

For a second Caitlin thought about hurriedly putting the papers away so as not to be caught snooping, but then she dismissed the notion. This concerned her land and she needed to know what was going on.

'Caitlin…' His voice trailed off as he reached the office door and saw her sitting behind his desk. 'What are you up to?' he asked warily as he noticed the papers spread out in front of her.

'I was just about to ask you the same question.' Her voice was brittle.

He came further into the room. 'The papers you are rooting through are private,' he said, an edge of annoyance creeping into his tone.

'But they concern me, don't they, Ray?' Her heart

started to thump with painful rapid strokes, but it wasn't with anger, it was with cold dread. The mood between them earlier had been so playful and tender. She remembered the way they had actually teased each other about having ulterior motives…and now suspicion and distrust were twisting everything inside her. 'You led me to believe that you wanted my property because it was a minor inconvenience having to drive across it towards one of your many entrances. But that wasn't the truth, was it?' Her eyes drifted to the plans lying by Murdo's will. 'I'm blocking more than an entrance to your house, aren't I?' Her voice was icy with realisation. 'In fact I'm obviously a major headache…that's why you've gone to so much trouble getting a copy of Murdo's will so you could find out how to get rid of me before the six months were up…that's probably why you've invited me here…' As everything tumbled into place her eyes darkened with pain. 'And it's probably why you've taken me to bed—'

'Caitlin, that isn't true,' he cut across her quietly. 'I invited you here because I wanted to spend time with you—'

'Just cut out the smooth talk, Ray, because it's not going to wash with me,' she intercepted him fiercely. 'I'm not stupid—I can see exactly what has been going on here.' She flicked the paper on the desk contemptuously. 'I knew there would never be anything deep and meaningful between us. But I never thought that you would stoop to this.'

'Caitlin if you would just listen for a moment—'

'I don't want to listen to anything you say ever again.' Her eyes blazed with fury now. 'And don't flatter yourself that you can get round me with platitudes, because, to be honest, going to bed with you was a light-hearted fling, something to take my mind away from the real love of my life.' As she said the words she noticed how his eyes narrowed on her and she hoped vehemently that she had struck a blow to his arrogant male ego. But also at the same time something twisted inside her painfully, and she knew that her words were anything but honest. Sleeping with Ray had meant so much more than that. 'But I thought we were at least truthful with each other,' she finished huskily.

'I have never made any secret of the fact that I wanted to buy your land.' Ray's voice was terse now.

'But you didn't tell me about this.' Furiously she swept the papers off the desk and onto the floor.

'I didn't tell you because I didn't think it would help matters.'

'Well, you were right there, because the answer to your offer is still no.' She stood up. 'And what the hell is this marriage solution that Philippe has written about?'

'You have been digging, haven't you?' Ray said calmly.

'What is it, Ray?' she asked again, fixing him with a rigid stare.

He bent and retrieved the papers to put them back on the desk. 'Apparently the only way around the six-months stipulation for selling is if you and I marry.' He watched as her skin blanched, then went on tersely. 'Apparently Murdo specified that if we marry the house will be mine and, what is more, he has placed a large amount of money in a trust fund somewhere as a wedding present for us.'

'So what were you planning, Ray—a whirlwind romance and wedding followed by a lightning divorce?' Her heart was thundering so hard against her chest that it felt tight with pain. 'I hope you were planning to get down on one knee when you ask me,' she added darkly. 'That way it will feel so much more satisfying when I say no.'

His lips twisted in a mirthless smile. 'I think you are getting a little ahead of the game, Caitlin,' he said coolly. 'Because I haven't asked you to marry me.'

'Saving that for a cosy night in with me on Wednesday?' She tossed her hair back from her face as she marched past him. 'Well, you can go to hell, Ray. I'd rather marry the devil incarnate than take any vow with you.'

She had almost reached the door when he caught hold of her arm. 'Just hold it right there,' he said angrily and swung her around to face him. 'Just for the record, it was Philippe who came up with the marriage suggestion and I told him to go to hell. And I didn't tell you about the land development because I didn't want to put that much pressure on you to leave. And thirdly I invited you here for purely personal reasons.'

Caitlin swallowed hard. She wanted so much to believe him...but she just couldn't.

The sound of the doorbell cut through the silence.

'That will be my taxi.' With a supreme effort of will she pulled away from him.

Ray followed her out into the lounge and watched as she picked up her bag from behind the door.

'Caitlin, you are making a big mistake,' he said quietly.

'I don't think so.'

'The fact is that I could have had you out of that house quicker than you think.'

The arrogant confidence of his tone made her pause with her hand on the door handle. 'The house is mine,

Ray—' she glanced around at him angrily '—and there is nothing you can do about that.'

'I think there is. Go back to your house and find out where your water supply comes from.'

'What the hell are you talking about?' Caitlin frowned. 'I know I'm not connected to the mains, if that's what you mean, but I've got my own well.'

He shook his head. 'Correction, you've got *my* well. You see, I could have cut you off from your only supply of water ages ago. I just chose not to because it seemed like a very unpleasant thing to do. I preferred the gentle approach. But…' he shrugged '…if you want to take the gloves off and play rough, then fair enough. It's your choice.'

Caitlin stared at him. 'Are you threatening me?'

'No. I'm telling you a point of fact. Any water you have comes courtesy of me. Go back and check it out.' He shrugged. 'Then when you've come to your senses and you realise that I am trying to play fair with you, we'll talk.'

'I don't want to talk to you ever again,' Caitlin said furiously. She turned and opened the door. 'Cut the water off if it makes you feel better.' She tossed the words back at him over her shoulder. 'It won't get you anywhere.'

Then she closed the door behind her, gently but very firmly.

All the way to the airport Caitlin's blood boiled with anger. She was seething with Ray and she was furious with herself for having ever gone to bed with him. How could she have been so stupid? Why hadn't she realised what he was up to?

She reran conversations in her head, searching through for the signs that she had missed. And she remembered especially how he had hesitated when she had asked him directly if there were any hard feelings about her not selling to him. How he had looked amused by her passion for Murdo's house. What was it he had said? 'Some advice, Caitlin… Never fall in love with a business project. You should be objective and unemotional at all times.'

Those words burnt through her mind now and she felt stupid and used and cheap. She had obviously been the business project and he had wined and dined her and probably taken her to bed with only one purpose in mind.

The pain that knowledge caused her was unbelievable. She kept telling herself that she didn't care, that she had no feelings for him anyway. That it had just been a light-hearted fling on her part. But the words were hollow inside her. And the pain just wouldn't subside.

CHAPTER TEN

THE sun rose over the mountains and slanted through the olive grove in a yellow misty haze. Somewhere a cockerel crowed its distinctive notes clear on the silent early morning air. But Caitlin was already awake. She hadn't been sleeping well since her return from Paris and that was a week ago now. Despite the fact that she felt lethargic, she threw the covers of the bed back and went into the kitchen to turn on the tap.

It had become a daily routine. The first thing she did every morning was check the water and she did the same again at regular intervals throughout the day, and sometimes she even got up in the middle of the night just to turn on the tap to check it again. Each time after a few seconds' delay cool water gushed freely and it was the same this morning, a few tense seconds waiting, then water flowed with forceful pressure into the sink. Hastily Caitlin put the kettle under the tap so as not to waste a precious drop. Then she set the kettle on the stove and opened the back door.

It was a glorious morning; the sun was milky warm against her skin and a little bird sat in one of the branches of an almond tree and sang joyously as if life was full of promise. But life wouldn't be full of promise around here if Ray got his way, Caitlin thought darkly. The olive grove would be demolished along with the house and there would be no almond tree for the little bird to sing in. She bit down on her lip and tried not to think about it. Ray was a monster, she told herself sharply, an absolute monster.

So why hadn't he cut the water off? That was the question that plagued her most these days. As soon as she had returned to the house she had lost no time investigating his claims that the well was on his land, and she had found that he was telling the truth. The well lay half a mile inside his boundary. This meant he could have cut her off ages ago. And yet he had chosen not to.

Obviously he had decided that it wouldn't do him any good, she told herself firmly. And he was right, it wouldn't, because no matter what he did she wasn't going to give in and sell. She had already made provisions for the water crisis. All the buckets and the bath had been filled and she had ordered a water tank that should arrive some time next week. As soon as that was installed and filled it would give her some breathing space. She wasn't going to go down without a fight.

But the fact that she should have to fight Ray still astonished and hurt her. She couldn't believe how calculating he had been. Especially when she remembered how passionately he had kissed her and held her. When she lay in bed at night she squeezed her eyes shut and tried to forget how good it had felt to be in his arms. But the memories were hard to erase.

The really strange thing was that she had thought her breakup from David had hurt, but it was nothing to the torment inside her now.

'You are really very bad when it comes to choosing men, Caitlin,' she told herself angrily. 'You'd be better advised to give them up totally. Join a nunnery.'

The shrill whistle of the kettle made her return to the kitchen. As she made herself some ground coffee she tried to switch her mind away from Ray and think instead about the day ahead. There was a local market on in the village today and she wanted to go down and buy some fresh vegetables and provisions.

She turned the immersion on so that she could have a shower. Then she sat at the kitchen table and sipped her coffee as she made a shopping list. She had just finished when the phone rang and she picked it up expecting it to be her mother or Heidi.

Instead it was Ray's lazily relaxed tone that echoed down the line. 'Hi. Are you ready to talk yet?' he inquired, and instantly every nerve inside her seemed to tense.

'I'm surprised you've got the nerve to phone me.' She felt strangely breathless as she spoke, her emotions twisting inside her as if she were pulling them through a wringer. But the really dreadful part was the weakness inside her that was glad to hear his voice; she fought against that furiously. 'And, no, I am not ready to talk to you and I never will be.'

'Come on, Caitlin, this is silly,' he said impatiently. 'I've given you a whole week to cool off and think about things and that's long enough. Now I think we should meet up and talk about this like civilised adults.'

His tone grated on her. How dared he talk to her as if she were some recalcitrant child? 'Just go to hell.'

'What are you doing today?' he asked as if she hadn't spoken.

'I'm going down to the market to do some shopping, not that it is any of your damn business.' She frowned and wondered what on earth had possessed her to even tell him that. 'Look, I never want to see you again, Ray,' she continued swiftly. 'And I'm going to hang up now. So goodbye.' She disconnected him and sat drumming her fingers against the table, trying to gather her senses. How did he manage to churn her up so easily? Just the sound of his voice made her literally go weak at the knees and it really irritated her.

Hastily she got to her feet and went to have her shower. She wasn't going to give Ray one more thought. Not one.

Why was it, she wondered a few minutes later as she stood under the forceful jet of water from the shower, that every man in her life had let her down? It had started with her father, he had walked out of her life when she was twelve and she hadn't seen him for five years. Then there had been Julian, who had said all the right things but been as insincere as hell—then David—and now there was Ray to add to the list. And it was strange because, of all the betrayals, Ray was the one that hurt the most. She felt kind of numb inside. It was inexplicable because she hadn't known him that long. But the memory of his kisses, his caresses, his whispered words of passion were emblazed on her mind along with the way he sometimes looked at her, with that quizzical intensity, that tender gleam of humour...just thinking about it now made her insides wrench with longing.

She raised her head to the jet of water and fiercely tried not to think about him. And that was when the water flicked off.

At first she thought that she had leant back against the switch and then it dawned on her: she hadn't switched it off, she had been cut off.

With shaking hands she reached for a towel and wrapped it around her. And just to check that it wasn't the shower that was faulty, she walked over to the sink and turned the tap on. Nothing happened.

Caitlin was furious; she could hardly believe that Ray

had actually stooped so low. Then she reminded herself that this was the man who had cold-bloodedly set out to seduce her to win her around to his way of thinking. Of course he would stoop that low.

Her mobile phone rang and she snatched it up.

'Have I got your attention now?' Ray asked coolly.

'I won't be bullied into submission, Ray.' To her dismay her voice shook slightly.

'All I'm asking is that you meet me down in the village for lunch,' he continued as if she hadn't spoken. 'You told me you were going down there anyway, so it's hardly out of your way.'

'I don't want to meet you for lunch,' she said stonily.

'Do you want your water back on?'

'You know I do.' Her voice was tightly controlled now.

'Okay, so repeat after me. Yes, I will meet you for lunch at one-thirty at the restaurant in the main village square.'

Go to hell, were the words Caitlin wanted to say. She was silent for a long moment as she tried to think rationally. Cold water dripped down her face and her back from her wet hair and the hand that held her mobile was tight. She wanted to hang up or tell him she had made contingency plans and she would get through this. But then she found herself backing down. 'All right, I'll meet you.' Maybe she should talk to him, she told herself firmly. If only to tell him to his face what she thought of him. 'But just for a coffee,' she added hastily. 'I couldn't eat lunch—it would choke me.'

'Always so dramatic,' he said, a hint of amusement in his tone now. 'I'll see you later, Caitlin.'

A few minutes later the water started to run in the shower again.

An hour later Caitlin was driving down the narrow country roads towards the village.

She was going to tell Ray exactly what she thought of him, she told herself all the way down and around the hairpin bends. There was no way she would ever back down now.

Caitlin parked her car on the outskirts of the village under the shade of some trees and glanced at her watch. She had an hour to kill before their meeting. Trying to ignore the little prickles of apprehension that burst inside her, she found her shopping list, and taking her bag, stepped out of the car.

The village of Ezure was perched on the side of the mountain and was picture-postcard perfect. Shady lanes with cobbled surfaces wound steeply down past quaint old houses before finally opening out into a wide tree-lined square.

Although the community was only thirty miles from the tourism of the coast it was completely unspoilt; there was an air almost of stepping back in time about it. There were only a few shops, a couple of restaurants and one bar. And when Caitlin had ventured down during the week the place had been virtually deserted; the only sound had been the gurgle of water from the fountains and the soft thud of boules as some elderly men had played the traditional game under the shade of the giant eucalyptus trees.

Today, however, the village seemed to have awoken from its dreamlike trance and it rang with the sound of children laughing, and people talking. As she rounded the corner into the square she found it was alive with the colourful, vibrant buzz of the local market. The stalls were covered in wide awnings that created a shady place to shop, but even so the heat was intense and Caitlin was glad she had put on a lightweight summer dress as she pressed through the crowd to wander along the stalls.

There were mountains of juicy black and green olives and a range of fresh vegetables that looked as if they had just been pulled fresh from local gardens, goats' cheese and fresh preserves and a mouth-watering array of freshly baked bread. The smell of cooked chickens mingled with the scent of fresh herbs and ground coffee in a way that was somehow uniquely French. Caitlin enjoyed browsing along the lines of wares. She bought some ingredients for a salad and was queuing up to buy some crusty bread when suddenly she didn't feel very well.

The wave of dizziness and nausea hit her from no-where and hastily she turned and left the stall, her one thought to get to somewhere cool and sit down quickly before she fell down.

It was a relief when she emerged into the open space at the other side of the square. There were views across the rolling countryside towards the sea from here and a soft breeze blew in that helped quell the sick feeling. She sat down on the wall under the shade of one of the eucalyptus trees and closed her eyes for a moment.

'Caitlin.' Ray's voice instantly made her alert and she looked up quickly.

'I thought it was you,' he said as he strolled across towards her. 'I saw you hurrying out of the market...' He trailed off suddenly and his eyes raked over the pallor of her skin with a look of concern. 'Are you okay? You look terrible.'

'Thanks.' Her voice was dry.

'No, I mean it. You really don't look well.' He sat down beside her on the wall and reached to put a hand on her forehead.

The touch of his skin so cool against the heat of hers sent a million different reactions spinning through her, and amidst the confusion the one overriding emotion was the weakness of longing. She flinched away from him appalled by such a pathetic reaction. This was the man who had used her for purely mercenary reasons, she reminded herself fiercely. And maybe he did sound concerned but all he really cared about was his land and his business. 'I'm fine, Ray, don't fuss. The heat just got to me for a moment, that's all.'

He dropped his hand back down to his side. 'Are you drinking enough water?' he asked. 'Because in these temperatures it's very easy to dehydrate.'

'Coming from the man who cut my supply this morning, that is a bit of a joke, isn't it?' She glared up at him.

'You should be drinking bottled water, not the stuff that comes from your tap,' he reminded her quickly. 'And I cut the supply for five minutes, Caitlin, so let's not exaggerate this.'

'It was still a lousy thing to do,' she said furiously. 'How did you manage to do that anyhow?'

'The connections have been set up like that for easy maintenance and I have control over them.'

'Well, I won't forgive you for it.'

For a moment his eyes moved over her face contemplatively. The colour had returned to her cheeks and her eyes glistened with vivid green fires of passion.

'It got your attention, though, didn't it?' he said softly. 'And I wanted to see you.'

The words and the way he looked at her made her emotions dip dizzily. Confused, she looked away.

'I've missed you this week,' he continued softly.

She looked up at him then and her heart lurched crazily. The truth was that she had missed him as well, missed him more than she could ever have believed possible.

There was no doubt about it; there was a powerful chemistry between them. It was uncurling now in waves that seemed even more forceful than the sun. But it didn't mean anything, she told herself furiously. And his words were insincere. All he cared about was her land.

The strong reminder gave her the courage to shake her head. 'Well, I haven't missed you,' she said huskily. As she made to look away again he reached out and caught hold of her face, forcing her to hold his gaze.

'I've thought about you every day and every night.'

The whispered words sent her emotions into total chaos.

Her eyes moved to his lips and she found herself remembering how wonderful they felt against hers, how easily he could stir up a wild, uncontrolled passion that she hadn't even known existed inside her until the day he'd taken her into his arms. *She loved him.* The knowledge sneaked unbidden into her subconscious and it shocked her so much that she felt dizzy with fear.

Ray watched as her skin drained of all colour and his hand dropped from her skin, his eyes narrowed. 'Caitlin?'

Released from the touch of his hand, she lost no time in moving away. 'Look, I shouldn't have agreed to meet you,' she said breathlessly. 'You can throw as many compliments and soft words at me as you like but it won't make me change my mind. I've got your measure, Ray, and—'

As she made to stand up he caught hold of her arm, forcing her to sit.

'The little exercise with your water this morning was

to show you that if I'd wanted you out of that house and off that land I could have made life much more difficult for you ages ago. But I haven't.'

'Only because you knew it wouldn't work.' Her heart was slamming fiercely against her chest. And she wanted to put her hands over her ears like a child and block out his words.

'I've also pulled a few strings to get your electricity supply restored quickly.' His eyes hardened on her. 'Do you think I would have done that if I'd wanted you gone?'

'Stop it, Ray.' She tried to pull away from him but still he wouldn't release her. 'I don't want to hear any more of your lies. You are just a user and—'

'I know you've been hurt in the past, Caitlin.' He said the words softly. 'I can see it in your eyes sometimes when you look at me. But I'm not David...and I'm not anyone who is going to use you, or hurt you, or deceive you...because I love you.'

For a heart-stopping moment Caitlin thought she had misheard him. She stopped struggling to escape from him and then he let her go.

'I asked you to come to Paris with me because I wanted *you*. There were no ulterior motives concerning your property...no shady deals...just a desire to be with you and hold you in my arms.'

Caitlin stared up at him wordlessly. She wanted so much to believe him.

'From the first moment when you opened the door to me at Murdo's house I felt drawn to you. You blew me away Caitlin. It was like...' He trailed off for a moment.

'What was it like?' she asked him huskily, her eyes wide with puzzlement and bewilderment.

'It was like history repeating itself,' he said softly.

Then he reached out and stroked her hair back from her face with a tender caress. 'It was the same way I'd felt about Hélène, and it was an emotion I didn't think I would ever experience again… It scared me.'

The husky timbre of his voice startled her. Ray was so powerfully controlled and always so confident. To hear him say he'd been scared by anything astonished her.

'I found myself making up all kinds of excuses to keep myself away from you. Told myself that you were probably just a gold-digger, that you had fooled Murdo into thinking you were a decent, caring person. And then you arrived…' He trailed off. 'And I found myself running out of excuses to keep away from you, because you are decent and caring and wonderful. In fact you are everything I love.'

She didn't say anything for a long moment. Her heart was thundering so loudly that it was deafening her. 'You're just saying this.' Her voice felt stiff. She wanted so much to believe him, but she was really scared now. How did she know that she could trust him? He could hurt her so badly and she didn't think she could bear it… 'Look. I've got to go.' She stood up abruptly.

'Caitlin…'

She was aware that he called out after her but she didn't look back.

CHAPTER ELEVEN

As CAITLIN made her way through the crowds Ray's words pounded through her brain. 'I'm not David…and I'm not anyone who is going to use you, or hurt you, or deceive you…because I love you.'

She wanted so much to believe him, but she couldn't allow herself to. 'You are a sensible and mature woman, Caitlin Palmer,' she told herself firmly. 'You know very well that Ray has everything to gain by sweet-talking his way around you, and nothing to lose. *You can't trust him.*'

She repeated the mantra over and over again until she reached the safety of her car. Once inside she took a few moments to compose herself before starting the engine. She had done the right thing walking away from him, she told herself firmly. There was no way she was going to leave herself wide open to being hurt again. She'd been there and got the T-shirt. Only a fool went back for more.

What about the fact that you've fallen in love with him? a little voice whispered inside her, cutting through all the strong, angry words with a force that was overwhelming. She tried desperately to close it out. Of course she didn't love him—that was ridiculous, absolutely ridiculous. But even as she denied the words she was remembering again the way Ray had looked at her, the things he had said—*'I've thought about you every day and every night.'*—and her heart was turning over with a raw need to believe him because she loved him so much. She had thought of him every day and every night as well and the thought of being without him was the worst feeling ever. It was as if someone had blown a great big hole inside her and the vast gap would never, ever be filled.

How was she going to go on without him? How was she going to cope with this raw ache inside her? Her eyes misted with tears and fiercely she brushed them away. She had coped before and she would cope now. Angrily she put the car in reverse and looked behind her. A car pulled up, blocking her way, and she waited patiently for a few minutes for it to move. But it didn't move and as she watched in her mirror the driver's door opened and someone stepped out.

And that was when she realised it was Ray and her heart started to thunder wildly against her chest.

Taking a deep breath, she wound her window down. 'Will you please move your car? You are in my way.' She was amazed by how cool and composed she sounded.

'I'm not going anywhere, Caitlin, because we haven't finished our conversation.' He sounded just as coolly composed.

Caitlin watched in the mirror as he came closer and hurriedly she pushed the button that would lock all her doors. 'I've said all I've got to say, Ray. So please go.' She gripped the driving wheel with tense hands and didn't dare glance sideways at him as he crouched down beside the door.

'I'm not going, Caitlin. So you may as well get out of the car and talk to me.'

'If you don't move your car I'll make a scene,' she warned him shakily.

'Will you?' She could hear a faint edge of amusement in his tone now. 'What are you going to do?'

Angrily she leaned on her car horn and the sound reverberated loudly down the empty street. 'There, that is what I will do.' She took her hand off the horn and glared at him through the open window. 'And I'm going to keep doing it until you move.'

His lips twisted in a roguishly amused smile. 'Well, go ahead. I wouldn't mind an audience anyway. A few witnesses might come in handy.'

'A few witnesses for what?' she asked warily.

He held up a sheaf of papers. 'These are the legal papers for the land deal with Philippe.'

Caitlin bit down on her lip. 'I don't care what they are, Ray, I just want you to move your car so that I can go home.' She leaned her hand on the horn again and a few people started to gather on the pavement behind them.

Ray ignored the noise and the people completely as he held the papers for her to see. 'Look at them,' he demanded, pushing them further in front of her face so that she had no alternative but to see they were the same papers that had lain on his desk in Paris. Then slowly he started to tear them up with forceful, positive strokes.

Caitlin's hand fell away from the horn as she watched pieces of papers fluttering down beside her in jagged chunks.

'This is what I think about the land deal with Philippe,' he said steadily. 'Listen to me, Caitlin. I love you and there are going to be no *gîtes,* the deal is off.'

She didn't answer him immediately; her heart was thundering so loudly against her chest that she could hardly hear herself think.

Ray allowed the rest of the papers to fall onto her lap.

Then he turned to the few people who were watching with interest. 'I'm in love with this woman,' he said loudly in French. 'And I want the whole world to know it.' There was a ripple of applause and a few whistles of encouragement as a few more people rounded the corner to listen. 'And I want everyone to know that there will be no *gîtes* built anywhere near her land, because the last thing in the world I would ever want would be to hurt her.'

'Ray, will you stop it?' Caitlin murmured as there was another round of applause. 'You're making a scene.'

'I thought that was what you wanted,' he said, looking back at her.

As she looked up at him her eyes blurred with tears and a drop rolled down her cheeks and landed on the paper. 'I don't know what I want,' she admitted huskily. 'All I know is that I don't want to be hurt again, Ray. I…couldn't bear it…'

'Just unlock the door, Caitlin, and get out of the car,' he said gently.

After a moment's hesitation she did as he asked and paper fluttered down around their feet like confetti as she stepped outside.

She stood and looked up at him and he reached out and wiped the tears from under her eyes with tender fingers. 'I'm so sorry, Caitlin,' he whispered gently. 'I never wanted to make you cry and I never wanted to hurt you. But what I said to you before is the whole truth…I invited you to Paris because I wanted *you;* there was no other reason—and no ulterior motives. I promise you that, sincerely.'

There was no doubting the honesty of his tone and suddenly all her defences came tumbling down around her. She believed him but couldn't find her voice to answer him; it seemed choked under a weight of emotion that was far too heavy for her.

'All I'm asking is that you give me a chance to prove myself to you,' he said, his voice earnest and pleading. 'I know you still love David. I know this is all too soon for you but I'm prepared to wait for you, Caitlin. I'll wait for as long as it takes.'

'Philippe is not going to be pleased.' She managed the words hoarsely.

'To hell with Philippe,' Ray said sweepingly. 'And meanwhile I've organised contractors to come out and connect your property to the main water supply. They should be with you tomorrow.'

'And you are doing all this for me?' she whispered huskily.

'I'd do anything for you, Caitlin,' he said seriously. 'And anyway I've decided you are right—Murdo's house is full of character and potential. A person would have to be mad to knock it down.'

She looked up at him and suddenly she started to laugh and at the same time another tear trickled down her cheek. 'I never thought I'd hear you say something like that.'

'And after Hélène I never thought I would fall in love again.'

The gentle words caused more tears to stream down her cheeks.

'Don't cry, my love.' He reached out to wipe her tears away with a soothing hand. And the next moment she was being cradled in his arms. 'I never wanted to hurt you,' he whispered fiercely. 'I admit, when you first got here, I told myself that my priority was to get you out and get the land. But the idea started to crumble within an hour of being in your company. From time to time I tried to rekindle it, told myself I was a businessman first and foremost, and then you'd look at me with those adorable green eyes and honestly I couldn't have cared less about business…'

'I can hardly believe you are saying all this,' she whispered breathlessly. 'I keep wondering if I'm dreaming—'

She pulled back. 'And if it's a dream it is the most wonderful one.' Caitlin looked into his eyes and she felt her insides melt with the heat of desire and suddenly she was reaching up to kiss him.

For a long moment they were wrapped in each other's arms, their kisses growing more and more heated and passionate. It was only as they became aware of the cheers and applause from the crowd gathered behind them that Ray pulled back from her. 'Let's get out of here,' he said softly.

Wordlessly she allowed him to lead her back to his car. She slipped into the passenger seat and then watched as he locked her car before getting in beside her and driving slowly up through the winding narrow streets.

'I should really have driven my own car home,' she murmured, trying to think sensibly as they rounded a corner away from it.

'I'll get someone to pick it up for you later,' he said as he continued on until they were out into the countryside. 'You aren't in any fit state to drive anyway.' He slanted a glance across at her and watched as she found a tissue and dabbed at her eyes. 'How are you feeling now?'

'Shell-shocked,' she admitted wryly. 'I was so hurt and angry when I drove down here this morning, I can hardly take in what you have said.'

'But it is the truth,' he said softly.

The car rounded a corner and Murdo's house came into view.

'We are friends again, aren't we?' he asked as he pulled the car to a halt by the front door.

She didn't answer him immediately.

'Caitlin?' He looked over at her anxiously.

'I thought we were a little more than friends,' she whispered softly. 'Didn't you say something about being in love with me?' She slanted a shy look across at him. 'Did you say you'd wait for me?'

He gave that lopsided smile that she knew so well. 'I love you with all of my heart and I'll wait for you until the end of time.'

She swallowed on a deep knot of emotion. 'And I love you,' she whispered unsteadily. 'With all my heart.'

For a moment there was a deep silence as he stared at her, his dark eyes intense, a muscle flexed in his cheek.

'I...I thought that maybe the deep feelings I was experiencing with you meant that I was on the rebound,' she continued, her voice so low it was barely audible. 'But the truth of the matter is I've never felt this way about anyone before. In fact I realise now that I was never truly in love with David, whereas with you it's the real thing. I adore you, Ray, and I'd do anything for you...' She shrugged hopelessly. 'So if you are stringing me a line...you know about the house...' a tear trickled down her cheek. '...well, you don't have to. You can have the property because right at this moment it is singularly unimportant.'

'Caitlin.' He reached and folded her into his arms. 'I want *you* and nothing else matters, so please get that into your mind.' His lips found hers and he kissed her with the hungry passion that she had been craving all through these long, lonely nights apart from him.

'God, I love you so much…' She wound her arms up and around his neck. For a long time they just kissed, their caresses filled with the anguish and relief of a love that knew no bounds.

'Shall we go inside?' she whispered tremulously as his hands grew more passionately insistent and her body cried out for so much more.

He smiled. 'Where is the young woman who practically ran from me the last time I drove her home?'

The return of that teasing humour in his eyes made her smile.

'She's given in to a power much stronger than herself…' she whispered.

Ray reached for the door handle and they climbed out into the sunshine. He waited for her to come around and join him, then he held out his hand and took hold of her.

'Caitlin, before we go inside I've got something to ask you,' he said solemnly.

She looked up at him. 'What is it?' she asked nervously.

Then suddenly he got down on one knee by the front door of the property.

'Caitlin, will you do me the honour of becoming my wife?' he said huskily. 'I want us to grow old together…have children together and fall into bed together every night from now until eternity.'

Her eyes misted with tears and she dropped down on her knees beside him to wrap her arms tightly around him. 'Just name a day and I'll be there,' she promised softly.

EPILOGUE

IT WAS early summer in Provence and sizzling hot. Caitlin walked out of the kitchen door and looked down over the garden. Thanks to the new irrigation system that had been installed, the orchard looked lush and the vines had started to bear fruit. It was delightful standing in the shade admiring the difference that the last few months had brought to Villa Mirabelle…her inheritance. There was a new red roof that glowed in the sunshine. The windows had all been replaced, their style lovingly in keeping with the period of the property. The interior was even more impressive. Polished wooden floors ran throughout and there was a superb new kitchen fitted around the trusty wood-fired stove and, what was more, the water was now properly connected to the main supply. Upstairs the bedrooms had been restored and furnished with antiques and decorated with stylish simplicity that was unique to a French country cottage.

'I think you would be pleased, Murdo,' Caitlin whispered as she watched a little bird fluttering down to sit in the almond tree. 'It is my last morning here, but Villa Mirabelle feels like a home again.'

'Caitlin?' Her mother's voice drifted out from the house. 'Caitlin, where are you? Flowers have arrived.'

Caitlin smiled. 'Oh, and I forgot to tell you. My mother is going to be living in your house…just for a while. She wants to be close by so that she can see her first grandchild.' Caitlin put her hand on her stomach, still flat as yet. 'The baby is due at the end of December,

Murdo, so Christmas is going to be very busy this year. What do you think of the name Paris, by the way? I thought it was appropriate…'

'Caitlin?' Her mother appeared at the kitchen door and caught her breath in a gasp. 'Oh, darling, you look so beautiful!'

Caitlin turned. She was wearing a full-length pale gold dress that clung to her slender figure and shimmered as the sunshine caught it. Her hair was caught up on top of her head, held with fresh flowers.

'The most beautiful bride ever,' her mother said, taking out a tissue and dabbing at her eyes.

'Now, Mum, don't start blubbering just yet,' Caitlin said with a smile as she headed back towards the house.

'I can't help it,' Elaine Palmer said as she blew her nose noisily. 'I'm just so happy for you. Ray is such a wonderful man and you are both so much in love. What are you doing out here anyway?'

'Just having a few moments' quiet reflection.'

'The cars are here.' Heidi appeared behind Elaine and smiled at her friend. 'It's time to leave.'

As Caitlin stepped out of the cottage for the last time as a single woman she couldn't help but feel a pang of nostalgia. She found herself remembering the first day she had arrived here in that terrible storm and the way Ray had caught her in his arms and held her. Then she remembered the way he had proposed to her out here by the front step. And it had been here a few weeks later that she had told him about their baby.

She smiled at that memory. Ray had suggested that they wait six months before they got married. 'I think it's a good idea, Caitlin, because that way you'll know without a shadow of a doubt that this wedding has nothing to do with the terms of Murdo's will and everything to do with how much I love you.'

'I know that anyway,' she said gently. 'And I think waiting six months is a terrible idea.'

'Well, it does seem a long time away…' He shrugged.

'Yes, it does.' She smiled up at him. 'And in six months I might not be able to fit so easily into a wedding dress.'

Ray frowned at that. 'What on earth do you mean?'

'I'm pregnant, Ray. Our baby is due at Christmas.'

She remembered the look of surprise on his face, and then the intense joy. He had held her so tightly, kissed her so tenderly and the moment had been so poignant and so perfect that just thinking about it now made tears of happiness come into her eyes.

Caitlin closed the door quietly behind her. The future beckoned, a future that promised to be wonderful in every way.

PRICELESS

KELLY HUNTER

Accidentally educated in the sciences, **Kelly Hunter** has always had a weakness for fairytales, fantasy worlds and losing herself in a good book. Husband…yes. Children…two boys. Cooking and cleaning…sigh. Sports…no, not really, in spite of the best efforts of her family. Gardening… yes, roses of course. Kelly was born in Australia and has travelled extensively. Although she enjoys living and working in different parts of the world, she still calls Australia home.

Visit Kelly online at www.kellyhunter.net Don't miss Kelly Hunter's scorching new novel. *Untameable Rogue* is available now in Modern Heat™!

CHAPTER ONE

ERIN SINCLAIR WAS used to traffic. Rush hour traffic, gridlocked traffic, rainy-day traffic…and, right now, airport traffic. Sydney was a vibrant, picturesque city with an iconic bridge and a bluer than blue harbour, but Sydney roads at eight a.m. on a Monday morning were congested.

Taxi drivers knew these things.

Her passengers had been running late, but she'd delivered them to the international departure terminal in record time thanks to a run of green lights. They'd tipped big, too rushed to wait for change. Probably not the best start to their day, thought Erin, but it was certainly an excellent way to start hers. Now all she needed was a fare back into the city.

Her pick-up area, the one for luxury taxis, was directly outside the arrival terminal doors. There were no other taxis and no one was waiting for a ride but that didn't stop her from sliding the car to a halt, popping the boot, and getting out. She wouldn't have to wait long.

As requested, she was wearing black. Black hiking boots, semi-regulation black trousers, black T-shirt. A perky black chauffeur's cap sat ignored on the front passenger seat.

The man who came striding through the arrival terminal doors was not wearing black but, boy, he would have looked good in it. He'd opted instead for scuffed steel-capped boots, green cargo trousers and a grey T-shirt, but that was where Mr Average ended and the fantasy began because the body beneath the everyday clothing was superb.

He was broad-shouldered, slim-hipped, every-thing about him lean and powerfully muscled. His hair was black and carelessly cut and his face was as near to perfection as the gods would allow. He looked tired. Tired in a way that had nothing to do with a long haul flight and everything to do with a weariness that went soul deep. He was all shut down, which was probably just as well. Because heaven help womankind if he smiled.

He glanced around and started towards her so she headed for the back of the car and pushed the boot open with her fingertips. He was beside her now, and up close she could see that his eyes were the colour of toffee and more than a match for the rest of him. She shot him a smile, reached for his bulky canvas carryall.

'I'll do it.' His voice was deep and quiet.

'Is this a gender thing?'

'I prefer to think of it as a weight thing.' The look he sent her might have been swift, but what it lacked in longevity it made up for in intensity. She felt the force of it, of him, clear through to her soul. 'You're not very big, are you?' he said finally.

Erin blew out the breath she hadn't realised she'd been holding and pushed a wayward strand of short brown hair from her eyes. So she was five feet four and a little on the slender side. This wasn't news. Maybe he hadn't seen clear through to her soul after all. If he had he'd have known better than to comment on her size.

By the time he'd shut the boot on his luggage she had the passenger door open and was waiting for him to get in. He looked at her, looked at the door, and the faintest of smiles crossed his lips. Obviously he wasn't used to having car doors opened for him either. 'Are you sure you're after a *luxury* taxi service?' she asked him dryly. 'Because the regular taxis are just over there.'

He glanced at the long line of regular taxis, glanced back at her. 'Will a luxury ride get me into the city any faster?'

'Only in your imagination.'

His smile widened fractionally.

'On the upside, I have three different newspapers you can read on the way and I can order in coffee.'

'Good coffee?' he asked.

'Exceptional coffee.'

'Espresso, black, two sugars,' he said, and got in. Men were so easy.

She shut his door and headed for the driver's seat. 'Where to?'

'Albany Street, Double Bay.'

Nice. She picked up her mobile, called in his coffee order, pulled out into the traffic, and set about making his journey a luxury one. 'Newspaper?' she asked. 'I have the *Sydney Morning Herald*, *The Australian*, or the *Financial Review*.'

'No.'

'Music?' There was something for everyone.

'No.'

O-kay. He didn't look as if he wanted conversation either but she gave it a whirl, just in case. 'So where'd you fly in from?'

'London.'

'Been away long?' His accent told her he was Australian.

'Six years.'

'Six years in London? Without a break? No wonder you look tired.'

'Maybe I will have that paper,' he said, his gaze meeting hers in the rear vision mirror.

'That would be a "no" to conversation, then?'

'Right.'

She handed him the *Sydney Morning Herald* in

silence. Maybe he was an elite athlete. A soccer player returning home at the end of the European season after his team's final crushing defeat. Maybe he'd missed the winning penalty goal and was barely able to talk through the weight of his despair. Yeah, that would work. 'You're not a soccer player, are you?'

'No.'

'A poet?' That would work too. Because he could have taught Byron himself a thing or two about looking sexy, unreachable, and sorely in need of comfort all at the same time.

'No.' He opened the paper. Rattled it.

Fine. Maybe she should forget about her taciturn passenger and concentrate on her driving. She could do that. No problem.

Five minutes later she pulled up outside Café Siciliano, lowered the rear window, and a curvaceous young waitress handed her passenger an espresso in a take-away cup along with two straws of sugar. 'The sugar's already in it,' the girl said. 'This is extra, just in case.'

'You're an angel,' he said in that soft, deep voice and the girl blinked and blushed prettily.

Harrumph! Erin jabbed at the controls and watched as the tinted window slid smoothly closed. He hadn't called *her* an angel for seeing to it that he got coffee in the first place. Ungrateful sod. Her gaze clashed with his in the rear vision mirror and she could have sworn she saw laughter flicker in their depths.

'Pixies can't be angels,' he said solemnly. 'Different fantasy altogether.'

'Gee,' she said. 'Glad we've cleared that up.' He had such glorious eyes. Such a heart-stopping face. She pulled out onto the road a little more abruptly than usual. Forget service with a smile. It was time to deliver the man to his destination.

And then the engine coughed. Not good. It coughed some more as she swung the car around the nearest corner and into a side street and then, with a well-bred splutter, the late-model luxury Mercedes died altogether.

'We seem to have stopped,' he said.

Oh, *now* he wanted to talk. 'Drink your coffee,' she said, and tried to start the car. The ignition turned over but the engine spluttered like an old maid choking on hot tea.

'Could be a fuel problem,' he offered.

'Could be lots of things.' Erin drummed her fingers on the steering wheel and considered her options. First things first. 'I need to get you another ride.'

'No, you don't,' he said. 'You need to pop the hood so we can take a look at what's wrong.'

'You're a mechanic?'

'No, but I know cars.'

'That's close enough.' Erin liked cars. She

enjoyed driving them. But she didn't know a whole lot about fixing them. She released the bonnet, got out of the car, and joined him in staring down at the immaculately clean engine. 'What can you do without tools?'

'Check fuses and connections,' he said and set about doing so with a confidence she found reassuring. He had nice hands, hands that looked as if they knew both strength and gentleness. She looked for a ring, a wristwatch, but he wore no jewellery of any kind. Some things simply didn't need embellishment.

'And I thought chivalry was dead.' There wasn't much she could do to help except stay out of his light so she leaned back against the grille and waited. 'Rescue people often? You're not a firefighter, are you? Emergency services?'

'Do you always measure a man by his occupation?' he asked absently, his attention still on the engine.

'Not always. Sometimes I measure him by his sweet words and pretty face, but that doesn't always work out.'

'I can imagine.'

'Of course, there's always star signs,' she said thoughtfully.

'You mean you judge a person by his *birthday*?' She had his attention now; his complete and utterly incredulous attention.

'Hey, the measurement of man is a tough one. A girl needs all the help she can get.'

'Yes, but *astrology*?'

'I'm thinking Scorpio for you. Moody, intense…' Unbelievable in bed. The mere thought of which was making her fidget. 'But I could be wrong.'

'I suspect you often are.'

He hadn't, she noted, come right out and told her she was wrong. That was interesting. 'You *are* a Scorpio, aren't you? I knew it.'

He regarded her with exasperation. 'It means nothing.'

'Nope, it means that without any more information whatsoever I can start to measure the man. At least, that's the theory.' And after a moment, 'We're quite compatible.'

'Hard to believe,' he murmured dryly.

Erin suppressed a chuckle. 'Yep, with that pretty face it's a good thing you're low on sweet talk otherwise I might be lost.'

His smile was slow in coming but when it arrived it scrambled her brain. 'I try to save the sweet talk,' he said.

'What on earth for?'

'Later.'

Oh, boy. 'I can see how that could work,' she said breathlessly. He should be carrying a sign, she decided. One that said 'Danger! Engage at own risk'. It would be a service to womankind, a necessity really, because if he ever did decide to go after a woman in earnest she'd probably melt. Already there was heat in her cheeks and a fire in the pit of her stomach as a result of that lazy smile and he wasn't even trying. Not really.

'You've got a blown fuel injection fuse.'

Make that not at all. 'I have?'

'Good thing there's a spare.'

'Yeah.' He leaned over to replace it and there was nothing for it but to watch him some more and try not to lose her breath all over again.

'You can try starting the car now.'

'Oh. Right,' she said, and headed for the driver's seat. The car started at once, purring like a well-fed kitten. 'It works.'

'Try not to sound so surprised.' He lowered the bonnet.

'I'm not surprised. I'm grateful. Really.' And after a pause, 'Is it going to happen again?'

'Hard to say,' he said as he got back in the back seat.

So much for a definitive answer. The easiest solution was to drive the car and see. If it stopped again she'd call it in. Meanwhile, Mr International Man of Mystery wanted to go to Double Bay.

With a swift U-turn and a quick corner they slipped seamlessly back into the Sydney morning traffic.

* * *

The pixie chauffeur was right. Six years was a long time to be away from home, Tristan Bennett thought as he downed the last of his lukewarm but surprisingly good coffee. He'd settled into London easily enough; he had his work and his apartment, and his sister was over there too now, but there was no denying that it had never really felt like home. He'd gone to London because of his work, travelled all over Europe because of it, but somewhere along the way youthful enthusiasm had given way to weary cynicism and an increasing sense of futility. The fire was gone, the blade had dulled. And then there'd been that last investigation, the horrors of which had left him tired and hurting and wondering if he had it in him to go back for more.

It had been Hallie, his sister, who'd suggested he take some long overdue leave and head back to Australia for a while. Heartland, she told him. The perfect place to fight demons and find peace. The only place.

So here he was. Haunted by nightmares he couldn't shake and fairly sure he was asking too much of the old house that held its own share of memories, both sweet and painful.

'It's this one on the right,' he said as they drew level with the old two-storey weatherboard with its wraparound verandah, and the pixie nodded as she pulled smoothly into the driveway and cut the engine.

'Is anyone expecting you?' she said with a frown.

'No.' His father was on sabbatical in Greece, his siblings were scattered across the globe, but it didn't matter. They didn't need to be here for him to feel their presence. He was home.

'I know of a good cleaning service if you need one,' she said.

Okay, so the house was a little neglected and the garden was overgrown. Nothing he couldn't fix. 'I can clean,' he said. It wasn't as if he was going to have much else to do.

'You have no idea what those words do to a woman, do you?' she said as she turned towards him, and he felt the impact of a pair of lively brown eyes and a smile that promised equal measures of passion and laughter. 'I swear it's better than foreplay. If you can cook I'm yours. You're not a chef are you?'

'There you go again,' he said. 'Focussing on what a man does, rather than what he is.'

'Isn't it the same thing?'

'No. And I'm not a chef.'

Her expression was one of mingled relief and disappointment. 'Probably a good thing,' she muttered.

'Probably,' he said, unable to stop his lips from curving, just a little bit.

She wasn't his type. Not that he could say he had a type exactly, just that she wasn't it. She'd surprised him, that was all. When the car had stopped he hadn't expected her first thought to be about how best to get him to his destination. It suggested a generosity of spirit and a focus on others that was uncommon. And then she'd blind-sided him with her smart mouth and easy smile, battering away at his defences with the force of butterfly wings and the impact of an armoured tank and before he knew it he was aware of her in a way that was truly disquieting.

His body wanted to know why she wasn't his type. His body seemed to think that she was.

His *body* had spent the last twenty-two hours trapped in a flying tin can and would have normally been at rest right now. He was prepared to allow it a little leeway. 'How much do I owe you?'

'No charge. You fixed the car.'

'I replaced a fuse,' he corrected. 'It's a thirty-minute drive. I have to pay you something.'

'Nope. I've got it covered.' There was a phone ringing somewhere in the car and by the look on her face she badly wanted to answer it. 'Do you mind if I take this call?' she asked on the sixth ring. 'My brother's been trying to contact me all morning and I keep missing him.'

'Go ahead.'

She shot him a quick smile, found the phone. 'Hello?'

'Erin, it's Rory.'

Finally. Erin popped the boot so that her passenger could unload and stepped from the car to give him a hand. Not that he wanted it. 'What's up?'

'It's about the gem-buying trip next week. I'm going to have to bail.'

'What?' Her voice rose. 'Why?'

'New task orders came through this morning. We leave for Sumatra in three days' time.'

'Dammit, Rory. I knew this would happen! Why you? Why now? What about the leave they approved two months ago?' Erin paced the length of the car, turned, and paced back. Rory was an Army Engineer and wedded to his work. Questioning his choice of career or the Army's decision-making was pointless. 'Scratch those questions. Does Mum know?'

'We're only rebuilding infrastructure, Erin. It won't be dangerous.'

'So she doesn't know.'

Rory sighed. 'I'll tell her tonight. At dinner. You will come, won't you?'

'No!' She ran a hand through her hair, knowing full well that her refusal to go to dinner would be short-lived. Rory always took them out to dinner whenever notice to move orders came in. It was a family tradition. Her father, a Rear Admiral, always took them out to dinner whenever *his* deployment orders came in too. Hell, the defence forces probably had a protocol booklet outlining exactly how to deliver such news to loved ones. It probably said, *Make sure you're in a public place and feed them first.* 'Dammit, Rory, it better be somewhere expensive because you owe me big. My collection's due in a month. I need those stones!'

'I'm sorry, Erin. If you can find someone else to go with you, preferably a eunuch with the protective instincts of a Rottweiler, you can still take the car.'

'Gee, who to ask? The list is so long.'

'I see your point,' he said. 'Okay, you can widen the search criteria to include females. But she still has to be capable of covering your back.'

'I could go alone.'

'Only if you intend paying by card and getting the stones shipped to you. That could work.'

'Don't do this to me, Rory.' He knew as well as she did that the best stones were found in the most unlikely places—the one-man mines where you could forget bank cards and delivery options. Out on those claims they traded stones for cash and that was it. 'There's no one in your unit staying behind who you could con into coming with me?'

'Absolutely not!'

Erin sighed. She had an ironclad resistance to military men. Why Rory felt the need to protect her from them was a mystery. 'Maybe I'll put an ad in the paper.'

'Over my dead body,' he said. And then, 'Dinner's at Doyle's. Just so you know.'

Harbourside views and the best seafood selection in Sydney. He did have guilt. 'What time?' she countered. 'Just in case I can make it.'

'Seven-thirty, and if you're not there I'm coming to find you,' he said, and hung up.

Great, just great. Erin scowled as she ended the call and tossed the phone on the front seat. Her passenger had retrieved his bag and was regarding her with a tilt to his lips that told her he'd found the show amusing. Lucky him.

'Problems?' he murmured.

'Yeah, but I'm working on a solution.' She had other options. She could buy stones at auction or off the Internet. But she wouldn't get value for money and her chances of finding something that little bit different would be slim. No. Not good enough. The design competition she'd entered was a prestigious one. Reputations were made there. Careers forged. She needed six perfect pieces of jewellery and for that she needed perfect stones. 'You're not a eunuch, are you?'

'I'm not even going to ask where that question came from,' he said.

'It's just that I need a co-driver,' she said in a rush and his gaze slid to the chauffeurs cap on the front seat. 'Not for the taxi. For a gem-buying trip out west. And not just any driver. He has to be built like, er, well, like you. For bodyguarding and safe gem-keeping purposes. I don't suppose you'd be interested in coming along?'

He looked surprised.

And then he looked stern.

'You should be more careful,' he said. 'What would your brother say if he knew you'd just asked a complete stranger to accompany you on this trip?'

'I really don't want to dwell on it.' Desperation obviously did strange things to a woman. She had no idea who he was or what he did for a living and absolutely no idea what had possessed her to ask him on this trip. So she was impulsive, always had been. She wasn't normally *this* impulsive. 'You're right,' she said. 'Bad idea. Forget I asked.'

'I wouldn't recommend an ad in the paper, either.'

'You're not alone.' Ten to one he had a sister stashed away somewhere. 'Don't let me keep you.'

'How much do I owe you?'

'Nothing. The meter wasn't running.' He had that look about him, a stubborn slant to his chin that told her he was going to be difficult about this. 'Okay then. Answer a question for me and we're square.'

'You want to know what I do?'

'What makes you think that?' He levelled a look at her that made her want to laugh. Damn, but he was appealing when he wasn't being melancholy. 'I'd rather know your name.'

The silence that followed was awkward, to say the least.

He didn't want to tell her.

'Never mind,' she said with a rueful shake of her head. She should have known better. Did know better. There was just something about him that made her want to know more. 'Slate's clean. Have a nice day.'

'Tristan,' he said gruffly as she went to get in the car. 'Tristan Bennett.'

There was power in a name so carefully given. Erin halted and stared at him in silence. Those marvellous toffee-coloured eyes of his were guarded and the expression on his face was wry, as if he'd surprised himself with his revelation. Such a small, everyday thing, the giving of a name. Except that now that she'd won it from him she had no idea what to do with it.

'Well, Tristan Bennett,' she said finally. 'Welcome home.'

CHAPTER TWO

TRISTAN didn't want her to go. Maybe it was curiosity or maybe it was just that he was putting off stepping through that front door and into his childhood, but now that she was on the verge of leaving he was looking for ways to keep her there. 'What do you need the gems for?' he asked.

'When I'm not driving taxis I make jewellery,' Erin said. 'There's a competition coming up in four weeks' time, a prestigious one, and for that I need good stones.'

A jeweller? He wouldn't have picked it. 'You're not wearing any jewellery.'

'Company policy. There's less to rob.'

Good policy, he thought. 'So when were you planning on making this trip?'

'Next Monday.'

One week away. 'Well, if you can't find anyone you know to go with you, let me know. Maybe I can help.' What was he saying? Why was he offering to help her? He wasn't *that* good a Samaritan. Obviously he was more jet-lagged than he thought.

She was looking at him with her head cocked to one side. 'You're very sweet, aren't you? Underneath it all.'

Sweet? No one had ever called him sweet before. He tried the word on for size, found it an uncomfortable fit. 'No.'

'Suit yourself,' she said. 'Anyway, better get going. Places to go.'

She was leaving. 'You haven't told me *your* name yet.'

'You don't want to know my name.'

'I don't?'

'No. Not really.' Her smile was rueful. 'But I'll tell you anyway. It's Erin. Erin Sinclair.'

It took Erin five days to admit defeat. Friends, cousins, distant cousins…they were all busy. Maybe if she'd been able to give them more notice she'd have had better luck, but she didn't have that luxury. The competition pieces had to be ready in a month. She was running out of time, almost out of options. Almost.

There was still Tristan Bennett.

He was everything she needed. Tough, protective, and determined to keep his distance. He'd said he might be able to help.

Maybe it was time to find out what he meant.

Erin debated hard over what to wear. She wanted her dealings with Tristan to be business-like so she decided on beige trousers, flat sandals, and a collared shirt. Never mind that the shirt was a deep, vibrant pink and that the neckline dipped low. To her way of thinking, creamy skin and cleavage was simply a backdrop for more impor-tant things.

Like jewellery.

She opted for one of her favourite necklaces: a slim column of polished jade with a freeform platinum swirl oversetting it. Erin knew the history of jewellery all the way back to Mesopotamia. The materials, the motifs, the meanings and the making of them. Her designs were good. Different. In her more confident moments she even thought she had a shot at winning this competition.

With the right stones, the right design, flaw-less execution…

One step at a time.

To make a tough job easier you carved it up. You set goals and time frames, and attacked it systematically. Her father had taught her that when he'd tried to instil in her a respect for military ways and military ideals. He thought she hadn't listened, thought he'd failed her when she'd told him she wanted to design jewellery rather than weaponry, but he was wrong. He hadn't failed her and she had listened. First things first. One step at a time.

She needed the right stones. And for that she needed Tristan Bennett.

One-ninety-two Albany Street looked different with the lawn mowed and the garden tamed. He'd let the climbing rose have its way along the verandah, and he'd left the autumn leaves beneath the old oak trees, but it was big-picture tidy and all the more appealing for those things he'd let be.

It wasn't until Erin pulled into the driveway and brought the car to a halt that she saw him. He was on a ladder braced against the side of the house, scooping leaves from the gutter. Man at work. And then his gaze connected with hers as she got out of the car and the leaf scooping stopped.

'Erin Sinclair,' he said as she came to a halt not far from the ladder and Erin smiled up at him. He'd asked her her name out of pure politeness but at least he remembered it.

'You've been cleaning,' she said. 'You do good work.'

'You're back,' he countered. 'I wondered if you would be.'

'You're a hard man to forget.' Easy to dream about though.

'You couldn't find anyone to go with you on your trip out west, could you?'

'No,' she admitted as he came down the ladder, first his boots and then the rest of him. 'But you are hard to forget.' He was bigger than she remembered him, his skin a touch browner. A sun-kissed dark angel, she thought, and wondered if every woman who saw him got that little bit breathless or if it was just her. He slipped his heavy-duty gloves off and slung them over a rung of the ladder, revealing his strong, square hands. Hands that would know their way around a woman's body.

'I still need a co-driver,' she said, trying hard not to think about how those hands would feel rushing all over *her*. 'And I was wondering if you'd be interested in the position. I'll pay for your meals and accommodation, of course, and maybe we can come to some arrangement regarding payment for your time. It wouldn't be much, but if you're currently, er, looking for work, every little bit helps, right?'

'I don't need your money,' he said. 'Save it for your purchases.'

'So you're not out of work?'

'I'm currently on leave from my work.'

Whatever that was. Not exactly forthcoming when it came to talking about himself, she'd noticed that before. 'I'm expecting the trip to take four or five days, depending on what I find and when. The first stop is Lightning Ridge for opals. After that I want to head over to Inverell to look at the sapphires.'

'I can manage a few days.'

'You can? Just like that?'

Her smile was like sunshine, her warmth drawing Tristan in even as he moved away. She was too open, far too trusting. Everything he wasn't.

'There's just one problem,' she said. 'I don't know you all that well. I'll need to run some sort of check on you.'

Maybe not that trusting, he amended, applauding her good sense. 'How?'

'I'm thinking of taking you to dinner.'

Dinner? Tristan stared at her in disbelief. 'You call a *dinner* date a foolproof method of taking a man's measure?'

'You're right,' she said. 'It needs tweaking. We'll have it at my mother's.'

'Your…' What? 'Oh, no. No.' He shook his head for emphasis. 'I don't do dinner with other people's families.'

'It's just my mother,' she said soothingly. 'Possibly my grandmother as well.'

Two mothers. 'Absolutely not!'

'Well, I can't very well go haring off with a complete stranger for a week without someone in my family knowing who I'm with, can I?'

'You should meet my sister,' he said darkly. 'What about your father? Can't I meet him instead? Or your brother?' Brothers he could deal with. He had three of them.

'They're out of the country. Besides, they can be a little overprotective about these things. Mothers are far more reasonable. Say seven o'clock tonight?'

'No.'

'When, then?'

Never. 'What if I gave you my driver's licence?' he said. 'You can discover a lot about a person from their driver's licence.'

'Like what? That they can drive?'

'Their full name and address. Their date of birth. With that you can access other records.'

'You're not a criminal, are you?'

'Not yet.'

She looked at him through eyes that were clear and thoughtful and not nearly as guileless as she would have him believe. 'Okay, I'll cut you a deal. Sunday brunch but it's still at my mother's. In the interests of fairness you can bring your mother too.'

Tristan shook his head. 'My mother died a long time ago.' He'd been twelve.

Startled silence greeted his statement and Tristan waited warily for her reaction. This wasn't information he usually offered up. He hated the sympathy that came with it; that soft, nurturing look women got in their eyes when they found out. He was thirty years old. He did not need mothering.

'Guess that's out of the question, then,' she said at last. 'What about your sister?'

'She lives in England.'

Erin Sinclair sighed and the pretty little pendant dangling from the chain around her neck seemed to sigh right along with her. 'I don't suppose you have a spinster aunt nearby who loves nothing more than to talk about your childhood escapades?'

'No, but the next-door neighbour's cockatoo remembers me. I could bring him.'

'Now we're getting somewhere,' she said. 'Bring the neighbours as well.'

Relentless wasn't usually a word he applied to whimsical women with laughter in their eyes, but in this case it seemed to fit. 'Couldn't you just trust your own judgement?'

'I am. It says never trust a man who refuses to meet your mother.'

She had a point.

'Last chance,' she said. 'Brunch tomorrow morning. You can even set a time limit. Say, half an hour?'

Still he hesitated.

'If I have to find someone else to come with me on this trip, I will.'

'You're bluffing.'

Her hands went to her hips; her gaze was steady. She bluffed very well. He found, disturbingly, that he kind of liked the idea of a week out west, hunting down gemstones with Erin Sinclair. 'How many mothers?' he said at last.

'Just the one if it makes you any feel better.'

It did. Surely he could manage one mother for half an hour. It wasn't as if they were dating. No. All he had to do was meet the woman, reassure her that he'd look out for her daughter, thank her for the coffee, and leave. 'One mother, half an hour,' he said firmly. 'Maximum.'

'No problem.' Her smile was warm. 'I'll pick you up at ten o clock?'

'Give me the address and I'll meet you there.' His father's car was in the garage. It could use the run. Although… He turned his attention to the five-point-seven-litre, eight-cylinder, factory-modified Monaro sitting in his driveway. Now *that* was a very sweet ride. 'Yours?'

'Rory's,' she said and started towards it. Tristan followed willingly. 'I don't have a car. He offered to let me take it on the trip but I figured if I did, the sellers would take one look at it and triple the price of the stones. I've decided to take my mother's Ford instead. She can drive the Monaro.'

'I think I'm going to weep.'

'You would if you had to put fuel in it.'

'You see, that's where you're wrong. We're talking sledgehammer acceleration and a top speed guaranteed to make your eyes water. The price of fuel is secondary.'

'You sound just like my brother,' she said as she fished a cardboard drink coaster and a pen from the Monaro, set the coaster face down on the roof of the car, and started writing on it. 'What is it with men and fast cars?'

Tristan winced. 'Mind the duco.'

'I swear, it's like an echo,' she muttered, her attention still on her task. 'Why do you think I'm using a coaster?'

'This is a good idea, right?' asked Erin the following morning as she set a packet of freshly ground coffee and a bar cake down on her mother's kitchen bench. She hadn't lived at home for over two years but she'd never quite kicked the habit of visiting her mother's kitchen on a regular basis. It was the perfect place to sit and chill and, when necessary, grill potential travelling companions. 'It seemed like a good idea at the time.'

'Very sensible, dear.' Lillian Sinclair regarded her daughter over the top of a pair of purple-framed reading glasses. The glasses bordered on the theatrical; the eyes behind them were shrewd. 'What was his name again?'

'Tristan Bennett.'

'I knew a Tristan once. He was a dance choreographer. Darling man.'

'I don't think this one's a dance choreographer.' Not that she knew for sure, but the thought of Tristan Bennett mincing the floorboards in tight tights and a V-necked T-shirt didn't really work for her. 'Tristan's a misleading name for this particular man.'

'Oh? What name would you have given him?'

'I'm thinking Lucifer.'

Her mother's eyebrows rose. 'That's quite a name.'

'He's very handsome.' She thought her mother needed at least some advance warning.

'What about wicked?'

'I hope not.' Erin hesitated. 'Instinct tells me he's a good man. It also tells me he's no stranger to the dark side.'

'A man doesn't have to be part of the darkness to walk through it.' Big fan of Chinese poetry, her mother. 'What does he do for a living?'

'No idea.'

'You should have asked.'

'I intend to ask.' Erin slit the packet of coffee open with a knife. No more waltzing around the subject. She needed to know. 'He's just so… elusive.'

The doorbell rang. It was ten o clock. 'Punctual, though,' said her mother. 'I like that in a man.'

'How do I look?'

'Fresh. How do you want to look?'

She was wearing casual green trousers and a sleeveless cotton top in pale pink. A dozen thin Indian-style gold bangles danced along one wrist. 'I was aiming for businesslike with a twist.'

'I think you overdid the twist,' said her mother. 'Do you want me to answer the door or will you?'

'I'll get it,' she said with a sigh, and headed up the hallway.

He was wearing a white business shirt. The top two buttons were undone and the sleeves were rolled to his elbows, but it *was* a business shirt. The rest of his clothes were what she'd come to expect: comfortable-looking cargo trousers, well-worn boots…

There was sulphur-crested cockatoo sitting in a cage at his feet.

'This is Pat,' he said. 'Unfortunately the neighbours had to go to church.'

O-kay. 'Come on through.'

He picked up the birdcage, followed her through to the kitchen, and Erin watched with fatalistic resignation as her mother took one look at Tristan and Pat and fell in love with them both. When the introductions had been made, when Tristan was sitting at the breakfast counter with Pat sitting next to him, and Erin was brewing up the coffee, Lillian Sinclair sat opposite Tristan and favoured him with a long, assessing look from over the top of her glasses.

'Cake?' she offered.

'Thank you.'

She cut him a thick slice. Pat got wholegrain bread with a slather of honey.

'No swearing,' said the parrot by way of thank you.

'Not in my kitchen,' said Lillian affably. 'So, Tristan, Erin tells me you've been living in London.'

'Yes.'

He looked uncomfortable, Erin decided. He hadn't touched his cake. She brought the coffee pot over to the counter, found mugs for everyone. 'Black, two sugars, right?' she said as she poured the coffee.

'Right.'

'Eat,' said Lillian, gesturing towards the cake. 'You look like you could use some nourishment.'

With an oddly defenceless glance in her mother's direction, Tristan picked up his piece of cake and ate. 'It's good,' he said after a man-sized mouthful.

'It should be,' said Erin. 'I bought it from the corner deli.' There were shadows in his eyes this morning. Shadows under them. 'You look like you could use some sleep as well.'

'I sleep fine.' He finished his cake, reached for his coffee. 'I eat plenty.'

'Hell,' said Pat. 'Purgatory.'

'He's Catholic,' said Tristan.

'He's forgiven,' said her mother. 'What brings you back to Australia?'

Tristan shrugged. 'Whim. I had some leave owing. I decided to come home.'

There was more to it than that, thought Erin. Maybe he'd been worked over by a woman. 'How long will you be staying?' she asked him.

'Six weeks.'

Six weeks was a lot of time to be away from a job. Any job. She knew it was rude to ask a person what they did for a living, but she had the feeling that if she didn't ask him outright he'd evade the subject for ever. 'What exactly is it that you do?'

'I work for Interpol.'

Erin stared at him, open-mouthed. *Not* what she'd been expecting. 'Paper pusher?' she asked finally.

'No.'

No.

'Damnation,' said the parrot.

'Now, now, Pat. It's not that bad,' Lillian told the bird. 'He could have been Navy.' That would have really annoyed her.

'An Interpol cop,' said Erin flatly. 'You.'

'Why? Is that a problem?'

'Only for your future *wife*.' He was watching her intently. Her mother was eyeing her with something very close to sympathy. Tristan

Bennett was a cop. Serve and protect and all that went with it. Another man with secrets to keep and a job that came before family. Why on earth hadn't she seen it sooner? All the signs had been there. The strength, the aloofness, the quiet authority…

'At least you'll be safe on your trip,' said her mother.

'Yeah.' *Damn* him. Why couldn't he have been a stockbroker or a tax accountant? 'Why police work?'

'I like justice,' he said quietly. 'I enjoy the chase.'

'Do you always get your man?'

'No. Not always.' He looked away but not before Erin had seen the frustration in his eyes, along with an underlying anguish that clear took her breath away. Ditch the failed-relationship theory. Tristan Bennett had been worked over by his work.

Great, just great. Now she wanted to *comfort* him. So did her mother. Her mother cut him another piece of cake. Her mother had been married to a military man for twenty-eight years; her firstborn had followed in his father's footsteps. Taciturn, soul-wounded warriors were Lillian Sinclair's speciality.

'Here's where I need to get to,' said Erin, fishing a map from a pile of papers and spreading it out on the counter. She knew a thing or two about distracting wounded warriors herself. 'I was thinking we could take the inland road.'

'You'll be driving straight past the Warrambungles, then,' said her mother. 'You could go climbing.' She eyed Tristan speculatively. 'You're about Rory's size, give or take a couple of kilos. You can use his gear.'

'You climb?' asked Tristan, looking from her mother to her.

'Sinclair family sport. I've been climbing since I could crawl.' It wouldn't hurt to pack the gear in the back, just in case. 'Do you climb?'

'No.'

'Would you like to? We can go as easy or as hard as you like. Your call. I figure you for the vertical limit, do-it-or-die-trying type, but I could be wrong.'

'Wonderful sport, climbing,' said Lillian. 'Challenges the body, clears the mind, and then there's all that spectacular scenery thrown in for free. I don't know why it isn't more popular. More cake?'

'Who *are* you people?' said Tristan.

'Hey,' said Erin indignantly. 'You're the one who brought the parrot.'

Half an hour with Erin and her mother passed quickly. Lillian Sinclair had a knack for making even the wariest of people relax, decided Tristan, even if she had been persistent about feeding him. Sandwiches had followed the cake. Thick crusty Vienna loaf sandwiches with rare roast beef, salad greens, homegrown tomatoes, and mustard. She'd made him two of those and he'd made short work of them. He'd been hungry. Hungrier than he thought.

Oh, they'd grilled him. Lillian Sinclair knew of his father through some art gallery who'd consulted him on Chinese pottery pieces so they talked about him for a while. He'd told them of his three brothers, all of them older, and his younger sister. They'd talked about London and Kensington Gardens, the River Thames and the gentrification of Chelsea, where he had his apartment. Rock climbing, yoga, children's book illustrations, and the merits of super-sharp kitchen knives. All had been touched on and considered.

Not your average family.

'See?' said Erin as she walked him and Pat out to the car. 'That wasn't so bad, was it?'

'It was bearable.'

'Nah, you liked sitting in my mother's kitchen. Everyone does. You just won't admit it.'

She was right. But he still wasn't going to admit it. 'So you've taken my measure. What now?'

'Pack for a week and I'll pick you up in the morning,' she said as he bundled Pat into the passenger seat. 'Unless you've changed your mind.'

'I haven't,' he said, but he thought she might have. 'Have you?'

'No.'

She looked pensive. He thought he knew why. 'You don't much like what I do for a living, do you?'

'I'm sure you're very good at what you do,' she said coolly.

She smelled of sunshine and lemons, and her slim little body seemed tiny when compared to his, but he had her measure now, just as she had his. She was pure steel. 'You haven't answered my question.'

Her eyes grew stormy. 'Arrest me.'

She had a smart mouth. Lush, unpainted, sexy. He liked looking at it. He was looking at it now. 'What is it that you don't like?'

'It doesn't matter,' she said with a toss of her head. 'I only want you for your gem-guarding skills. I've decided against wanting you for anything else.'

'Really?'

'Yes. You're an intriguing man, don't get me wrong. But you're not my type.'

'Are you quite finished?' he asked silkily.

'I think so.' She tucked a stray strand of shiny brown hair behind her ear and nodded. 'Yep. All done.'

'Good, because I have this theory.'

'Scientists have theories.'

'Cops have them too. You see, I think you're attracted to me. Lord knows, for some strange reason I'm attracted to you. Want to test my theory?'

'No.'

But her cheeks were flushed, and when he traced her lips with his fingers they parted for him. Soft, so soft, he'd known they would be. The pulse at the base of her neck was beating frantically, he found the spot with his fingers and watched with no little satisfaction as her lashes fluttered closed and her breathing grew ragged.

'I don't want you,' she said.

'I can see that.' He gave her every opportunity to move away as he slid his hand around the back of her neck and closed the gap between their lips. She didn't move towards him, not one little bit, but she shuddered when his lips touched hers and that was all the encouragement he needed. Once. Twice. And then again.

It was the third time that did it.

He thought he was in control. Just a quick taste of her, that was all he'd take. Just to prove that she was no different from any other woman, certainly no sweeter. That it was all in his imagination. He was still in control when she slid her hands to his shoulders. Still coherent when he pulled her towards him. And then their bodies touched and fire streaked through him as her lips opened beneath his and then he knew.

She wasn't sweet.

She wasn't like any other woman he'd ever known. And his control deserted him.

Deeper, she took him there and he thought he

might drown in her desire. More, she gave it to him and he shuddered at the extent of her generosity. She reached up and sank her fingers into his hair and offered him more again. Nothing mattered but the woman in his arms and the magic they created. Nothing.

He'd been kissing women for half a lifetime, but not like this. Never like this.

Abruptly he released her.

Her lips were swollen, her eyes bewildered, as they stared at one another in shocked silence.

'*Hell*,' he muttered, taking a giant step back and shoving his hands in his pocket to stop himself reaching for her again. 'You're not my type either.'

Erin made it back to her mother's kitchen without her legs giving way. That was the good news. The bad news was that her mother took one look at her and just plain *knew* what she and Tristan Bennett had been up to. 'I think I just had an epiphany,' she said as she slumped down onto the stool Tristan had vacated. 'Seriously. The earth moved, fireworks lit up the sky, and I'm pretty sure I heard harps playing in the heavens.'

'That's interesting,' said her mother. 'Tristan hear them too?'

'I don't know. He left in a hurry.' Nought to sixty in three seconds flat. In a Corolla.

'I liked him,' said her mother.

'He's all wrong,' countered Erin. 'I should ring him and cancel the trip. I'll just have to buy stones at auction, that's all. There's one on Friday.'

'Good idea,' said Lillian. 'You might even find stones you like that you can afford this time round. Not that you ever have before.'

Erin sighed heavily. 'He's a cop.'

'An elite cop. A Criminal Investigation Officer, I think you'll find.'

'Go on. Rub it in.'

'The trouble with you is you can't see past his occupation.'

The trouble *was* she'd been intrigued by him from the start and his occupation didn't seem to matter a damn. Now she was even more fascinated by him, and that was a bad idea for a girl who wanted a husband who came home every night and wasn't compelled to keep secrets from his family. 'Is it so bad to want to fall in love with a man whose work *doesn't* take him all over the globe hunting down bad guys?'

'Not at all,' murmured Lillian. They'd had this conversation before. 'I'm the first to admit it can wear thin at times. But a passionate crusader won't be satisfied with menial work, Erin. The two just don't go together.'

'I don't want a passionate crusader.'

'Sweetie, you imprinted on them at birth. I doubt you'll settle for anything else.'

'I'll marry a doctor, then. At least they get to stay at home while they save the world.'

'Yeah. Those doctors have it so easy. Eighteen-hour days, life or death decisions to make, needy patients… Their wives have it easy too. Special occasions are never interrupted by a call from the hospital and their husbands are always home at six every night, bright, cheerful, and ready to help cook dinner.'

'Okay, so maybe that wasn't such a good example.'

'Life's a balancing act, Erin. You have work that you're passionate about too. Find the right man and the balance will come, no matter what he does for a living. As for Tristan Bennett, he's available, suitable, and willing to help you achieve your goals. He's exactly what you need. Make sure he eats.'

Oh, please! 'He's a grown man. He'll eat when he's hungry.' Erin frowned and drummed her fingers on the counter. There was something else bothering her about Tristan Bennett apart from his incredible kisses—something big. 'He's running from something,' she said finally. 'A botched case. A bad call. He's hurting.'

'I noticed that.' Her mother eyed her steadily. 'He responds to you.'

'Reluctantly.'

'But he does respond.'

CHAPTER THREE

HALF an hour. That was all it had taken Erin and Lillian Sinclair to unravel him, thought Tristan darkly as he wove his way home through the leafy suburban streets. Hell, the last time he'd been played so skilfully was in his Interpol recruitment interview six years ago; back when he'd been naive, idealistic and a whole lot more malleable than he was now. He liked to think he'd matured a little since then. He liked to think he'd grown smarter. Not that the last half-hour was any indication. Anyone witnessing that little debacle could be forgiven for thinking he wasn't smart at all.

He thought back, tried to pinpoint how they'd slipped through his guard, but he came up empty. He'd sat down on that stool, Lillian had looked at him, Erin had dumped two loaded spoonfuls of sugar into his coffee cup, and he'd been history. 'See what stress does to you?' he told the cockatoo. 'You don't eat, you don't sleep, and you say yes to things you'd never usually agree to.' Like brunch and week-long gem-buying trips. 'Then you go and kiss a woman who doesn't like cops, mainly to annoy her, and end up misplacing your mind.' Tristan slowed for a roundabout. 'Stay away from women, Pat. That's my advice to you.'

Pat ignored him completely. Pat was busy preening feathers. It occurred to him, belatedly, that Pat might just be a *female* cockatoo—which meant that from the tender age of nine he'd been spilling all his innermost secrets and no few kissing fantasies to a *girl*. '*Patricia?*'

Pat stopped preening feathers to look at him with a beady eye. 'Hallelujah, brother.'

Whoa! Definitely a female. How could he have *missed* it? All of a sudden, Tristan's world had tilted off course and it didn't seem to matter which way he looked, nothing was what it seemed.

He'd been looking forward to this road trip. Opals, sapphires, miles of road, and the company of a beautiful woman with a smart mouth and an easy smile…He'd wanted the distraction, wondered where it might lead, and he'd fanned the spark between him and the pixie deliberately. Hell, he was only human.

But he'd been thinking light-hearted. A pleasant diversion, for heaven's sake, not full on enslavement.

She didn't like what he did for a living.

Snap. Right now, neither did he.

He lived in London.

In a two-bedroom flat with the city all around him and no room to breathe. If he quit his job there was nothing keeping him in London. He could go anywhere, do anything. He could come home.

He was scared witless of giving his heart to a woman and then losing her.

There was that.

Sometimes a man's fear was buried so deep that it couldn't be reached and it couldn't be conquered. It just was. It certainly didn't need a reason for being, although Tristan figured his was tied up with losing his mother and watching his father crumble. Oh, his father had rallied, they all had, but there was no denying that the loss of his mother was engraved on his heart. Then he'd watched Jake marry young, watched his brother struggle to keep his dream alive and Jianna happy, only to have her leave him six months later. Sweet, loving Jianna, who'd been a part of their lives since before he could remember, had turned tail and fled, taking the best part of Jake with her.

Tristan liked women. Warm, smart women who could make a man laugh. Sharp, serious women who knew what they wanted to do with their lives and weren't afraid to work towards it. He liked them all, liked being with them, enjoyed making love to them. As long as they didn't get too close.

With Erin it was different. He looked at Erin and something stirred inside him. Something potent and unfamiliar and powerful enough to declare war on his old and constant companion that was fear.

Not love. Not yet.

Desire, maybe. The kind that went soul deep and left a man aching and needy. Not love, never that. His brain shied away from the notion, determined to resist it.

While his heart trembled.

Erin couldn't sleep. The memory of Tristan's kisses and her newfound knowledge of his occupation kept her tossing and turning long after she should have been asleep. He was all wrong, no matter what her mother thought. Her mother was wrong. He was too intense, too intriguing, too much *everything* for her peace of mind.

He kissed like an angel.

Erin glanced at the clock. Not quite midnight. She should call him. Tell him she'd changed her mind about needing his company on this trip. She was a grown woman. A smart woman. Far better to make this trip alone and take her chances than lose her heart to the likes of Tristan Bennett.

No. He'd looked tired. It was far too late to call him now. What if he were asleep? What if this was his first decent sleep in weeks and she woke him? Besides, she didn't have his number. Maybe *she* should go to sleep. There was plenty of time to call him in the morning. Erin turned over, rearranged her pillow, and closed her eyes.

Nope. Not working.

Two minutes later she had Tristan's number, or more accurately his father's number, and was standing by her bed, cordless phone in hand, listening for a dial tone. She punched the numbers in quickly, before she changed her mind, and waited for him to pick up. She could do this. All she had to do was calmly tell him the trip was off, everything would go back to normal, and then she could get some sleep.

Five rings. Six rings.

And then the ringing stopped.

'Bennett.' Tristan's voice was a sleepy rasp. The downside was that she'd woken him. The upside was that he'd get to sleep late tomorrow morning. She was pretty sure he'd appreciate the trade off. Eventually.

'It's Erin,' she said, starting to pace the room. 'I'm having second thoughts about this trip.'

'Fine,' he muttered. 'Goodnight.'

'Wait!' So much for calm. 'Aren't you going to ask me *why* I'm having second thoughts?'

'No.'

'I mean, you can't just kiss a girl like that and expect her to carry on as though it never happened. I think I deserve an explanation.'

'There is no explanation,' he said. 'It's one of life's little jokes.'

'Not laughing.'

'Trust me, it won't happen again.'

'Damn right it won't!'

'Pixies don't swear,' he said.

'I'm not a pixie. About this trip—'

'Does that mean we're done with the kissing talk?'

'Unless you'd like to tell me that our kiss was absolutely perfect and that you can hardly eat, breathe, or sleep for thinking about it, yes.'

'Moving on,' he said.

Right. Where was she? Oh, yeah. What to do about the trip. She stopped pacing in favour of sitting cross-legged in the middle of the bed. 'I'm thinking of cancelling this trip.'

'Because of the kissing?'

'Not at all. We're done talking about the kissing, remember?'

'Sorry. My mistake.' He sounded slightly more awake, a whole lot more amused. 'Why are you cancelling?'

Because of the kissing. Because of the potential for more kissing. 'I heard there were some good stones coming up for auction this week. I figure I'll get those instead.'

'Liar,' he said. 'But it was a good try.'

'How do you know I'm lying?'

'I'm a cop.'

She hadn't forgotten. 'What kind of cop?' She didn't expect a straight answer. She just wanted to see what he'd say. 'What exactly is it that you do?'

'I investigate international car theft.' He was all the way awake now; she could hear it in his voice.

'Do you ever work undercover?'

'Sometimes.'

'Ever talk about it?'

'No.'

Surprise, surprise. Maybe she *could* manage a week in his company. Clearly, he had no intention of following through on that kiss. And if *he* kept his distance, then surely she could. Maybe she'd been a bit hasty about cancelling the trip; maybe she *wouldn't* lose her heart to him after all. 'It probably wouldn't hurt to take a look at those opals out at Lightning Ridge, anyway. Just in case.'

Tristan sighed heavily. 'Why don't you sleep on it and call me in the morning?'

'Well, I'd like to. Really. It's just that I'm having a little trouble sleeping. I'd rather sort it out now and then sleep.'

'Wouldn't we all?' he said darkly.

Not a man bent on seduction. That was good. And she hadn't once pictured him lying there in a big old bed, on a mass of white cotton sheets, surrounded by fluffy white pillows that were a perfect foil for his eyes, that face, and that gloriously hard body of his.

'Erin?'

His voice was soft, sexy. Pity about the underlying thread of impatience. 'What?'

'Make up your mind.'

Cue the unmistakable air of command. Not that she was impressed by that. She was immune to weary warriors who wore command as if they were born to it and reticence like a shield. 'We're going.' There, she'd done it. She'd made her decision.

'Are you sure?'

'I'll pick you up at eight o clock. Just like we planned. This morning's kiss was an aberration. I see that now.'

'That's a relief,' he said, and hung up.

Erin was awake before dawn the next morning. Now that she had her feelings for Tristan sorted out—breathtaking, but not the one for her—she was eager to be underway. She had their lunch prepared and the car packed in record time and only iron control stopped her from hightailing it over to Tristan's two hours earlier than planned.

There was something magical about the start of a trip. Something marvellous about possibilities just waiting to be discovered. The perfect stone and the design she might dream up for it… A long straight stretch of road and a beckoning horizon… People to meet, places to go… Erin glanced at her watch for the umpteenth time in the last fifteen minutes. Five forty-six a.m. She wondered if Tristan was awake yet. Wondered if she should call him and find out.

Probably not. One embarrassing phone call a day was plenty.

It was just on seven-thirty when she reached his house. She was half an hour early but it couldn't be helped. Surely he'd be awake by *now*. She saw an old brass doorbell by the front door, rang it energetically, and stepped back to wait. Twenty seconds, thirty seconds, and then she heard the sound of footsteps coming to the door and then it opened and Tristan stood there wearing nothing but jeans, with his hair wet and tousled and a towel in his hand. Freshly showered and shaved was a *very* good look for him. 'Good. You're nearly ready,' she said, trying hard to ignore his superbly sculpted chest, complete with a sprinkling of dark hair that tapered to a vee. 'Not that I want to rush you.'

'You're early.'

'Only a little.'

Tristan stood aside, silently inviting her to come in. He looked past her, towards her mother's late model Ford, and sighed.

'It's a comfortable ride,' she said reassuringly.

'I know,' he said. 'But it's not quite the Monaro, now, is it?'

'It'll still get us from A to B,' she said firmly. 'Do you have any idea how much attention the Monaro draws on the road? What with the rumble, and the racing wheels… I swear it's a guaranteed trouble magnet.'

'I know.' His grin was swift and decidedly dangerous. 'Why do you think we like it so much?' he said as he shut the door behind her and padded back down the hallway, leaving her to follow in his wake.

Watching Tristan's back muscles flex and ripple as he towel dried his hair on the way down the hall made Erin's hands itch and her mind fog, so she dragged her gaze away from the half-naked Tristan and turned her attention to her surroundings instead, hoping for a distraction. The house was masculine; there was no other word for it. Dark-wood floorboards, a navy hall runner, wood panelling halfway up the walls… The painted part of the walls was a cool forest green. She followed Tristan into what she figured was the living room, only to discover more dark furnishings and walls lined with books. Tristan had mentioned that all his siblings had left home and that his father lived here alone now, but the house still bore the marks of a loved and lived-in family home. She spotted a karate belt behind glass in a cabinet. Now there was a distraction. 'Who's the seventh Dan black belt?'

'Jake. He runs a Martial Arts dojo in Singapore.'

'And the aircraft books?'

'They're Pete's. He's flying charter planes around the Greek islands at the moment. Summer job. It's only temporary.' Tristan didn't seem to mind offering up information about his family, she noted. Just not about himself. There was a photo on the sideboard of a young man in Navy whites who looked disturbingly like Tristan. 'That's Luke,' he said, before she could ask. 'You'd like him. He's a Navy diver.'

Erin bared her teeth. 'So much testosterone,' she said sweetly. 'Anyone in your family have a normal job?'

'Hallie buys and sells ancient Chinese artwork,' he said. 'That's normal.'

Yeah, right. At least he'd stopped towelling his hair. Only now it spiked in places and lay flat in others, framing his face in a way that was boyishly endearing and affording him an innocence that was deceptive. *Very* deceptive. There was nothing innocent about Tristan Bennett. Nothing at all innocent about her body's reaction to his near nakedness and, judging from the way his eyes had darkened and his sudden predatory stillness, he knew exactly what sort of effect he was having on her.

Oh, boy. Not good. Must remember to breathe, she thought, and hurriedly turned her attention to an old framed *The King And I* poster hanging on the wall above the mantelpiece. It was the only vaguely feminine thing in the room. Deborah Kerr teaching Yul Brynner how to waltz. 'I'm assuming the poster belongs to your sister?'

'It's here under sufferance,' said Tristan, seemingly willing to be distracted. 'It used to be Hallie's favourite movie.'

The governess who tamed a proud and strong king. A motherless young girl growing up in a houseful of alpha males. No wonder *The King and I* had been his sister's favourite movie. She'd needed a role model. 'My mother and I caught a rerun at the cinema a few years back,' she said with a wistful sigh. 'It was lovely. I've been a sucker for bald-headed men ever since.'

'Gimme a break,' he said.

Erin eyed his tousled hair critically. Maybe if he didn't have quite so much of it, she wouldn't have this overwhelming urge to bury her hands in it. 'You know, you could use a haircut.'

'I am *not* shaving my head for you.'

'Of course not,' she said soothingly. 'Although—'

'No.'

Right. In that case the bare skin definitely had to go, because if he didn't cover up soon she was going to start drooling. 'Shouldn't you be getting ready?' she prompted. 'Putting a shirt on?'

'I would if you'd stop asking questions.' His voice was long-suffering.

Erin smiled sweetly. 'I'll wait here. Don't mind me.'

Tristan sent her a warning glance that she decided to ignore and headed for the door. He'd almost reached it when she spoke again. 'So who collects the little toy cars?'

'Models,' he said firmly as he disappeared out the door, taking his tousled hair and his near-naked body with him. 'They're scale replicas.'

'Got it,' she said, not bothering to hide her grin.

The little toy cars were his.

It was like driving with an optimistic fairy, thought Tristan some three hours later. He'd tried silence. He'd tried quelling glances. He'd taken over driving duty. None of it had the slightest impact on Erin's general effervescence. They were aiming for Lightning Ridge that evening, a nine-hundred kilometre trip from Sydney. They weren't even halfway there.

'We could play I Spy,' she said.

'No.'

'Break for lunch?'

'It's not even midday.'

Erin sighed. 'Want to change drivers again?'

He'd been driving for less than an hour. It was nowhere near time to change drivers again. 'No. Put a CD on.' They were between towns. They'd lost radio reception twenty kilometres ago.

'I'm not in the mood for music right now.'

'Perhaps a nap?' he suggested hopefully.

'Maybe after lunch.'

He slid her a sideways glance to see if she was playing him. She was.

'Tell me about yourself,' she said.

'What happened to "Let's not get to know one another"?' he said dryly. They'd decided on that particular tactic about half an hour into the journey. He'd needed something to counteract her effect on him. That ready smile, those laughing eyes. Something, anything, to keep her out.

She was wearing a bright blue T-shirt and casual grey trousers, and there was nothing overtly sexual about them, nothing innately feminine, except that every movement she made *was* feminine, and graceful, and sexy. And then there was the dainty charm bracelet on her arm that accentuated the slenderness of her wrist, the earrings dangling from her ears that drew attention to the delicate curve of her neck, and the pulse he knew he'd find beating there if he put his lips to it.

How on earth was he supposed to get through a week or so of *this*?

'I'm having difficulty with the let's-not-get-to-know-each-other plan,' she said with a sigh. 'I figure if I get to know you I won't find you anywhere near as intriguing. I figure if I'm *really* lucky, I might not even like you.'

There was merit in the idea, he decided warily. Maybe he could even help her out a little. 'What would you like to know?'

'Tell me how you ended up working for Interpol.'

'They had an opening in their stolen car division. They were looking for someone who knew cars. Someone they could send undercover. I qualified.'

'And was it what you expected?'

'It was the wildest game in town. For a while.' He'd thrived on the excitement and the danger, the adrenaline rush that came with each and every takedown.

'So what changed?' she said, her eyes shrewd and far more knowing than he would have liked.

'The odds grew longer, the stakes grew higher, and it stopped becoming a game,' he said quietly. 'I grew up. End of story.'

'That's a terrible story,' she said. 'Don't you have any uplifting stories?'

'Yeah. There was this stolen car ring operating out of Serbia once. Family run business. We knew all the players. We just couldn't touch them. The old man died of a heart attack, the brothers took each other out in the ensuing fight for control, and everyone else lived happily ever after.'

'Gee, thanks for that,' she said with a grimace. 'The kids are going to just love *your* bedtime stories.'

'What kids?'

'Your kids. You are planning on having children, aren't you?'

'I hadn't really thought about it.'

'Not ever?'

'Not yet.'

'You are such a bad bet for a husband.'

'I know,' he said solemnly, stifling a grin. She looked so disgruntled. 'My strengths lie elsewhere.'

'I can't imagine where.'

'Yes, you can.'

She blushed furiously, opened her mouth to speak, caught his eye, and looked away.

Silence. Finally. Tristan grinned, savouring the moment. He loved it when a plan came together.

They stopped for lunch at Gulgong, changed drivers again at Gilgandra, and rolled into Lightning Ridge just as the sun was disappearing behind a desert horizon of red dirt and saltbush. The road sign on the way into the town said, 'Lightning Ridge, Population—?' because, bottom line, no one knew. Rumour had it somewhere between two and twenty thousand. More or less. Lightning Ridge—in the middle of nowhere and chock-full of eccentrics, opal miners, optimists, and fortune seekers—was the perfect place to hide.

'Where are we staying?' he asked.

'We're very flexible in that regard,' she said,

shooting him a smile. 'Now would be a good time to decide.'

'I see,' he said, and wondered why the notion that Erin was perfectly comfortable embarking on a journey with no fixed destination in mind disturbed him so much. He *always* travelled this way. His undercover work demanded the flexibility and he just plain preferred it. Women, at least in his experience, did not prefer it. Women always wanted to know where they were headed and when they were going to get there—be it a conversation about a weekend away, or the terms of a relationship. That was just the way it was. 'Let's try this one,' he said, motioning to a motel coming up on their right.

'Done.'

The motel offered air-conditioning, satellite TV, and standby rates. The woman behind the reception desk was frighteningly forthright. 'I can give you a family suite with two rooms and a kitchenette,' she said when Erin asked after accommodation.

'Not two separate rooms?' he asked.

'Take it or leave it.'

'We'll look at it,' he said, and the woman took a key from the hook rack behind her and thumped it down on the desk.

'Last door to the left.'

Erin liked the family suite. It was clean, functional, comfortable, and right there waiting for them at the end of a long day's driving. The bedrooms and bathroom were upstairs, the kitchenette and living area downstairs. If it had been Rory with her on this trip she wouldn't have hesitated, she'd have agreed to stay there without another thought, but it wasn't Rory, this was Tristan and there was a privacy issue to think about. 'What do you think?' she asked tentatively.

Tristan's expression was guarded. 'It's fine.'

They'd just managed nine hours in a car together without finding a whole lot in common apart from an annoyingly persistent physical awareness of one another. Chances were that if he left the lid off the toothpaste and his towel on the bathroom floor, even that would fade. 'Because we can try somewhere else if you'd rather.'

'This is fine.' In that remote way of his that promised distance no matter how aware they might be of one another.

'We'll take it,' Erin told the woman back at reception.

'What name?'

'Sinclair,' she said.

Tristan said, 'Smith.'

'Sinclair Smith,' said the woman dryly. 'Is that hyphenated?'

'Yes,' said Tristan.

'I'll need a car registration number as well,' she said, and Tristan rattled it off.

'Handy,' said Erin.

'Occupational hazard.'

'Who's paying?' asked the woman.

'I am,' said Erin, fishing her credit card from her wallet. Tristan frowned and looked as if he was going to protest and Erin shot him a warning glance. She was paying for the accommodation. They'd discussed it already. 'Two nights should do it.'

'Stay three and I'll throw in a free double pass to the town pool as well.'

Gee, the town pool. Huge incentive.

'Maybe three nights,' said Tristan with a lopsided smile that had the formerly forthright receptionist smiling coquettishly and patting her beehive hairdo into place, never mind that she was old enough to be his grandmother. 'We'll let you know.'

It didn't take long to unload. Tristan had his carryall. Erin had a backpack full of clothes, a cotton shoulder bag with her jeweller's loupe and a sketchpad and pencils, and a box of assorted groceries to bring in. Two trips, except that Tristan hauled her backpack out of the car along with his carryall, which left her with just the groceries and the shoulder bag. Rory would have done the same and Erin would have accepted his assistance automatically and thought nothing of it. That was what brothers did.

When Tristan did it she grew decidedly weak at the knees.

'Do you want the room with the double bed in it or the one with the two singles?' he asked from upstairs as she unloaded the grocery box in the kitchenette.

'What colour are the sheets on the double bed?'

'White.'

Damn.

'They're all white,' he said, appearing in the kitchenette doorway. 'Is that a problem?'

'Not really.' Who was she kidding? It didn't matter what colour the bedsheets were, Tristan Bennett would look sensational on them. Of course, he'd look a lot less sensational wedged into a single bed but she didn't really have the heart to make him sleep in one. He was bigger than she was. Gloriously, mesmerisingly bigger. She took a deep breath, blew it out again, and pushed all thoughts of white sheets, big beds, and Tristan Bennet aside. 'I'll take the single.' There. Bedrooms sorted. Bedroom doors firmly closed. 'What shall we do about dinner? Eat in or go out?'

'What's in the box?' he asked.

'Breakfast food, mainly. A few snacks. A couple of bottles of wine. Nothing that could constitute dinner. It's more a question of bringing take-away back here or finding somewhere to sit down and eat. Depends what you feel like eating. And before we go any further, I'm paying for it.'

'You don't need to do that.'

He wasn't comfortable with a woman picking up the tab for him. The deeply hidden, feminine part of her soul, which saw a man as both provider and protector, applauded him. But she wasn't about to let him pay for his own meals. Not without an argument, at any rate. 'Think of yourself as a business expense,' she said. 'Me, I'm thinking hamburgers. How about you?'

'A works hamburger, heavy on the BBQ sauce,' he said. 'And your accountant is *never* going to see me as a business expense. Just so you know.' He fished a fifty-dollar note from his wallet and set it on the counter beside her. 'You provided lunch and breakfast is in the box. I'll pay for tonight's dinner. Don't argue.'

It wasn't his quietly spoken words but the cool, steady gaze that accompanied them that warned her not to push him. Pick your battles and never use all your ammo in the opening salvo. Her father had taught her that too, bless his military soul. 'Okay,' she said with a cool and measuring gaze of her own. She picked up the fifty-dollar note and headed for the door. 'Good hamburgers heavy on the BBQ sauce requires local knowledge,' she said. 'I'll go ask the receptionist where we can find some.'

The receptionist, whose name, Erin discovered, was Delia, gave more than advice. She called the shop, placed their order, and arranged for it to be delivered to the room. Two works hamburgers, one with extra BBQ sauce, and an extra large serve of hot chips with chicken salt.

'Who are the chips for?' asked Erin.

'Your man. He looks hungry.'

Great. Another woman hell-bent on feeding him. 'He's not my man,' she said firmly. 'He's just a travelling companion. A chauffeur.'

Delia cackled. 'Honey, if that man's a chauffeur, I'll eat both your burgers *and* the chips.' And after a pause, 'Mind you, he'd look mighty fine in the uniform. Any uniform.'

'Yeah, well, thanks for that.' Erin did *not* want to picture Tristan Bennett in uniform. Unfortunately, she couldn't help it.

He looked fabulous. Cool, confident, heartbreakingly remote…

'Where were we?' said Delia.

'Uniforms,' she said wistfully. 'Navy formals. The dark blue with the gold braid.' She had no idea what the Interpol uniform looked like, so she'd gone with what she knew.

'I knew you'd catch on,' said the older woman. 'By the way, there's a twenty-minute wait on that order. Sol's always backed up this time of night.'

'I don't mind waiting.'

'Why would you when you have a man in uniform to think about?' said Delia. 'You can use the time to visualise just how you'd go about getting him out of it.'

Five minutes later Erin was back in the motel suite. The burgers were on their way, she told Tristan, eyeing him darkly before following up with the somewhat puzzling statement that she wasn't the slightest bit interested in the type of dress uniform Interpol cops wore. 'Not a problem,' he said and watched with no little amusement as she banged around in the kitchen, setting plates on the table, and searching the cupboards for wineglasses for the bottle of white she handed to him.

'We're drinking?' he asked.

'I am,' she said. 'I'm in need of a distraction.'

'From what?'

'You.'

'Care to expand on that?'

'Absolutely not,' she said, finally finding some wineglasses and setting them down on the table in front of him. 'Pour.'

He poured generously, for both of them. Maybe she had a point. Maybe wine would dull the senses and cloud the mind enough so that he could get through the night without doing anything monumentally stupid like acting on the awareness that lay thick and insistent between them. Or maybe not. 'What if the wine doesn't distract you?' he asked. 'What if it makes you even more focussed on what you're trying to avoid?'

'Let's not dwell on it,' she said, lifting her glass. 'To opals and the buying of them. To brilliant designs, worldwide recognition, and restraint when it comes to acting on impulse with men in uniform.'

'I don't wear a uniform,' he said.

'Not sure I needed to know that.'

Tristan shrugged, stifling his smile. 'To your success,' he said.

'Thanks.' She touched her glass to his and drank.

The food arrived some ten minutes later and although the burgers were good, the chips were better. 'Good idea,' he said, indicating the chips piled high on a plate between them.

'Delia's idea,' said Erin wryly. 'She thought you looked hungry.'

He was hungry. 'Who's Delia?'

'The receptionist.' Erin regarded him curiously. 'Women really like the thought of feeding you, don't they? Why is that?'

'It's some sort of nurturing instinct,' he said. 'Also the way to a man's heart. You should know this.'

'So has Delia captured your heart?'

'Not yet, but she's certainly in the running. These are good chips.'

'Anyone else cook for you back in England?'

He knew what she was asking. Thought it as good a time as any to let her know his thoughts on the subject. 'Not on a permanent basis.'

'How about a regular basis?'

'Not even that.'

'I don't feel an overwhelming need to feed you,' she said solemnly.

'No nurturing thoughts?'

'Not one.'

'This is a good thing,' he said.

She smiled. 'Nope, when I think of you it's all about wild passionate sex and losing my mind. I suspect you've heard that before.'

Not in this lifetime he hadn't. 'Don't you have any sense of self-preservation at all?' he demanded. Because his thoughts were already there, his body tense and hard as he undressed her in his mind, roughly, urgently, and took her right there in the kitchen. 'Dammit, Erin!' He closed his eyes, muttered a prayer, and tried to remember exactly why it was that he didn't want Erin Sinclair in his bed or anywhere else he could think of to take her.

Because she was dangerous, his brain reminded him. Whether she was gunning for his heart or not, Erin Sinclair had the power to reach out and engage him on every level he could think of and a few more he couldn't even name and he didn't want that. No, he couldn't risk that. He wouldn't. 'Drink

your wine,' he commanded, burning up with the
knowledge that if she pushed him, heaven forbid,
if she even looked at him with an invitation in her
eyes, he'd never be able to keep himself leashed.

'Good idea,' she said, and picked up her wineglass with hands that trembled ever so slightly.
'Geez. Who knew?'

Exactly.

'I think we need another distraction,' she said,
setting her wineglass carefully back down on the
table, and headed from the room without another
word. When she returned she had her sketchbook
in one hand and a fistful of pencils in the other.

'What are you doing?'

'Your portrait.'

'Why?'

'You, me, a sketchpad between us…' she said,
setting it on her lap and using her knees as an
easel. 'I'm going to objectify you.'

It sounded reasonable. 'Who taught you to
draw?'

'My mother, at first. Then I took classes. It's
a useful skill for any designer to have.' Her
pencil moved sure and swift across the page.
'Brood for me.'

'Excuse me?'

'You know. Brood. Think about whatever it is
that's bothering you.'

'You mean apart from the thought of wild,

unfettered sex with a woman who doesn't want to feed me?'

'Not that,' she said quickly. 'You need to think about something other than that.'

'Not sure that's possible,' he muttered.

'Think about your work.'

Tristan glared at her.

'Perfect.'

Tristan glared at her some more. 'How long is this going to take?'

'Not that long. I'm almost done. This is a speed portrait. I only want the lines. The essence of you is something I'm trying to avoid.' She lifted her gaze from the paper and her pencil paused as if momentarily distracted. 'I have a piece of tiger-eye the exact colour of your eyes,' she said at length. 'If I set it in a ring for you, would you wear it?'

He doubted it.

'I was thinking of something like this.' She turned to a fresh page in her sketchbook, set it on the table, and the picture of a ring began to take shape. The design was simple: a wide band with a squarish insert of polished stone. With a few strokes of her pencil she managed to make it look both elegant and bold.

Tristan shrugged.

'Your enthusiasm overwhelms me,' she muttered, picking up her wineglass. 'I'll make it for you anyway, as payment for coming opal-hunting with me. I'm thinking white gold for the band. Platinum if I can get hold of it.'

'Are you always this generous with people you hardly know?'

'You give some, you get some.'

Tristan wanted some. Badly. And he didn't know how long he could hold off before he reached out and simply took. 'Erin—'

'I know,' she said breathlessly. 'You know, maybe this portrait business isn't such a good idea. Maybe I should go for a walk instead.' She stood abruptly and reached for his plate.

'Leave it.'

'Oh, boy.' She reached for her wine.

'Refill?' He reached for the bottle.

'No!' And then more calmly, 'Thank you. I'm going to take that walk now. Then I'm going to come back and take a shower and go to bed. Alone.'

'It's a good plan.' His voice was rough, strained, his control was close to non-existent. 'But if you're still here by the time I get these dishes to the sink, it's not going to happen. You and me naked on the table will happen, and then maybe, *maybe*, we'll make it to the shower. You know that, don't you?'

She nodded. Swallowed hard. 'I'm not quite sure I'm ready for that to happen.'

Neither was he. 'Enjoy your walk.' He stood up, reached for the dinner plates and took them to the counter. By the time he'd scraped the scraps into the bin she was gone.

What in hell was wrong with him? He never lost control when he was with a woman. Not ever. He hoped Erin's walk was a long one. He hoped she had the quickest shower in history and that she went to bed directly afterwards, just as she'd said. He would stay up late, watch some TV. And then, when she was safely tucked away for the night, sound asleep, and he'd watched all there was to watch on the television, and read all there was to read in the newspaper, when his mind was foggy with fatigue and his body was aching with tiredness, maybe then he'd think about going to bed.

CHAPTER FOUR

TRISTAN was dreaming of the dockyards of Prague and row upon row of shipping containers. They were slick with sea spray and shrouded in mist that twisted and eddied around his feet as he walked towards that last unopened container. Cars; he was looking for stolen cars; the permit to search was in his partner's pocket, and they were onto something. He could feel it in the air, see it in the eyes of passing dockyard workers.

Cars. Shiny, expensive, luxury cars, that was what they were looking for. The hour was late and he was tired, deathly tired, but there'd been something in Jago's voice when he'd talked about this latest container load that no one wanted to pick up that had had him breaking deep cover and calling it in. Jago was frightened; something had gone badly wrong. And scum like Jago didn't frighten easily.

'Tell me why we're doing this,' said Cal when

he'd collected him and hightailed it down to the yards. 'Tell me why you just blew off months of undercover work on one lousy container load of stolen cars.'

He couldn't say. He didn't know. 'Something's wrong.'

'Yeah, your judgement. Seriously, man. We nearly had the whole damn lot of them, the entire cartel.'

'The big dogs bailed this morning. It's time.' It was past time.

Death. He could smell it as they drew closer and it made his hair stand on end. 'Has anyone checked the container?' he asked the night watchman who padded alongside him, grim and wary.

'Hell, no,' said the man. 'The men are spooked. You can see that for yourself.'

Not cars. Not just cars. He knew that as surely as he knew his own name, and all of a sudden he didn't want to open up that container, didn't want to know what was inside. 'We should wait for backup.'

'You going soft on me, old man?' This from Cal.

Not soft. But gut instinct had kept him alive too many times for him to ignore it, and right now instinct was telling him to stay the hell away from that container. 'I don't like it.'

'Hey, you're the one who dragged me out of bed

and down here.' Cal reached the container and started sliding bars into their open position. Bars that had kept whatever was in that container in. The dockworkers of Prague had the right of it, but Cal couldn't feel it. Cal who was young and fearless and hadn't yet seen the things that Tristan had seen.

'Cal! Wait!'

But Cal hadn't waited. He'd thrown that door open and the smell had poured over them like a wave. Death. He should have called this in days ago, when the missing container had finally arrived. He'd known something was going down but he'd bided his time. Not just cars, no cars at all, just filth and mattresses and shapeless, nameless lumps and then he knew what this container had been trafficking and why the cartel had spooked when it hadn't come in on time. His eyes watered, he couldn't see for darkness, didn't want to see. 'Call the paramedics,' he said as Cal stumbled back, white-faced and clumsy with his need to get away. 'Some of them might still be alive.'

He should have called it in earlier. Three days ago, when the container had first hit the dock. He'd known something big had gone down, he just hadn't known what. So he'd waited.

And waited.

Erin woke to the echo of a noise reverberating in her head, not entirely sure if she'd been dreaming or if a sound really had woken her. She lay in the little single bed in the unfamiliar motel room, hardly breathing, just waiting. Waiting for what?

She didn't know.

Uneasiness came quickly, spreading over her like a blanket as the noise came again; a harsh, anguished cry of grief and desperation that was universally recognisable, never mind that it was wordless.

Tristan.

Erin hadn't been dreaming. But Tristan was.

What to do?

Her first instinct was to go to him, hold him, and let him take from her what comfort he could. Her second instinct was to feed him. Damn! She lay in bed, listening to him thrash about, and then the noise stopped abruptly and light crept into her room from the gap beneath the door. He was awake.

She heard his bedroom door open, heard him go into the bathroom and then there was the splash of running water and she figured he was dousing his face. She wanted to go to him then, and ask him what was troubling him, but she stayed where she was, motionless in her indecision. He wouldn't thank her for her interference. He'd close up tight, stare at her with eyes as fierce as any mountain cat and tell her that it was nothing, that he was fine, and that she should go back to bed.

Damned if he'd tell her anything. She knew the breed.

Damned if he would.

She heard him turn the tap off, heard the click of a light switch as he turned the bathroom light off and padded quietly down the hallway.

He didn't turn his bedroom light off. She could picture him sitting on the bed with his elbows on his knees and his head in his hands and cursed him afresh for being what he was. For making her care that he was hurting.

She wanted to go to him. She desperately wanted to help him. And knew that she could not.

Maybe he was reading. She hoped that was what he was doing.

Or maybe he simply slept better these days with the light on.

CHAPTER FIVE

BREAKFAST the following morning was a subdued affair; never mind that the sun was shining and the prospect of hunting down the perfect opal loomed bright. Erin watched in silence as Tristan, freshly showered and shaved, slotted two bits of raisin bread into the toaster. He knew his way around a kitchen, that much was certain. The dishes from last night had been washed and stowed away, and the tea towel had been hung to dry. What was more, the bathroom was tidy too, not a toothpaste smear or a dropped towel in sight. Just the lingering scent of soap and man, and the memory of a cry in the darkness that she couldn't forget. 'Sleep well?' she asked casually.

'Fine,' he said. And after a moment, 'You?'

'Like a baby.'

'Good.' He nodded, waited for the toast to pop.

He wasn't going to tell her about his night-mare. Wasn't even going to acknowledge its existence. Her father and Rory were the same.

Forever shutting her out and telling her every-thing was okay when, clearly, all hell had broken loose. Trying to protect her, she knew that. Trying to shield her from the darkness that came with war, and she appreciated their concern, she really did, but she resented it too. She was stronger than they gave her credit for. Strong enough to listen. Plenty strong enough to help.

Toast popped and Tristan slid the pieces onto a plate and slathered them with butter, before loading up the toaster again. 'Want some?' he offered, gesturing towards the plate.

Sighing, Erin took a piece. 'Coffee's hot,' she said by way of contribution to the breakfast cause. Given the night he'd just had she figured he was going to need a couple of cups before he'd be ready to seize the day. 'There's a one-man mine about forty kilometres northeast of here,' she said. 'I thought we might head out there first up this morning.'

'You don't need to phone ahead?'

Erin shook her head. 'Can't. Old Frank's not one for phones. The upside is that he does love his opals.' Another thought occurred to her. 'Er, he likes his guns too. You're not going to get all righteous about him having unlicensed firearms on the premises, are you?'

'Only if he's waving one of them in my face,' said Tristan.

This was a distinct possibility. Frank and his twenty-two tended to meet potential customers shortly after they pulled up on his plot. Mind you, that particular gun probably was licensed. 'Maybe you could wait in the car while I go and find him.'

'I don't think so.' Tristan's voice was implacable.

'Ooh, tough guy. Be still my beating heart.'

The tough guy favoured her with a look that could have frozen Sydney harbour and Erin sent him a sunny smile in return. She'd worry about who went and found Frank when they got there, she decided, because there was obviously no sense talking about it *now*. One thing was for certain, she thought smugly. Tristan wasn't thinking about whatever was giving him nightmares any more. No. He was thinking about ways to chain her to the car.

Tristan's eyes narrowed. 'I know that smile,' he said warningly. 'My sister has one just like it.'

'Really?' Erin's smile widened. 'More toast?'

An hour later they rolled onto Frank's patch of dirt, studiously ignoring the barrage of no-trespassing signs and the bone-white cow skull mounted on a stake by the front gate.

'Colourful,' said Tristan as he got out of the car and came to help her drag the broken-hinged farm gate closed behind them. 'How did you come across this place again?'

'Rory and I were out this way about two years back and stopped to help Frank with a busted radiator hose. Of course, we didn't know who he was back then, but we got to talking and one thing led to another.'

'I can imagine.'

'Next thing you know we're getting a tour of his mine and I'm sifting through a handful of rough-cut opal and doing business. I think it was fate.'

'Not horoscopes?'

'That too.' Erin scoured the desolate landscape in front of them and waved energetically in the general direction of the old silver caravan in the distance. 'I think he's home. I just saw a glint of sunlight on steel.'

'Where?'

'Over by the caravan.'

'Great,' said Tristan. 'Get in the car.'

She got in the driver's side, held out her hand for the keys, and when Tristan somewhat reluctantly handed them over she headed for the caravan.

'Do you think he'll remember you?' asked Tristan

'I'm pretty sure he will,' she said, with a nod of her head for good measure. Eventually.

Frank West did remember her. The grin on his sun-battered face and the lack of a twenty-two in his hands confirmed it. He didn't remember Tristan.

'Who's the muscle?' he wanted to know.

'Frank, this is Tristan. Tristan, meet Frank.'

Tristan nodded.

Frank eyed Tristan curiously. 'Seems a bit uptight,' he said.

'We're working on it,' said Erin, and smothered a smile when Tristan sent her a glance that told her she could work on him forever; he still wasn't going to bend.

'Got me some nice black opal,' said Frank.

'Sorry, Frank. The budget won't run to the blacks.' There was a ten-thousand-dollar limit on the cost of materials for the competition pieces, to even the playing field. Anyone could make a million dollars' worth of Argyle diamonds look good. 'I'm after some rough-cut boulder opal.'

'Got some good quality blues,' he said. 'What shape?'

'Freeform.'

Frank's eyes brightened considerably. Freeform was a harder sell than the more common oval and square shapes. 'Better come into the office,' he said, and sat them down at the table in the little silver caravan that doubled as both living quarters and business premises. 'Sure you don't want to take a look at the blacks?'

'Bring them out by all means,' she said with a

grin, 'but unless you have any for sale under two thousand, all I'm going to do is admire them.'

Frank sighed and turned his attention to a row of opal-filled jam jars high up on a shelf. He bypassed the first half a dozen jam jars on the ledge in favour of a selection from further along, eventually taking down three jars and setting them on the table. He opened one up, and poured the contents carefully onto the table. 'Homebrew?' he asked Tristan. 'I figure you're going to need it before she's through.'

'Go ahead,' murmured Erin as she started sorting through the opals, piece by piece. 'This could take a while.'

'She was here for three hours last time she came,' said Frank.

'*How* long?' said Tristan.

'I figure that's a yes,' said Frank and opened the fridge door to reveal a tub of margarine, half a tomato, a row of empty beer glasses where the milk should be, and a twenty litre steel keg, complete with tap. He filled three glasses with beer from the keg, one for each of them, and took a seat.

'How long do you think she'll take this time?' asked Tristan.

'I've gotten smarter in my old age, see? That there first jar is to help her get her eye in. It's a practice jar, so to speak, to remind her what she's not looking for.'

'Gee, thanks, Frank,' said Erin, not bothering to look up from the opals she was sorting. 'What's in the second jar?'

'You'll find some nice opal in the second.'

'And the third?' asked Tristan.

'My best boulder pieces. She'll find what she's looking for in the third.'

'Why not give her the third jar first?' said Tristan.

Frank eyed him pityingly. 'You don't know much about women, do you, son?'

Tristan sighed, and reached for his beer.

'Would *you* like to see some black opal?' Frank asked Tristan speculatively. 'Got a stone there that'd make a fine engagement ring for a non-traditional kind of woman.'

Tristan froze with his beer halfway to his lips and Erin sniggered. 'Frank, you're scaring him.'

'A man needs to contemplate the future every now and then,' said Frank with a toothless grin as he headed past a curtain of faded blue cloth and into the bedroom section of the caravan. He came back with a small roll of red velvet cradled gently in the crook of his arm and Erin sighed and abandoned the opals on the table in favour of scooting over, closer to Tristan. Frank was determined to show off his blacks to someone and it was useless to pretend she wasn't interested.

There was a fortune in opals nestling on that there red velvet strip, she thought in awe as the old miner unrolled his best onto the table in front of him. Enough to buy Frank a mansion if he wanted one. Five mansions.

'This here's the latest,' said Frank proudly, turning over an opal the size of a twenty-cent piece. It was turquoise on black, shot through with yellow and a brilliant fiery red. 'Haven't seen colour like that in thirty years. Not since old Fisty dug up the Sorcerer's Stone and you know what happened to that.'

Tristan didn't.

'It vanished,' said Frank. 'Disappeared into thin air. One minute it was there on its pedestal and the next minute...*poof.* Gone! Saw it happen with my own eyes. That's why I never put my stones on display under glass. They don't like it. They disappear.'

'Someone could have taken it,' said Tristan mildly.

'That there room was locked down tighter than a Russian submarine the minute it disappeared, and everyone in the room was body-searched. Nothing!'

'Maybe someone swallowed it,' said Tristan.

'It was the size of a tennis ball.'

'Or hid it.'

'In that room?' Frank shook his head. 'It was one of them contemporary museums. You couldn't hide dust in that place.'

'Which museum was that?' asked Tristan and Erin lifted her gaze from the opals to stare at him with amused exasperation. His interest in the opals set out in front of him was cursory. His interest in Frank's story was all-encompassing. 'You can't help yourself, can you?'

'What?' he said.

'Doing the cop thing. Aren't you supposed to be on leave?'

'I am on leave.'

'Yet you're sitting here asking questions about a legendary fire opal that's been missing for, what, twenty years?'

'More like thirty,' said Frank.

'Just curious,' said Tristan.

'You were working it,' she said sternly. 'Trying to solve a thirty-year-old crime in your spare time.'

'Don't you have boulder opal to look at?' he countered.

'I'll get back to them eventually.' Just as soon as she'd finished ogling the blacks and making her point. 'You know what your problem is? You've lost your balance. You're all work.'

'Really?' said Tristan coolly.

'Yes, really.' Erin stood her ground. 'You've been so busy chasing villains that you've forgotten how to chase rainbows.'

'I know perfectly well how to chase rainbows,' he said.

'Oh, yeah? When was the last time you acted on impulse? When was the last time you let whimsy have its way?'

Tristan's eyes lightened as he sent her a lopsided smile she couldn't even begin to resist. 'I'm here, aren't I?'

Erin found the perfect opal pieces in the third jar she looked in, just as Frank had predicted. There were three of them altogether. Two halves of the same opal, expertly cut into slim columns of shimmering blues and greens and perfect for earrings. The third piece showed similar colour and form; only this one had a thin streak of potch running through it like a silvery grey river. This one would form the basis of the necklace, she decided, never mind its irregularity, and when Frank named a price that was more than reasonable, she was decided.

'There's better than that in there,' he said bluntly.

'I know…' Erin picked up the stone and held it up to the light, turning it this way and that. 'But the colour's exquisite and there's just something about it.' She paid cash for the stones and stood just inside the caravan door, rubbing the opal between her fingers as she watched Tristan wander over towards a rusty old ute that Frank seemed to be using as a storage cupboard. There

was something about Tristan too. An almost irresistible blend of vulnerability and strength that
called to her, even as she railed against it. 'I know
it'll be a challenge,' she said absently, 'but that's
the one I want.'

'Women,' muttered Frank, and Erin tore her
gaze away from Tristan to raise an eyebrow in
silent query.

'You give that boy some room to move, y'hear?
It don't always help to have a woman pointing out
the obvious. Sometimes a man needs to solve
things his own way, and in his own good time.'

'What if his way's not working,' she countered,
thinking of Tristan's nightmare.

'Then ya gotta get sneaky.'

'You mean subtle.'

'Subtle. Sneaky. Never could tell the difference, between the two.'

'It's a good thing we women can tell the difference then, isn't it?'

Frank snorted, handed her a plastic Ziploc bag
to put the opals in and with the deal done they
headed over towards Tristan, still standing there
eyeing the ute.

'It's a thirty-nine Ford,' said Tristan.

'Bought that old girl from a broke miner for a
hundred dollars,' said Frank. 'Look at the lines on
her!'

Tristan was looking. 'Is it for sale?'

'Depends what you wanted to do with her,' said Frank. 'I wouldn't sell her to just anyone.'

'I want to restore it,' said Tristan. 'I'll give you six hundred for it.'

'Twelve hundred,' said Frank.

'There's a lot of rust,' said Tristan.

'Surface rust,' said Frank.

Surface rust? Erin bent down and picked at a flake of it with her index finger and stifled a giggle as it fell to the ground leaving a hole the size of a twenty-cent piece.

'Five hundred,' said Tristan, and Erin stared from the rusted wreck to Tristan in bemusement. The man lived in England. In London. In an apartment. What on earth was he going to do with a thirty-nine Ford ute?

'Does it run?' she asked as Frank wrestled with the bonnet to reveal one of the biggest engines she'd ever seen.

'Had her purring like a kitten fifteen years ago.'

'Yes, but does it purr now?'

'Four hundred,' said Tristan as he worked his way around the old engine. 'Know anyone who could get her to Sydney for me?'

'That'll cost you an extra two hundred,' said Frank. 'Six-fifty all up should about cover it.'

'Done,' said Tristan, and shaking hands with Frank, became the proud owner of a rusty paddock junker.

'What are you going to do with it after you've restored it?' she asked him. 'Have it shipped over to London?' By the time he'd finished restoring and transporting it, the old heap would have cost him a fortune.

Tristan shrugged. 'I haven't really thought about it.'

'That's ridiculous!'

'No,' he said, the ghost of a smile hovering around his lips. 'It's a rainbow.'

They visited three more opal mines after that, two of them on Frank's recommendation, and Tristan suffered the shopping in stoic silence. He didn't rush her, distract her, or try to influence her. If it took an hour to sort through a tinful of boulder opals, then that was what it took. Cops obviously acquired a lot of patience in the course of their work, Erin decided approvingly. Rory's would have run out around midday.

It was after five by the time they reached the motel and Erin was no richer for opal than she had been when they'd left Frank's. Not that it mattered. She had three pieces; three extraordinary pieces of opal and the jewellery that would come of them would be stunning. As far as opal-buying was concerned, she was done.

'We won't be needing that third night after all,' she told Delia, when they stopped by reception on the way back to their rooms. 'We'll head off in the morning.'

'Checkout's at eleven,' said Delia, eyeballing them both. 'You look spent. You need to go and have a soak in the hot pool. Here.' She reached beneath the counter and came up with a small gold-coloured entry coin. 'A two-night stay'll get you a single entry into the pool complex. Try it.'

'I didn't bring any bathers,' said Erin, turning to Tristan. 'Did you?'

'No.'

Delia's eyes brightened. 'Of course, there's always the secret pools hereabouts. The ones we don't tell the tourists about. You can skinny-dip in those.'

Skinny-dip? As in get naked with Tristan Bennett in an isolated hot pool? Erin didn't think so. But Delia was insistent.

'Here.' She found a map for them and marked it with an X. 'It's quite the picture, especially at sunset. I dare say you'll have the place to yourselves.'

'No,' said Erin, shaking her head. She'd made it through the entire day without letting the sexual tension escalate. For dinner she was thinking the bowling club, carvery food, plenty of people and lots of noise. She was into awareness expulsion, not isolated hot pools at sunset.

'I could swim,' said Tristan, with a lazy smile that was pure challenge. The smile had Delia

fanning herself with a tourist brochure. She fanned
Erin too.

'Relax,' said Delia. 'Go for a swim.' And with
a chuckle, 'Don't forget to breathe.'

The hot pool didn't look particularly inviting from
a distance. Someone had gone to the trouble of
bringing in a few flat rocks and scattering them
around the edge of the pool but otherwise it was
as bleak as nature could make it. A scattering of
stunted greenery, miles and miles of flat grey
ground and a sun that looked like a fireball about
to ram into the horizon. 'I'm not sure why the
locals feel the need to keep this one a secret,'
muttered Erin as she stepped from the car.

'It has a certain elemental appeal,' said Tristan
from the other side of the car, door open as he
stood there surveying the landscape. 'Water looks
good.'

'Yeah.' Pity about the thin film of grey-brown
clay that covered everything, including the surface
of the water. A desert oasis it wasn't. Maybe if she
closed her eyes she could rearrange reality and
pretend it was a desert oasis. Add a few palm
trees, white sand instead of the superfine clay
beneath her feet. There, much better. She opened
her eyes to find a shirtless Tristan just about to
shed his trousers. Definitely *not* on her list of
oasis improvements. 'Er, we're not really

planning to skinny-dip, are we?' she asked, eyeing his trousers with equal measures of what she was pretty sure were lust and apprehension.

'I'm easy,' he said.

That he wasn't. Not even in her imagination. In her imagination, he was a wild and reckless lover, chasing pleasure, and taking it, with breathtaking intensity. 'Underwear needs to stay on,' she said firmly.

Tristan shrugged and moments later he'd stripped down to boxers and was in the pool and heading for the far side of it, explorer-style. Men! So much for sitting back and rejuvenating the mind while the water washed away the dirt of the day. Sighing, Erin stripped down to her black cotton panties and matching singlet and waded into the pool. The water temperature was just short of hot, and if she discounted the squish factor of the clay beneath her feet and not being able to see what was on the bottom, it was really quite pleasant. The water got deeper fast and Erin pushed off and swam lazily to the middle of the pool before turning onto her back and floating. 'I'm picturing myself in a desert oasis,' she murmured as Tristan appeared at her side.

'You are in a desert oasis,' he said mildly. 'This is great.'

'You wouldn't understand.'

He regarded her with a tilt to his lips that she

tried to ignore. 'Are you alone at this desert oasis?'

'No, there's a waiter. He looks a lot like you.'

'Tell him to swat that mosquito next to your ear. It's the size of a bus.'

'I would,' she said, waving away the mosquito herself, 'But he's busy seeing to the horses.'

'Horses? What kind of horses?'

'A fiery black stallion and a dainty white mare. The stallion's my ride.'

'You should reconsider,' said Tristan lazily. 'That horse is far too powerful for you. Some things are best left to men.'

'I can handle him.'

'Don't say I didn't warn you.' He sighed and sank below the surface, reappearing moments later. 'Don't suppose your waiter has a cold beer handy?'

'Good idea. I'll get him to bring two.' She rolled over and swam towards the side of the pool. 'Hey, there's a ledge to stand on.'

'Handy,' said Tristan, coming to join her on it.

She shifted over to give him some room, lots of room. Lucky for her it was a long ledge. She closed her eyes and concentrated hard on ignoring the effect a superbly muscled Tristan was having on her senses.

'Erin?' he murmured, his voice sliding over her like a caress.

'What?' Breathe in. Breathe out.

'Open your eyes and turn around. Slowly.'

Erin's eyes snapped open and she eyed him anxiously. 'What is it? It's not a snake, is it?' She wasn't fond of snakes.

'No.'

'Goanna?' She wasn't exactly fond of goannas either. Something about those razor-sharp claws.

'No.'

'Emu?' Now emus she liked.

'Turn around. You're missing the sunset.'

Oh. The sunset. At the secluded hot pool. With Tristan.

With as much indifference as she could muster, Erin turned around.

The sky was ablaze with colour. Fiery oranges, and reds streaked with indigo, and a smattering of wispy grey cloud. Not your typical tropical island sunset, nothing like it, she thought in awe. This sky was all about power and raw, undiluted glory over an earth that was stark and barren. It was primitive and overwhelming and it slammed into her like a fist, daring her to be as bold when it came to living her life and making the most of the moments she was given. Like now, beneath a cinnamon sky at a secluded oasis. With a man she couldn't even look at without wanting. And wondering what it would take to chase the shadows from his eyes.

She sank beneath the surface, searching for answers and some sort of direction and surfaced instead with a handful of mud. 'Tristan?'

He looked at her in silent query, so solemn and restrained that it made her heart bleed. And then...

Splat!

The mud hit him square in the shoulder and Erin was racing towards the edge of the pool in search of more accessible ammunition, laughing helplessly at his astonishment. 'People pay good money to be covered in this stuff. Honest, it's supposed to have healing powers.'

'Well, hell. Why didn't you say so earlier?'

Splattt! His aim was good; his hands were large. One strike and she was all but covered in the stuff and still she laughed as she reached the shallows and tried, unsuccessfully, to nail him again. She turned sideways and crouched low in response to his next volley, flinging mud over her shoulder at random; out-manned, outgunned, but in no way outmanoeuvred as she disappeared beneath the water only to be snagged by the ankle and brought up spluttering, chest to chest with an amused and muddy Tristan. The sun was behind him, accentuating his darkness, but the shadows in his eyes had gone. 'Hey, it works! You're almost smiling.' She was almost whimpering as her hands slid to his shoulders, finding sinew and muscle beneath mud-slicked skin.

'Maybe we should bottle some. Bring it along for the ride.'

'Can the oasis come too? Because I really don't think the mud's going to work without it.' His eyes were darkening as he spoke, the amusement fading, replaced by something a whole lot more intense. Not shadows, not yet, but a flame of something that licked over her, licked over them both, and set her heart to hammering.

Be bold, she thought as his eyes grew heavy with intent and his hand brushed the curve of her cheek and slid to the curve of her neck as he drew her closer. And then his lips were on hers, soft and coaxing, and she wasn't thinking at all because the fire in the sky was in her as well, burning her up from the inside as she melted in his embrace.

She sought the wildness in him and found it. Tasted it on his tongue, felt it in his touch as he dragged her closer until there was nothing between them but the thin cotton of her singlet, her panties, and his boxers, and it was still too much to have between them and Tristan was in full agreement. Her top went, and then his hands were on her, rough and urgent, but his lips were in her hair, the curve of her neck, the hollow at her throat, and his lips were gentle.

'I thought you said you weren't ready for this,' he muttered.

'That was yesterday.' His hands were at her hips, anchoring her against his hardness, and it was exactly where she wanted to be, exactly what she needed, and then his hands moved lower, positioning her against him more fully as he surged against her. More. She sought it. Found it in the slickness of his skin, in the slide of that hard, muscled body beneath her hands, and then her hands were in his hair and she was offering him everything she was, everything she had to give.

He groaned, deep in his throat, and shuddered hard. There was no gentleness in the arm that snaked round her waist like a steel band, binding her to him while his other hand came up to cup her breast. Nothing gentle about that rough, urgent hand at her breast, kneading and teasing with ruthless skill. She wanted more, wanted his mouth on her skin, and she nipped at him to break their kiss, and dragged his head lower.

He couldn't get enough of her, of the sleek feminine curves beneath his palm. Couldn't get enough of her flavour, her flesh, and she was with him every step of the way; he could feel it in the hard little tremors that ripped through her body, hear it in the mindless whimper he drew from her as he devoured her breast with his lips.

He wanted to stop. He desperately wanted her to do something or say something that would make him stop before he drowned in her, drowned them both, but passion held sway here now; passion and raw, unfettered need and it was merciless.

He wanted her naked, couldn't see how to get her that way without drawing away from her and that was impossible. 'Stop me,' he muttered. 'For God's sake, Erin, make me stop.'

'No.' As she wrapped her legs around his waist and water swirled around them and the sky caught fire.

There was nothing gentle about the kiss that followed. It was mindless and brutal and it was all that mattered. Nothing but this man and this moment and she matched him, need for violent, desperate need while the pleasure built and built. He was all darkness and greed and he was all she'd ever wanted. Everything she'd never wanted. Too strong, too wounded.

Too much.

She hesitated, just for an instant, wondering what she'd done, what she was doing, and he felt her withdrawal, he must have done, because the hands that held her so tightly released her. He broke their kiss and pushed her away to stare down at her with eyes full of anger, frustration, and a hint of pain that nearly destroyed her. He uttered a harsh, one-word expletive and turned away.

Not what a woman hoped to see in a man after the most intense sexual experience of her life.

'I'm sorry,' he said gruffly.

Not what she wanted to hear.

'I was rough on you. I lost control. There's no excuse for that.'

'I didn't mind,' she said, trying desperately to break down walls as fast as he built them. 'I liked what you did to me. I liked it when you lost control.'

He speared her with a glance. 'I didn't.'

She could see that.

'I didn't hurt you, did I?'

'No. Tristan—' What could a woman say to a man who was hell-bent on re-establishing his emotional and physical distance? 'I'm fine. Don't worry about me.' She didn't want his guilt. There was no need for it. No reason he should carry it. 'What do you normally do?' she said, with a tentative smile. 'After you've kissed a woman and she's melted in a puddle at your feet.'

'I'm not normally in a hot pool,' he said.

'Wing it.'

'I might dry off,' he said, his eyes lightening, just a little. 'I might bring her a towel so that she can dry off too.'

'That would be a good start.'

'Then I might find her that beer she was after on the way home. Or wine. Whatever she wanted.'

'I'm really liking where your head's at.'

He smiled at that, really smiled, and Erin bit back a sigh of relief. She didn't want his apology for what they'd just shared. Didn't want him to stew and to brood over something that neither of them had been able to control. 'It's not such a big thing, you and I and a couple of kisses.' She was lying through her teeth.

'You don't want to know where all this is heading?'

'No.' She was heading for heartbreak, she knew that much already. One step at a time.

CHAPTER SIX

TRISTAN was in turmoil. He didn't know what to think. Damn sure he didn't know what to say to the woman who'd just destroyed him with her kisses and then blocked his retreat with nothing more than clever words and a warm smile. He was used to keeping people out. Never revealing too much, never caring too much, always staying in control. His work demanded it, and when it came to his private life *he* demanded it.

He never lost control when he was with a woman. Not ever. He certainly didn't ravage them beneath a blood red sky with no thought of tenderness or care. No thought at all, truth be told, beyond sheer animal need.

He didn't want it. Didn't want Erin Sinclair filling needs he'd never known he had and leaving memories that would haunt him for the rest of his life. Erin in his arms, lost to everything but sensation, and the only thing that saved him from complete self-loathing was the knowledge that she'd been as much at the mercy of their love-making as he had. That she'd wanted him as mind-lessly as he'd wanted her.

She just handled the afterwards a hell of a lot better.

So he would follow her lead and be an adult in the aftermath of near catastrophe. Nothing he didn't want to give, but he could show her some tenderness, he could do that. He could be civil and buy her a meal and act the gentleman.

It was the least she deserved.

He bought beer on the way back to the motel, and Chinese take-away to go with it, and she didn't object to him paying, not by so much as a glance. She hadn't objected to him doing the driving either. She was reading him, he thought grimly. Reading his need for some small measure of control with disturbing accuracy.

They ate back at the motel, in the little kitch-enette, and he worked hard to make the evening almost normal and the conversation almost easy. It was the little things that tripped him up. Her delight at the spicy heat of the Mongolian lamb, never mind that her eyes were watering. Her un-abashed appreciation for a cold beer straight from the bottle. The way she moved, the way she smiled. She was sensualist; he'd known that from the start. From the moment he'd kissed her in the driveway outside her mother's house, and vowed to stay away from her.

'So where to next?' he asked when they'd eaten their fill and cleared away the plates, and even that small domesticity carried with it an intimacy he didn't want. 'Inverell for sapphires?'

'In the morning.' She regarded him steadily. 'You don't have to come with me, you know. You could head back to Sydney tomorrow if you'd prefer.' Her lips curved into a slight smile. 'You could drive your ute home. You'd cut quite the dashing picture. Very James Dean.'

'James Dean drove a nineteen-fifty-five silver Porsche Spyder. I'm not quite seeing a connection between him in that and me heading down the highway in Frank's old Ford.'

'You'd probably have to be female to see that particular connection,' she said dryly. 'You men are far too literal. My point is that there are plenty of ways to get back to Sydney from here if you have a mind to.'

She was giving him an out, but damned if he was going to take it. Damned if he'd let her see how much she affected him. 'You still need sapphires for your competition pieces, don't you?'

'Yes, but if you're not comfortable—

'Don't,' he said curtly. 'Just…don't.'

She nodded once and looked away. 'Two more days ought to do it.'

And two more nights. He didn't know what to do with himself, with all this time between now and morning. There was too much Erin in it.

'I thought I might work on some designs,' she said as she hung the tea towel to dry. 'Now that I have the opals.'

'I might take a walk into town.' She was the one who'd taken a walk last night. It seemed only fair that he be the one to do the walking tonight. 'I could be a while.' He might find a game of eight ball somewhere, or better still a rumble. Pity Luke wasn't here. Luke was always on for an argument involving fists. Or Pete. Two against one. Just enough to take the edge off his hunger for Erin, and if that didn't work there was always Jake.

Nobody messed with Jake.

He was halfway to town when he took it in his head to call his oldest brother. In Singapore.

'You in trouble?' said Jake, the minute he'd said hello.

'No.' *Yes.* 'I'm in Lightning Ridge.' Playing bodyguard to three opals and a beautiful woman whose body he wanted with a ferocity that left him aching.

'And?' said Jake.

'And what?'

'Ask me how I am and I'm likely to strangle you.'

'There's a woman.'

Dead silence at that, and then, 'Is she a criminal?'

'No.'

'Psychopath?'

'No.'

'Married but nonetheless pregnant with your child?'

'No.'

'I'm not seeing a downside here. You're going to have to help me out. Have you slept with her yet?'

'No.'

More silence. A long, long silence, after which Jake sighed heavily. 'Dammit, Tris. Please tell me you're not calling for advice about women. Call Pete. He's always in love.'

And never in love. 'She's in my head.'

'This is bad,' said Jake. 'You need to get her out of there immediately. You need to head butt something.'

Typical martial arts solution. 'There's the tele-graph pole.'

'Perfect. You'll feel much better afterwards. Call me from the hospital.'

'I was wondering,' he said doggedly, 'if you ever managed to get Jianna out of your head.' They'd never talked about Jake's ill-fated marriage, not once. He'd never known how,

'You want my advice? All right, then, you've got it. Walk away. Stay away.'

'You haven't answered my question.'

'You don't want to hear my answer to that question.'

'I think I do,' he said quietly.

He didn't think his brother was going to answer. He'd pushed too far. And then Jake spoke.

'You want to know if I still bleed? If I still think of Ji every day and dream of her at night? The answer's no.' And with a dark and biting humour, 'Sometimes I go days without thinking of her at all.'

Tristan was dreaming of the dockyards of Prague and a decision he'd taken too long to make. Again.

He woke in a lather of sweat and a tangle of sheets, with his heart thudding in his chest and his soul full of bile. He shoved the sheet aside, flicked the bedside lamp on, and sat there on the side of the bed, breathing hard. When was he ever going to make peace with these memories? How was he ever going to shake them loose?

They'd said it wasn't his fault. That he'd played it by the book, and that much was true. He'd played it straight down the line, both the undercover work and the takedown. He hadn't known what was in that container, he couldn't have known. And still the nightmares came.

A shower would help, he thought wearily, and

with his next breath wondered if taking a shower at this time of the morning would wake Erin. No. The shower was adjacent to his room, not hers. He would be quiet. He would sluice away the sweat and the memories and by the time he was clean he'd have thought of something else to do with the rest of this night.

The water was hot but the spray was weak and he stood there beneath it, wishing it were fiercer while his heartbeat steadied and he shoved those memories back in their box. By the time he'd tugged on a pair of track pants and padded downstairs he was almost back in control. He headed towards the kitchen for something to eat, belatedly wondering why the light was on. He'd been the last to bed and he'd turned that light off; he could have sworn he'd turned it off.

He had. Someone else had turned it back on.

'Morning,' said Erin, abandoning her latest design in favour of taking a good long look at Tristan. He looked tired, she thought. Defeated. His demons were riding him hard.

'What are you doing here?' he said abruptly.

Not exactly the warmest of greetings, but then, she hadn't expected one. 'I had some designs I wanted to get down on paper,' she said by way of explanation, and it was true to a point. She *had* been working on her designs. But she'd been waiting for Tristan.

He looked at the drawings, looked at her. 'At four-thirty a.m.?'

She shrugged. 'Why not? I was awake.'

'I'm sorry if I woke you,' he said awkwardly, and she bled for him even as she cursed his reticence.

'Kettle's boiled,' she said, indicating the cup of hot tea in front of her. 'And last night's leftovers are in the oven.'

'You're feeding me?'

'Not at all.'

'Are you sure?' he muttered. 'It feels like you're feeding me.'

'I didn't cook it so it doesn't count.' Tristan's hair was tousled, he was shirtless again, and she tried to ignore the quickening of her blood and the warmth that blossomed low in her belly when she looked at him. She knew the feel of him now, knew it and craved it, but she wasn't out to seduce him. She wanted to help him. 'Do you have them every night?'

'Showers?'

'Nightmares.'

His silence spoke volumes.

'You want to talk about it?'

'No.'

'Ever heard the one about problems shared?'

'I've heard it,' he said. 'I just don't hold to it.'

Erin smiled ruefully. 'Yeah, well, maybe that's your problem.' She'd been expecting him to shut her out. She was used to it and not just from him. From her father. From Rory… Talking through their troubles wasn't an option and it wasn't just a gender thing. It was a warrior thing. 'Tough guy.'

'Not even close.'

So vulnerable, she thought with a catch in her throat. So heartbreakingly defiant as he stood there like some dark angel and dared her to breach his defences. His demons were his own; he would not share them. And still she tried to reach him. She was a warrior's daughter; she could do nothing less. 'Any ideas on how to make those nightmares go away?'

He reached for a glass, filled it with tap water and drank deeply. Stonewalling her deliberately, she thought with a sigh.

'I'm thinking of handing in my resignation,' he said gruffly. 'Finding another job.'

Erin blinked and leaned back in her chair. Not what she'd expected to hear. And *not* what she thought would help him, for all that the notion appealed mightily to *her*. 'Do you really think that's going to help?'

Tristan shrugged. 'Maybe.'

'What would you do?'

'I don't know.'

'What about internal transfer options?'

'Desk jobs,' he muttered.

'No one works on the frontline for ever,' she said carefully. 'How long have you been there?'

Silence.

Too long, she thought as she stood and headed towards the oven, hoping that the aroma pervading the room meant that the food was hot enough to serve because it was either feed him or take him in her arms and soothe his hurt in a different way. 'I think it's ready,' she said as she took the dishes from the oven.

'Are you sure you're not feeding me?'

'Don't dwell on it.'

'What if I put the food on the plates?' he said. 'That might help.'

Only to make her want him more. But she let him do it anyway, careful to keep some distance between them as she picked up her loaded plate and took it to the table. Food was good. Food occupied hands that could otherwise be engaged in touching and caressing. 'Are you planning on getting any more sleep tonight?' she asked him between mouthfuls of lukewarm fried rice.

'No.'

'And we're done talking about work options?'

'If there's a God.'

She ignored his fervour and concentrated on the big picture. Eating would take all of ten minutes. After that it'd be her, Tristan, a motel suite, and three empty beds. 'The thing is, I'm

experiencing a powerful need to help you take
your mind off your troubles,' she confessed. 'I
have a couple of options I think you might be
interested in.'

'I'm listening,' he said.

'We pack up and drive. Move on. Men like
running from their problems.'

Tristan ignored the jibe. His thoughts had taken
a sensual turn as he imagined another way in
which Erin might think of to ease his troubled
mind. A timeless, instinctive way. 'What's the
second option?'

'Of course, we'd have to backtrack a bit.'

He was already there. Back at the hot pool,
right where they'd left off. With Erin in his arms
and a fire in his blood.

'I don't suppose you'd like to go rock climbing?'

CHAPTER SEVEN

'GOOD thing we didn't take the climbing option,' said Erin some two hours later as they drove towards Inverell. She was in the passenger seat, bright-eyed and clearly in the mood for conversation, which suited Tristan just fine. He wasn't against small talk as such. Just so long as he didn't have to provide it.

'I was thinking Cornerstone Rib because it's a brilliant climb no matter how experienced you are,' she continued. 'But it's a two hour walk-in from the closest car park and over two hundred metres of vertical. Then there's the descent. It can get slippery in the rain, and Lord knows it's raining now.'

This was true. Wind whipped at the car and the wipers struggled to keep water off the windscreen. The weather had turned mean. 'What else do you do in your spare time?' he asked her as he checked to see if the windscreen wipers could go any faster. They couldn't.

'You mean besides scale vertical crags and drive thousands of miles in search of gemstones?' She paused to consider. 'Movies are good. And Rory's talking about rally-car driving. That could be fun. Matter of fact that might be something you should consider. Some sort of car racing.'

He'd considered it. For a few years there he'd considered nothing else, but in the end he'd gone a different way. 'You mean as a vocation?'

'I mean as a sport. Something simple to take the edge off the stress that comes with your real work.'

'You think car racing is simple?'

'Well, yeah.' She slid him an impish smile. 'You get in a car, you drive very fast and you win. How hard can it be?'

'Harder than that,' he said dryly.

'All the better,' she said cheerfully. 'Seriously, you need to find a way to relax. Maybe you could go to the raceway when we get back to Sydney. Take a test drive or something.'

'Let me get this straight. You're against the armed forces—and policing for that matter— because of the dangers involved but you encourage mountaineering and motor sports? I don't get it.'

'I'm not against someone choosing a danger-ous occupation for a living,' she said loftily. 'I'm against secrecy, the tyranny of distance, and putting duty to country or mankind before family.'

'You don't think duty to country or mankind is important?'

'I didn't say that. Someone's got to do it. I appreciate that.'

'Just not *your* someone.'

'Exactly. And don't you look at me like that. I gave at the office.'

And every step of the way throughout her childhood, he thought, remembering her seafaring father. He *knew* how much the absence of a parent could colour a lifetime, knew that the scars she carried were real for all that they were internal. 'I'm not looking at you like that,' he said gently.

'And don't you pity me either!'

No. It would be a mistake to do that. But he did think he'd just gained a slightly deeper understanding of her. 'So what kind of someone are you looking for?'

'One who loves me and isn't afraid to admit it.'

Ouch. 'Besides that.'

'One who's in our relationship for the long haul,' she said next. 'I want laughter, even if it's sometimes mixed with tears. I want a lifetime of it.'

'What if it's not working out?'

'Then we both give a little more, bend a little more, and we make it work out.'

'What about money?'

'Money is good but it's optional. Workaholics

need not apply. I can contribute to moneymaking endeavours.'

'What about military men? Can they apply?'

'No. Their passion for their work is admirable and they have many fine qualities but the cost to their families is unacceptable. I won't be shut out,' she said fiercely. 'I refuse to be.'

'Even if it's for your own good?'

'Do I look like a powder-puff to you? Do I look like I need protecting?'

He slid her a sideways glance. 'Yes.'

'Excuse me?' Her eyes narrowed and if she hadn't been sitting in the passenger seat he was pretty sure her hands would have gone to her hips. 'This is a size thing, isn't it?'

'No.' It was far more complicated than that. 'It's an instinctive thing. Men protect what they cherish.'

'And women nurture what they love!'

'I think this is where the "give and take" philosophy comes into play,' he said dryly.

Erin scowled. 'Yeah, well, there's a lot to be said for a passionate, no-strings-attached and extremely short-lived love affair these days too.'

'Hell!' He rounded a curve at speed, overcorrected, and the car almost ended up in a ditch. 'Can Interpol cops apply for those?'

It was mid-afternoon before they reached Inverell. The streets were wide country thoroughfares and the architecture of the older buildings was early colonial, but the rest of it was a mixture of modern architectural styles and the city centre was armed with every convenience. Built on the back of sapphire-mining and agriculture, Inverell had grown big enough to hold its own.

Choosing a motel was harder this time but eventually Tristan pulled into the one deemed most suitable by them both; the one with under-cover parking next to the reception area and carports next to each room.

'We need a couple of rooms for the night,' Erin told the young girl behind the reception desk as she ran her hands up and down her arms. It was cold in Inverell. Far colder than in Lightning Ridge.

'Adjoining?'

'Er…' Erin slid him a sideways glance.

'Separate,' he said. He couldn't do another night that close to Erin and not take her. He knew he couldn't. And for all her fast talk of a passion-ate, no strings attached and extremely short-lived love affair, he knew damn well that it wouldn't satisfy her. When Erin Sinclair gave, she gave ev-erything. She deserved a man who could give something back.

'Rooms number eighteen and nineteen are free,' said the girl, 'and you won't get soaked bringing your stuff in.' She reached to one side for the keys as Erin filled in the paperwork. Tristan busied himself by picking up a brochure on sapphire mines in the area. He still didn't like it that she was paying for the accommodation. 'Are you interested in sapphires?' asked the girl as she turned back around and handed him a key, placing the other one on the bench next to Erin. 'We have some very reputable mining operations here-abouts. Here,' she said, picking up a flyer and handing it to him. 'This one's open today and they're having a sale.'

'Why the sale?' he asked.

'No idea,' she said. 'They're just having one.'

'What are the regular prices like?' asked Erin.

'It's popular with locals; that's always a good sign,' said the girl with a grin. 'I got my engage-ment ring there.' She held out her hand to show them the ring.

'It's lovely,' said Erin, leaning forward to examine it more closely even as Tristan took a hearty step back. 'Congratulations on your engagement.'

The girl beamed. 'We didn't want to spend much cause we're saving for a house, but I wanted something I could look at in fifty years time and still love as much as the man who gave it to me.'

'That's the master plan.' Erin's smile was wistful.

'About those rooms…' he said.

'Halfway along on your right,' said the girl. 'Checkout's at eleven and let me know if you need anything meantime.'

'Thanks.' And because she really was a sweet kid, even if she was far too young to be getting married, 'Nice ring.'

Tristan's room was functional and impersonal. He'd stayed in hundreds of rooms just like it over the years. A bed was a bed. A room was a room. It had never bothered him before. But it bothered him now. There was no warmth in it, no welcome. No... Erin.

Damn but he had it bad.

Jake would tell him to run, he knew that already, and Pete would ask him what he was waiting for. Luke would ask him searching questions he didn't want to answer—no way was he ringing Luke—and as for Hallie, there was no way he was calling her either. Hallie was crazy in love with her new husband and happier than he'd ever seen her...she'd be delighted that he'd finally let someone in.

As if he had a choice.

Erin knocked on Tristan's door as soon as she'd unpacked. It was only three-thirty and she wanted to visit some sapphire mines before the end of the day. She was anxious to find what she needed. Anxious to be on her way. She'd thought she could keep her distance from Tristan but, the more she knew of him, the harder it was. She'd thought she was resistant to such men. She'd thought he would keep *his* distance from *her*.

'I'm just going for a drive out to this place with the sale on,' she said when Tristan opened his door. 'You don't have to come, though. You'd probably rather stay here and catch up on some sleep.' They'd been up so early and he'd done most of the driving—nasty, rainy-day driving. He looked exhausted.

'I'll come,' he said.

'No, really. I'm just going to browse. You don't have to take your bodyguarding duties that seriously.'

'I'll come,' he said in a way that warned the discerning listener to beware the steel beneath. And that was the end of that.

Twenty minutes later they pulled into the car park of Wallace Sapphires, a medium-sized mining operation with its own onsite shop. There was a 'thirty per cent off marked price' sign on the shopfront door. Thirty per cent off everything.

The woman who looked up at them from behind the counter as they entered had a faded loveliness that matched her vintage clothing. Her eyes were shrewd but her smile was friendly as she greeted them with an invitation to look around and call her if there was anything they wanted to take a closer look at.

'I might get you to help me from the start,' said

Erin, skirting a large tank of brilliantly coloured tropical fish that held centre stage in the shop. She pulled the opals from their Ziploc pouch and set them on the counter. 'I'm looking for sapphires the same colour as the blue in these opals. And I'm looking to buy in bulk.'

'May I?' The woman indicated a large magnifying glass set on a stand on the counter, and, at Erin's nod, set the opals beneath it. She peered down at the opals. 'They're quite beautiful, aren't they? Such a vivid blue.' And with a sigh, 'Most of our stones are darker. For this colour you really should be looking at Ceylon sapphires.'

'I know.' But she couldn't afford Ceylon sapphires. Not in the quantities she was after. 'I thought it was worth a try.'

'We did find colour like this once,' said the woman hesitantly. 'Came from a seam my late husband discovered more than twenty years ago. Good-sized stones they were too, but a terror to cut. We left most of them in the rough.'

'I don't mind buying rough stones.' Erin was sufficiently intrigued by the notion of gloriously coloured rough sapphires to want to see them. Even if they were hard to cut. 'Do you still have any?'

'You know, I think I might,' said the woman. 'Mind you, I have no idea where they are. Take a seat.' She gestured towards two stools on the customer side of the counter. 'This could take a while. My memory's not what it used to be. You wouldn't believe the things I've misplaced since Edward died. Gems, scissors, even the fish food… Why, if it wasn't for Roger I'm sure all the fish would be dead.'

'Who's Roger?' asked Tristan.

'A young work-experience boy we had here a few years back.' She was rifling through drawers as she spoke. 'He used to help us out in the school holidays when we were busy. Since Edward died he's been coming in every week to do the fish. He's due any minute and not a moment too soon. Those fish are starving. Ah, here they are. I'd filed them under "T". Probably for "Tragedy Waiting To Happen". Did I mention they were hard to cut?'

'Yes,' said Erin as the woman emptied the packet of stones onto the counter. 'But I'm feeling very optimistic about these stones.'

'What about the cutting of them?' asked Tristan.

'I'm optimistic about that too.' Rough sapphires were nothing like the finished stone. It took a discerning eye to predict the final colour of the stone and an even more discerning one to figure out how to cut it. She'd lose up to seventy-five per cent of the original weight of the stones in the cutting, but these stones were big. They'd still cut out at over half a carat and that was exactly what she wanted. Provided she could cut them.

The bell on the entry door tinkled and a young man in unironed clothes and a shabby baseball cap entered, carrying buckets, aquarium equipment, and a bag of multicoloured pebbles under one arm. This, decided Erin, was Roger.

'Afternoon, Mrs Wal,' he said, his cheerful nod encompassing them all as he headed for the fish tank. 'Afternoon, Lucinda.'

'Who's Lucinda?' asked Tristan.

'Lucinda's an angelfish,' said Roger, tapping the tank. 'This one here. Hello gorgeous.'

'Edward's pride and joy,' said the woman.

'Edward being Mrs Wal's deceased husband,' muttered Erin before Tristan could ask.

'I knew that,' he said.

'I got you some more fish food pellets,' said Roger, setting a small tin on top of the tank.

'Darling boy. How much do I owe you?'

'It's all right, Mrs Wal; it didn't cost much.'

'I wish you'd let me pay you,' she said, and Erin was in full agreement. Roger didn't look as if he had a lot to spare. 'How's the baby?'

'Fever's down and she's on the mend. She'll be right again in no time. I'll bring her out with me next week if you like,' he said as he set to work scooping pebbles from the tank. Mrs Wal's eyes brightened.

'She's such a dear little poppet,' she told them. 'You hardly know she's here.'

'You mentioned you'd misplaced some stones,' said Tristan as Erin positioned the magnifying glass over the sapphires and started sorting them with an eye to clarity, colour and shape. Her ears, however, were on the conversation.

'Seems to be happening a lot lately,' said Mrs Wal. 'I'll have them out and be showing them to customers one day and the next time I go looking for them I can't find them. I've been running this shop for thirty years. You'd think I'd know where to put everything by now.'

'Maybe you're not misplacing them,' said Tristan. 'Maybe someone's stealing from you. Low-level theft on a regular basis happens a lot.'

Erin looked sharply at Tristan. Tristan was looking at Mrs Wal. Mrs Wal was watching Roger clean the fish tank, and her eyes were sad.

'It's usually an employee,' said Tristan gently.

'It's possible,' she said as she dragged her gaze away from the fish tank to bestow on Tristan a wry and faded smile. 'But you know I think I'd rather believe I've misplaced them.'

Erin got an excellent deal on the sapphires. Two dozen rough stones of her choice and six smaller ones thrown in for free for cutting practice. 'I'll keep my fingers crossed for you,' said the older woman as she bagged the stones. 'If you can cut them you'll have some beautiful stones.'

'If I figure out the knack before I've used up all my practice stones I'll send those ones back to you, cut,' said Erin.

'You will not!' said Mrs Wal. 'Use them in your competition pieces and mind you let me know when you win.'

'*If* I win.'

'Is that one of your designs?' Mrs Wal gestured towards the tiger-eye pendant at Erin's throat.

Erin nodded.

'You'll win. The combination of those sapphires and those opals will be magnificent. You'll see.'

Erin did see. And lost herself in the vision.

'She's gone,' said Mrs Wal. 'I know that look.' Tristan smiled, and Mrs Wal blinked. 'My, you're a handsome one when you lose the sternness, aren't you? You should smile more often.'

'She's right,' Erin told him, coming back to the conversation with a sigh. 'You really do have the sweetest smile, but unlike Mrs Wal I'll not encourage it. Brood, be stern. You save those smiles.'

Tristan's smile widened.

Damn.

* * *

'You think Roger's stealing from Mrs Wal, don't you?' she said as they walked across the car park towards the car. Tristan's questions were rarely questions for the sake of small talk. He'd sensed something amiss back there in that shop. She knew he had.

'I think someone's stealing from her,' he said, shooting her a sideways glance. 'I don't necessarily know that it's Roger.'

'She could just be misplacing them, you know.'

'She didn't strike me as particularly forgetful. It took her all of two minutes to find those stones for you and I'm betting she hasn't had them out for years. No, she knows her stock and I suspect she knows she's not forgetting where she left it.'

'But that's terrible!' she said. 'Why doesn't she do something about it? *You* could do something. We could go back tomorrow and work through it with her.'

'What happened to forgetting about work for a while and chasing rainbows instead?'

'This is different.'

'No.' Tristan's smile was grim. 'It's just the same. There's a victim—in this case Mrs Wal—and there's a perp. Let's for argument's sake say that Roger is the perp. Roger's been helping out at Wallace Sapphires for years, possibly being paid for it, maybe not. He doesn't have much but he doesn't need it either. He makes do. And then one day he gets into a bind with money and the banks won't touch him and no one in his family's got it to give. He borrows a few thousand from the wrong kind of people and all of a sudden life takes a turn for the worse. He can't get work, his lenders want their money back, and he has a kid of his own and she's a sickly little thing, which means medicine and it ain't cheap. And there's Mrs Wallace with more sapphires than she can sell in a lifetime and surely she won't miss one little stone… So he takes one. And then another,' said Tristan savagely. 'Before he knows it he's thieving regularly and vowing that one day, *one* day, he'll give it all back. Meanwhile he'll give it back in help and somehow try to convince himself that he's not really hurting anyone, that it's not such a crime as far as crimes go, and that it's the only way he can survive. Who's the victim, Erin?' said Tristan bleakly. 'And how the hell are you going to go back in there tomorrow and fix it?'

She'd wanted this, she remembered belatedly. She'd wanted Tristan to open up and talk about his work. Well, now he had.

'It might not be like that,' she said in a small voice.

'No,' he said. 'It might not.' But it was clear that his faith in the justice system he'd sworn to uphold was badly damaged.

'This is what happens when you go undercover, isn't it? You get too close, too involved.'

Tristan was silent, his features grim.

'And then you have to turn around and make
impossible decisions about impossible situations
and it doesn't always make things right, does it?
Sometimes all it does is make things worse.'

Nothing.

'It can't always be like that,' she said a touch
desperately. 'Sometimes you make things better.'

'Yeah,' he said with a weary smile that pierced
her to the core. 'Sometimes we do.'

It wasn't supposed to be like this, thought Erin
grimly. She wasn't supposed to stare at him in
dismayed silence because his problem was too
big and there was no fixing it. She should have
been able to comfort him. With wise words and
compassion or whatever it was that he needed.
She should have been able to help.

A bad call. Maybe even the right call but the
wrong result. *This* was what Tristan dealt with on
a daily basis. This was why the nightmares and the
disillusion, and she had no answers other than for
him to step back and not care so much and let
someone else enforce society's rules, at least for
a little while.

She wanted to help him. Needed to think that
she could.

She simply didn't know how.

They got in the car in silence. Tristan the driver and she in the passenger seat. It was her turn to drive but she didn't push the issue. He'd broken his silence and would see it as weakness. And curse himself for letting her see it.

His features were stern and forbidding as he started the car and pulled out of the car park. The rain had stopped but there would be no sunset this night. No hot pools or mud fights to ease the tension. She wanted it gone. Contrary woman that she was she desperately wanted to win a smile from him. But how? She stared out the window at the passing landscape, thinking.

They were in granite country, sheep country for the most part, and that meant rolling grassland punctuated by the occasional stockyard and shearing shed. No inspiration there, she thought glumly. Unless… 'Hey, there's an old bomb just like the one you bought off Frank.'

'Where?' Tristan slowed the car.

'Over by the shearing shed. To the left. Half buried in grass.' Now that she looked more closely it didn't really resemble the car he'd bought from Frank at all.

'It's an FJ Holden ute,' said Tristan. From the tone of his voice, this was a good thing.

'We've stopped.'

'We have to take a closer look at it.'

She got out of the car willingly enough and followed Tristan towards it. There was something in his eyes when he looked at that old wreck that she wouldn't destroy for the world. It was hope.

'Look at the lines on her,' he said when they were standing beside it.

The lines that remained were lovely. The rest were the product of an impressive imagination.

'I could restore it,' he said. 'I wonder if it runs?'

Erin was wondering if it had an engine at all.

It didn't.

'I could put a BBQ under the bonnet,' he said, in no way deterred. 'Or a pizza oven.'

'You could turn it into a garden ornament,' she said. 'A water feature with water sheeting down the windscreen and the wipers wiping it off. The neighbours would love it.'

'I could use it for storage,' he said, sticking his head inside the body of the car. 'Like Frank was using the Ford.'

'You'd need doors, of course,' she said. 'But the lack of seats would be a definite advantage.'

'I could turn it into a dog kennel.'

'I didn't know you had a dog.'

He walked around the old truck a few times and finally stood back to admire it from afar. 'I think I'll make an offer on it,' he said.

Erin nodded, flashed him a grin. 'I think you should.'

* * *

'Dinner,' said Erin, 'should be about celebration.'

'You mean balloons?' said Tristan. He'd tried to retreat, tried to pull back when they'd returned to the motel, but Erin was blocking him every step of the way.

'I mean good food, good wine, a pleasant atmosphere and lively company. But I'll take three out of four.'

'You don't think the food will be any good?'

'Ooh, a joke. I'm *very* impressed. I'm thinking we should eat at the pub. Best char-grilled steaks and pleasant atmosphere in town. It says so right here on the flyer.'

'It's called promotion,' he said dryly.

'And it's very effective,' she said. 'Because my mouth is watering as we speak. What do you say?'

She was in his room again, perched on the edge of the table and wielding sunshine like a sword. 'I'm really tired,' was what he said.

'And so you should be. Which is why we're heading down there now rather than later. Imagine how well you'll sleep on a stomach full of steak and potatoes.'

He did like steak and potatoes. 'Do I need to get changed?'

'No, perfection is fine.' She eyed his jeans and T-shirt and sighed. 'How do I look?'

'Fine.' She was wearing a sky-blue sundress,

strappy little sandals, and half a dozen thin gold bracelets at her wrist. She was beautiful.

'You know how you were saying you liked to keep the sweet talk for later? I'm guessing you like to save the compliments for later too.'

'You want a compliment?'

She nodded firmly. 'And sweet talk too.'

'I like your shoes,' he said.

'I'm taking that as the sweet talk. Now for the compliment.'

Tristan stifled a smile. 'May I think about it over dinner?'

Her eyes narrowed. 'Certainly. But I have to warn you, I'm not a patient woman.'

'I noticed that,' he said amiably. 'Good thing you're so beautiful.'

'That wasn't a compliment.'

'No,' he said. 'I'm still working on that.'

'Good thing *you're* so beautiful,' she muttered. 'Shall we go?'

The Brasserie at the pub was all dark carpet, wooden panelling, and comfortably mismatched furniture. The lighting was friendly rather than intimate and the bustle from the bar and the thoroughfare to the poker machines and gaming area gave it a relaxing informality. It was just what Tristan needed, Erin decided.

Sometimes it was nice to sit back and watch the world go by.

'I'm for the rib fillet and salad,' she said after examining the blackboard menu. Tristan chose rump and three veg. 'Shall we argue about who's paying for this now or later?' she said.

Tristan shrugged. 'I'm easy.'

That he wasn't.

'We can argue about it whenever you like.'

She chose now. 'I'd like to thank you for coming on this trip with me,' she said earnestly. 'For your time and effort. I would like to buy you a meal. *This* meal. And the drinks.'

Tristan regarded her steadily. 'You never give up, do you?'

'You're wrong,' she said. 'I'm fairly focussed on what I want to achieve, yes, but the truth is my resolve has never really been tested. I've never, for example, been in a burning building and had to pull out even though I knew there were still people inside. Rory was the one who had to do that.'

'Nothing else he could have done,' said Tristan.

'Try telling him that.' She wasn't finished yet. 'Nor have I ever lost two men in a mine clearing operation and the following day sent another team in to replace them. My father has. I think I'd have given up and gone home.'

'Your father's been trained to make tough decisions.'

'He has, and he does. It's the living with them afterwards that's the problem. My father's a good man. A strong man. So's Rory. I'm proud of them both. But sometimes they hurt in places that I can't reach, and I can't help them and it drives me nuts.' She took a deep breath and said it plain. 'I look at you and you're just the same. Hurting in places I can't reach. And it drives me nuts.'

'You help,' he said quietly. 'By being there. By being you.'

God! If they didn't change the topic soon she was going to cry. 'Was that your compliment?'

'No. Still working on that.'

'Work faster—I'm feeling a little fragile.' There was a folded newspaper on the chair beside her. She picked it up, opened it out. Horoscopes. Tristan, if she remembered correctly, was a Scorpio. 'It says here that you'll be receiving a boon, and that power mixed with love will give you grace.'

'Humph.'

'You're right,' she said. 'You've already got the grace thing covered.'

She moved on to the Virgo section. 'It says here that *my* power this week lies not in understanding but in giving. It says that rich rewards will come to Virgos who learn this lesson. Well, I guess that settles it.'

'Settles what?' he asked warily.

'I am definitely paying for this meal.'

* * *

The food was good, the wine was excellent, and the atmosphere was indeed very pleasant. Erin was halfway through her meal when she saw Roger the fish-tank cleaner walking into the room carrying a little blonde poppet who couldn't have been more than a year old. He nodded to the barman, who angled his head towards the poker-machine room. Roger said something to the tot, who nodded and gave him a watery smile and then the pair of them disappeared into the gaming room. 'Was that Roger?' she said to Tristan.

Tristan nodded.

Five minutes later, Roger reappeared. He still had the little girl cradled in one arm, but walking beside him, holding his other hand, was a young woman with big sad eyes and a pinched face. She looked defiant. Dejected. Roger looked resigned. They were halfway across the room when Roger spotted them. Recognition crossed his face before he quickly looked away.

She thought that was it, that he wouldn't look back, but then Roger's eyes sought Tristan's again and something passed between them. A question maybe, or an answer. She didn't know.

It seemed an age before Roger's gaze cut to her. He gave her what might have once passed for a smile if not for the misery in it, and then he and his little entourage moved on.

'You *do* think it was Roger who took those sapphires, don't you?'

'Yes,' said Tristan.

'What would the police do if they caught him?'

'Arrest him. Send him to court.'

'What would the court do?'

'Send him to prison.'

'What would *you* do?'

'I just did it.'

'Leaned on him? Is that what that look between you was about?'

'No,' he said, his lips tilting ever so slightly. 'You'd know it if I decided to lean on someone.'

'Well, what was it about?'

'Recognition. It was about knowing what he was. Maybe even knowing why he was doing it. And letting it go. Mrs Wal herself doesn't want to follow through on this one, Erin. And neither do I.'

She stared at him solemnly. Saw the strength there and the compassion. And without any thought for an audience of strangers she put her hand to his cheek and kissed him softly on the lips. Not passion, not this time. This was something else.

'What was that for?' His sudden stillness was disconcerting; those glorious amber eyes of his were intent.

'For doing what you do,' she said. 'For being the man you are.' And because she was in love with him.

* * *

Erin paid for their meal. Paid for their drinks and
Tristan let her. It was written in the stars, she'd
told him loftily. Besides, she'd said next, it was
either that or a tiger-eye signet ring.

She twisted him with words, spun him into
knots. And with laughter on her lips and wisdom
in her eyes, spun him round again.

Work talk, when he never talked about his work
with anyone.

Encouraging him to buy another old car wreck.
What the hell was he going to do with two of
them? He didn't even know what he was going to
do with one.

Rock climbing! Enough said.

'What time do you want to get up in the
morning?' she asked him as they headed for the car.

'No more sapphires?' he asked gruffly. She'd
kissed him gently in the pub and stopped his heart.

'No,' she said solemnly. 'I have everything I
need now as far as making jewellery is concerned. We can go home. We could have an
early night, get up in the morning, and drive
back to Sydney.'

She'd looked at him with pride and something
else and he'd damn near wept.

He made it to the car, to the door of his motel
room before he stopped her. He thought it showed
a remarkable degree of restraint. 'I have nothing

to give you,' he muttered. 'I'm not what you want.' And still he reached for her.

'I know,' she said. And still she came.

Tender, he could be that, at least for a little while as he pressed his lips to hers. Slow and easy as he gave her every chance to pull back while she still could. While he could still let her. 'I don't know where I'll be in a month's time or what I'll be doing. I don't want to hurt you.'

'I'm glad to hear it.' She punctuated her words with a nip to his bottom lip and desire ripped through him, fierce and needy. He wanted to be in control. Needed to think that he could be. His words were meant to keep her at bay. To keep them both safe, and she was playing the game, heaven help him she was. He found the frantic pulse at the base of her neck with his lips and nipped with his teeth, darkly pleased when she gasped and arched into him. Maybe he did want to hurt her, just a little bit. Maybe he wanted her burning up for him the way he burned for her. Filling him, dammit, with everything that she was.

Her eyes were dark and fey as she pulled his head back to stare up at him. 'I won't ask you for tomorrow, Tristan. Nothing you don't want. But I will ask something of you tonight.'

'What is it?'

'When we're making love… When I'm wrapped around you and I can't feel anything but you inside of me, can't see anyone but you above me…don't you dare try to control it. Don't you dare hold back.'

'*God!*' he muttered.

He managed to get the door open, managed to get her inside before he pushed her back against the wall and savaged her mouth. He was undone, he couldn't think. There was nothing but Erin and his need to have her and it was overwhelming. The room was in darkness once he'd slammed the door shut but he didn't reach for the light switch. He wanted it dark as he hiked up her dress with greedy hands and ripped the thin, lacy barrier of her panties aside. Her hands were at his T-shirt, pushing it up his chest, and then it was off, and her lips were at the base of his neck and moving lower. He freed himself, lifted her against the wall and her legs came around him and he cursed her, cursed himself, and then the gods for good measure as he slammed into her where they stood.

She cried out when he entered her, not in shock but in sheer outrageous pleasure. She was ready for him, had always been ready for him, and she wrapped her arms around his neck as sensation piled in on her and she surrendered to wherever he wanted to take her. Wherever he wanted to go.

Harder, he drove her there and she met him thrust for vicious thrust. Deeper, she took him there, darkly delighted when he cursed again, even as his hands curved around her thighs and he positioned her for still more. He was greedy and desperate and he was all that mattered. All she'd ever wanted.

She thrust her hands in his hair, she wanted to see his face, and caught her breath when she did because he wasn't in control. She was his and he was lost. Mindlessly, magnificently lost. And then his mouth was on hers again, hot and wild as he took her higher and higher still, took her to the very edge of pleasure. And tipped her over.

She was like quicksilver. Gloriously, unashamedly wanton as she came apart in his arms and there was nothing for it but to follow her. Nothing he could do but pour himself into her, over and over, as he found his own pulsing release. He felt her go limp in his arms. Felt himself tremble as he slapped his hand against the wall for balance. She was breathing hard and shuddering in the aftermath. So was he. 'God, I hope that was what you had in mind,' he muttered.

Her smile was shaky, but it was there. 'It was perfect.'

'Good.' Because he wanted more.

CHAPTER EIGHT

THEY made it to the bed this time and Tristan was careful with Erin as he tugged the cover aside and lowered her onto the sheets. 'I don't know whether to get you out of that dress or not.' He came down on the bed beside her, leaning on one elbow to look at her. 'You look so incredibly wanton in it.' It would have to come off, of course, but for now…for now he thought he might be able to move a little slower if she left it on.

He needed to touch her this time and to linger. He needed to show her that he could be careful with a woman. That he knew tenderness as well as insatiable need. He wanted light this time too, and the dim glow of the bedside lamp was just enough. He needed to see her eyes.

'I could keep it on a while longer, I guess.' Her eyes were dark and full of lazy satisfaction. 'But sooner or later it's going to come off. You know that, don't you?'

He knew.

'I want your skin against mine. All of it.'

'You'll have it,' he muttered, for he could deny her nothing. 'Later.' He slid his hand beneath her dress and trailed it up her body, and everywhere he touched he drew a response. A gasp, a shudder, a plea. And then he slowly brought his hand down to where she was hot and wet and open for him.

He knew how to pleasure a woman, thought Erin hazily as he found her with his fingers. Knew exactly how to please her as his lips found the curve of her jaw and his fingers worked their magic. Too much, too soon, and there was nothing she could do about it. She was his. Utterly and ir-revocably his, to do with what he wished, and if that meant he wanted her to come for him again with nothing but the stroke of his fingers and a layer of clothing between them then she would. Again and again and again.

That didn't mean she couldn't try and change his focus somewhat.

She put her hand over his and arched into both, and then she was trailing her fingers up his arm, revelling in the contrast of silky skin over hard, hard muscle. His was a warrior's body, tough and lean, and she couldn't get enough of it. Couldn't resist tracing the sculpted contours of his chest, and all the time he was playing her with *his* hands. Playing her to perfection.

She felt the heat rising through her, felt her breath quicken, and resisted. Not yet, not like this. She wanted…more. She slid her hand to his shoulders, to the nape of his neck, and then she was drawing him towards her. She wanted his lips on hers, and then they were and it was so much more than she'd ever dreamed of. He was all darkness and heat and his mouth took her so deep, so fast, that she came apart in his arms for the second time that night. And cursed him in the aftermath.

'What was that for?' He was half indignant and wholly amused. 'Shouldn't you be thanking me?'

'Thank you,' she said grudgingly. '*Now* can I take my dress off?'

'No. I'm *trying* to show you a little consideration here. Slow things down. You're not cooperating.'

She started to laugh. 'Kiss me less. Touch me less. That might help.'

'Not sure that's possible. I'm thinking of kissing you more. Stand up.'

'I *know* that's not possible.' But she did it anyway and stood there before him in a crumpled blue dress with an ache for this deep, brooding man that she knew now would never fade. He came to her then, circled her like a hawk, with an eye to weakness, but the only weakness was her heart and that was in strong hands already. His hands.

She lifted her chin high as he looked his fill and then he was behind her, his fingers barely brushing her skin as he found the zipper of her dress and slowly drew it down. He smoothed the straps from her shoulders next and then the dress was gone, pooled in a puddle at her feet and she was naked. 'Finally.'

'You know, maybe you shouldn't talk at all,' he said. 'Comments like that could make a man want to rush things.' He punctuated his words with a feather-light kiss to the sensitive curve of her neck. Maybe he had a point. He could be gentle when he wanted to be, she thought, and trembled when he ran his fingertips slowly down her spine and over her behind. And then he was in front of her, shucking off his trousers and then they were both naked and he was drawing her closer, skin on skin, and his mouth came down on hers, dreamy and magical as he took the time to savour her.

She gave too much, he thought, when he thought at all. So warm, so smooth in his arms as he took the time, this time, to learn what she liked. His lips at her collar-bone made her tremble. Trailing a finger across her breast and over her tight little nipple made her gasp. She copied his movements exactly, tracing her fingers over his nipple and letting them linger and *he* gasped. And then, with a wicked little smile, she took his nipple in her mouth and he almost lost his mind. Again.

So generous, too generous, and her laughter was dark and damning as he tumbled her onto the bed, coming down over her, all thought of tenderness forgotten as passion roared through him. He couldn't get enough of her, the taste of her skin, the scent of her, her slightness and her strength. She was fearless, and fascinating, and, heaven help them both, she held nothing back, offering him whatever he wanted, and he wanted it all.

He took her breast with his mouth and she screamed her approval. Set his lips to her waist and she jackknifed in his arms as if she'd been shot.

'Hurry,' she said, but he was already there, pinning her to the bed and dragging her hands above her head even as her legs came around him and he buried himself inside her. 'Tristan, please…' Her eyes were wild with need, her body taut with it. 'I can't wait—'

'Yes, you can,' he commanded. 'Look at me.' He brushed her lips with his. 'Feel me.' He kissed her again and felt his control slip away. 'Come with me,' he whispered, and, locking eyes with her, he began to move.

Tristan dreamt of the dockyards of Prague and a night that was rife with despair. A thick mist eddied around his feet and the air was sharp with salt and the unmistakable scent of death. Anguish rolled over him like a wave, spinning him round, working him over, and he turned away abruptly. He'd waited too long.

'No.' Shudders racked his body, even as he clenched his fists and willed himself to stop. To make his face impassive as he watched the team from the coroner's office bag the last of the bodies. He was a cop. He *knew* the depths humanity could sink to. But he'd never seen the likes of this.

The drone of a ship horn melded with another sound, an inarticulate cry of anger and grief. The sound was close; it might have come from him; he didn't know.

'Shh.' There was another voice in this nightmare, a different voice, and it was Erin, smoothing his hair from his face with gentle fingers as she leaned over him. 'It's all right. It's just a dream.'

'No.' He was still caught in sleep but it wasn't a dream. That much he did know.

'It's all right,' she murmured, and put her palm to his heart as if to stem the frantic beating of it.

He reached for her, gathered her close and drew a deep and ragged breath, breathing her in, the warm, feminine scent of her that chased away the memory of a raw and fetid stench. 'Erin, they're dead,' he said hoarsely. 'They're all dead. I was too late.'

'Shh.' Her arms came around him tightly, protectively. 'It's all right now. It's over.' He felt her lips in his hair as she cradled him into her body and it was shelter from the darkness and the home he'd never found. 'I've got you,' she whispered.

With a shuddering sigh, Tristan slept.

CHAPTER NINE

TRISTAN woke with the dawn the following morning, took one look at the sleeping woman curled into his side with her head on his shoulder and a hand on his heart, and felt a fear so big and overwhelming that he simply had to escape. He dressed fast and silently and hightailed it out of that room as if a horde of demons were after him. She gave too much. And he who'd spent a lifetime never taking too much had taken it all.

He'd dreamed last night; at least he thought he had. The same nightmare, only this time he hadn't woken in a sweat. He'd slipped out of it somehow and that was Erin's doing; he knew it instinctively, even if he couldn't remember how it had happened.

Not love. He repeated it to himself fiercely as he took to the sidewalk and headed towards the town centre. Never that. As he replayed last night's events over and over in his mind.

And knew himself for a liar.

* * *

When Erin woke the following morning she was in Tristan's motel room in Tristan's bed. Alone. She rolled onto her back and stared up at the dreary grey ceiling, not sure if she was grateful for the solitude or hurt by it. Making love with Tristan had been more than she'd ever dreamed of. Wilder, faster, more intense than anything she'd ever known. More…everything. She stretched experimentally and felt her body protest. Her body ached because of him, and damned if it didn't still ache *for* him, even after last night.

Especially after last night.

Clothes. She found her dress by the bed, her shoes and panties over by the door. Right where she'd left them. There was no sign of Tristan's clothes, although his carryall was still there. No sign of Tristan either. She needed a shower. Didn't know whether to take one in his room or head next door to hers. A door between them would have been useful. An adjoining door.

Her room would be better. Fresh clothes were there. Her toiletries. And when Tristan returned to his room she would not be there; she thought that bit was important. She was standing in the middle of the room, naked, just about to get dressed when she heard the sound of a key in the door. Moments later she was face to face with Tristan and feeling incredibly self-conscious, which was ridiculous given the liberties he'd taken with her body last night.

'You're back,' she said awkwardly.

'I, er…yes.' He came in, shut the door carefully behind him and set the bakery bag on the table.

'I was just—'

'I just went out for—'

They spoke in unison. Stopped in unison.

He tried again. 'I didn't mean to…' he gestured towards her nakedness, trying hard to stay unaffected '…ah, interrupt whatever…'

'The shower,' she said hurriedly.

'In there.' He was pretty sure that was where it was.

'Yes,' she said. 'Yes, it is. I'll, er, go, then.' And with a glance that was half mortified and half amused, she fled into the bathroom.

The minute she shut the door Tristan cursed and ran a hand through his hair. He wasn't a boy. He was thirty years old. He was no stranger to waking up with a woman in his bed. Nothing permanent, but he was civilised enough to offer them the use of his shower and have coffee made by the time they reappeared. Backing off easy, keeping it casual.

Jake had once asked him how the hell he got away with it and his reply had been simple. You laid down the ground rules beforehand. Jake had snorted and shook his head. And asked him how he ever got a woman to agree to *them*.

He *had* laid down the ground rules last night, hadn't he? He was pretty sure he had. Right there, just outside the door. Just before he'd gone insane. So now all he had to do was re-establish them and figure out a strategy for keeping his distance for the rest of the day.

Concentration was important. He planned to drive a lot. Keep his mind on the road and off the woman who sat beside him. She was good at sneaking past his defences. She was the daughter of a military man. She knew the value of strategy and the element of surprise. Of laughter and mis-direction. She was smart.

Sneaky.

She was ten minutes in the shower.

Ten very long minutes during which time he tried very hard to forget what they'd shared during the night. He made the bed. That helped. Packed his duffel and sat it by the door. Also a good move. Coffee came next and he set about boiling the jug, ripping coffee and sugar sachets open and dumping them into mugs. He'd almost managed to get his thoughts back in order when she emerged from the shower and scattered them again as he tried to remember what it was he was supposed to be doing. Keeping his distance. Well, he was, wasn't he? He hadn't reached for her at all yet. He was doing just fine. As well as could be expected.

After a night like that.

She looked beautiful in her crumpled blue dress. Rested. How on earth she pulled *that* off he didn't know, because she certainly hadn't had much sleep. She smiled at him and her smile was warm and easy, which was both good and bad. Her awkwardness seemed to have disappeared. His, on the other hand, seemed to be growing. 'Juice?' he offered.

'From the bar fridge?'

'From the bakery. Breakfast roll?'

She looked at the bakery bag on the counter, looked at him. 'You're feeding me?'

Damn. He knew walking into that bakery had been a mistake. 'Don't dwell on it.'

She smiled and reached for the bag of bread rolls and the tension in his stomach eased. 'I've been thinking,' she said, and the ache in his stomach was back, only this time it was multiplied tenfold. He hated it when a woman got to thinking. Especially the morning after. 'You didn't give me a compliment last night at dinner.'

'I didn't?' He narrowed his eyes. 'You're very smart.'

'Backhanded compliments don't count,' she said, shaking her head. 'I want a genuine one.'

'Working on it.'

Her smile was pure challenge. 'I'm glad to hear it. Is that coffee?'

'I wasn't sure how you took it.' He had all the fixings there. He just hadn't made it.

'White, no sugar.'

Girl coffee. He made it fast and set it on the table beside her, deliberately not handing it to her directly, because handing it to her meant touching her and touching her was out.

'So…' she said, after she'd sipped her coffee and nibbled on her bun, 'I'm thinking we need lots of inane morning-after conversation.'

'Silence is good,' he countered. 'Silence is golden.'

'No.' She eyed him steadily. 'We do not want golden this morning. We want casual and meaningless. At least, I'm assuming that's what you want.'

It was. He was desperate for it. Whether they could manage it was a different matter altogether. 'Nice day outside,' he said doggedly. 'Rain's gone.'

'That's good.' She smiled at him and sipped her coffee. 'Did you know that Inverell has an old-car museum?'

'That's not inane,' he said indignantly. 'That's important.'

'Hmm. It opens to the public at nine a.m. When did you want to leave for Sydney?'

'When do *you* want to leave?'

'It's an eight-hour drive, straight down the New England,' she said matter-of-factly. 'We could leave at lunchtime and still get home this evening. If you wanted to.'

'Or if you wanted to,' he said.

'Mmm.' She handed him a glass of orange juice. 'Cheers.'

She was doing it deliberately. Holding off until *he* said something about where they were going and when. As if *he* knew.

'Had any more thoughts about that compliment?'

'No.' He wasn't currently thinking complimentary thoughts about her at all and one look at the smirk she was trying to hide behind her orange juice told him she knew it. Damned if she didn't think she had the upper hand in not-nearly-as-inane-as-it-seemed conversation this morning. The fact that she *did* didn't improve his mood any.

It was half eight already. It would take half an hour to eat, shower, and get underway. After that it was straight down the road. He *did* want to get back to Sydney today. Didn't he?

'Here's the plan,' he said. 'First the car museum, then a quick stop at Wallace Sapphires. After that we hit the highway and head for home.'

'Why Wallace Sapphires?'

Tristan rubbed the back of his neck. For all that this wasn't his beat or his business he couldn't let Roger keep stealing from the widow Wallace. 'I thought I might speak with Mrs Wallace about protecting her sapphires from theft. Simple measures like a security camera in the shop, for instance.'

'Or finding another fish-tank cleaner.'

'That too. The point is, she has options. She should know that.'

'I like it.'

Erin's smile warmed him through. Spun him round. He didn't want it. Didn't need it. He told himself that as he stood there watching her and wondering just what it was about her that made her so different from any other woman he'd ever known. 'I need a shower,' he muttered.

'And I'm off to pack.' She downed her coffee, collected her shoes, and started to leave. Her steps slowed as she drew level with him and her smile faltered as her eyes searched his face. 'If I thought I could pull it off I'd kiss you good morning,' she said solemnly. 'One of those quick, thanks-for-the-good-time-last-night kisses. One that said I was used to feeling the way I felt when I was in your arms. That's the kind of kiss I'd give you this morning. If I thought I could pull it off.'

'Erin?' She was halfway out the door before he spoke. 'If I thought I could pull it off I'd let you.'

Erin didn't mind taking a wander through the old-car museum. There were other things there to look at besides cars. Old petrol-station pumps and shopfront signs. Porcelain dolls.

Tristan…

She really, really liked seeing the boyish side of Tristan come out to play. She'd tease it out more often if he were hers. Make sure it appeared at least once daily to counteract the seriousness of his work.

No! She had to stop thinking about what she would do if he were hers. He wasn't hers. He didn't want to be hers. And that was a good thing because he was everything she didn't want in a partner. Work he couldn't talk about. Hurt she couldn't heal. And a dedication to duty that he simply couldn't shake.

Oh, he was trying, she thought with grim humour. He was hurt enough, and tired enough to wonder about finding another job. A more menial job. And two months into that he'd wonder what on earth he was doing there. His need to make a difference, to make the world or at least the part of it he walked through a better place, was too strong.

So they would call in to Wallace Sapphires on the way home today and he would do what he did. With compassion and with grace he would serve and protect.

It was ten-thirty before they left the museum. He'd immersed himself in yesteryear and lingered longer than he should have, thought Tristan, but the old jalopies, some perfectly restored and some not, had been impossible to resist. Erin could have

hurried him along but she hadn't. She'd given him
space and walked her own path through the
museum, an easy wander that had taken in the
little curiosities more so than the cars, but if her
aim was to put some distance between them, both
literally and figuratively, she hadn't succeeded.
Even surrounded by a hundred classic cars he
always knew where she was. He knew when she
was watching him, and he knew when she looked
away. It was then that he looked at her. She was
in his head. And he couldn't get her out.

It was almost eleven before they pulled into the
Wallace Sapphire mine car park. 'What are you
going to do if Mrs Wal isn't in the shop today?'
asked Erin as he opened the car door.

'Find her. Wait in the car.'

'I'm coming with you.'

'No.'

'Clearly one of your favourite words,' she
muttered as she got out of the car and met his gaze
over the roof of it. 'It's like this. You can try and
tie me to the car—and under different circumstances I might enjoy letting you—or I can come
with you. I won't interfere—'

'Then stay in the car!'

'But I won't be left out. This isn't some
official investigation, Tristan. You know it isn't.
It's you and me trying to help an old lady with
an employee problem.'

His glare was his blackest and he knew for a fact that it could reduce grown men to stuttering, but not Erin. Hands on her hips, she traded him glare for glare before dismissing him and heading for the shop.

He was one step behind her when she reached the door. One step ahead of her as he reached for the door handle and turned it for her. 'One of these days I really will shackle you to the car,' he muttered.

'Bite me.'

'That would come after,' he said, and meant every word of it.

Erin's eyes grew dark and slumberous. The grin she gave him was lethal. 'Promise?'

'Keep your mind on the job,' he muttered. 'That way maybe I can keep my mind on it too.'

'I'm on it,' she said, and with a deep breath, 'sorry.'

'First rule of policing.' She looked so contrite that he couldn't resist bringing his hand up to tuck a wayward strand of silky brown hair behind her ear. 'Never hit on your partner.'

'Right.' She took the hand he'd used to touch her with and brushed her lips against his knuckles, sending a jolt of desire straight through him.

'Why are we doing this *now*?' he muttered.

'Because right now we're safe. We know we have to stop,' she said with a tiny tilt of her lips as she let go of his hand and drew away.

Her words made a frightening amount of sense.

'Looks like we're in luck,' she said, peering through the door. 'There's Mrs Wal.'

'She's probably wondering why we're making out on her doorstep,' he muttered as he pushed the door open and ushered Erin into the shop. 'If she asks, *you* explain it.'

'If she asks, I will. Morning, Mrs Wal,' she said cheerfully.

'Oh, dear,' said the older woman with a tentative smile that didn't quite reach her eyes. 'It's going to be one of those days, I can tell. You've changed your mind about the sapphires, haven't you?'

'Not at all,' said Erin. 'Those sapphires are perfect.'

The widow Wallace looked relieved. 'Well, if there's anything else I can help you with…'

'Actually, we haven't come to look around,' Tristan said gently. 'I'm in law enforcement, Mrs Wallace, and I'd like to talk to you about some options you might like to think about with regards to those missing sapphires. Nothing official,' he said at the older woman's look of alarm. 'But if they're being stolen rather than misplaced there are things you can do to protect your stock.'

Her eyes watered and she gave him a tremulous smile. 'You've a good heart,' she said. 'I knew it the first time I saw you. And I thank you for your concern, but it's not necessary.' She looked down at a closely written sheet of paper beside her on the counter.

'I found this tucked underneath the front door when I came in this morning. It lists every stone he ever took from me along with dates, prices, and calculated interest.' She looked as if she was about to cry. He hated it when they cried. He looked to Erin. Maybe she could help when it came to the tears. Nope. She looked as if *she* was going to cry. This was a disaster.

'This next sheet's a repayment schedule,' said the widow Wallace, picking it up and handing it to him. 'Starting today, of how he's going to pay it back.'

'Roger?' he asked gently and she nodded.

'These,' she said in a slightly firmer voice for which Tristan was truly thankful, 'are *my* calculations, using the cost price of the stones instead of retail price. I've used a lower interest rate as well. I knew he was in trouble, not that he ever said. That wife of his…' She shook her head. 'I'm offering him a job. I should have had someone in to oversee the business well before now. Lord knows my heart's not in it, not since Edward passed on. Besides, it's about time someone offered that boy a chance.'

'You'll be running a risk,' he said as he set the sheet on the counter beside her. It was a solution, yes. But it wasn't one he would have advised.

'I know.'

'What if he steals from you again?'

Mrs Wallace looked down at Roger's letter, at his estimate of what he'd taken and what he owed her, and smiled through her tears. 'He's a good boy,' she said. 'I know he is. Sometimes you've just got to have faith.'

'That went well,' said Erin when they reached the car. 'Not quite what I expected, mind, but it certainly *feels* like a win for the good guys. I feel good about this. Mrs Wal feels good about this.' She stared at Tristan's stern profile. He was doing the driving again. 'Do *you* feel good about this?'

'I'm not unhappy about it,' he said after a while. 'I believe in giving people a second chance.'

'I'm hearing a but,' she said.

'But I'm not a big believer in happily ever afters either,' he said quietly. 'I don't see it.'

'What about hope?' she asked him. 'Do you see that?'

'Yeah,' he said. 'Lately I do.'

They stopped for a late lunch in Tamworth and even after they'd lingered over coffee they were making good time. Erin took a stint at the wheel and then it was his turn again, as the sun slipped behind the horizon and the night unfolded. They would get home that evening, without a doubt, thought Tristan. They would get home and say goodbye and he would walk away unscathed and so would she. That was what he wanted. What they both wanted. Wasn't it?

She didn't like what he did for a living.

Yet she understood it instinctively. She knew the heaviness that came with duty and by God she knew how to fight it. With laughter and hope and a hefty dose of distraction, she brought balance into a world that was too often too dark.

He lived in London.

But he wouldn't be going back there. Not to live. He wanted a transfer back to Australia and a break from undercover work. He could make it happen.

He was scared witless of giving his heart to a woman and then losing her.

There was that.

No woman had ever captivated him so completely, or made him fear so much. He didn't know how she did it, she just did and she was everything he'd ever needed and everything he'd never allowed himself to dream of.

'Whoa!' she said suddenly.

'What?' he said, alarmed. 'What is it?'

'Kangaroo,' she said. 'A big grey one. Huge. It was just about to hop out in front of us.'

'I didn't see it.'

'Could have been a wombat, I guess.'

'A *wombat*?'

'Big grey one.'

He saw the tilt of her lips out of the corner of his eye. He was too busy looking for kangaroos and oversized wombats to look at her properly.

There was nothing there.

'Dangerous business, this driving down the highway at dusk,' she said conversationally.

'Yeah.' Particularly with a madwoman in the car.

'There's a motel a few kilometres up ahead. We passed a sign a couple of kilometres back.'

'Was that before or after you saw the mutant kangarombat?'

'I'm pretty sure it was just before.'

He chanced a glance at her. Her smile was wicked.

'Maybe we should consider spending the night at the motel,' she said. 'For the sake of the animals. I'm all for protecting rare and endangered wildlife.'

He had to smile. Even as he cursed her and surrendered to the inevitable. He didn't want to make it home tonight. He didn't want the trip to end, didn't want to have to say goodbye to her. Not…yet. 'You're right,' he said. 'We should do our bit for wildlife conservation.'

'I do like conviction in a man.' She stretched languidly and sent him a smile that slid through him like a hot knife through butter. 'How many rooms do you think we'll be needing?'

'One.'

They made it to the room without touching. He managed to get their bags in and the door closed before he reached for her. 'Kiss me good morning,' he muttered as her arms came around his neck, and her eyes grew dreamy.

'I looked for you this morning, when I woke,' she whispered as she brushed her lips across his. 'I wanted your lips on mine. I wanted mine on you.' She set her mouth to his and her kiss was deep, and drugging, and seemed to last for ever. 'I watched you at the car museum and I wanted to kiss you then. Right there by the straight-eight Ford you fell in love with.' Her fingers were at his shirt, unbuttoning it and smoothing it over his shoulders and he let her, helplessly following the flow of emotion that bound him to her. 'I watched your gentleness with Mrs Wallace and wanted it for myself. I still want it.' And then her lips were on his again and he was slowly drowning in her. He felt the edge of passion rip through him and fought to control it. Not yet. Mindless desire didn't always rule him. He could be gentle, *would* be gentle. Because this time he needed to give as well as take.

So he slowed his hands as he slid them over her,

slowed his movements as he drew her down onto the bed and took the time to savour what he held.

She sighed, shakily as he undressed her, his hands gentle and sure. There was passion in him, there always was, but this time he kept it leashed. Only his eyes gave him away for they blazed hot with every whimper he drew from her lips, every tremor he coaxed from her body.

She wove her hands in his hair and lost herself to sensation when his lips followed his hands to her breast and he sucked gently. Her nipples peaked for him and she arched against him, wanting more, craving more, but he wouldn't be rushed. He took his time, with long, slow strokes of his hands and with hot, open-mouthed kisses down her body; he took the time to know her.

'Tristan—' She was trembling with the effort of holding her body in check. 'Tristan, please—'

'You want me to be more gentle?'

'No!' She didn't know what she wanted. The passionate intensity he brought to his lovemaking could shoot her so high so fast she could hardly breathe. She'd thought to avoid that this time, she'd thought she wanted tenderness, but his tenderness was destroying her. 'Yes,' she whispered brokenly. She wanted it all.

She opened for him and finally, he moved lower and took her with his tongue. She tried to hold back, heaven help her she did, but within moments she was convulsing around him. Too fast, all of it. The speed with which he'd captured her heart and the road they were travelling on, but she couldn't slow down, not with this man. He was everything she'd ever wanted. Everything she'd never wanted. And she would give him anything he asked.

He waited until her body was limp and her breathing had steadied before kissing his way back up her body. She smelled like sunshine, tasted like sin as he set his lips to her heart and felt it thundering beneath his lips. He moved over her, into her, and the soft, slick slide of his body in hers was almost his undoing. She kissed him then. Put her hand to his cheek and her lips to his and kissed him with emotion so pure it made him tremble. He moved against her, inside her, in a dance he knew would send him soaring.

She was in his head, in his heart, and right now, right now, she was in his arms. His to hold.

And his to love.

CHAPTER TEN

WHEN Erin woke the next morning she was in
Tristan's arms and it felt like heaven. She lay there,
perfectly still, watching the steady rise and fall of
his chest. He was still asleep. It had been late before
he'd finally surrendered to sleep. Late, or early,
depending on what one called the wee hours of the
morning, but when he *had* slept he'd done so dream-
lessly. She knew because she'd been watching him,
watching over him. Not all the time, she'd caught
her own sleep in snatches. But enough.

He wouldn't have wanted that. He'd hate the
very thought of it.

She wasn't about to tell him.

She came up on one elbow and eased slowly
away from him, trying not to wake him, and found
herself caught instead in paying attention to his
face in a way that she'd never allowed herself to
do when he was awake, not even when they'd
been making love. Beautifully male, he was that,

with a mouth that spoke of passion tempered by restraint and it mirrored the man exactly. Strength tempered by compassion, sternness softened by humour. A beautiful, unfathomable contradiction.

She didn't know what she would find this morning when he woke. Not yesterday morning's awkwardness, they were past that, or at least she prayed they were. Retreat was more likely; she doubted he was past that. He didn't trust easily. He didn't love easily either.

When he finally did fall in love, she thought wistfully, he would love hard.

She was in the bathroom, filling the kettle with tap water, when he found her. She looked up, startled by the hand that snaked around her waist, and then he was drawing her back against him and locking eyes with her in the mirror. His hair was tousled, boyish, and his eyes, as always, were intent, but it was his tentative smile that commanded her attention.

Lord but it was sweet.

'Breakfast,' she said gravely, 'should be about celebration.'

'You mean food,' he said.

'I mean a gluttonous abundance of food crammed onto trays in the middle of a warm bed with me on one side and a man who makes love like the devil and smiles like an angel on the other. But I'll take three out of four.'

'You think food will be scarce?' His smiles came easily this morning and she delighted in them. 'What if we ordered everything on the menu?'

'Yeah, but what are *you* going to eat?'

His smile grew lazy as his lips brushed her ear. 'Guess.'

Her eyelashes fluttered closed and her breathing grew short. 'Tell you what,' she said. 'You order while I shower and maybe I'll share.'

'You're very generous,' he said as he trailed his hands across her stomach. 'There's just one problem.'

'You think we're going to get crumbs in the bed?'

'No.'

'Spill our drinks?'

'No, although I can see how that would be a problem.'

"What, then?'

'You don't really think you're getting into that shower all by yourself, do you?'

They ordered breakfast once they were clean, and it was double servings all round of scrambled eggs and bacon on Turkish bread, with freshly squeezed orange juice to finish. They were in Branxton, less than two hours from Sydney, and would be home—if they had a mind to be—by lunchtime.

'There's something we need to do before we

get back to Sydney,' he said. 'Otherwise it's going to haunt me for all eternity.'

'Really?' This sounded interesting. They'd already managed a fair few things that were going to haunt her for eternity. Hot pools at sunset. Morning showers with Tristan… 'What do we need to do?' He was sitting on the bed opposite her wearing nothing but grey cargo trousers and he was relaxed and easy and there was a teasing glint in his eyes that was irresistible.

'We need to go and climb something.'

'It's called the Ladder of Gloom,' said Erin some two hours later as they stared up at a twelve-metre-high rock face situated on the edge of Kuringai National Park, just north of Sydney. 'It's a lovely, fingery, sports climb and just about perfect for our purposes. Not too high, not too easy, and lots and lots of fun.'

Tristan looked up at the vertical cliff face, at the bulges in the rock, and sighed. 'Who suggested this idiocy?'

'You did. And when you get to the top you'll know why.'

She showed him how to harness up, and went over the equipment with him with relaxed efficiency, explaining as she went. Then she drew him back from the bottom of the cliff face and pointed out their route.

'The first bit's the hardest. If you can climb the first two metres you can climb the rest, so here's what we're going to do. I'll spot you from below to start with, then come up past you and take lead. It's just like climbing a ladder.'

'Although gloomier.'

'Don't worry if you slip. Everyone slips. We'll be roped into ringbolts all the way up.'

'You really like this, don't you?' he asked.

'I really do.'

'You're an adrenaline junkie.'

'I am not!' And with a toss of her head, 'I'm really very sedate when you get to know me. Ask anyone in my family.'

'Not sure that's necessary,' he said dryly. 'Erin, you're not sedate. You move fast, think fast, and make love…fast. Even when you're going slow.'

'Was that a complaint?'

'Hell, no,' he said with a grin. 'That was a compliment.'

Erin's eyes narrowed.

'You'd probably have to be male to understand the depth of that particular compliment,' he said sagely. 'If you'd rather a different compliment I'll keep thinking.' He was, after all, just about to follow her up a twelve-metre vertical rock wall that bulged alarmingly towards the top.

'I'd rather a different compliment,' she said. 'Maybe a sonnet.'

A *sonnet*? Not in this lifetime. 'I might be able to manage a limerick,' he said. 'I'll think about it on the way up.'

Up.

The first two metres were what Erin called skinny. Tristan's interpretation was somewhat more colourful. Five-mil-deep handholds that were nothing but cracks in a rock weren't exactly his idea of a ladder, but up he went. And after Erin had swung past him, bright-eyed and sure-footed, he went up some more. Erin was right. It wasn't a big climb. Twelve metres wasn't that high, but it was strenuous enough to bring a sheen of sweat to his body, and different enough to have him wondering how a climber's arms and hands held up on longer, more difficult climbs.

He was over halfway up before it occurred to him that he, who rarely trusted anyone, had trusted Erin to take the lead. She had the skills. He didn't. That part was logical. That he'd willingly handed over responsibility for their safety wasn't so logical.

He always took point position in the course of his work. He always moved to protect. And here he was, clinging to a cliff face, and if Erin slipped, if she fell, there wasn't a thing he could do about it. He didn't like it. *He* was safe. He was roped in all the way. But she wasn't. Not until she reached each consecutive ringbolt. 'What stops *you* from falling?' he said grimly as she prepared to climb to the next ringbolt.

'Ah,' she said, shooting him a quick smile. 'The mountain strikes its first blow. I wondered if it would. I probably forgot to mention that climbing's all about trust. Trusting yourself, trusting your equipment, and trusting your lead man, or woman, to get you to the top.'

'Don't turn this into a gender argument. It's not.'

'No.' Her gaze was oddly sympathetic. 'In your case it's probably not. It's that overdeveloped protective instinct that's giving you trouble, isn't it? You can't protect me from there and that bothers you.'

'You're vulnerable,' he snapped. And he hated it.

'It's just a little climb,' she said. 'I'll be fine.'

Tristan scowled.

'Apart from that, what do you think?' she asked him as she reached for the next handhold. 'Do you like it? What if you were leading? Would you like it then?'

'Yeah.' Then he would like it. 'Be careful.'

'I'm always careful,' she said, stifling a grin at the glare he sent her. If he'd just relax a little he'd have a much better time of it. He was climbing well for someone who'd not climbed before. His movements were sure; he had no fear of heights. He was strong and agile and he would climb the ladder all the way to the top. She had every confidence in him. He just needed to have the same confidence in her. And that, she realised belatedly, was asking a lot of him. 'We don't have to keep going,' she said, trying to gauge his feelings, but she couldn't read him. He was doing the 'inscrutable cop' thing and doing it well. 'If you're not comfortable the best thing to do is go back down.'

'I'm comfortable enough,' he said gruffly. 'Just don't fall.'

'It's not part of the plan.' She wasn't a reckless climber, but she wouldn't deal in absolutes halfway up a crag. Climbing was a dangerous sport. A challenging sport. Most serious climbers had a tumble or two under their harness. She'd taken a few tumbles herself although now clearly wasn't the time to mention it. She sent him a reassuring smile before turning away to focus on the next leg of the climb, a textbook shimmy up to the next ringbolt.

She made fast work of it and then it was Tristan's turn. He was strong, leanly muscled and in perfect control of his body. 'Beautiful,' she said when he was beside her once more. 'You're a pleasure to watch. That was a compliment, by the way. Just in case you've forgotten what they sound like.'

'Don't you have places to go?' he muttered. 'People to see?'

'I do,' she said. 'I'm going up to the top. And I will see you there.'

The last leg of the climb was Erin's favourite. She liked the bulge in the rock, liked the exhilaration that came with approaching the top of a crag, no matter how high or difficult the climb. She just plain liked getting there. The final move was a scrabbly toe-in and a full stretch to reach the top. She made sure that top hold was secure, that she hadn't grabbed a handful of loose ground, and drew herself up. Her hold was secure, no problem there.

But she was eyeball to eyeball with a brown snake.

Its body was coiled; its head was raised. It didn't look happy. And it wasn't backing down.

She reacted instinctively, snatching her hand away, jerking away, wanting to get out of striking range. She lost her balance, lost her grip, and that was the end of coming back down gracefully.

She wouldn't fall far, she was secured to the lower ringbolt, but she'd hit the wall hard. Better than a brown snake bite though. Much, much better.

He saw her reach the top of the climb. Saw her jerk away from the edge as if stung. He saw her let go and his world stopped. The rock beneath his fingers was hard and unforgiving, his hold on it not nearly deep enough as he reached for her with one hand, reached out to break her fall. He felt his hand brush her shirt, brush her body, but there was nothing to grasp, nothing to clasp. He couldn't stop her. She was tumbling straight past him. And then she reached out to him and he grabbed her and held on tight.

She was falling, falling awkwardly, and it felt as if everything were happening in slow motion. She flung her hand out, looking for purchase and finding nothing, and then Tristan had hold of her, hand to forearm, in a grip that was punishing. She hit the wall, shoulder first but not hard, not nearly as hard as she'd expected to. Tristan had her. Held her.

'Brown snake,' she said, when her heart stopped trying to choke her and she had the breath for speaking. 'At the top.' She looked up at Tristan, at his position. He wasn't secure. She looked at the wall, looked for a handhold or foothold, but there was none. They were all further down. 'Let me go,' she said. 'I won't fall far. Just a couple more metres. I'll pick up a hold further down and come back up.'

'No.' His muscles screamed in protest, and his hold on the rock was perilous, but he would not let her go. It was unthinkable.

'It's okay.' Her eyes were huge. She was dangling in midair, ten metres off the ground, and damned if she wasn't trying to reassure him. 'The rope will stop me. I won't fall far.'

'No.' He would not lose her. Could not. 'Climb.'

So she climbed, using him as her anchor, and

when she was secured to the rock beside him and he'd finally released his grip on her arm, she cursed him. 'What was that?' she demanded. 'Have you no concern for your own safety whatsoever? You should have let me go! You could have dislocated your shoulder! What on earth were you thinking?'

'Shut up!' His breathing was ragged, his face was white beneath his tan, and his eyes blazed with a temper that was raging. 'Just shut up. Don't you dare tell me I should have let you go! Do you have *any* idea what watching you fall from the top of that damned rock was *like*?'

That he had a temper was no surprise. That he was letting it rip on the side of a mountain was. She'd scared him, she realised. He hadn't known that her fall would be broken and that she'd be banged up but otherwise fine. He'd only seen her fall. 'I'm fine.' She was starting to tremble. Reaction was setting in. She needed to get to the top before it got the better of her and turned her muscles to mush. 'Tristan, we need to get to the top. Now.'

'What about the snake?' He was calming down. Starting to think ahead, which was good. She needed him calm. She needed him climbing. They needed to get to the top.

'I'll flick some rope up. Scare it away.'

'Why not go down?'

'We can't rap from here. The top's closer.

Safer.' Apart from the brown snake and she was going to make damn sure it wasn't waiting for her this time. She was going to bomb that piece of dirt with enough rope and climbing hardware to persuade an elephant to move. 'I'm going up,' she told him. 'Before my muscles give out.' He didn't look convinced. 'Trust me. Please.'

'Are you hurt?' he said gruffly.

'No.' Yes. Her shoulder wasn't in good shape but she could still hold, and if she could hold she could climb. 'We'll check for injuries at the top. You and me both.' And up she went.

She reached the top, bombed that piece of dirt above her with unladylike zeal, and finally, finally hauled over the edge. The snake was gone. She tied off on the double ringbolt at the top and called for Tristan to start climbing.

He came up fast. He'd make a damn fine climber if he had a mind to. Not that he seemed to have a mind to, judging by the rigid set of his jaw and the stern set of his mouth. His introduction to the sport had left a lot to be desired.

She let him settle while she drew up the rope and collected her scattered hardware. When that was done and he still hadn't said a word she sat down a little distance away from him and set about examining the damage. She'd scraped her leg, a series of long thin gouges that stung like the devil, but they weren't bleeding much. It was her shoulder she was worried about. It was banged up plenty from where she'd rammed into the wall. She rotated it gingerly. She still had full movement; it wasn't dislocated. She felt around her collar-bone, worked her way over her shoulder and upper arm. Nothing *felt* broken.

'You need ice,' he said gruffly.

'Maybe when we get back to the suburbs we can stop by a petrol station.'

'Or a hospital.'

'It's not that bad.' She thought she saw a flash of temper in those glorious golden eyes, but then his jaw tightened and he looked away and the moment was gone.

'It's your call,' he said.

She felt it then. The loss of his protection, the loss of him, clear through to her soul.

The view was superb. The snake was gone. And so was Tristan. He'd retreated deep inside himself. Not shock. She knew the symptoms of shock and he didn't have them. His eyes were clear; he was in control. But he wasn't with her the way he'd been before they'd started to climb. 'I wouldn't have fallen far,' she said, desperately trying to reach him. 'Our second position was still secure. You were still secure.' He looked at her, looked away as if she hurt his eyes. 'Tristan?'

He didn't answer.

'Thank you for catching me.'

'It was instinct.' He still wouldn't look at her. 'I'm sorry if you'd rather I let you fall.'

'No,' she said. 'No. It was better that you caught me, of course it was. I was just scared for you, that's all. We were scared for each other.' She reached out and put her hand on his forearm and he flinched as if struck. 'What is it?' And with a sinking feeling, 'You've hurt your arm.'

'The arm's fine.'

'What, then?'

'It's nothing.' He stood. 'We should head back down.'

'Yes. Yes, we should.' She couldn't get through to him. Not this time. The walls he'd built around himself were too strong. She would try again when they reached the bottom. Maybe once they were off the crag he'd come back from wherever he was. Yes, maybe then he'd be all right.

They rappelled back down to the base of the wall without incident. They packed the climbing gear back into the two packs it had come out of, Tristan covering her hand with his when she reached down to pick one up to carry it to the car. He didn't say a word. He didn't have to. He hefted one pack over his shoulders, held the other like a carryall and started for the car. Erin walked beside him carrying nothing.

'So, I'll drop you at your place, shall I?' she

said, when they reached the car, desperately striving for some semblance of normalcy.

'You can't drive with that shoulder,' he said, and opened the passenger door for her. 'I'll drive.'

He was probably right, she thought as she sat in the passenger seat. Her shoulder was really starting to throb and sagging back into the car seat and keeping it motionless felt like heaven. She reached for the seat belt, wincing as she did so, but his hands were already there.

'I'll do it,' he said gruffly, his hands gentle as he drew the seat belt across her body and clicked it into place.

He was so close, so careful of her that she reached out to him again, brushing her fingers against his cheek, and for a moment she thought he would respond. His hand covered hers and he seemed to turn into her caress, but then he was pulling her hand away and placing it gently in her lap. 'Tristan, what is it? What's wrong?'

'We'll go to your mother's,' he said, ignoring her question as he moved away and headed for the driver's seat. 'Patch you up there. You're going to need rest. Looking after.'

'Okay.' She leaned back against the seat and closed her eyes, willing away the tears. Her shoulder hurt, and the scratches on her leg were stinging, but they were nothing compared to the pain in her heart.

She couldn't reach him.

* * *

They stopped for ice for her shoulder at the first petrol station they came to and Erin was glad of it. It must have shown on her face because Tristan's eyes grew dark with concern. 'We're going to the hospital,' he said. 'Now.'

She didn't protest.

He drove like a demon to get there. Waited with her in silence, tension radiating from him in waves until her name was called. He walked with her to the door of the examination room, and the look he gave the young intern would have fried a lesser man.

'Take care of her.'

'That's the plan,' said the younger man dryly, and to Erin, 'Come on in and we'll take a look at that shoulder.'

The shoulder was fine, the intern told her when her X-rays came back some half an hour later. She'd torn some muscle and she'd have severe bruising and stiffness, but otherwise she'd be fine. He gave her some painkillers, strapped her shoulder, and ushered her from the cubicle.

Tristan had been sitting, waiting. He stood abruptly when she came out, his focus absolute as he searched her face. He didn't say anything when she approached. He didn't have to. His eyes spoke for him and they gave her hope. He cared for her. Maybe he didn't want to, but he did. It was there in those bruised and shadow filled eyes. She wasn't the only one who'd been beat up by that mountain. Tristan had taken a hammering too.

'The shoulder's going to be fine,' she said gently. 'I've torn a few muscles and bruised the rest, that's all.'

'Best to be sure,' he muttered, shoving his hands in his pockets.

'Yes.' Her smile was gentle too. 'Let's get out of here.'

She gave him directions to her mother's house as they drew closer to it and he followed them in silence. He was silent when they pulled into her mother's driveway as well. Big surprise.

'Here we are,' she said. It was inane but it was the best she could do.

'Head on in,' he said. 'I'll bring your gear in and call for a taxi.'

'Take this car,' she said. 'I can call round for it tomorrow.'

'No.' He shook his head. 'I'll take a taxi.' He gathered up her things and followed her into the house, greeting her mother with a politeness that was as sweet as it was awkward.

'What happened to your shoulder?' asked her mother.

'We went climbing this morning. I gave it a nudge.'

'How big a nudge?'

'Not that big. Nothing's broken. We stopped by

the hospital on the way home. Everything's fine. I'm fine.'

'You don't look fine,' said Tristan.

'He's right,' said her mother.

Two against one. 'Honestly, I'm fine. I just need to sit and rest for a bit, that's all.'

'I'll call for that taxi and let you,' said Tristan.

'*I'll* call for the taxi,' she said. 'I can have one here in less than two minutes. I have connections.'

He smiled at that, just a little. 'I'll wait for it outside.' He nodded to her mother, nodded to *her* as if they were nothing but casual acquaintances and headed up the hall. He almost broke her heart.

He felt something for her; she knew that. But whatever it was, it wasn't enough. He was pulling back. Had pulled back. And nothing she said or did seemed to make any difference.

Lillian Sinclair wasn't slow on the uptake. She gave Erin a quizzical look and inclined her head in Tristan's direction as he headed up the hallway. '*I'll* call for the taxi.' Follow him, her look said. Taking a deep breath, Erin did.

She stood back as he unloaded his carryall from the boot and set it at his feet. 'It's over, isn't it?' she said in a small voice. 'Whatever we had, it's over.'

'I don't know,' he muttered. 'Erin, I need time. I need some space. I can't think when I'm near you. You spin me round. You shake things loose that shouldn't be.'

'I don't mean to.'

'I know,' he said. 'I know you don't. I'll call you. In a few days.'

'Really?' She sounded desperate. Men hated that. *She* hated it. 'Well, you know. If you ever need a taxi…'

'Erin, don't,' he said quietly, and she blinked rapidly and looked away.

She couldn't look at him. If she looked at him she was going to cry. 'There's your ride.' She watched him walk up the driveway. She refused to watch him get in the taxi and leave. With a small wave she turned and headed back into the house.

Her mother was waiting for her in the kitchen with the kettle on and coffee beans grinding in the grinder. 'Well?' she asked. 'Did you get the stones you wanted?'

Erin nodded and tried to smile. It didn't work. 'Oh, Mama, I'm such an idiot,' she said. And burst into tears.

CHAPTER ELEVEN

TRISTAN'S Ford arrived at his father's house two days later on the back of a truck that was almost as old as the Ford itself. Frank was driving it. 'How about putting her over to one side of the garage, underneath that elm tree?' said Frank. 'It'll look quite the picture.'

Yeah, thought Tristan. The colour of the rust was a near perfect match for the colour of the falling leaves. He could sweep them into a heap around the old jalopy and no one, his father included, would ever know it was there. 'Good idea,' he said and set about helping Frank unload it. 'You heading back to Lightning Ridge straight away?'

'Nope. I'm gonna get me some culture. I'm booked into a downtown hotel and tonight I'm off to the Opera House to hear Beethoven's piano sonatas numbers one, three, and fourteen.'

'You're a Beethoven fan?'

'Isn't everyone?'

'No.'

'Erin is,' said Frank, nodding his head for good measure. 'That girl knows her classics. How'd she go finding more opal?'

'Nothing caught her eye.'

'Ha!' cackled Frank. 'She knows what she wants; I'll give her that. She caught you yet?'

Tristan gaped at the sun battered older man with his baggy town clothes that hung loosely on his once powerful frame. Age had caught up with Frank's body but it certainly hadn't withered his mind. He was sharp. He saw too much.

'Guess not,' said Frank. 'Pity, 'cause I brought those black opals along, in case you were in the market so to speak. She's a firecracker all right. Just like my Janie. Best twenty years of my life, married to that woman.'

'What happened to your Janie?' asked Tristan.

'She up and died on me. Her heart gave out. I nearly died right along with her.' Frank's face creased into a bittersweet smile. 'Life doesn't come with guarantees, boy, and neither does love. When you find it you hold to it. All you can do. For as long as you can.'

'Wouldn't you rather not have found it at all?'

'Hell, no. A man starts thinking like that and he's only half alive.' Frank eyed him shrewdly. 'You alive, boy?'

'I guess I am.' He eyed Frank right back. 'But I'm still not looking at any black opal. If I was thinking of asking someone to marry me—and I'm not saying I am—I'd take diamonds along for backup.'

'If you're thinking of Erin—and I'm not saying you are—you'd best be looking at the Kimberley Argyles. I've heard her talk about them. She had that look women get in their eyes. You know the one.'

Tristan sighed heavily. He was trying not to think of Erin at all. Problem was he couldn't help it. 'I'd need a fistful of them.'

'Oh, ho!' Frank cackled some more. 'You blew it, didn't you?'

'Big time.' Tristan shoved a couple of bricks behind the wheels of the old car to stop it from going anywhere, not that it seemed to want to. 'I need to call her but I don't know what to say. I don't know where to start.'

'I don't normally give advice without a beer in my hand,' said Frank, 'but for you I'll make an exception. Start with an apology.'

It sounded like good advice. He could use some more of it. 'There's beer in the fridge,' he said. 'Lots of beer. How long before your show?'

The following morning Tristan set about pulling the Ford engine apart. He hadn't called Erin.

Not…yet. He would, though. Soon. Just as soon as he was clear on what he was going to say.

Frank was right; it would start with an apology. Yes, it would start with that. The next step was to explain why he'd backed off so fast on the top of that damned cliff and *there* was the rub. The thought of losing her had terrified him. Still terrified him. But walking away from her was impossible, so he was going to have to park his fear somewhere and walk away from *it*. He had to tell her that. He had to open up and talk about his feelings out loud.

He'd do it. He would. Soon.

Just as soon as he got this motor apart and built up the courage for it.

Two hours later he was still no closer to calling her. His shirt was off, his jeans were filthy, and so was just about everything else he'd touched. He wanted to keep the innards of the engine halfway clean but it just wasn't happening. He was swearing like a trooper, and Pat—who'd screeched at him from her cage on the fence line until he'd let her come over—was with him every step of the way, perched on the edge of the Ford's front grille, watching him work while she extended her vocabulary.

'I'm a moron,' he muttered.

'Moron,' said Pat.

'A fool.'

'Fool,' said Pat.

'And how I ever figured you for anything other than female I'll never know,' he said, eyeing the bird darkly. 'Spanner.'

Pat passed him a screwdriver with her claw.

He put it down, picked up the spanner. 'Spanner, Pat. Spanner. *This* is a spanner.'

'Moron,' said the bird.

'She's too impetuous for starters,' he said. 'Asking a complete stranger to go gem-hunting with her for a week. How sensible is that?' Pat handed him another spanner. 'Thank you. She's fearless, Pat. She gives too much. Have you any idea what that does to a man?' Pat handed him a bolt. Tristan had no idea where it had come from. 'Thank you.' He sighed heavily. 'She doesn't want a burnt-out cop in her life. Who would?'

Finally a reason for not calling her that actually made sense.

Until he remembered her innate understanding of the pressure that came with his work. She didn't deal in platitudes, she understood impossible situations and difficult choices and she knew full well they weren't easy to live with afterwards. Sometimes the system asked too much, she'd told him passionately, and he'd known it for truth. She saw into the heart of things. She'd seen into the heart of *him* and she hadn't seen failure. She'd given him strength when he'd needed it, and in return he'd surrendered his heart.

'I'm in love with her, Pat. All the way in love.' There, he'd said it.

Now what?

'I'm putting in for a transfer back to Australia. I'm here to stay.' He still needed to find a place of his own. He still needed to *get* the transfer. But distance was one obstacle he could remove.

'And no more undercover work either. I'm taking a desk job.' He was tired of working undercover. He didn't want to deal in secrets any more. He wanted to be up front about his work. He wanted the people he dealt with to know what he was and what he did. 'From now on I'm living a balanced life.' He needed to be able to offer it to the woman he loved.

'Hobbies.' He punctuated the word with a wave of his spanner.

'Sport.' Another wave of the spanner.

'Hell, Pat, I might even get a pet.' He was on a roll, dreaming big.

'Children.'

Whoa! Children. Where had *that* come from? Perhaps he'd better put the spanner down.

He needed to call Erin. He needed to call her *now*. He held out the bolt Pat had given him earlier. 'Where did you get this?'

Pat bit him.

* * *

'He hasn't called.' Erin was sitting at the counter in her mother's kitchen eating lemon meringue pie, heavy on the double cream, and watching her mother paint an illustration for a children's book of verse. Today's picture was the dark, dark house. The gloomy menace of the dark, dark house suited Erin's mood to perfection. Being in love was difficult enough. Being in love with a soul-wounded, work-weary, overprotective and uncommunicative Interpol cop who hadn't called her in three days was murder. 'He's not going to call.' Her mother dabbed her paintbrush in the grey and started to darken the sky. More menace. Excellent.

'Why don't you call him?' said her mother.

'No.' Erin shook her head vigorously. No. 'My falling down that damned rock face brought everything to a head but he'd have backed off anyway.' She dug her spoon into her piece of pie with a vengeance. 'At the end of the trip or even just before he went back to London. Sooner or later he'd have pulled back. The fall just made him do it sooner, that's all. He doesn't want to love me. He doesn't want to love anyone.'

'You've never known loss,' said her mother. 'You've never known the death of someone who's a part of you. Tristan does. My guess is that when he does love he does it passionately, deeply, and for ever.'

'Go on,' said Erin. 'Rub it in.'

'You made him care for you. And then you took him up that crag and, in falling, made him face his greatest fear. He thought he'd lost you. And he couldn't handle it.'

'You need more black in the sky,' said Erin. 'God, I'm so depressed.'

'Do you love him?'

'I do.'

'Are you prepared to fight for him?'

'I am. But I'm not calling him. I can't.' She shook her head. 'He has to want to fight for me too.' A phone started ringing. Her phone. The one in her handbag. Her handbag was sitting on the counter. Erin stared at the bag as if it had sprouted fangs, her heart suddenly pounding with equal measures of terror and hope. 'What if it's him?' she whispered.

'What if it's not?' her mother countered dryly.

'What do I do?'

Her mother set her paintbrush on the palette and stared at her with no little amusement. 'Answer it.'

Right. Of course. Yes. First things first. She needed to answer it. She found the phone. Took a deep breath. 'Erin Sinclair.'

'Erin, it's Tristan.'

Erin covered the phone with her hand. 'It's him.'

Her mother rolled her eyes. 'Well, talk to *him*, not *me*.'

Right. Of course. She was about to make a

complete fool of herself, nothing surer, so with a wave for her mother she headed out onto the deck. Best she didn't have an audience. 'Hello.'

'I, ah, hope I didn't interrupt anything,' he said.

'No.' No, that didn't sound right. That sounded as if she'd been moping around waiting for him to call. She needed to sound busier. 'That is, I've been working on my competition pieces this morning, but you didn't interrupt. I was taking a break.' A long one. At her mother's.

'Good,' he said. 'Good. Er, how did the sapphires cut?'

'The tally so far is three shattered practice stones, three shattered big stones and nine that have cut up beautifully. I still have twelve more of the bigger stones and three more practice ones to go.'

'Will you have enough?'

'I'll make it enough.' Excitement crept into her voice. 'Tristan, they're stunning. You should see the colour. It's perfect!'

'I'd like to see them,' he said. 'I'd like to see you. Maybe take you to dinner.'

'You mean like a date?'

She sounded wary, thought Tristan. After the way he'd treated her, she had every right to be. 'Or a movie,' he said quickly. 'Dinner and a movie. Or, we could do something else. We could meet for coffee or go on a picnic.' Whatever she wanted.

'We could go climbing.'

Except that. Tristan raked a hand through his hair and looked to the sky for inspiration. 'We could,' he said carefully. 'We could do that. I might even manage a civil word afterwards. Provided you didn't fall.' If she fell, all bets were off. 'How's the shoulder?'

'Sore. And, to be honest, climbing's out for a while on account of it.'

'Shame.'

'Liar.'

There was laughter in her voice. A warmth that slid straight through him and he relaxed enough to say what was foremost on his mind. 'I hurt you. We got to the top of that rock and I couldn't shake the image of you falling. I wasn't there for you. I couldn't deal with the thought of losing you. I'm sorry.'

'You didn't lose me.' There was no laughter in her voice now. It was so small he could hardly hear it. 'I'm still here.'

He needed to see her face. He desperately needed to see her eyes. 'I'd like to start over,' he said, his heart hammering in his chest. 'I'd like to go slower this time and get it right. I'd like to take you to dinner. '

'I'd like that.' Her voice was slightly stronger now. 'When?'

'Tonight?' No. She only had a couple more weeks to prepare her competition pieces. He didn't want to jeopardise her chances by monopolising her time. 'Any time,' he amended. No, that sounded too casual. 'But tonight would be good.'

'Tonight it is. What time?'

'Seven.' Seven sounded about right. Except that it was five hours away. 'Six. I'll pick you up at six.' He was as nervous as a teenage boy asking a girl out for the very first time. He didn't even know where she lived. 'I'll need your address.'

She gave it to him. And then she hung up.

It was four-thirty when Erin pulled up in Tristan's driveway. She'd started cutting two more sapphires, shattered the third, and decided she needed the rest of the afternoon off. She wasn't sure where they were going for dinner but she'd dressed casually in anticipation of somewhere fairly relaxed. Okay, that was a lie. It had taken her over an hour to decide what to wear and although at first glance her attire could be mistaken for casual, on second glance it was not. Her shirt was a rich and flattering shade of watermelon and clung in all the right places, her skirt was a cool forest-green with a gauzy black undersheath, designer cut to whisper around her calves as she walked, and her shoes, well, they were black and strappy and they weren't made for walking at all. They were made for seduction. She wore half a dozen slim gold bangles

at her wrist for music, a watermelon tourmaline
pendant at her neck for luck. She was ready for
anything.

She saw Frank's old Ford, Tristan's Ford now,
off to one side of the garage. The bonnet was up.
And then she saw Tristan.

One look at him in his torn work jeans, with
his hair tousled and his muscled torso gleaming
in the sunlight, and she damn near forgot her
own name, let alone what she was wearing. He
flashed her a smile and reached for what she
thought was a rag, but it wasn't a rag, it was a T-shirt
and he was dragging it over his head and down
across his body.

Okay, so he hadn't known she was coming over
early. He'd still heard her pull into his driveway,
hadn't he? She'd driven the Monaro; he'd have to
be deaf not to. He could have covered up before
she'd stopped the car and started looking for him,
but no. He'd waited until she'd seen him without
it and *then* put his shirt on.

He was torturing her deliberately.

She took her time getting out of the car, making
sure her skirt rode way up and that he had a clear
view before leisurely smoothing it back into
place. Two could play at that game.

'Afternoon,' he said.

'Isn't it. Afternoon, Pat.'

Pat moved along the edge of the car, closer to Tristan, and fixed her with a beady eye. Protective.

'I cut three stones and got the fidgets so I came on over. I'm interrupting, aren't I? You're busy... bonding.' She eyeballed Pat right back. 'You *do* realise that bird is in love with you?' Tristan looked at Pat. Pat moved closer. The look on Tristan's face was priceless. 'Guess not.'

Tristan had never seen anything more beautiful than Erin Sinclair, dressed to stop a man's heart. That she knew she could stop it didn't lessen her appeal one little bit. The only thing stopping him from dragging her into his arms there and then was the small matter of him being covered in dirt and grease and smelling like a farm animal. 'I need a shower.' He put a protesting Pat back in her cage and all but ran for the kitchen. He pulled a beer from the fridge, cracked it open, and handed it to Erin. 'I'll be right back.'

'Handsome, you just take your time. I'm not going anywhere.' Her smile was Gidget but her words were pure Mae West.

He managed to saunter down the hallway, at least until he was out of sight.

He hit the shower at a dead run.

By the time he made it back to the kitchen, showered, shaved, and dressed for dinner, he'd calmed down somewhat. Until she went to the fridge, pulled a beer from it, cracked the top, and handed it to him. The beer went on the counter and his arms snaked around her. She came willingly, eagerly, as her lips met his for a kiss that was staggeringly potent. He let her go almost as abruptly as he'd reached for her. He wanted to do this right this time. He wanted to take his time.

He didn't have a chance in hell.

'Dinner,' he muttered. 'We're going out to dinner. Now.'

He took her down to Circular Quay and they chose a busy seafood restaurant that overlooked the Quay and the Opera House. It was lively and casual as opposed to intimate and romantic. He was almost certain he could keep his hands off her for the duration of the meal.

'I love this place,' she said as she browsed the menu. 'I never know what to order. I want it all.'

'What about the seafood platter?'

Her eyes grew dreamy.

He ordered the platter and a bottle of white to go with it. 'How are your competition pieces coming along?' he said, and she seemed to come back down to earth with a thud.

'I hadn't counted on having so many sapphires, or having to cut them myself,' she said with a worried frown. 'I figure if I work day and night for the next two weeks I might just get everything I want to get done, done.'

'Are you driving taxis next week?'

'Three shifts.'

'Can you get someone else to drive them?'

'Yes, but there's this small matter of rent.'

'There's also the small matter of your future. You need to prioritise.'

'I am. I will.'

'I'll cover your rent for a couple of weeks.'

'You will not!' Her eyes flashed fire. 'But thank you for offering.'

She was as hard to help as his sister, he decided glumly. Women. 'Okay, here's the plan. It supersedes my original plan, which was to take you to bed and keep you there for the next twenty years or so.'

'What about your job?' she said. 'You know, the one in *London*?'

'I'm putting in for a transfer to Sydney.'

'Oh.' She seemed taken aback. 'Well, why didn't you say so?'

'I did. Just then. Do you want to hear the new plan or not?'

Her smile was slow in coming but when it did it damn near fried what was left of his brain. 'I'm all ears.'

'The new plan,' he said doggedly, 'involves taking you home at the end of the evening and staying away from you until your competition pieces are done.'

Erin sighed heavily. 'I liked your original plan

better.' She picked up her wineglass, toyed with it. 'Are you really putting in for a transfer to Sydney?'

'Cops' honour.'

They were back at his place by eleven. He didn't ask her in. Instead, he leaned down and brushed his lips against hers in the briefest of kisses. She had a rainbow to chase. And he had to keep that in mind.

'What was that?' she said indignantly. 'Because whatever it was it wasn't nearly enough.'

His smile was slow in coming and he hoped it fried her brain. 'That was goodnight.'

Strawberries arrived from Tristan at breakfast the following morning. The day after that it was bodysurfing with him at Bondi Beach at dawn. He took her home after that. Took her home so she could work.

The days passed slowly. Erin drove taxis and worked on her pieces. Tristan tracked down car parts and worked on his Ford. His Holden arrived, he told her on one of his brief visits, and he was pulling that apart too. Pat was helping him.

The weekend arrived and Erin finished the earrings for the competition. Tristan took her fishing from a friend's houseboat on the Hawkesbury to celebrate. They stayed there half the day and he never once looked tempted to move from the fishing deck to the bed inside and make use of it. He was sweet; he was sexy. He was a perfect gentleman.

He caught three fish.

The following afternoon she took him to the Opera in retaliation. Three solid hours of Berlioz. She delighted in the sight of him in a suit almost as much as she delighted in his suffering.

Her need for him grew claws but she didn't give in to it. She took that shimmering sexual tension he could create in her with a glance and poured it into her work.

She finished the bracelet and the brooch, and the daintiest of hairclips.

She finished the necklace with two days to spare.

She slept for an hour, lay in a steaming hot bubble bath for almost as long, and throwing on some clothes and rolling her finished pieces in velvet and tucking them into her handbag, she went in search of an audience.

She found Tristan and Pat—deep in conversation—as they did whatever it was they were doing to the Ford. They made a pretty picture, it was a pretty spot, but it wasn't quite the unveiling location she had in mind. She collected them up and with food, love, and an audience of more than mere man and bird in her sights she headed for Lillian Sinclair's kitchen.

Her mother was painting when they arrived. Erin wasn't the only one working to a deadline. Today's illustration was for 'Tiger, tiger, burning bright'. Erin stared hard at the glowing golden eyes and strong, sinewy lines her mother had created and sighed her approval. 'He's so beautiful,' she said. 'He's so…' Familiar was the word she was looking for. Her gaze slid from the illustration, to Tristan, and then back.

Her mother smiled angelically. 'Wonderful thing, inspiration. You never know where you'll find it next.' She saw Tristan seated at the counter and Pat—in her travelling cage—seated beside him. 'You look well,' she told Tristan, studying him from over the top of her purple-framed glasses. 'You're getting more sleep. And *you*,' she turned her attention to Pat, 'are positively glowing.'

'It's the love of a good man,' murmured Erin, *sotto voce*. 'I should be so lucky.'

'Was there a reason for bringing us here other than to practise your comedy routine?' asked Tristan dryly.

'Indeed there was.' Erin delved into her bag for her roll of buff-coloured velvet and rolled it out along the counter. When Tristan studied them intently, her mother's expression grew reverent, and even Pat looked at them in silence, Erin knew she'd surpassed herself. Win or lose, she was satisfied with her efforts. Of course, she would prefer to *win*.

'You finished them,' said Tristan slowly.

'So I did.'

'We need champagne,' said her mother and headed for the fridge. Grinning, Erin went in search of champagne flutes. A girl had to love a mother who kept champagne in the fridge, just in case.

'Any news on your transfer?' she asked Tristan, just in case there was more than one reason to celebrate.

'It came through a few days ago.'

Erin paused, midway through opening the champagne. 'And you didn't think it worth mentioning?'

'I was waiting for the opportune moment.'

She narrowed her eyes. 'It's here.'

'I'm not working car theft any more,' he said. 'I'll be tracking down stolen diamonds.'

'Get out of here!'

'Seriously.'

'Is it undercover work?'

'Not for me, although there will be men in the field. I'll be running the show from a desk here in Sydney.'

'It sounds demanding.'

'It will be,' he said, his gaze on hers, intent and searching. 'But it's what I do. Part of who I am.'

'I know that.' She shot him a smile. Maybe they could open the champagne after all. The cork popped and she reached for the flutes. Pat got a grape from the fruit bowl.

'You don't mind?' he said.

'Mind? I think I'm jealous.'

'There'll be travel involved, particularly at the start,' he said, and Erin nodded. He would need to be hands on to begin with; she expected no less of him.

'You like to travel, remember?'

'I do, but I distinctly remember you objecting rather strenuously to the tyranny of distance when it came to relationships. Not to mention secrets. I may not be working undercover but there'll still be things I can't talk about. And there'll still be things I *won't* talk about,' he said quietly. 'I know what you want in a partner, Erin. I know I'm not it.'

Her mother was quiet. Even Pat was quiet. They were all looking at her, but it was Tristan she looked to. Tristan who was laying his life out in front of her, warts and all.

'Yes, well, I'm currently reviewing my criteria with regards to what I want in a partner.' She looked to her mother and sent her a grateful smile for her wisdom and for the example she set. 'I'm thinking that if you find the right man the balance will come.'

'I have to go to the Kimberleys in the morning,' he said gruffly. 'I'll be gone for a few days.'

He still wasn't convinced of her sincerity. But he would be, Erin decided firmly. Eventually. 'If

I'm starting to look a little green don't be alarmed. It's just envy.'

'You could come with me.'

Erin groaned. 'It's very, *very* tempting, don't get me wrong. But maybe you should go alone this time. Ask me again when there's less pressure on you to get your operation set up.' He'd encouraged her to focus on her work when she needed to. She could do no less in return.

He smiled at that. 'I'll look around on your behalf. Take notes. Anything in particular you're interested in?'

'The flawless whites. No, the cognacs. No… *The Pinks*.'

'Jezebel,' said Pat.

'Where *does* she get her vocabulary?' said Erin.

'Second book of Kings,' said her mother. "And the dogs shall eat Jezebel in the portion of Jezreel, and there shall be none to bury her."'

'Amen,' said the bird.

'Oh, go eat your grape,' said Erin.

'Don't look at me,' said Tristan. 'Pat and I don't talk religion. I only teach her modern language skills.'

'Moron,' said Pat affectionately. And gave him her grape.

Tristan drove Erin home from Lillian's after dinner and she fell asleep on the way. She'd had a glass or two of champagne over the course of the evening but that wasn't it. She was exhausted. He didn't know how many hours she'd put in on her competition pieces but he suspected it had been enough this past week to bring her to the point of exhaustion. She was still driving taxis. She'd still managed to spend time with *him*. But it had cost her.

'Stay,' she whispered when he picked her up as he would a sleepy child and carried her to the door.

'You need sleep,' he muttered. 'If I stay you won't get it.'

'Stay anyway.'

'What is it about timing?' he muttered.

'What's wrong with the timing?' She stifled a yawn. 'The timing's perfect.'

'Just a few more days,' he muttered. '*Then* it'll be perfect.' He set her down, kissed her on the forehead. 'I'll miss you,' he said, and then he was gone.

CHAPTER TWELVE

IT WAS official. Erin Sinclair was not a patient woman. Oh, she *could* have been a patient woman, thought Erin darkly. If Tristan had come to her bed when she'd asked him and spent the night making wild, passionate love to her she could have been positively saintly when it came to waiting for him to return. But he hadn't. And boy was she going to make him pay.

She spent the three days he was away driving taxis and plotting her next step. She submitted her competition pieces and cleaned Rory's car, polishing and detailing it until it gleamed. She adored the easygoing, laid-back Tristan. She looked at him and saw for ever and it was bright with rainbows and sunshine after rain. She looked at him and saw a man who loved hard and loved deeply. She wanted him to love her like that.

He was staying in Sydney, building a life. He seemed to be building one with room for her in it.

He was being such a gentleman and she loved that about him. Really. She did.

But if he didn't make love to her soon she was going to explode.

He called her the following morning to tell her he was back. He asked if she was busy and when she said she wasn't he asked her over. It was time to put her plan in motion.

He was sitting on the top step of his father's verandah when she arrived, drinking coffee and looking sexier than any man had a right to look. She pulled into his driveway with a five-point-seven litre V8 rumble and he smiled and shook his head. When she shimmied her way out of the car his smile grew rakish.

She was wearing a little blue dress that was short enough and tight enough to make a man beg.

And he *was* going to beg.

'Welcome back,' she said when she reached him, leaning over to settle a whisper-light kiss on his lips. It didn't stay whisper-light for long. His hand came up to cradle the back of her head, he slanted his lips over hers, and unleashed a deep and urgent passion that left her weak and wanting more.

She ended the kiss with a nip to his lower lip and watched his eyes blaze with no little satisfaction. '*Tiger, tiger, burning bright.*' She was about to pull this one's tail.

She settled down on the step just below him, making sure he had an excellent view of her cleavage. 'There I was this morning,' she said. 'Sitting there staring at the Monaro—as you do— and all of a sudden I had this hankering to see how fast it went.'

Tristan's smile widened. 'You got a speeding ticket, didn't you?'

'Not at all,' she said airily. 'A girl in my line of work can't be going around collecting speeding tickets. I'd be out of a job. No, I phoned an old friend of the family who has a dirt racetrack in western Sydney. It's mine for the day.'

'Your brother's going to kill you.'

'He owes me. I figure this will make us about even.'

Tristan looked at her. Looked at the car. 'No, he's going to kill you.'

'Yes, well, I was wondering if you'd like to join me.'

'To stop him from killing you?'

'He's not here. He's not even in the country. Forget the killing part. Because, seriously, you're way too focussed on death.' This wasn't going according to plan. He was supposed to jump at the chance to put the Monaro through its paces. 'Do you, or do you not, want to come and drive this car at speed around an empty dirt racetrack this morning?'

'It's bait,' he said. 'You're up to something.'
'Cops are so suspicious. I hate that.'
'I'm right, aren't I?'
'I hate that too.'

'I love this car,' said Erin an hour later, pitching her voice above the throaty roar of an engine that was being put through its paces. They were midway round the bottom curve of the figure-eight dirt racetrack and Erin was driving, her hands sure and firm on the wheel. The Monaro's front wheels were currently tracking a tight line around the bend. The rest of the car was following. She handled the car with a confidence born of fearlessness and a hefty dose of devilry.

She was doing it deliberately.

Tristan's nerves were good. He hadn't cracked yet. And then she hit the straight and hit the accelerator. The speedometer hit two-hundred kmph three quarters of the way down the two kilometre straight and Tristan started praying. 'There's a corner coming up,' he said with as much nonchalance as he could muster. 'Just thought I'd mention it.'

She hit the brakes and slid into the corner, taking an outside line this time with spectacular sideways results. He knew cars, knew she was in perfect control of this one, but it didn't seem to make a jot of difference. She was precious to him;

he was dying a thousand little deaths, not because of what *was* happening but at the thought of what *could* happen. He wanted her to pull over and park the car. Instead, he attempted to be rational and park his fear instead. He was doing it. He was. And then she spoke.

'I know,' she said, slanting him a naughty pixie smile. 'Let's talk about us.'

'You mean *now*?' He couldn't believe the way a woman's mind worked. 'Wouldn't you rather—oh, I don't know—concentrate on your *driving*?'

'Not at all.' But she didn't accelerate quite as aggressively out of the corner this time. Thank God.

'Are you sure you wouldn't rather talk about this over coffee? Or beer? What about scotch?' he said. 'I know this bar. It's quiet. Private. *Stationary*.' The last word was a roar to match the engine.

'When are we going to make love again?'

That did it. 'Pull over.'

'Pardon?'

She'd heard him, nothing surer, but just in case she hadn't he roared a little louder. 'I was *going* to do this the traditional way. There was going to be moonlight and music, palm trees and a hot pool. Maybe even a horse or two.'

'It's a pretty picture, to be sure,' she said. 'But let's face it. It's been done before.'

'I was *going* to come for you in a meticulously

restored thirty-nine Ford, bearing a picnic basket full of food—'

'Presumably some time this decade,' she said. 'When were you going to get around to the love-making bit?'

'And propose to you then, but—'

'Propose?'

She hit the brake hard and they came to a sliding, screeching halt amidst a cloud of smoke and dust. 'There go the brake pads.'

'Define *propose*.'

'You know. Ask the woman I love beyond reason to be my wife, but no. You had to rush me. So now you're just going to have to make do.'

She was staring at him with what looked a lot like dismay. It wasn't exactly reassuring. 'I know I'm not what you want,' he continued raggedly. 'I'm overprotective. There'll be details of my work that I can't share with you, won't share with you. But I will always put you first and I will always love you.'

Erin's eyes filled with tears.

'Don't cry,' he said. 'You're not supposed to cry. I'm doing this all wrong, aren't I?'

'No.' Her tears started to fall. 'No, it's perfect.'

He hadn't bought her an engagement ring. He dug in his pocket for what he had bought for her. 'Hold out your hand.'

Wiping the tears from her eyes, Erin did as she

was told. Her hand was trembling, her whole body was trembling, and when he turned her hand palm upwards and poured a fistful of rough diamonds into it she shook even more.

'The big one's the pink,' he said. 'But there's whites and champagnes and cognacs as well. Whatever you don't want for yourself I thought you could use for your business.'

She couldn't see them through her tears but it didn't matter. She would ogle them later. Right now she had more important things to do. 'I love you,' she said fiercely. 'You're all I'll *ever* want and don't you dare think otherwise.' She closed her fist around the diamonds he'd given her, holding them tight. 'Tell me what you want.'

He took a deep, ragged breath. His heart was in his eyes. He was the most beautiful thing she'd ever seen. 'I want you to be my wife. I want laughter, even if it's sometimes mixed with tears. I want a lifetime of it. With you.'

'Yes,' she said.

His smile was the sweetest she'd ever seen. He was going to kiss her now, nothing surer. And then he was going to make wild and passionate love to her, just as she'd planned. She loved it when a plan came together. He looked out the window at the deserted racetrack, looked back at her, and this time his smile was rakish. 'And I'd really, *really* like to drive.'

millsandboon.co.uk Community

Join Us!

The Community is the perfect place to meet and chat to kindred spirits who love books and reading as much as you do, but it's also the place to:

- **Get the inside scoop from authors about their latest books**
- **Learn how to write a romance book with advice from our editors**
- **Help us to continue publishing the best in women's fiction**
- **Share your thoughts on the books we publish**
- **Befriend other users**

Forums: Interact with each other as well as authors, editors and a whole host of other users worldwide.

Blogs: Every registered community member has their own blog to tell the world what they're up to and what's on their mind.

Book Challenge: We're aiming to read 5,000 books and have joined forces with The Reading Agency in our inaugural Book Challenge.

Profile Page: Showcase yourself and keep a record of your recent community activity.

Social Networking: We've added buttons at the end of every post to share via digg, Facebook, Google, Yahoo, technorati and de.licio.us.

www.millsandboon.co.uk

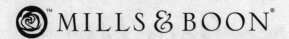